Tip the Piano Man

by

Rosetta Diane Hoessli

Tip the Piano Man

Cover Art by *Debbie Taylor*

The Wild Rose Press, Inc.
PO Box 708
Adams Basin, NY 14410-0708
Visit us at www.thewildrosepress.com

Publishing History
First Edition, 2024
Trade Paperback ISBN 978-1-5092-5441-5
Digital ISBN 978-1-5092-5442-2

Published in the United States of America

Dedication

To my Tabin, whose love has supported me for the last 49 years and who grew into the best dad ever. And to our Missy, whose courage and determination has kept us all going. I love you both with my whole heart.

Acknowledgments

This book has undergone so many changes over the years that it would be impossible for me to thank everyone who helped me. But *Tip the Piano Man* could never have been written without the following individuals: Texas Ranger Jerome Preiss, now deceased but still a huge part of my memories; retired Judge Jim Rausch, a Guardian Ad Litem attorney for a sexually abused child I worked with; retired psychologist Michael Aaron, PhD; my dear friend/advisor/reader retired police detective Patrick Boyd, and good friends who encouraged me and believed in my work along the way.

Prologue

Piper Callaghan pushed the concealed sliding door in the back of the closet to one side and squeezed through the small opening, listening closely before she finally stepped into the bedroom, just as Mama taught her. The house was silent. When she spied the twisted body lying in a pool of blood on the cracked linoleum floor, she crossed the room slowly and stared down at it. An icy numb feeling slid into the pit of her stomach and settled there.

Poor Mama…

As she gazed down at the familiar form on the floor, Piper couldn't cry. Mama looked just like she was sleeping—except for the tiny bit of blood still oozing from the deep wound across her throat. She knew Mama was dead, but it was okay. Being dead was something Mama had wanted for a long time.

Mama explained once about getting dead, and Piper still remembered what she said. She'd said it was something you looked forward to, like a birthday party or Christmas, and it came unexpected-like and carried you off to a place so beautiful it took your breath away. Mama had always wanted to go somewhere beautiful, and Piper was glad she got to go. She'd looked forward to it for so long.

Still dry-eyed and chilled inside, Piper moved toward the dresser. She didn't bother to look into the mirror because it was so old and blurry that she could hardly see herself. Besides, she always looked the same—dirty blonde hair straggled to her shoulders, and her dark eyes were too big for her skinny face. Doe-eyes, Mama called them, just like Daddy's.

Mama always talked about Daddy like he was something special, but Piper knew he wasn't. Men weren't special. They laughed too loud, drank too much, and liked to hurt little children. And no matter what Mama said about Daddy, Piper knew he wasn't any different. If he was so special, he would've come back a long time ago…like Mama promised.

Piper couldn't understand men anyway. They always came here to her house or to that secret place, and they always watched those stupid movies. Tony's camera had been nearby for as long as she could remember. So had the blood and the screaming—men liked that. Piper didn't like it, but she didn't matter. No one ever listened to her.

She looked away from the mirror, waiting. Before today, she could go next door and cuddle with Tia Carly until she felt better. Before today, Tia Carly always took care of her until she had to go home and take care of Mama. But now Mama was gone, and no one would be around to protect Piper. Tony would bring back his camera, there would be more blood, and no one would listen to her.

She shrugged when she heard the distant police siren cutting through the night silence like that rip in Mama's throat. Mama must've screamed too loud, but it was okay. Nothing mattered anymore because she wasn't going to talk about it. In fact, she was never going to talk again in her whole life.

Ever since she was a little kid, people made her do things she didn't want to do. But from now on, no matter what else happened, they couldn't make her talk.

Besides, no one ever listened. Why should they?

Tony always laughed at her. "You're just a baby," he'd say with that ugly look on his face. "Who's gonna believe you anyways?"

At long last, the tears came, and Piper closed her eyes. Tony was right. Nobody would believe her. There wasn't any reason why they should.

After all, she was only six years old.

Chapter One

Sitting stiffly in a narrow, straight-backed seat with his long legs jammed up near his ears, Luke Callaghan gazed through his window into fog so dense it completely obscured the wing of the Delta 747. The murky cloud cover, as thick and nasty as coagulated potato soup, fit his mood perfectly. If the plane went down and splintered into a million fiery pieces, it would be no more than he deserved.

His fingers tightened protectively around the dog-eared, blue-penciled manuscript in his lap. No matter how evil he was or had ever been, his actions didn't warrant the destruction of this first draft of his latest novel.

On the other hand, he thought, relaxing, it might be poetic justice if these pages were discovered charred and blowing in the wind. Other pages like these had created the havoc he was going to meet on this night of December 15, 2022 in San Antonio, Texas. If he hadn't been so selfish in the beginning, so consumed by his need to write The Great American Novel, none of this would've happened.

But no, he had to play the part of best-selling novelist/playboy/celebrity and head up to New York City. There he'd hung out with other pseudo-artist types in Greenwich Village and rented a ridiculously priced, shoebox-sized condo in Hudson Square on the west side of SoHo.

A breathless feminine voice beside him interrupted his thoughts. "Excuse me, sir. Aren't you Luke Callaghan, the mystery writer?"

"Who, me?" He shook his head. "Never heard of him."

"But…isn't that a manuscript in your lap?"

"This? My love, I'm a professor at a junior college in Queens, and these are the term papers of my students who haven't yet learned to write beyond a second-grade level."

"Oh." She gave him an arch, come-hither look tinged with more than a little disbelief. "Well, with that gorgeous silver hair and beard… I saw Luke Callaghan on *Late Night* about a week ago, and you could pass as his twin."

"Lucky devil."

He gave her an intimate glance—more for her ego than because he was interested. She squirmed, blushed, then finally looked away. He grew bored and looked out the window again. *That's the trouble with women these days. They're either ballbusters or too damn easy to get.*

He was finished with all of them.

His stomach lurched as the plane began its slow descent through the thick clouds toward the San Antonio International Airport. Then, against the midnight sky, like little stars hanging upside down, were the welcoming lights of the city he hadn't seen in several months. Over the intercom came the pilot's voice crackling unintelligible instructions as he prepared to complete his landing. Luke deliberately blocked out the irritating static as he pushed his seat forward, then fastened his safety belt and locked the manuscript in his briefcase.

He gazed at the glittering skyline far beneath him. He couldn't believe how much San Antonio had grown.

Everything changes, yet nothing ever seems to change at all...

Like Lacy. She'd been dead for three days, probably murdered by a pimp or a drug connection, but he refused to play the role of a grieving ex-husband. He wasn't surprised in the least—he was only surprised it hadn't happened sooner. He'd attend her funeral a few days from now, then decide about the kid. A kid he'd never laid eyes on. A kid Lacy once swore was his. A kid the neurotic Dr. Madison Wagner said didn't even talk.

How the devil could any kid of his not *talk*?

The blood pounded in his head as he thought about Dr. Wagner. He didn't have a clue about why she'd called him or how she'd found him in the first place, but she apparently didn't believe in explanations. The instant he answered his cell phone, she'd lit into him about how he had to return to San Antonio to take responsibility for some hysterically mute kid named *Piper*. *His* kid, she'd claimed. When he asked what made her think that, she'd said someone had murdered the child's mother and there was no other family member to contact.

When Luke had googled *Dr. Madison Wagner, San Antonio, Texas*, on the internet later that evening, he'd learned she'd graduated from high school at age sixteen, received her Ph.D. in Clinical Psychology by the time she was twenty-two, and managed to complete a postdoctoral fellowship while writing tons of papers on child abuse, the effects of child abuse on adults, the connection between childhood trauma and dissociative identity disorder, *blah, blah, blah, ad nauseum*—all before she was thirty.

Luke was unimpressed. He'd graduated from the School of Hard Knocks, to coin a trite but accurate phrase, and he'd pit his world experience against her liberal ivory-tower education any day.

Now this same Dr. Wagner would be waiting for him at the airport, ready to pounce on him with platitudes about his selfishness and lack of paternal instinct. But she'd realize soon enough that the letters after her name meant nothing to him. She had to have more going for her than that.

"Did you say something, sir?"

Luke's face grew hot with embarrassment, but airplane tires thudding and skittering on the runway prevented him from answering. He pressed himself against the seat, eyes squeezed shut, and waited for the plane to coast to a halt. When it finally stopped, he breathed a sigh of relief.

The young woman stepped into the aisle and tossed her paper pillow into the luggage rack overhead. Slipping her expensive alligator handbag over her shoulder, she gave him a long smoldering look. "It was so nice traveling with you, Mr. Callaghan."

He sighed and stood up, pushing a lock of prematurely silver hair off his forehead. He had to stoop to maneuver his six feet, two inches from beneath the luggage rack, holding his briefcase close to his chest as he worked his way out of the airplane and into the Delta Airlines lobby. One of these days he would fly first class.

He stood off to the side for a moment, admiring the glass, circles, and chrome of the new terminal. Even at midnight it was teeming with people: passengers, pilots, flight attendants. The color and bustle of an airport was always exciting to the writer in him. He could spend hours imagining where folks had come from and where they were going…

"Hello, Mr. Callaghan. Did you have a good flight?"

He looked down at a tiny woman standing in front of him. She scarcely reached his chest, and the bones in that youthful, heart-shaped face were so delicate he thought they might break. A radiant cap of short, wavy hair the color of burnished copper accentuated a creamy complexion, and a light sprinkling of freckles played over her tip-tilted nose. Clear blue-green eyes surrounded by long, thick, black lashes searched his face curiously, as if she couldn't quite work out which planet he was from. Her slender body didn't weigh a hundred pounds sopping wet and was quite effectively concealed in snug blue jeans and an oversized University of Texas sweatshirt.

This is Dr. Madison Wagner?

"Luke Callaghan?" Her husky voice was sharp as she tapped a sneakered foot impatiently against the smooth concrete floor.

He honored her with his famous lopsided grin and bowed. "Yes, ma'am."

She didn't even smile and gestured in the direction of the incoming baggage. "My attorney would've met you, but his car broke down—as usual. So here I am. On a Saturday night, of course, right at the beginning of the Christmas holidays. As if I don't have anything else to do. If you don't mind hurrying, I'd really appreciate it. I'm exhausted." She paused and looked away. "I'm sorry, Mr. Callaghan. That was uncalled for. But the fact is we have a lot of work to do."

He shrugged. "*You* have a lot of work to do. I don't.

I'm leaving Tuesday morning."

"So soon? What could you possibly hope to accomplish here in such a short time?"

"The heck if I know, but I can't stay. I have a deadline."

She looked up at him with one cocked eyebrow and eyes frosty with contempt. "So do I, but mine is court enforced. That means my deadline is more important than yours."

He chose not to argue. "All right, it's your ball game. We'll play by your rules...for now."

"That's a very intelligent decision. Right now, *my* rules are the only ones that matter."

****

Madison started the engine of her fairly new pearl-white SUV and turned on the heater, then leaned back against her seat and took a deep breath. She was bone-weary. As the warmth began to toast her icy feet, she yawned and cast a sidelong glance at Luke Callaghan.

The headlights of other cars leaving the parking lot illuminated his silver hair, and his eyes were smudged by purple shadows. He sat pensive and tight-lipped, holding his briefcase close to his body. She pulled out of the parking lot.

What's he thinking? Probably plotting his next book, lost in a world of murder and intrigue having nothing to do with this reality. Still, she had to admit she'd been too hard on him when they talked on the phone. Maybe she was being too hard on him now.

"Do you have a place to stay?" she asked.

"Not yet."

"Do you mind if I make a suggestion?"

"I doubt if I could stop you."

She chuckled. "You're probably right. I have a shelter for abused and neglected children on Woodridge Drive called Hope's Home. I live there full time. The thing is Piper's there, too. I have an empty room, and I thought you might like to... Well, what I mean is...I thought you might want to stay with us and meet Piper."

"Thank you, I appreciate that. I haven't made any hotel reservations. I was going to rent a car and go home tonight, after I talked with you—"

She frowned. "I thought you lived in New York City."

"I do, but I also own a home out near Medina Lake. I thought I'd look in on it while I'm here. But that's about forty miles away, and I'm really tired. So I'll take your offer and leave in the morning—if that's all right with you."

She took a deep breath. "Mr. Callaghan, I owe you an apology for the way I talked to you on the phone the other night. I had no right to say those things. I was tired and frustrated, and I took it out on you. I was unprofessional."

"Not to mention rude...but no worries."

She fought a yawn. This wasn't going to work. What they felt about each other personally wasn't important. Nothing and no one mattered—except Piper. She had to make him understand that.

But before she could speak, he changed the subject. "What's the name of your shelter again?"

"Hope's Home."

"Why is Piper there?"

She summoned the last of her remaining energy to answer his question. "We keep abused, neglected, and abandoned children who've been taken from their homes by the Department of Family and Protective Services or the police. Sometimes they're runaways and come to me on their own. The children can stay with us up to six months—most shelters usually only allow three—during which time we try to find foster families for them if the courts deem it necessary. Of course, we do everything in our power to place them back with their own parents, but that isn't always possible—or even preferable."

"Impressive."

She glanced at him again. Like so many people, he couldn't seem to believe that she, a respected child psychologist, might prefer to spend her hours and money in public service instead of private practice. She decided to let it pass when he spoke again.

"You still haven't told me why Piper's staying with you. I understand she discovered her mother's body— and I agree that's horrible—but where's the abuse connection?"

She took the Woodridge Dr. exit, came to a smooth stop at a red light, and stared at him in disbelief. "Are you serious? This is your child we're talking about."

"You don't know that."

"Good God. Are you so cold that—"

His eyes narrowed. "Lady, I can be *ice* if it's necessary. I've run away from more social workers than you've ever met in your life. I didn't run back to this city because *you* ordered me to. I came back here for one reason."

The light changed, and she made a slow left turn through the intersection, trying to gather her wits. "I'll bite," she managed finally. "What reason?"

"*You* call her *my* child, but I don't know that. Until I do, I'm not taking any parental responsibility for her.

11

I've never even seen her."

She swallowed hard. She'd prayed this wouldn't happen, but she wasn't surprised. As far as legal documentation was concerned, Piper Callaghan didn't exist. She had no birth certificate, no state aid, insurance, or school report cards. No real proof at all. Still, this child desperately needed her father—*a* father, *any* father—especially now. She was far too fragile to maneuver her way through a callous foster care system alone.

Madison made a snap decision and turned right on Main Street, heading toward the world-famous downtown San Antonio Riverwalk. She drove several miles, passing landscaped parks, old churches, and historic hotels before the real inner city began to emerge.

Here, roads were deteriorating into little more than enhanced alleyways. Streetlights were broken, and graffiti—some displaying undeniable talent—decorated the run-down exteriors of empty houses and abandoned buildings. Now primarily gang territory, this area was the stronghold of a seedy underground that had long ago declared victory over law-abiding citizens and complacent peace officers.

Turning onto an unnamed, unlit street, she drove slowly, bloody images of Lacy Callaghan swimming through her fatigue. With tortured memories of the malnourished, mute Piper Callaghan clouding her vision, she barely managed to maneuver her vehicle around scattered garbage cans and potholes deep enough to consume a tiny car. Sparse strings of peeling Christmas lights occasionally outlined a roof. Somewhere a dog howled.

Madison double-checked the electric door locks, then turned onto an even more neglected side street. She drove past small homes that had years earlier been known as *tarpaper shacks* but were now generally used as crack houses. She squinted through the darkness, searching for Lacy's vacant residence.

She spoke quietly. "Do you think there's a chance that Piper *is* your daughter? I'd hate to think I'm wasting my time…or yours."

"I wouldn't be here otherwise."

"Well, that's encouraging." She finally spotted Lacy's house, slowed, and pulled in behind a red pickup truck parked in front of the driveway. "What do you think of this place?"

She peered at him closely as he looked out the window. The front porch sagged, and the roof over the living room had caved in. She'd gone inside with a police officer just once, so she knew the linoleum was rotten, there were few furnishings, and the glass was broken in several of the windows. According to city records, the place hadn't had electricity or water in more than two months.

She didn't care how manipulative she was being. She had to make him understand. "This is Piper's house. What do you think of it?"

A muscle twitched in his jaw, but he didn't answer.

She persisted. "Do you know who's in this pickup?"

"Of course not, but I bet you're going to tell me."

"You're right. It's a homicide detective watching for a pimp/drug pusher named Antonio Davila. He's wanted for questioning because the police think he might've killed your ex-wife. Also, he likes little kids, if you know what I mean—but don't worry about it. Cops lose interest in cases like this real fast. He's probably in the wind by now."

"What do you mean—little kids? What little kids?"

"Davila used to own a nightclub called La Ninfa, and he was suspected of prostituting children out its back doors. He's a predatory pedophile and a serial sadist. Years ago, he passed nasty Polaroids of children through underground pedophile networks. Back then, they traded kiddie porn like baseball cards, not that anyone really cared. But now, with the internet, or actually the dark web…well, that's another story, and not a pretty one. Anyway, this is the guy who raised your child. Pardon me. Your maybe-child."

"You're enjoying this, aren't you?"

"I beg your pardon?"

"You want to show me how the other half lives, while I'm out playing on my yacht or hiding on my estate making up stories without social messages. Well, catch this bulletin, Dr. Wagner. I lived in a house just like this, and I got out of it, so this little game you're playing doesn't impress."

Tears of fatigue and embarrassment burned her eyes. She was so transparent, always had been…

"I just want to know where the money went," he continued quietly. "I sent Lacy a lot of money over the years, but she clearly didn't spend it on living conditions. Or on Piper. Do you know where she spent it? You seem to know everything else."

Madison was bewildered. He'd sent money? Why? When? Where?

She tried to cover her mounting confusion with righteous anger. "What money? Jared Ross, our attorney, gave me a copy of a court order the police found in the back of her kitchen cabinet. It was dated about six years ago, and it demanded you pay Lacy a hundred dollars a month for three months. Was that partial support until your divorce was final? Whatever it was, the order didn't mention any child support, and there weren't any papers showing you ever paid her anything after those three months were over. I think it's a fair assumption that for the last six years, your ex-wife supported herself—and her child—in whatever manner she could."

"Stop." He actually chuckled. "You're breakin' my heart. Listen, you can judge me—I don't care. But I don't have to justify myself to you. You don't know anything about me, or about Lacy, so whatever I tell you is because I think you might need to know it. Not because I think you have a right to know. There's a huge difference. Are we clear on that?"

She ducked her head. "You're right. I'm sorry."

He continued as if she hadn't spoken. "So you could assume Lacy was forced to support herself and Piper— but you'd be wrong. I've sent her money orders totaling nearly $40,000 *a year*, and I sent that money under the table so she never had to pay taxes. I sent that money when I barely had two nickels to scrape together for myself. She never had to work if she didn't want to. It was free and clear money, Dr. Wagner. *My* money. I have receipts in this briefcase for every single payment I ever made to Lacy Callaghan."

Madison was stunned silent.

"So let's look at *another fair assumption*. We both know Lacy was a junkie and a hooker, so I think it's also fair to assume she spent all that money on dope or gave every last dime of it to her pimp or both. But no matter what happened to it, my responsibility to Lacy ended when I dropped that money in the mailbox. Piper is apparently a by-product of her mother's unfortunate lifestyle, and I'm very sorry about that, but I don't see what it has to do with me. If she's my child, I'll take care of her. If she's not, I won't."

"Wait—"

"And one other thing."

She sighed.

"Why—and how—did you call me in the first place? There has to be more than one Luke Callaghan in this country. Just because you saw that name as part of a divorce decree—"

She sighed again. "Lacy wrote on the court order *In case something happens to me, call Luke Callaghan*...and your cell phone number. We didn't know how long ago she wrote that, so we didn't know if the number was still good, but it was all we had. And thank God you answered."

Madison eased her car away from the curb. The drive home was silent, but unspoken questions and unresolved emotions screamed to be voiced in the stillness. Finally, when she pulled into a long drive beside a Victorian-era mansion currently housing twelve children, including Piper Callaghan, his deep voice broke the stillness.

"Hold up."

She blinked back those ever-ready tears of frustration, defeat, and exhaustion. They'd never find a place of common understanding. They were too different, too rooted in their own opposing perceptions of the world.

"What?"

"I want you to know you and I actually agree on one thing."

"I doubt that."

He ignored her sarcasm. "No child should ever have to live in a house like that. And every child deserves decent parents. I know because I spent years being tossed from foster home to foster home—never anywhere as nice as your Hope's Home, by the way. To this day I wouldn't know my parents if they spit on me, which they'd undoubtedly do. But I know my responsibilities, and I've never shirked them. Like I said, if you prove Piper is my daughter, I'll do my best to take care of her. That's a promise."

She didn't know what to think—or how to communicate with him. One minute he was cocky, arrogant, rude, only talking about *his* money, *his* viewpoint, *his* childhood. Then he flipped around and apologized with such sincerity she couldn't help but believe him.

Maybe in the morning, when she wasn't so exhausted, she'd figure him out.

She turned off the ignition with an irritated snap of her wrist. "The only thing you can do is let me get some sleep. We'll run a paternity test on you right away, but the results take time. So please don't tell Piper anything. Let her believe you're just a guest in my house. If I'm going to help her—and that's *my* goal—we *have* to call a truce. If you can't cooperate, go back to New York or wherever you live, because I need you to help me, not fight me. I have to release a child from demons you and I know nothing about."

"Demons? Aren't you being a little melodramatic?"

"No. And when you see her, I think you'll agree."

Luke touched her shoulder. "I want you to know, Dr. Wagner, that whether Piper's my daughter or not, I'm really glad you're in her corner. So you want a truce, and

17

I agree. Let's make a pact. If you promise not to talk down to me like I'm a spoiled two-year-old, I promise I won't make any jokes about how short you are."

As their eyes met and he grinned, she managed a little smile. Thank God he could hold on to his sense of humor—it would make her job easier. But she didn't think he could hold on to it for long. Still, if he was willing to shelve their differences for the time being, she wasn't going to stand in his way.

"I couldn't agree more," she said softly. "Truce…"

Chapter Two

Wrenched from sleep by her thundering heart, Madison leaped from her bed and clawed her way to reality. In the far distance, millions of miles away, someone was screaming—a wild, mindless, gut-ripping outburst of terror. Disoriented, she stared blankly around her room. Icy fingers of fear whispered up the back of her neck.

Once more the scream slashed through the dawn, and someone pounded frantically on her door. She slipped into her bathrobe and flung the door open.

Luke stood before her, wild-eyed. "What in God's name is that!"

She didn't answer but brushed past him, tying her sash around her waist as she dashed to the room next to hers. She pushed the door open and entered on tiptoe. As the rising sun bathed the room in soft pinks and grays, a shaft of silver streaked through a small window next to a twin bed placed kitty-cornered against the wall, facing the door. A towheaded little girl slept peacefully with one fist curled against her pale cheek. Madison walked quietly to the bed and sat down, every muscle taut with tension. She pulled her robe more closely about her, shivering in the early morning chill. Her bare feet felt like glaciers.

As the dawn illuminated Piper's face, spidery blue veins were visible beneath transparent flesh pulled too tightly over sharp cheekbones. Her arms and shoulders were painfully thin against a rose-patterned comforter, and a tiny pulse throbbed in her throat. Madison leaned forward, watching Piper carefully.

What a beautiful child...

A familiar sadness invaded her as she gazed at the little girl. Piper's long lashes swept against her cheeks like curling threads of silk, and her parted lips were delicate, tender. She was so tiny, so vulnerable...

Suddenly, Piper clenched her fist, and her body went rigid. The peaceful expression on her face vanished as her lips pulled away from her teeth in a grimace of horror. When Piper opened her mouth to scream, Madison leaned in and whispered in her ear.

"Piper, you're dreaming. Wake up, honey. It's Miss Madison. Wake up now. Can you hear me, sweetheart?"

Piper shuddered, relaxed, opened her eyes. An uncertain smile trembled on her lips.

Madison reached for a small stuffed puppy at the foot of the bed and tucked it against Piper's cheek. "You're safe now, baby girl. See? You're safe now."

Piper kept her gaze on Madison's face.

"You've had a scary dream is all, buttercup, but you're in your own bed, and I'm with you."

Piper didn't answer.

"You just close your eyes and go back to sleep." Madison stroked her cheek, her forefinger moving hypnotically against the petal-soft flesh. "I could stay with you for a little while and hold your hand. Would you mind that?"

Piper's chin quivered. Then suddenly, without any warning, she jerked the comforter over her face and screamed.

Madison whirled around to see Luke Callaghan standing in the doorway, white-faced and gawking. He stumbled backward, Piper's shrieks following him. Instinctively, Madison gathered the fragile, stick-thin body in her arms and rocked her, crooning in her ear. Tears streamed down her cheeks.

Damn him! Blast and damn him! I'll have to start all over…

But Piper's arms crept around her neck and held on with ferocious determination. Madison didn't move until the child's breathing became gentle and rhythmic once again. Finally, she lowered Piper back against the pillow and breathed a sigh of relief.

She pulled the comforter up under Piper's chin, then stood beside the bed for a few more minutes. When she was satisfied the little girl was sound asleep, she left the room and closed the door softly behind her. She sagged against it, legs shaky with fatigue and tension, until strong fingers gripped her elbow.

"Let me help you to your room."

She looked up into Luke's concerned face and bit back anger. "I'm fine—no thanks to you. Just give me a minute to catch my breath."

"I'm sorry I came in like that. She looked like… It was just… I thought maybe I could help…"

She stared pointedly at his fingers curled around her elbow. "I'm tired. I'm going back to bed."

He released her. "Wait. Has she had nightmares like that before?"

"Every night for the last three nights. She just lives and relives…something."

A low, throaty voice interrupted them. "Excuse me, folks. Are you all right, sweetie?"

Madison managed a smile as she nodded in response to her best friend and chief assistant, Whitney Patterson, and gave a dismissive gesture toward Luke. "This is Luke Callaghan. He might be Piper's father."

Whitney barely acknowledged him as she glanced at her watch. "Howdy do, Luke. I've got the kettle going downstairs. Would either of you like some herbal tea?"

Madison started to refuse, but Luke touched her arm. "Please, Dr. Wagner—if you don't mind. I need to show you something."

"It's five o'clock in the morning. Can't it wait?"

"I'd really like to get this over with."

Her words dripped sarcasm. "And it's all about you, isn't it? Do you mind if I shower first?"

"I'm sorry—of course not. But I think you'll agree this is important."

"Then go on down and have some tea. I won't be long."

About thirty minutes later, settled in at the kitchen table, Madison felt just a tad more human with her feet toasty in fuzzy slippers, her face scrubbed clean, and her hair freshly brushed. As she sipped her tea and waited for Luke to speak, she gave him a sidelong glance. He'd changed into a pair of black jeans and a gray pullover sweater that emphasized platinum streaks in his wavy hair. She was painfully aware of her bloodshot eyes and the dark-purple shadows beneath them. He had no right to look so refreshed when she was so exhausted.

Finally, he scooted his chair closer to the table and pulled his wallet from his back pocket. His hand trembled slightly as he removed a creased and yellowed picture from an inside pocket and handed it to her. "Please look at this."

She felt his eyes boring into her as she examined the photo. She frowned, confused. "This is a really old picture. Who's this child?"

"One of my social workers told me it was my mother when she was a little girl. I wouldn't know. But her resemblance to Piper is uncanny, don't you think?"

"Oh, so now you believe Piper's your daughter?"

"I believe it more now than I did earlier."

Whitney tossed a paper towel into a recycling can under the sink and cleared her throat. "Listen, I'm through here. The kids will get up soon, and they'll drive you crazy, so I'll keep them out of your hair."

"Well, they're not up yet, so don't leave on my account," Luke responded. "I doubt if there are too many secrets between you and Dr. Wagner anyway. You should hear this now so you don't have to hear it later."

"But if it's confidential—"

"Doctor-patient, you mean?" he interrupted with a chuckle. "I'm not in therapy. You can stay if you want."

As Whitney seated herself at the table, Madison leaned forward and fixed a penetrating gaze on Luke. "We'll order a DNA paternity test off the internet first thing tomorrow morning. It shouldn't take over a week to hear back. Are you still planning to leave this Tuesday?"

"No. I need to know the results."

"Good, I appreciate that. What do you want to do in the meantime?"

"Whatever you tell me to do. I don't even know where to begin."

She thought a moment. "Do you have any questions? We can start there."

He shot her a look of gratitude and didn't hesitate.

"How did you get Piper?"

Madison answered immediately. "After your ex-wife was murdered on December 12, the State of Texas automatically took Piper into protective custody until we could find you. There'd been reports of child abuse on her in the past, and the Department of Family and Protective Services had kept an open file on her because nothing was ever validated. I work closely with them, the police department, the sheriff's office, and the district attorney's family violence unit. Anyway, our attorney, Jared Ross, often represents my kids in court. So one of the cops on the scene called him and asked if we had room. Jared called me because there wasn't room anywhere else. I guess that doesn't surprise you."

He nodded, stone-faced.

Her brain felt hazy, like a fogged-up windshield. "Anyway, Jared brought Piper here that night. The next morning, we had an emergency hearing with Judge Paul Leonard. He's a family court judge who tries to stay available to us. He asked if I'd help him make a solid decision concerning Piper's future. He also drew up the necessary paperwork putting her into my custody."

"Back up a minute. You said, *Abuse reports that were never validated.* What does that mean?"

"It means someone reported some type of abuse to protective services at some time in the past—or even several times. But when the caseworker investigated, she discovered the reports were unfounded. That doesn't mean the reports were lies or inaccurate, only that protective services couldn't find enough evidence to warrant removing the child. Whenever that happens, the reports are filed away until another one comes along and they have to investigate again."

"Do you know who makes the reports?"

"Sometimes, but the reporter can remain anonymous. That's what usually happens."

"What about in Piper's case?"

"I don't know yet. Jared's going to try to bring her file over tonight, and I'll see then, but my gut says they're all anonymous. You probably know more about Lacy and her child than we do."

He drummed his fingertips against the tabletop. "I'm curious about something. Lacy's house obviously should've been condemned years ago. You told me about Davila and his record. If *you've* been able to find all that out in just a couple of days, certainly someone in protective services knew it, too. So how can they call those abuse reports *unfounded*? Since when is it all right for a child to remain in a house that's clearly falling down, living with a mother who's a known junkie and prostitute, and a pimp who's into kids?"

She closed her eyes wearily. "I have no idea. Jared told me about Davila on the morning of our emergency hearing, and he got it from the cops. Neither of us could figure out why protective services hadn't immediately removed Piper from that house. But I do know the system loses children right and left. They don't just fall through cracks—they fall through *crevices*. Piper was one of those children."

"Is anyone looking for answers?"

"Jared is. He has a friend in protective services who's going to try to make a copy of Piper's file. Like I said, he'll bring it tonight if he can."

"Good. How are you supposed to help your judge friend make this so-called *solid decision*?"

She could hardly hear her own words over the

fatigued ringing in her ears. "Judge Leonard wanted me to find you and bring you here. Then, if you were interested, you'd work with me and protective services to help us decide whether or not you're fit and capable of parenting Piper in the future."

"Am I named as the father on Piper's birth certificate?"

"There *is* no birth certificate—at least, not that we've been able to find. There's no record of her birth at the courthouse. But like I said, they *did* locate Lacy's divorce papers stuffed in the back of her kitchen cabinet. Judging from those, Piper's age was close enough that you could be her father. Also, the protective services file is in the name of Piper *Callaghan*—the name Lacy must've given when they opened their first investigation. And then there's your cell number we found written on the court order. We had no choice but to start there."

"What happens if I don't pass your inspection or I decide I don't want to do this?"

Madison's shrug sapped the last of her remaining strength. "You just move on. We'd legally terminate your parental rights, and Judge Leonard would put her in foster care until we find an adoptive family. That won't be easy, though. Piper's six years old, and she has problems."

Whitney spoke up. "What about grandparents? Aunts or uncles? *Any* relatives besides you?"

He shook his head. "I don't know anything about my family, and Lacy didn't know hers, either. We never cared enough to find out. That's a dead-end street as far as I'm concerned."

"I get that." Whitney gave a self-mocking chuckle. "Someone left me at a fire station when I was eight weeks old, and I think the cook there actually named me after the town he was born in. I was in foster care until I aged out."

He stared at her in astonishment. "No kidding!"

"Sorry, I don't know why I told you that. I never talk about it..."

"Your secret is safe with me. I'm just saying...if I *am* Piper's father, I'm all she has. For whatever that's worth."

"It may be worth a lot," Madison said softly.

"Oh, I doubt it. Knowing me doesn't usually work out well for people. Can I ask one more question?"

"Of course."

"How did Lacy die?"

She closed her eyes, revisiting the blood-red nightmares that had wrenched her awake bathed in clammy-cold perspiration. She hadn't seen Lacy's body herself, but Lacy's baby had.

"She was stabbed in the throat. Expertly, Jared said. That's all we know right now."

"My God." It wasn't an exclamation or a whispered blasphemy; it was just a simple statement of fact. "My God."

"I believe Piper knows a lot more than we think, and that's what we have to find out."

"How?"

Madison shook her head. "She's just a little girl, and we can't imagine what she's been through. We have to let her know she's safe with us and no one will ever hurt her again. When she's secure enough, I think she'll tell us. But that won't come overnight."

"No wonder she was so terrified when she saw me..." His voice trailed away.

"Don't beat yourself up over that," Whitney interrupted briskly. "Right now, she's not connected to anyone, anywhere. She refuses to talk, and we can't blame her. Bless her heart, she's just trying to hold on to a little power and control."

As he sat at the table, he seemed very vulnerable to Madison, very human, like a man who'd struggled with his own demons for so long it had never occurred to him to think of anyone else's.

"I'm sorry," she whispered. "I'm really so, so sorry."

Immediately, he straightened his shoulders, and his voice became distant, efficient. Once more he was a man in charge. "No worries. Listen, I'd like to visit the funeral home where Lacy is. Will you need me for anything this afternoon?"

"No. I've cleared my schedule of all appointments for the next two weeks, just in case you or Piper need my help. Would you like me to come with you?"

When he met her gaze, she glimpsed the curtain of pain that shadowed his face. "I'd appreciate that."

"Then we'll go, just as soon as you're ready."

****

Since the funeral home didn't open until noon on Sundays, Luke and Madison decided to take a nap, leaving the children in Whitney's care and that of the skeleton staff arriving at nine o'clock. So it was eleven thirty in the morning when Luke awoke. Even though his sleep had been restless, he felt much stronger and more in control.

He stretched and grinned. His feet hung a good three inches past the foot of the twin bed, and both his legs were numb. He wriggled his toes and yawned. Finally, he dangled his legs over the edge of the bed, wincing. His muscles felt like knotted fists.

He took a snug pair of gray brushed-denim jeans from his suitcase and stepped into them, then eased them over his narrow hips. He pulled a pale-blue sweater over his head, then tugged on a pair of dark-gray scuffed-up cowboy boots he wore anywhere he couldn't wear sneakers. Finally, after he'd combed his hair and brushed his teeth, he left his room and strode toward the staircase at the end of the hall. He stopped at the top of the stairs.

A long, narrow window looked down on a fenced-in area in the yard that contained a large pile of cut logs and three tricycles. A colossal elm tree reached toward the sky, its barren branches gray and gnarled with age, and a vacant birdhouse dangled precariously from a limb near the windowpane.

How he would've loved growing up in a house like this! Ghosts would've whispered through the corridors at night, and he would've concocted spine-tingling tales about their unfulfilled loves and bloody demises. But there'd been no Dr. Wagner to take him away from the pain and poverty that had marred his childhood. There'd been no haunted house to explore, no elm tree, not a single bird…

Slamming the door on these memories, he made his way quickly down the stairs and found himself in a wide, chilly foyer. His gaze was drawn immediately to a life-sized portrait of a nineteenth-century woman.

"She was Madison's great-great-grandmother. Wasn't she something?"

Whitney Patterson had joined him without a sound and spoke in a soft Texas drawl as comfortable as warm syrup poured over hot, buttered pancakes. That low, throaty voice gave him a double shot of masculinity, and he straightened his shoulders in response to it.

"She certainly was. I'm just not sure exactly what."

When Whitney chuckled in response, he gave her an admiring once-over. Tall and slender, she wore her silver-blonde hair in a single braid down her back, and her wide blue eyes were the vivid color of Texas bluebonnets. She seemed casual and easy-going, the perfect temperament for her high-pressure position.

She broke the silence. "Would you like some coffee?"

"That'd be great, thanks. Has this house been in Madison's family for a long time?"

"Ever since the early 1880s." Her expression was proud, as if Madison's heritage were her own. "Old Stephen Wagner, Madison's great-great-grandpa, started out in the mercantile business, but he ultimately became one of the most prosperous bankers in this city. He bought this land back in the 1850s or so, and for a long time there was only a little adobe house here. But when he married Miss Henrietta Madison, she didn't think his place was good enough, so he built her this house. It reminds me of a mausoleum. I'm not crazy about it."

"And it was passed down to Dr. Wagner?"

"Yeah, on her father's side. Her mother died when she was born, and her father raised her here. She's never lived anywhere else."

Luke couldn't imagine living in the same house with the same family for one's entire life. Until he was about ten years old, he hadn't stayed in the same place, with the same people, for longer than two months. Being passed around from family to family had established within him a wanderlust he'd never been able to shake.

Yet as he thought about it now, he realized he preferred the constant change to no change at all.

"What exactly do you do around here—besides take care of Dr. Wagner?" he asked, following Whitney from the foyer.

"Well, that's my main job. She wouldn't remember to eat or sleep if I didn't remind her. I'm also the den mother and general fixer-upper. I don't mean to sound conceited, but I can honestly say it wouldn't run without me."

"I believe that. This must be one expensive place to keep up."

"You can say that again. Bryan Wagner, Madison's father, was a very famous heart surgeon. So, fortunately, when he died a few years ago, he left her some money and a maintenance fund to help keep up this house. If he hadn't done that, she'd never have realized her dream of opening this shelter. She gets paid for much of her work, of course, and we get a lot of private donations, but she wouldn't be able to accomplish near what she does if her father hadn't helped her."

"Did he know what she wanted to do with his house?"

"Oh, absolutely! He backed her totally. They were very close." Then, abruptly, she changed the subject. "Are you going to stay with us awhile?"

"I haven't decided yet. I have a place out near Medina Lake I should check in on, but there's really no reason not to stay here. I could help, I think."

She tucked her hand cozily into the crook of his arm and smiled up at him. For a split second, he wondered if she was flirting with him, then was almost ashamed of the thought. She was just friendly, he decided, sort of like an overgrown puppy with a new playmate.

"Well, Lord knows we could use another adult around here," she confided. "One of the male species, that is. The kids can get kind of wild. Sometimes I'd give my right arm for a deeper voice, if you know what I mean."

He chuckled and followed her into the kitchen. He hadn't even noticed during their predawn meeting what a warm and cheerful room it was, one that encouraged lengthy visiting by permitting sparkling sunshine to pour through large windows. The long table was still cluttered with breakfast dishes, and an old coffeemaker burped and gurgled on the counter.

He kicked a blue rubber ball out of his way and crossed the kitchen to stand in front of the sink. He looked out a wide window that afforded an excellent view of the fenced-in backyard, beyond which was a slightly overgrown alleyway wide enough for a small vehicle to navigate. Several children laughed and shrieked as they played on a sprawling jungle gym and swing set, chased by an enormous barking dog that looked more wolf than canine—maybe an Alaskan malamute. Another youngster was engaged in a solitary game of hopscotch on the driveway. A basketball hoop was attached to the garage, and a plastic-covered, aboveground swimming pool was installed near the back fence.

As he watched the children playing together, a familiar empty sadness seeped through him. He'd spent most of his thirty-five years running from that sensation, yet nothing helped. Success, drinking, drugs, women, even writing only intensified this cavernous void in his life.

Then he saw her. Her pipe-stem legs crossed Indian style, she sat alone beneath a barren ash tree. Her face was expressionless, and her dull blonde hair was caught up in two ponytails, one on either side of her head. Dark shadows encircled her eyes, and her lips curved down in a dejected little droop.

He thought of the worn photograph tucked snugly into his wallet. This little girl looked so much like his mother that it hurt to look at her, but he couldn't understand that pain. He'd never known his mother, had never even *wanted* to know her.

He felt a soothing hand on his arm.

"She'll be all right, Mr. Callaghan. Kids are resilient, you know."

He remembered himself—a vulnerable, frightened, lonely little boy—and shook his head. "Not all of them, Whitney. Some of us just fake it."

"You're right. That was a stupid thing to say. What I mean is all Piper needs is some love and tenderness. Just the slightest feeling she might be wanted and assurance that she'll be safe will make a world of difference. She'll get that here."

"But Dr. Wagner said she could only keep the children for up to six months."

"That's true, but where there's a will, there's a way. Madison usually gets what she wants." She patted his arm again. "If you dare to risk it, your coffee's ready."

Luke heard a chair scrape against the floor, then the clatter of dishes as Whitney began clearing the table. He turned away from the window and the heart-tugging sight of the little girl's unhappiness.

As he carried juice glasses to the sink, he fought tears and couldn't understand why. He hadn't cried in years, but now he had to struggle to speak past the lump in his throat. "Are you the only staff that's here today?"

She forced the glasses into the packed dishwasher. "Well, Trudy, our cook, came in this morning while you were sleeping. She does meals and freezes them for the week. Thank God for her because Madison can't boil water without burning down the kitchen. In about an hour, I'll have Stacy, a local college girl who interns here as part of her sociology curriculum. She only lives about five miles away, so we can call on her if there's an emergency. Then during the week, we have a wonderful housekeeper who comes in every Monday, a gardener who comes in on Saturdays, and of course the volunteers that we rotate. Everyone else works with Madison on a per-case basis. The kids all have their own chores, so we manage."

"Well, that sounds efficient." He paused. "Is there anyone special in *your* life, Whitney?"

She chuckled and closed the dishwasher door. "Jared and I are engaged to be married in the spring. We get loose pretty much whenever we want to be. Madison's easy to work with."

"Did I hear my name?"

Whitney pointed to the coffeemaker without looking around. "Grab some, sweetie. It tastes horrible, as usual, but it'll wake you up. Did you get any sleep?"

"I think so. Finally." Madison wore white tailored slacks and a V-necked, peach silk blouse. She looked fresh and restored, like she'd enjoyed a full night's rest. She poured herself a cup of coffee, then walked to the window and stood very still, watching the children. "How's Piper today?"

"Quiet," Luke answered, standing beside her and

admiring the way the sunlight played over the gold and copper streaks in her auburn hair. "And alone. Is she always alone?"

"For now, by her own choice. She doesn't trust anyone." She turned and looked up at him steadily. "Are you ready to go, Mr. Callaghan?"

"As ready as I'll ever be."

"We'll grab something to eat while we're out, Whitney. Did you have any plans today, pet?"

"Well, I wanted to do a little art therapy with Piper as soon as Stacy gets here." Whitney wiped her hands on a damp dish towel. "Not that it's done any good so far. She won't communicate at all."

"Then leave her alone," Luke said abruptly.

Madison glanced at him, obviously surprised at the protective note in his voice. "I'm not sure when we'll be back, Whitney. If Jared comes early, call me on my cell and don't let him leave. I have to see that file."

Chapter Three

Madison was surprised by how deserted the usually bustling Broadway Street was as she drove toward the Sunrise Funeral Home. Even though the strip centers, exclusive boutiques, and sidewalk cafes were open for Sunday business, the high-rent district of Alamo Heights might as well have been unpopulated. She reached over and turned on the radio, locating a soft rock station. The Beatles' melancholy hit song, "Yesterday," filtered through the back speakers.

"They could've gone all day without playing that," Luke muttered.

"You don't like the Beatles?"

"Of course, I like the Beatles. I'm not un-American." He glanced at her with a smile. "Did you finally get some rest, Dr. Wagner? You look terrific."

She was inexplicably pleased by the compliment. "I did, thank you. Did you sleep?"

"On and off. I'm a bit long for those beds. My body woke up twenty minutes after I did."

"Oh, I'm sorry…I didn't even think of that. When you're as little as I am, you don't think about the length of beds and normal-sized people. After all, I can sleep in Sasha's doghouse without a problem."

"Sasha? Is that the malamute I saw playing outside with the children? She's a beauty."

"Thank you. She's my heart, and that's the truth."

She glanced over at him, a little embarrassed. "Actually, Sasha's a really valuable tool. She takes on my most traumatized kids and makes them her mission. She's amazing."

"Does Piper like her?"

"I think she's a little afraid of her. Sasha's so big, you know. But she'll come around. Sasha insists on it."

"And here I thought she was just the family pet." He shifted in the passenger seat until he was facing her. "I hate to bring up what might be an awkward subject, Dr. Wagner, but I really need to know."

"On one condition."

"What?"

"That you stop calling me Dr. Wagner. I keep thinking you're talking to someone a lot more important than I am. Even the kids don't call me that. They call me Miss Madison."

He chuckled. "Agreed, as soon as you start calling me Luke."

Madison made a left-hand turn from Broadway onto a wide residential street lined with older, more expensive homes and tossed him an impish grin. "All right, we're friends now. What'd you want to know?"

He drummed his fingertips against his knees, clearly uncomfortable. "Who's paying for Lacy's funeral?" he asked finally.

"I am. Or, rather, Hope's Home is."

"Why?"

"It's simple. When Piper came to me, even though she wouldn't talk, I knew she'd been very bonded to her mother. Children have different ways of grieving, as we all do. Some of us scream and go completely berserk. Others of us tighten up and hold it all inside until we explode. Piper holds it in. But I felt that later she'd want to know where her mother was buried and that loving people had buried her. So with my board's approval, I called Martin Gregory, who owns the Sunrise Funeral Home and is a close friend of mine, and asked him to take care of the details."

"Wasn't that going beyond the call of duty?"

She shrugged. "In my business, we have no call of duty. We do what's needed at the time. Later, when Piper's healthier, I'll take her to her mother's grave and let her put flowers on it. I want her to know her roots are something to be proud of."

There was a long silence. Finally, in a low voice, he asked, "How do you know they are?"

"How do I know they *aren't*? Your wife may have stuck needles in her arms, and she may have sold herself to pay for them, but that only makes her a *sick* woman. Not a *bad* one."

He didn't answer. When the disc jockey launched into a monotonous advertisement about overpriced sheets on sale somewhere, he switched off the radio, clearly irritated. "I'll take care of all this when we get there. Lacy's funeral isn't your responsibility."

"It's all right—"

He held up his hand. "No, it isn't. I *need* to do this. Will Mr. Gregory be around on a Sunday?"

"Oh yeah. I've never seen a man who loves funerals like Martin does. He takes great pride in his work. He's the last of a dying breed."

He laughed out loud. "That's a pitiful excuse for a joke."

She wrinkled her nose in wry amusement. "Actually, I wasn't joking. You'll understand after you meet him."

Once Madison had locked up the SUV, she and Luke walked slowly across the parking lot and stopped at the entrance as she steeled herself to go inside. Finally, he opened the door for her, and she entered the Sunrise Funeral Home, blinking rapidly to adjust her vision from the bright sunlight to the muted shadows of the sitting area.

Several plump love seats and overstuffed easy chairs were settled cozily around the room, fat pillows accenting the sage-green and soft peach of the decor, and Madison's feet sank into plush silver-gray carpet. The door swung closed behind Luke with a whispered *whoosh*, like a tiny gasp of air.

To their right, set unobtrusively at the entrance to a large foyer, was a black, white-lettered sign that read *Viewing: Lacy Callaghan—The Oakwood Room*. Madison thought of Piper and fought back tears. That simple sign made it all too real.

A young woman seated at the reception desk arose immediately and came to greet them. "May I help you?"

"We're here to visit Lacy Callaghan," Madison answered. "But first, is Mr. Gregory in?"

"Of course. May I give him your names?"

"Dr. Wagner and Mr. Callaghan."

Just then, Martin Gregory, an elderly man impeccably attired in a rich maroon suit and matching silk tie, entered the sitting area, arms outstretched. "Madison, darling! I thought I heard your voice."

The soft lamplight glowed beyond his thick waves of white hair, creating what appeared to be a peach-tinted aura around his head. When he gave Madison a fatherly bear hug, his goateed chin rested comfortably on her shoulder. He was perhaps an inch over five feet.

Releasing her, he offered his hand to Luke. "You must be Mr. Callaghan. My condolences, sir."

"Thank you. And I also want to thank you for all your help."

"You're welcome. When did you get back into town?"

"Late last night."

"I'm glad Madison found you. She was so worried she wouldn't be able to reach you in time."

"I'm glad, too. Sir, after I've seen Lacy, I'd like to go to your office and take care of some business. Will that be all right?"

"That's all been provided for—"

Luke's interruption was smooth but firm. "No, sir. I need to handle this myself. But once I've done that, I'd like for you to take care of the funeral details. I don't know any preachers, or what Lacy's belief system was at the end of her life, or if she even had one. I hope you can just take it over."

"I'll be happy to help. Do you want me to make the decisions without disturbing you?"

"Yes, please. I'd appreciate that."

"I'll handle it, then." Martin's pause seemed a little uncomfortable. "Would you like to see Mrs. Callaghan now?"

Luke shoved his hands into his pockets and stared at the carpet so intently Madison guessed he wished he could disappear into it. Her heart went out to him, even though she was certain the last thing he'd appreciate was sympathy.

He finally spoke. "Dr. Wagner tells me Lacy's death was...well, particularly heinous. If she isn't...if you couldn't..."

Martin placed a sympathetic hand on Luke's forearm. "She looks so beautiful you'd never know what happened. I think you'll be very pleased."

Luke nodded, still staring hard at the floor.

"Are you ready now, Mr. Callaghan?" Martin asked again. "I don't mean to rush you, but..."

Luke took a deep breath and nodded.

"Very good, sir. Follow me, please."

As he led them from the sitting area, Martin's surprisingly deep voice floated over his shoulder. "We've put her in one of our smaller rooms, so you'll be able to have a nice private visit with her. No one will bother you, and you can stay as long as you like."

Martin stopped before a heavy oak door and pushed it open, then stood to the side as Luke and Madison entered the softly lit room. He put a hand on Madison's arm, halting her, and spoke in a worried whisper as Luke walked slowly toward the casket.

"The white dress Mrs. Callaghan is wearing was brought to us by her next-door neighbor, a Hispanic woman whose name I can't remember. I didn't think you'd mind. The dress is so lovely and...covered everything so well... Nobody provided anything, you see."

"Oh my!" Madison was ashamed she hadn't thought of it herself. "I'm so glad. Are you sure you can't remember her name? Luke might want—"

"I'm certain the lady's name is written in the register. She's been here almost constantly."

"Thank you so much, Martin. You've been very kind."

"You're more than welcome, my darling." He patted

her shoulder and turned away. "I'll leave you now. Let me know if you need anything."

The door swung closed silently, and she stood alone. Dim track lights illuminated the white, rose-trimmed casket at the end of the room and the tall, silver-haired man standing beside it.

A lump grew in her throat as she watched him slowly bow his head.

****

Luke stood beside the casket, lost in long-forgotten memories. At this moment, even though her translucent pale beauty was too waxy to be life-like, Lacy Potter Callaghan wasn't dead. He touched her cheek, surprised to find the soft flesh so cold, and tried to study her as if she were a stranger…and not the other half of him.

Pale blonde hair tumbled over her shoulder and fell in shimmering golden waves to her waist, concealing how thin she was. She wore a simple white dress, high-necked and virginal, with a lacy bodice and long sleeves. In the soft lamplight, her full lips gleamed with just a touch of gloss, and her high cheekbones shone with the faintest hint of blush. Her hands, clasped prayerfully over her breasts, held a single pink rose.

Even though the delicate high neck of the dress covered it, Luke imagined the ugly wound across her throat. As frustration and futile rage choked him, he gripped the edge of the satin-lined casket and whispered, "Lacy, how in God's holy name did you come to this?"

But he knew the answer. She'd come to this because he hadn't been there to take care of her. She'd come to this because he'd been self-absorbed and determined to make it on his own. There were so many *if onlys… If only* she hadn't been so needy and he hadn't been so terrified of her needs. *If only* she hadn't been so self-destructive and he hadn't been so filled with rage. *If only* they'd been able to remain children…

And then, finally, against his will, Luke gave himself over to remembering.

He was ten years old, staying at Mrs. Spratt's house with several other foster children, including six-year-old Lacy Potter. Frightened, vulnerable, and angry, he played alone in a world of his own creation—a world where there was plenty to eat, parents tucked their children into bed, and there was no violence, pain, or terror in the dark.

Yet Lacy insisted on entering his make-believe, perfect world. Finally, without intending to or even realizing it, he let her in. As the years passed, he grew to love her long golden hair, her ever-ready grin exposing one slightly chipped front tooth, her long-legged body that was as slim as a young boy's but showed promise of curves to come. For some reason she followed him everywhere; he was the leader, she the disciple. They struck chords of recognition in one another, and as they grew older, they came to believe they'd been put together for a purpose. They were more than best friends; they were soul mates. They didn't know where one left off and the other began. It was natural they'd also become lovers…

Cool fingers on his hand hurtled him back into the present. He stared blindly down at Madison's anxious face.

"I'm terribly sorry to disturb you," she whispered, "but there's a lady here who insists on talking to you."

He tried to clear his brain as he looked toward the door. A short, very heavy woman stood in the shadows, twisting her hands together nervously.

"She was Lacy's next-door neighbor," Madison was saying softly. "Martin says she's been here almost constantly. She tells me she's been waiting because she has something for you. She can't leave until she puts it in your hands herself."

"What could she possibly have for me?"

Madison shrugged. "I don't know, but she says that if anything ever happened to Lacy, she was supposed to give it to you directly—Lacy's orders. So she refuses to leave until you see her."

Luke frowned as he waited for the woman to make her way down the aisle to join them, then led her to a small visiting area on the other side of the room. He helped her ease her enormous body into a softly cushioned sofa. He spotted a box of tissues on an end table and handed it to her, hoping she could stop crying. Too nervous to sit and too conscious of the casket nearby, he finally leaned against the wall and waited for someone to speak.

Madison broke the silence. "Ma'am, is there anything we can do to help you? What's your name?"

"I'm so sorry…" The woman hiccoughed and blew her nose. "I didn't mean to cry like this. I'm Carlotta Martinez."

As she mopped her cheeks with a tissue, Luke continued to wait for her to regain her composure and studied her from the corner of his eye.

If she were standing, she wouldn't reach his chest, but she was at least two hundred pounds of quivering flesh. Magnificent dark eyes, shadowed with grief, dominated an unlined face of indeterminate age. Raven hair was pulled tightly into a thick bun on top of her head, and her massive body was encased in a black Mexican peasant dress. A hundred pounds ago and twenty years earlier, she'd been a real beauty.

Her lower lip trembled for a moment before she spoke. "It's very good of you to meet with me, Mr. Callaghan. I was afraid you wouldn't."

Now he walked quickly to her side and rested a comforting hand on her shoulder. "Not at all, Carlotta. I'm grateful to you for caring so much."

She gave him a quavering smile, then looked over at Madison anxiously.

He understood her apprehension. "This is Dr. Madison Wagner. She's a good friend."

Carlotta visibly relaxed. "It's good to meet you, Miss Doctor. Now, Mr. Callaghan, I won't take much of your time—"

He patted her shoulder again. "It's all right. Call me Luke, okay?"

"Thank you. What I'm going to tell you may not be important, but I feel you should know. Lacy loved you very much, and I think she'd want you to know that."

"I hope you aren't in danger if you talk to me."

Her angry outburst was so sudden and ferocious he was startled.

"Danger, hah! I've been in danger ever since that piece of trash moved in with my Lacy. He frightened me once—because of Lacy and Piper—but no more. I won't keep quiet for him now."

Luke narrowed his eyes. "Excuse me. What piece of trash would that be?"

"*Tony Davila*, Mr. Luke. I'm not afraid of him anymore. Lacy's dead. He can't hurt me now. Only Piper matters."

Madison's chair squeaked as she sat up straight. "Do you know Piper well?"

"Pretty well, I guess."

"Carlotta, I'm a child psychologist, and I'm very concerned about Piper. Before we talk more about what's on your mind, is it okay if I ask you a few questions?"

"I'll try to help you any way I can."

"Carlotta, does Piper speak well? Does she talk a lot, like other children?"

Carlotta gave a soft, reminiscent laugh. "I don't know about 'a lot' because I didn't see her that often toward the end, but I do know she made full sentences by the time she was eighteen months old. She was very bright."

Madison met Luke's eyes for a moment, then leaned forward earnestly. "Did you see her often in the early days?"

"Until Davila stopped letting her come. But if she could get away, she'd come to my back door and say, 'I need a cuddle, Tia Carly.' That's what she called me. *Tia* is Spanish for *auntie*, you know. We'd cuddle until I sent her home or she thought she might get in trouble. Davila kept a firm hand on her."

"Can you remember how you met Lacy?"

Carlotta nodded with such vehemence her bun tilted. She pushed it back into place absently and tucked a straggling lock of blue-black hair behind her ear. "Lacy moved into the house next door to mine just a few months before she gave birth. She had Piper in that house, with only me and Juan to attend her."

"Juan?" Luke asked quietly.

"My husband. He's dead now."

"Oh. I'm sorry."

"Thank you. Anyway, Lacy lived alone and said she had no money, but I knew better. She spent her money on drugs. She had needle marks on her arms and then later behind her knees. She was afraid to have her baby in a hospital because she knew they'd never let her bring it home. And she wanted that baby."

So that's why there was no birth certificate, Luke thought, and no record at the courthouse. Considering Lacy's inherent distrust of the system, it was easy to understand why she would've wanted to keep her baby's birth a secret. She'd learned the hard way what happened when the state got its hands on a baby. It all made sense to him now. Yet to be pregnant and continue to do drugs—that was more than even Luke could forgive.

"Was Piper all right when she was born?" he asked hesitantly. "No sign of addiction?"

"None. She was a perfect, beautiful little baby."

Well, maybe there's a God after all…

Madison's voice interrupted his thoughts. "How did you know Lacy so well? Drug addicts don't usually get very close to people."

Carlotta's face softened. "My Juan thought that strange, also, but I understood. I'd had six babies, and I know a lost child when I see one. Lacy was old enough to have a baby, but she needed a mama herself. I learned much later she never had one, but that's all I know how to be. I was so happy to have Lacy to take care of, and then later, when Piper was born, I was overjoyed. I thought I'd get to take care of a new baby, but that didn't happen. At least, not after Davila moved in."

Luke cleared his throat nervously. "*When* was Piper born?"

"Six years ago, on October thirteenth. I bought her a present every year until…" Her voice trailed away, and her eyes filled again.

"Until what, Carlotta?" Madison prodded softly.

"Until last year, on Piper's fifth birthday. By then Davila ruled that house, and I seldom visited with Lacy anymore. She was terrified of him. My Juan had died, my children were grown and gone, and I lived alone. There was nothing I could do for her. One day Davila came to my house, not too long before Piper's fifth birthday, and warned me to stay away from them. I did what he said. Nobody ever argues with Tony Davila."

"Can you remember when he first came to live with Lacy?" Luke asked. The question was so crucial his voice actually seemed to echo in his ears.

As Carlotta thought about it, Luke began deftly calculating. He'd left Lacy six years ago in February 2016 and filed for divorce in March. In June the divorce was granted, and she'd given birth in October. Since Texas law didn't allow divorce if there was a child on the way, Lacy's tall, slender body must've concealed her pregnancy. She hadn't even told Luke there *was* a baby until December—the first time they'd spoken since he left her—and she'd sworn the baby was his.

And how had he responded?

He'd laughed out loud, called her a few choice names, and hung up.

Carlotta's voice startled him. "Davila came to live with them in December when Piper was about two months old. I remember because it was really cold. Lacy left Piper with me as much as she could until then. But one morning in early December, when Lacy appeared at my door to take Piper home, Davila was with her. Lacy

48

said he was going to live with them and I wouldn't have to worry about Piper anymore." Carlotta raised her head and thrust out her chin in defiance. "I looked into his eyes and knew he was the most dangerous man I'd ever meet in my life. Lacy tried to warn me—"

Luke shut out Carlotta's voice.

Davila came in December…

Those words rang in his ears, over and over—like the tolling bells of the death sentence he'd so selfishly passed down on Lacy. And Piper. Lacy had called him in December and begged him to come meet his child. He'd refused, and Davila had moved in.

In December.

Luke closed his eyes. Like so many other times in her life, Lacy had cried out for him, but this time she'd been too proud to say she needed him, too proud to ask for help with her baby. He'd turned his back on her and done nothing…

I did nothing except accuse her of trying to pawn another man's child off on me.

Suddenly, he was bathed in sweat and locked inside an airless, invisible space of panic and guilt. Madison's accusing gaze seared his soul, ripped him apart. She knew all about him now, if she hadn't known before…

A moment passed before he realized Madison didn't know a thing. She didn't even seem interested. She was focused only on getting the answers she needed. Luke tried to pull himself together before she figured out who and what he really was.

Her voice broke into the stillness. "Carlotta, you said Lacy tried to warn you. About what?"

"About Tony. My daughter, Consuelo, has two beautiful little boys. Piper was about a year old by then.

Consuelo worked at a butcher shop not far from my house, and she left her children with me during the day." The radiant smile returned for a fleeting moment. "I was so happy because taking care of my grandbabies kept me busy. I didn't have time to worry about my Juan, who wasn't well, or about Piper next door. That summer I bought a small plastic swimming pool and put it in the front yard for my grandsons to play in. They'd go outside in their little bathing suits and splash in the water. It was very hot..." Her voice trembled and trailed away.

Suddenly Luke felt it deep down in his gut—he didn't want to hear this. "It's all right, Carlotta," he interrupted quickly. "You don't have to say any more."

"It's just...hard to talk about." The sofa creaked as she shifted her enormous weight. "One afternoon, when my grandsons were playing outside in the swimming pool, I was in my rock garden pulling up the weeds. I had my back to them, but when I heard Davila's voice, I turned around and came out of my garden immediately. He was down on his knees in front of Felipe, my youngest grandbaby who was three years old. Davila was telling Felipe how handsome he looked in his little bathing suit. He had one hand on Felipe's waist, and while he was talking, his other hand kept moving up and down, over Felipe's bottom. I could see his fingers digging into Felipe's skin. The poor baby was stiff with fear. His mouth was open, as if he wanted to cry out, but he never made a sound. I would've gone after Davila with my weeding tool, but I move slowly...

"Just then, Lacy flew out of her house like a crazy woman. She grabbed Davila's arms and screamed about how he wasn't going to hurt any more babies. Davila is a powerful man, and he smashed her in the face so hard she hit the ground and lay there, still. I thought he'd killed her. My grandbabies were both crying, scared to death. I just stood there, so shocked I couldn't move. I couldn't believe he'd hit Lacy or touch my babies like that in front of me, but he just stared at me with those terrible black eyes and smiled. I knew he was daring me to stop him."

Luke fought to breathe. His heart slammed in his chest. He choked with fury.

"Three days later, when Consuelo brought the babies to my house, Lacy met her outside and told her to take them away and never bring them back. When Consuelo told me Lacy had done that, I knew it was a warning to me, also. She didn't want *any* children around Davila."

Luke's jaw clenched with rage, and he couldn't hold it back. "Except Piper." His low voice shook with anger. "Her own little girl… She didn't care enough to protect Piper."

Chapter Four

From the corner of his eye, Luke saw Madison shake her head and forced himself to swallow his fury. He cleared his throat.

"What about Lacy?" Madison asked quickly. "How did her life go after that?"

"Lacy was a very beautiful woman, Miss Doctor. The first time I saw her, I couldn't believe my eyes. My Juan once said she took his breath away, but I was never jealous because it was the truth. Even the drugs didn't seem to damage her beauty. But she was always so sad, so lost. After Davila moved in, Lacy changed. She seemed to crawl inside herself, like she didn't feel safe anywhere else. She worked all night and slept all day— Davila had her working almost constantly. Do you know what I mean by *working*, Mr. Luke?"

"I do."

"Who took care of Piper when Lacy was gone?" Madison asked in a strange, still voice.

"I'm not sure, Miss Doctor. Sometimes Davila stayed with her, but I don't think anyone really took care of her." Carlotta's expression clouded. Suddenly, she buried her face in her hands and broke into sobs. "I'm sorry… I've felt so guilty… I'm so terribly sorry…"

Luke couldn't move; he didn't know how to comfort her.

But Madison gripped Carlotta's hands and eased

52

them away from her face. "You're no more guilty than anyone else, Carlotta. We all failed Piper here, not just you."

"No, Miss Doctor, you're wrong. I failed Piper because I was more afraid for myself, my home, my husband, my grandsons…"

Madison handed her a wad of tissues and said grimly, "You had every right to take care of your family, Carlotta. You were right to be afraid."

"You don't understand, Miss Doctor. I loved Lacy very much, but an alley cat is a better mother than she was. She lived only for the drugs and couldn't see what was happening to Piper. Or maybe she didn't want to see." Carlotta blew her nose and dabbed at her tearstained cheeks. "But I saw, and I did nothing."

For the first time, Madison seemed to lose a little of that phenomenal control. Her voice trembled. "Tell me…*what* did you see?"

Carlotta sagged and suddenly appeared exhausted and old. She took another deep breath.

"The first few years Davila lived with them, Piper seemed all right. But by the time she was five, her life was terrible. She never ate, and she was so thin she looked like a little skeleton. She was always bruised—not like the bruises children get when they play hard, but ugly bruises on her face and body. I often saw cuts, too. One time a cut lip, another time a cut over her eyebrow. She never went to school or church or played with other little ones. I believe she was often beaten, but she never cried. Sometimes she came to see me, and we'd sit together on the couch. She'd curl up as close to me as she could get and hold my hand. She never said anything about what was happening to her, but I could see for myself."

"Cuts and bruises...no food...no school..." Madison's voice sounded far away. "Carlotta, are you sure you never reported this to anyone?"

Carlotta looked down, obviously ashamed. "No, Miss Doctor. It was wrong of me, but—"

"Well, somebody did," Luke interrupted roughly. "Dr. Wagner says the authorities received several reports from *somebody*. Did Lacy not have any friends?"

Carlotta shook her head. "Davila wouldn't allow friends. Piper and Lacy were completely alone."

Madison's frown deepened. "Did no one ever call the police?"

Carlotta gave an indelicate snort. "No one calls the cops in my barrio. Cops hardly ever go there. And if they do, they don't stay long. We don't waste our time with cops. We take care of our own business."

But Madison couldn't seem to let it go. "Haven't they talked with you about Lacy's murder? You knew her so well and live next door..."

"I haven't seen a single cop since it happened. I left my home a few hours ago to move in with my daughter, and I'm never going back. It's the way things work in the barrio—"

"It doesn't matter now," Luke broke in brusquely. "Carlotta, is there anything else you want to tell us?"

She hesitated, then nodded. "Early this morning, about three o'clock, my two dogs began barking and woke me up. I got up and started looking around my house. I saw nothing, but then...I heard noises coming from next door, from Lacy's house. I stood at my kitchen window—it looks right into Lacy's side yard—and watched. A man came outside, through the back door, and I knew it was Tony Davila. He moves like a cat. I'd know him anywhere."

Luke couldn't believe his ears. "Davila! Why would he risk that? Cops are looking for him. We saw a detective outside last night—"

"I don't know," Carlotta interrupted, "but I know it was him, and I know he was looking for *something*. Whatever it was, he was willing to get caught to find it. I don't know for sure, Mr. Luke, but it might be this."

Carlotta reached into an oversized handbag, pulled out a large manila envelope, and handed it to him. "Lacy gave this to me just two weeks ago. It was the last time I saw her alive. She told me if anything happened to her, you'd come home and I should give it to you. I don't know how she knew you'd come, but she was sure you would."

He didn't open the envelope. "Do you know what's in it?"

"She didn't tell me, but she said I had to give it to you. So…here it is."

"Carlotta, do you really think this is what Davila was looking for?" Madison asked.

"Not really, Miss Doctor. I think he's looking for Piper because she may have seen him murder Lacy." She gripped Madison's hands. "Miss Doctor, do you have her?"

"She's safe," Madison assured her vaguely. "She's completely safe."

"No, she's not. She's never been safe. She isn't safe now. Do you know where she is?"

Madison nodded.

"Then hide her away, Miss Doctor. He *will* find her. He *has* to find her." Carlotta's voice dropped to a whisper. "I believe his own life depends on it."

****

After Madison and Luke had put Carlotta safely onto the bus that would take her back to her daughter's home, they returned to the SUV and sat silently. Luke felt her speculative gaze on him, but he couldn't meet it. The last thing he wanted to know was what she was thinking.

Finally, she spoke. "I hope she gets home all right. I would've driven her."

"She'll be fine," he answered absently. "Listen, we need to reach Whitney and tell her to watch Piper like a hawk. Not to answer the door for anyone. Do you want to do that or should I?"

"I will."

"Okay." He opened the door. "By the way, I gave Carlotta our business cards, just in case she remembers anything else. I'm going to step outside and get some air. I need to think."

Nodding, Madison gave him an absent-minded wave and removed her cell phone from her purse.

Luke was oblivious to the light Sunday afternoon traffic as he thought about Carlotta's story. It chilled his blood, but it wasn't unfamiliar. He'd spent years hanging out with little victims just like Piper—most specifically, Piper's mother, Lacy Potter. What *was* unfamiliar was the sense of responsibility he felt now and the realization that his narcissism and anger could cost a little girl her life. He owed it to Piper and Lacy to provide a safety net…maybe even a home…

He slammed the door on that thought. It was too radical, and he wasn't ready to go there. Right now, he needed to figure out what Davila had been searching for.

He didn't have a clue where to begin, but he didn't agree with Carlotta that he'd been hunting for Piper. Davila was familiar with the legal system. He was bound to know that once Lacy's dead body had been discovered, the police would've removed Piper from that house.

Unless…

His eyes widened as one particular memory of his misspent youth hit him. He jerked open the SUV door just as Madison was sliding her cell phone back into her purse.

She greeted him with a shocked epithet. "What the hell? Have you lost your mind?"

He shook his head, slammed the door closed, and locked it. "Actually, I think I've found it." He turned to face her. "Listen, I need to go to Lacy's house. I need to get inside. Can we do that?"

"Absolutely not. It's still an official crime scene. Besides, what if Davila comes back and finds us?"

He shrugged. "Then he does and I'll handle it. But I don't think he was looking for Piper. That doesn't make any sense. He knew a little girl wouldn't remain alone in a house crawling with cops—they'd take her. Don't get me wrong. He probably wants her, and badly. But I think he was looking for something else, and I may know where it is."

"You've never even been inside that house."

"No, but I know Lacy. If she's hidden something, I may know exactly where it is."

"How would you know that?"

"Because I taught her."

"What do you mean, *you taught her*?"

"Madison, I don't expect you to understand this. But…do you trust me?"

"No."

He sighed. "Fair enough. But do you agree we need to find what Davila was looking for before he finds it? If he hasn't found it already?"

"Of course." She gave him a conspiratorial wink. "But why don't you open that envelope first? That's a lot easier than breaking into her house."

He'd completely forgotten the large envelope Carlotta had placed in his hands. He pulled it from beneath his seat, opened it carefully, and reached inside, touching booklets, papers, rubber bands. When he ripped the envelope apart, the contents showered into his lap and onto the floorboard.

In an instant, Luke knew exactly what Lacy had given him, and he understood why. These were bank statements, deposit books, receipts… And without even looking at the figures, he knew she'd banked every dollar he'd ever sent her.

Madison's awed whisper broke the stillness. "Is that the money you told me about?"

"Probably."

"It looks like an awful lot of money. What bank is it?"

He looked at a return address. "Centurion Bank in Boerne. I'll go through this when we get home."

"We should leave right now."

He shook his head. "Listen to me. I have to get in that house. Don't you see that?"

"No."

He shoved the bank items back into the envelope. "This was Lacy's way of telling me what a selfish idiot I am."

"Oh, I doubt that—"

"No, it is. And now I need to get in that house to find out what else she's trying to tell me. I can't go home until I do. Come with me or not, but I'm getting inside that house."

"But you don't even know *what* we're looking for."

"You're right, but I think Davila's willing to risk everything to find it. Lacy probably knew he would. I just pray I find it before he does."

****

The late afternoon had become much chillier by the time Madison turned into an alley that ran behind Lacy's house. While on their way, Luke had placed another concerned phone call to Whitney, who assured him everything was fine, and Madison had dashed into a truck-stop restroom to change from her tailored slacks and heels into a much warmer, blue running outfit and sneakers she kept in the back of her SUV. Now, as she watched gathering thunder clouds pass over a disappearing sun and noted the tiny droplets of drizzle skating down the windshield, she shivered and parked in the alleyway. She shut off the engine.

"There's a flashlight in my glove compartment," she said. "The house is about three doors down. We'll be going in the back. The house next door—I guess it's Carlotta's—has a chain-link fence. She said her dogs barked, so we need to watch out for them in case they're still there. You didn't see any cops on Lacy's street when we drove down it, right?"

He shook his head, took the flashlight from the glove compartment, and paused before he opened the door. "Anything else?"

Madison bit her lip, thinking. "I don't remember seeing any caution tape anywhere. Unless the police have actually barricaded it, which I doubt, there's no lock on the back door. But it won't matter either way. Some of the windows are broken, so hopefully we can squeeze through if we have to. Watch out, though. The roof's caving in over the living room."

Luke glanced anxiously toward the sky. "We may be in for a real frog-strangler."

"Are you sure you want to do this?"

"We *have* to do this. And we have to do it now, before someone spots us. You don't have to come with me. You could lie down in the front seat."

She chuckled. "This SUV is just two years old. They'd steal it with me in it. I'm better off with you."

"Was that supposed to be a compliment? C'mon. I hear thunder."

They closed their doors quietly and walked nonchalantly down the alley, as if they belonged there. A heavy raindrop plunked on the top of her head and rolled down her brow. She dashed it away and glanced at the darkening sky, worried. A streak of lightning zig-zagged through the charcoal-gray clouds in the far distance. It wouldn't be long before it would be too dark to see three inches in front of them.

Madison knew Lacy's house was on the left, but the backyards were so littered with trash, wind-tossed garbage cans, and isolated auto parts it was nearly impossible to distinguish one house from another. She picked her way carefully down the alley, trying to avoid broken beer bottles and bent tire rims. When they reached Carlotta's chain-link fence, Madison put a finger to her lips and pointed to the house next door.

Luke nodded and moved ahead of her. Sunlight struggled behind a dark cloud, and a few more heavy raindrops landed on her shoulder. She grabbed the back of Luke's sweater.

He stopped immediately and turned around. "Are you all right?"

She hid behind indignation. "Of course, I'm all right! Do you see any cops?"

He looked back at the house and shook his head. "No. God, this place looks terrible in the daylight!"

She didn't think it looked all that great in the dark, but she kept her opinion to herself and pointed to the far side of the little frame house. "There's a driveway over there. Do you see anything?"

He took a few steps in the direction of her forefinger, peered into the shadows, and shook his head again. "Nope."

"Let's go, then. It's now or never."

A steady shower of chilling rain began to fall as she followed him across the straggly grass in the backyard and up a winding path to a concrete slab that served as a narrow porch. They stood at the door and assessed the small house. A window to the right of them was broken—she knew that to be the bathroom—but it was too narrow for even a child to wriggle through.

He reached for the doorknob, turned it slowly, and winced as the door creaked open. Glancing over his shoulder, he leered at her. "Enter my boudoir," he invited, low in his throat, and gave a wicked chuckle. "I vant to suck your blood—"

"Oh, shut up and get inside, you idiot."

Their whispers screeched through the stillness. A dog barked nearby, and her heart stopped. As Luke walked into a small, dark kitchen and flicked on the flashlight, she remained close behind him.

What had possessed her to agree to this crazy stunt? They could be hauled downtown for breaking and entering, tampering with evidence, obstruction of justice, and anything else an irritated homicide detective could dream up.

An ear-splitting crack of thunder shattered the silence. But Luke seemed not to notice as he moved the flashlight beam over the rotting linoleum floor, past cabinets, up and down walls. She followed the light with her eyes, aghast, and hardly noticed as an enormous cockroach skittered near her foot.

She couldn't believe what she was seeing. Cabinet doors were open, and dishes had been flung carelessly to the floor. Slivers of broken glass were scattered everywhere. Dingy, grease-streaked paper had been ripped from the walls, the base of the pantry had been jerked free, and the shelves of an ancient ice box had been tossed near the back door.

"Luke, this place has been ransacked. It wasn't like this before."

He turned to look at her, his dark eyes as hard as steel. "I told you Davila wasn't looking for Piper."

"Then what?"

He shrugged. "Wait here. I'll be back."

"If you think I'm waiting here by myself, you're even crazier than I thought."

She followed him from the kitchen into the living area. In the cold beam of the flashlight, the interior looked even more forlorn than she remembered. Paint was peeling from the walls, great chunks of linoleum jutted from the floor, exposing rotted wood, and part of the ceiling dangled, threatening to fall through at any moment. She even detected the odor of spoiled fish.

This room had been ravaged as well, practically dismantled. The blinds, yellowed with nicotine and age, hung lopsided at the small front window. Stained pillows from an armchair and a sofa had been sliced and ripped apart; piles of fluff and stuffing littered the floor. The drawers from an old desk were tossed into a corner.

Thunder crashed again. Driving rain pounded and reverberated against the roof. Without even thinking, she grabbed Luke's hand and held on. His fingers were cold and clammy with sweat. He flashed the light up and down the walls so rapidly she was sick to her stomach, but he seemed oblivious. He was a man on a mission.

"Is there a closet in here?" he asked finally.

She frowned, trying to remember. "No. The only closet is in the back bedroom."

"Let's go."

She followed closely behind him as he moved carefully down the narrow hallway, flashing the light from one side of the wall to the other. He paused long enough to stare at an overhead vent, then walked on. She came to a sudden halt as his broad back obstructed the entrance to the bathroom. When she peeked around him, she gagged.

The walls were a nasty gray and smelled like mold. The inside of the toilet bowl was black with filth, and the base of the tub was splotched with rust-orange stains. He stepped inside but took only a moment to glance at the bare shelves in the open medicine cabinet and shine the light at a vent over the commode. The top of the toilet back was askew. He glanced into it without showing any real interest and turned back to her.

"Let's get out of here."

The bedroom was just a few steps away. He stood

immobile in the doorway for a long moment, then stepped inside and bowed his head. Once more, impulsively, she reached for his hand.

Age-yellowed, shredded shades covered the window beside a filthy mattress on the floor. Crimson blotches stained the cracking linoleum from the makeshift bed to the closet door, and dirty footprints were visible over the tape that outlined where Lacy's lifeless body had been discovered. Dresser drawers were yanked open, and flimsy undergarments littered the room. A cheap silk nightgown was still draped over a time-distorted mirror.

He seemed unable to speak, and she couldn't even imagine what he was going through at this moment or what his memories were. She squeezed his fingers comfortingly.

The movement seemed to bring him back around. "Is this the only bedroom?"

She nodded. Outside, the storm was growing worse, but inside, a throbbing malignancy seemed to move in waves of evil through the house. She'd never experienced anything like it.

All she wanted was out.

Once more, Luke began shining the flashlight around the bedroom, his brow furrowed in intense concentration. When he saw the closet, he walked toward it but then stopped, as if he was afraid to discover what secrets might be hidden behind that door.

Finally, he jerked the door open. "Will you come hold this flashlight for me, please? Shine it on the wall in the back."

She obeyed and stared inside the closet. This didn't make any sense.

Although the house was old and falling apart, each of the three walls in this large closet were paneled with comparatively new cedar. Everyone knew that cedar protected clothing, but only a few articles hung inside: three cheap bathrobes, one inexpensive blouse, two pairs of blue jeans. Why would Lacy want to protect that?

He shoved the clothing far to one side, then entered the dark closet and knelt before the back wall. She followed him with the flashlight, watching as he carefully felt along each panel of cedar.

Finally, she had to ask. "Luke, what *are* you looking for?"

"A door. Some kind of door." He thumped softly against the wall with the meaty part of his hand. "You can see this wood isn't original, right?"

"Sure."

"When Lacy and I were together, I built a makeshift closet *inside* the closet in our bedroom. We put wood over the side walls like normal, but we brought the back wall farther in. If you're strapped for money, all you have to do is mount some cheap paneling on ceiling-to-floor plywood and bracket it from behind. That gives you as much space as you want between your wood and the original closet wall. It's not going to stand up under a dynamite explosion, but it'll work in a pinch."

"What's the point?"

He grinned at her over his shoulder. "You hide stuff behind the wall."

"Stuff?"

He gave her a pitying look and went back to feeling the cedar panels. "Sure. Drugs, guns, jewelry, cash…whatever you want to hide. In our case, it was anything we didn't want the cops to find. Anyway, Lacy helped me build it, so she was perfectly capable of building another one. There's bound to be—" His voice caught. "And there is. Right here."

She knelt beside him and shined the flashlight near his right hand. "I see it."

He placed his hand flat against the wood and gave a gentle shove to his left. Four panels moved easily. Apparently unconnected to the ceiling and attached to a thicker slab of plywood only slightly in front of the rest of the clumsily constructed barrier, the paneled door opened to expose only the rotting wood of the closet's original wall.

Rocking back on his heels, he stared at her incredulously and gave a low whistle. "What a perfect place to hide a child."

Chapter Five

Madison held her breath as she thought about how terrified a child would be to be hidden in a space this small and dark. She released her breath in a long sigh. "Do you think Piper knew about this?"

"I think it's more important to wonder if Davila did." Then Luke answered his own question. "I'm sure he did. I actually came up with the idea after I saw a Clint Eastwood movie from way back—that's how old this trick is. What I don't understand is why Davila didn't tear this closet apart like he did the rest of the house—or why the cops didn't."

"The cops probably didn't care enough, and Davila probably didn't have time. Carlotta said her dogs started raising hell, remember?"

"Stop talking and look. You take that side and I'll take this one."

Luke grunted as he leaned forward and reached behind the wall. Madison touched the back corner of the original closet. What was she even looking for? Cobwebs wrapped themselves like sticky silk around her fingers, and a small insect swept across the top of her hand, but she gritted her teeth and continued feeling every inch of the floor in front of her. Suddenly, her fingers brushed against a hard object, and she gasped with excitement.

"Here…it's in plastic or something." She brought

the item from its hiding place and handed it to Luke. "It's a DVD."

He held it between two fingers warily, as if it were an unpinned hand grenade, then placed it carefully on the floor beside him. A muscle twitched in his jaw. "This can't be good."

"Maybe Lacy was blackmailing someone, or someone was blackmailing her."

He was silent, then shook his head. "No, this is for me. She left this DVD for me."

"You can't actually believe that."

"Oh, I do. Think about the kind of man Tony Davila is. Think about the condition Lacy was in. She was a lot of things, but she wasn't stupid. She had to know she was a dead woman. She also knew if anything happened to her, I'd come back and handle it."

Madison frowned. His voice sounded calm enough, but she didn't like his expression. He was rigid with tension, like a man battling repressed emotions he hadn't experienced in years.

She decided to try logic. "Luke, I find it hard to believe that Lacy left something like this in a hidden place on the off chance you'd come back and find it."

"That's what you don't understand—it wasn't an off chance. She knew I'd remember and I'd look for a hiding place like this."

A deafening clap of thunder shook the house, and Madison leaped to her feet. "C'mon, Luke. This whole place could come down on us. Please...let's get out of here!"

"Wait. I want to—"

"No! Now!"

"Oh, for God's sake..."

Luke shoved the DVD into his jacket pocket and grabbed Madison's hand, then pulled her down the hallway toward the back door. As thunder rolled overhead and a jagged streak of lightning illuminated the wretched kitchen for just a moment, Madison couldn't help but think of little Piper.

How many storms just like this had she weathered in this house? Maybe even all alone...hiding in that closet...

Luke seemed to read her mind as he pushed the door open. "Don't think about it now, Madison. Let's just go home."

****

Luke was lost in thought as Madison drove back to the shelter, and it was dark when they finally arrived. Although it still drizzled on and off, the thunderstorm had passed, leaving the cold night air heavy and humid.

She turned off the ignition and pointed to a late-model pickup truck parked by the curb. "Jared's already here, so he must've gotten the file."

"That's good," Luke said absently. He was going to ask her for a huge favor and didn't quite know how to word it. He decided to just plunge in. "Madison, could you do something for me?"

"If I can," she answered instantly. "What is it?"

"Could you just keep everything to yourself?"

"What do you mean?"

"Well, don't say anything about the DVD or the bank records, okay? I'm going to take everything straight up to my room and look at it later...if you don't mind."

He felt a little embarrassed about his request, but he wasn't ready to explain anything about his relationship with Lacy to people he didn't know. He needed to think, to try and understand it himself.

She grinned. "Of course. I never intended to tell my attorney we broke into a crime scene anyway."

He chuckled. "Thank you. I appreciate that."

"C'mon. I'm starving, aren't you?"

He wasn't, but he nodded and followed her inside, folding Lacy's bank envelope into his jacket pocket next to the DVD. As he made his way upstairs to his room, the packages seemed to burn right through his heavy sweater. On the one hand he was eager to study it all because he felt sure many of his questions would be answered, but on the other hand he dreaded it. No matter which way it went, he was sure it would be a lose-lose situation for everyone.

As he walked back toward the stairs, he heard children's laughter coming from a room at the end of the hallway. Without thinking or knocking, he opened the door just enough to see inside without being seen himself.

This was a cheerful blue-and-white playroom with floor-to-ceiling white shelves, blue plastic tables and chairs, and two large toy boxes pushed against one wall. Several children were seated on the floor, cross-legged, engrossed in an animated film. But only one child grabbed Luke's attention and held it.

Clad in fuzzy green pajamas, Piper sat off to one side of the group—clearly still not part of it, but not as isolated as she'd been earlier in the day. Her thin blonde hair hung over her shoulders, and her huge dark eyes were encircled by purple shadows. Her sadness seemed almost palpable to Luke, just as it had this morning, but there was one significant change.

Right beside Piper lay Sasha, the beautiful Alaskan

malamute Madison had explained always made the most traumatized children in the shelter her mission. Her huge silver-and-white head rested in Piper's little lap as she absently stroked one of her furry ears, and her eyes were closed. Both Sasha and Piper seemed at peace with the world.

Luke smiled and closed the door quietly. This was something he could relate to, a kid with a dog.

Whistling a soft tune between his teeth, he headed downstairs.

"Sit down and grab a bite," Madison said as he entered the kitchen. "This is Jared Ross, our attorney. Jared, Luke Callaghan."

Jared stood up instantly and offered his hand. Luke shook it and eased his long frame into the only vacant chair at the table.

"Glad to meet you," Jared said.

Luke didn't respond.

Whitney handed Luke a plate of cold cuts from her place next to him. "Want some potato salad?"

"No, thanks. A sandwich is fine."

As he prepared a ham-and-cheese sandwich, Luke tried to study the attorney without being too obvious. Jared Ross seemed like a normal enough guy, but Luke didn't trust lawyers and had never known one he could actually call *normal*. In his experience, they were all arrogant control freaks who couldn't care less about their clients. All they cared about was how many families they could break up and whether they got paid after they did it.

Whitney tapped his forearm with her fork. "Did you hear what I said, Mr. Callaghan?"

"No, I'm sorry. I was thinking."

"I said Sasha adopted Piper today. They're best friends now."

Luke met her gaze and grinned. Something about Whitney's wide-open, guileless face made him want to smile. "I know. I peeked into the playroom upstairs and saw them together. That's great, isn't it?"

Jared Ross answered in a deep, gravelly voice that didn't seem to fit his long, lanky frame. "Probably greater than you realize. Sasha has a sixth sense about who needs her the most." He paused and sipped his iced tea. "She's kind of like Mary Poppins. She'll take care of Piper until Piper doesn't need her anymore. Then she'll move on."

Luke looked at him gratefully. "Thank you for telling me that, Mr. Ross. I trust a dog's instincts before I trust that of any human being. If she's adopted my daughter, I see that as a blessing. And I'm grateful."

His words hung in the air. Luke couldn't take them back now even if he wanted to. *My daughter...*

Finally, Jared broke the stillness. "Why were you guys so worried about Piper this afternoon? Is everything okay?"

Madison glanced at Luke before she answered. "Sure. Just double-checking." She changed the subject quickly. "So, Jared, what does the file tell us?"

"Well, not much, really. That's what bothers me. There were abuse reports made—four over just the last year, as a matter of fact. Apparently, they were investigated by different caseworkers, tossed around in staff meetings, and then pretty much disregarded because she wasn't considered to be in immediate danger. I don't know why she wasn't, but she wasn't."

"I don't get that," Luke muttered.

Jared shrugged. "Neither do I, but it's the same old story, I guess. Too many kids, not enough workers, not enough funding, not enough foster families. But here's where it gets interesting. The last report was made a couple of weeks ago, on December second. This was one day *after* Lacy Callaghan was arrested down on Grayson Street for solicitation and possession of methamphetamine. Her attorney bailed her out a few hours later, and I guess she went home.

"But the next day another anonymous report came in, and protective services decided to act on it immediately. Finally. A caseworker went to the house, prepared to take Piper into emergency custody. But before she could even knock on the door, she received a phone call from her supervisor, who said Lacy's attorney had offered to take the child into his home. The caseworker was overjoyed, of course, because she didn't have to find a place for the kid after all. She went back to her office to handle the paperwork without ever contacting Lacy or going inside the house."

Whitney sat back in her chair. "Who was the supervisor?"

"I don't know. The name's redacted."

"Good grief."

"Then what happened?" Luke prodded.

"Well, a few hours later, this same attorney called the caseworker directly and asked where Piper and Lacy were. He said he was at the house to pick up Piper, but no one was there. Lacy and Piper were gone. That's pretty much where the file ends."

"Who was the caseworker?" Whitney asked.

"I don't know. That name's redacted, too..." His voice trailed away.

Madison looked baffled. "And the file ends there?"

Clearly frustrated, Jared ran his fingers through his dark wavy hair and nodded.

"Who was the attorney?" Whitney pressed.

Jared snorted. "You're not going to believe this. Ryan Neely."

"Are you serious?"

Luke cleared his throat. "Excuse me. Who's Ryan Neely?"

"The most expensive lawyer in San Antonio," Jared answered, "and he's not the philanthropic type. He'd never take a kid into his house—or represent a two-bit whore like Lacy Callaghan. I'm sorry, Luke, but that's how Neely would see her. You don't know this guy."

"No worries. Was he the one who bailed her out?"

"I had to run that down with a cop buddy this afternoon because the file doesn't say, but it looks like he was."

Madison held up her hand in exasperation. "Well, that makes no sense at all. If Neely bailed Lacy out and then offered his house to Piper before Lacy was killed, why didn't anyone call him *after* her body was discovered? He clearly would've taken her. Why call *me*?"

Jared shrugged. "I don't know. I didn't realize Neely had anything to do with this at all until this afternoon. It's probably just a detail that was buried in paperwork. I can call him tomorrow if you want me to."

"No, it's okay."

"Well, Piper is safe here now and in your legal custody, so you should be able to talk to anyone you want about her case. I'll call Quinn first thing in the morning."

Luke was beginning to feel a little left out. "Quinn?"

"Quinn Davis," Jared answered. "He's the director of the Department of Family and Protective Services."

"More like the Director of Nothing That Works, apparently," Luke mumbled.

Madison persisted, seemingly focused on a detail Luke couldn't see. "But all the incoming abuse reports are anonymous, right?"

Jared nodded. "And they all came in after-hours."

Whitney propped her elbows on the table and leaned forward. "How would Ryan Neely have known someone called in that last abuse report in the first place, or that protective services was finally going to move on it after all this time? How would he have known they were going to place Piper into foster care? Someone had to tell him. Who was it—and why?"

Jared shrugged. "No clue, but you can ask Quinn yourself. Do you want me to call him for you tomorrow?"

Whitney went pale. "No. Don't call him. If Lacy took Piper with her, then disappeared right after Neely offered to give her a home, she must've had a damn good reason. Leave it alone."

Luke knew Whitney was right. Lacy wasn't an idiot. If she didn't feel her child was safe around this man, she would've moved hell and high water to keep her from him. Lacy's own childhood had taught her to do that. The only time she seemed to have dropped that ball was if a risky situation also involved Antonio Davila.

Suddenly, Madison pushed her chair away from the table and stood up. "I think we've done enough for tonight, Jared. I really appreciate you coming here on such short notice."

"Sure."

"Can you leave that file with me?"

"Of course. It's just a copy." He reached for Whitney's hand. "Are we still on for dinner at The Tavern tomorrow night?"

"Of course, baby. I'll see you at seven."

Luke's chair scraped against the floor as he arose and offered his hand to Jared. "You've been a big help, Mr. Ross. I appreciate it."

Jared's handshake was firm and reassuring. "Please, call me Jared. Do you mind if I ask you a personal question?"

"Not at all."

"You seem fairly certain Piper is your daughter. Am I right about that?"

"I'll have a paternity test run in the morning, but I'm pretty sure she is."

"That's wonderful news, Luke. She's a very special little girl."

Luke straightened his shoulders proudly. He thought he might be feeling like a real dad, but he wasn't sure.

Finally, he answered quietly, "Thank you. I think so, too."

****

"Good morning, Whitney," Luke said cheerfully as he strode into the kitchen, heading straight for the coffee pot. "How are you this morning?"

"Very well, thanks." She carried cereal bowls to the children's table in a colorful room off the kitchen and returned with a wide grin on her face. "Look out the window, Luke. Look at Piper and Sasha."

He poured himself a cup of steaming coffee that looked dangerously black and moved to the window over the kitchen sink. He peered outside, noting with relief that the storm had completely passed. The early morning promised sunshine with a soft breeze, and delicate clouds floated across the azure sky like fragile spider-netting. It would be perfect weather for what he hoped to accomplish today.

His searching gaze finally found Piper seated on a swing, her stick-like legs thrust straight out in front of her as she tried to pump herself. Sasha lay off to one side, one front paw folded delicately over the other, watching the little girl attempt to do something that most kids could do by the time they were three. Clearly in her element, Sasha looked as regal as a queen surveying her domain from a perfect vantage point.

"I think I'll go help."

Whitney placed a restraining hand on his forearm. "I'd leave them be if I were you."

He glanced at her in surprise. "You would?"

"I'd give her a couple more days."

"Okay, you're the pro. Whatever you say."

He took a sip of his coffee and nearly gagged.

Whitney laughed out loud and turned away. "It's this hard water—destroys every appliance we have. I'll get a new coffeemaker the next time I go to the store. So what are your plans for today?"

"I'm not sure. Where's Dr. Wagner?"

"I think she's in her office, trying to answer some phone calls. I know she wanted to talk to Quinn Davis if she could."

"And I can't," Madison said from the doorway. "He's in Austin all day."

Luke frowned. He remembered the name but couldn't place it. "Who's he again?"

"The director of protective services," Whitney

answered. "I don't like him. Luke, I need to herd the kids in for breakfast. Would you see if you can get Piper in the house?"

"But I thought you said I shouldn't..."

"Just go tell her it's time to eat and walk away. That'll be fine."

He set his coffee cup on the counter and pushed open the screen door. As he walked across the back patio, he kept his gaze on Sasha, who had arisen slowly to her feet. Piper came to an immediate halt and jumped down from her swing. She stood as still as a granite statue, her huge dark eyes burning like black coals in her pale face. As Luke came closer, he heard the unmistakable rumbling of a low, warning growl. He stopped and looked away from the dog.

"It's okay, Sasha," he said in a quiet conversational tone. "You're a good girl. I'm not going to hurt you. Either of you."

Sasha's white plumed tail waved over her back, but she eyed him warily and gave him another warning growl.

He ignored her. "Piper, Miss Patterson says it's breakfast time now and you need to come inside."

As he turned and walked back to the house, he was intensely aware of Piper and Sasha following behind him, but he didn't acknowledge their presence. When Whitney pushed open the screen door and gave him a victorious thumbs-up, he felt ridiculously proud of himself.

"Can you come in my office for a minute, Luke?" Madison asked from her spot in the doorway. "Piper, you can take Sasha and go in with the other children for breakfast."

He turned to Whitney. "Thanks for the coffee."

"Don't mention it. I promise to buy a new coffeemaker this afternoon."

He made a mental note to pick one up, just in case she forgot. He wasn't going to survive if he didn't get his hands on a good cup of coffee.

Madison closed her office door behind her. "Take a load off for a minute, okay?"

"Sure." Luke sat in an overstuffed armchair and stretched his long legs out in front of him. His gaze followed her as she bustled efficiently around the office. "What's up?"

"I thought we'd do your cheek swab right now, before the day gets away from us." She pulled a DNA paternity test kit from the bottom drawer of her desk. "This is really just for your information, by the way. It wouldn't hold up in court if you want to fight the results."

The entire procedure didn't take but fifteen minutes.

"I guess this could be life-changing for some unsuspecting bloke, huh?" Luke observed with a chuckle as she finished packaging his specimen. He assumed she was doing it for the umpteenth time in her career. "I'm glad my life doesn't depend on the results."

"Well, if your life depended on it, the entire process would be court ordered and someone would be watching it every step of the way. But this is easy. Whitney will get it mailed out this afternoon, and we should get a response in about a week."

He continued watching her as she walked around her enormous oak desk, stacking files, dropping phone messages into the trash, ripping up single sheets of paper.

Finally, she placed one hand on her hip and looked

at him questioningly. "What?" she demanded. "Have I sprouted six eyeballs or something?"

He grinned. She wore a pair of tailored teal-blue slacks with a matching pullover sweater, and he couldn't help but admire how striking that vivid color was against the copper-toned highlights in her hair. Even though she stood on the other side of the desk, he could still see that her thickly lashed blue-green eyes were extraordinarily beautiful.

"Sorry, I didn't mean to stare. You look terrific. Are you going somewhere special?"

She dropped her gaze. "Oh! Thank you. No, not now. I thought I was going to see Quinn Davis today, but that didn't work out. Still, since I'm actually dressed like a grown-up, do you have any plans I can help you with?"

"I don't know. Maybe."

"What's up?"

"Well, I thought I'd rent a car and go to Centurion Bank in Boerne, just to see what's what with Lacy's account."

"That's not necessary. I'd be happy to take you."

"Well, I need to rent a car sometime today. Maybe after we're finished at the bank?"

"Sure, not a problem."

"What about Piper? I don't want... I mean, Whitney's going out to dinner with Jared tonight, so we need to be back here before they leave."

She smiled. "Spoken like a good daddy. Don't worry. I have a full staff here today, plus Sasha. Don't underestimate her—she's equal to the mafia all by herself. We'll be home before Whitney and Jared leave this evening."

He frowned, unconvinced. Madison might be a child

psychologist accustomed to dealing with people who shouldn't be parents, but he was positive Antonio Davila was out of her league. If Davila found Piper first, a staff of women and one large dog wasn't going to stop him.

She seemed to appreciate his concern. "I'll call Jared and let him know we'll be out of town a little while. He'll check in with Whitney throughout the day. We've also got a great security system and cameras. Please don't worry."

He held up his hand and chuckled. "All right, you win." His smile disappeared. "There's something else, Madison."

She met his gaze and nodded. "I know. We have to watch the DVD. I wish we could've watched it last night after Jared left, but I just couldn't bring myself to…well, you know."

"Let's do it tonight."

"Of course."

He eased himself from the overstuffed armchair and stood up. As she walked around the desk toward the office door, he held out his hand. "Come here a minute?"

She paused, then moved closer to him and allowed him to take her hand. Her head barely reached his chest, and for just a moment he felt the familiar surge of protectiveness he'd always felt with Lacy. It was an uncomfortable memory, but he refused to allow it to color what might be happening between him and Madison Wagner now.

After all, she wasn't Lacy Potter.

"I want to thank you for everything you've done for me, Madison. I don't deserve any help from you, and you've already done so much. I truly appreciate you."

She squeezed his fingers and looked up at him, blue-green eyes swimming with tears. A faint blush suffused her cheeks. "Stop. You're embarrassing me. I'm going to cry."

"I don't care if you cry. I need you to know how I feel."

"Okay. You've told me." She pulled her hand from his grasp and softened her response with a warm smile. "Let me get my jacket, and we'll go, all right?"

"Yes, ma'am." Needing to break the intimacy of the moment, he gave a mocking salute. "Sounds like a plan to me."

Chapter Six

Madison pulled into the Centurion Bank parking lot on Main Street in the small town of Boerne and looked at Luke from the corner of her eye. As usual, he seemed lost in another world, one he couldn't share with her. Was that because he was a writer, or did he just have too many memories?

He pulled his briefcase from beneath his seat and clasped it close to his chest, as if he feared he'd lose it if he let it go. She knew none of this was about the money—Luke Callaghan had more than enough money. It was about him struggling to understand the woman he'd always believed he knew so well.

She had a sudden thought. "You know, they may not be able to tell you anything without the death certificates. Martin said he wouldn't receive them at the funeral home for another week or so."

"I understand that, but my name is on these accounts as well as Lacy's. So that might help. Let's go in and see what they can tell us."

When they'd walked through the swinging doors, Madison stood to the side as Luke spoke quietly to the front desk receptionist, then opened his briefcase and pulled out a large envelope. He removed a document from it and handed it to the young woman. After looking it over for a few seconds, she finally nodded, smiled, and motioned toward a small sofa in front of an enclosed cubicle. Luke said something to her that made her giggle, and Madison stifled a grin.

The man can't help it, she thought in amusement as she followed him to the sofa and sat down. *His world could be ending, but if a pretty girl's around, he's not going to waste a minute.*

The door to the small cubicle opened, and a young man poked his nearly bald head out. "Mr. Luke Callaghan? I'm Bryan Wilkerson." He opened the door wider. "C'mon in."

Luke helped Madison to her feet, then followed Wilkerson inside the tiny office. He seemed to dwarf everything around them.

"Have a seat. How can I help you?" Wilkerson moved his computer screen off to one side of his desk and sat down.

Luke opened his briefcase again, pulled out the manila envelope, and pushed it across the desk. "I hope you can help me with this."

"I'll try." Wilkerson pulled a pair of glasses from a drawer and settled them on the end of his nose.

He removed bank statements, registers, official documents, and even a few old cancelled checks from the envelope and placed them in neat stacks in front of him. He didn't speak until he had gone through it all.

Finally, he looked up and pushed his glasses to the top of his head. "I'm very sorry, Mr. Callaghan. I didn't put you and Lacy...well, that is...I didn't realize..."

"Lacy? You're on a first-name basis with Lacy?"

"Oh yes. She comes in here at least once a month, and I'm the only person she ever asks for. She often speaks of you. I'm so sorry. I should've known."

"There's no way you could've. I haven't seen Lacy

in about six years, and we haven't communicated in all that time. I've just sent money. I know nothing about these accounts."

Wilkerson looked bewildered. "What did you want to know?"

Madison spoke up. "Mr. Wilkerson, I'm Dr. Madison Wagner. I hate to be blunt here, but are you aware that Lacy Callaghan is dead?"

His pale-gray eyes widened with shock. "Oh my God. No, I didn't know. I can't tell you how sorry I am."

Madison was so afraid he was going to cry that she jumped back in immediately, just to keep him on track. "Mr. Wilkerson, since Mr. Callaghan is a signer on these accounts, can you give us a total balance as of today?"

Wilkerson took a deep breath and nodded. "Sure. May I have some identification, Mr. Callaghan?"

"Of course." Luke removed his driver's license and social security card from his wallet. "Are these good enough?"

"Perfect, sir. Do you have a death certificate?"

"No. I understand there's a rush on them, but they tell me it'll be at least another week. I don't want to take any of the money out of here, Mr. Wilkerson, or make any changes. That money was for Lacy and her daughter. I'm just trying to wrap my head around what's happened."

For the first time, Wilkerson's banker-client mask seemed to slip. "Sir, Lacy was in here just a couple of weeks ago, and she was very ill at that time. I told her she needed to see a doctor, but she refused. I was so worried about her that I actually offered to loan her the money—even though I knew she had a truckload more money than I do—"

"That was very kind of you, Mr. Wilkerson," Luke interrupted quickly. "I truly appreciate that. Lacy didn't have many friends."

"Well, she had one. She just didn't realize it. I'll go get the information you need."

When Wilkerson closed the office door behind him, Madison looked at Luke in astonishment. "Well, Lacy clearly stirs up strong feelings in people, doesn't she? Look at Carlotta, and now this guy. Amazing."

"Not really. You didn't know her. There's no way you could be around her for even five minutes without having some kind of strong reaction, good or bad. There was no neutral with Lacy."

"Yet…when *you* were done with her, you were done."

"That was only because I had to be. I knew I'd die otherwise. In all honesty, it had nothing to do with Lacy. There wasn't a day that went by that I didn't miss her. She was everything to me. I just couldn't let her kill me."

Before she could respond, Wilkerson opened the door and returned to his chair. Without a word, he sat down, placed a key on his desk, and handed Luke a piece of paper. "Here's your total, Mr. Callaghan."

Madison had to look at the figure twice to be sure she was seeing it correctly. "Two hundred thousand dollars?" she asked in disbelief. "Are you sure?"

"I certainly am. It includes interest, dividends, cash back rewards…everything."

Luke stared at the key on Wilkerson's desk. "What's that for?"

"Lacy's safety deposit box. Do you have a key? You're on all of her documentation, you know. You're included in everything."

Luke shook his head.

He was beginning to look a little sweaty, so Madison stepped in once more. "Can Mr. Callaghan still check out its contents without a key or a death certificate?"

"Of course. There'll be a lost key fee, but other than that, it'll be fine."

"Thank you," she said softly. "You should probably know, Mr. Wilkerson...Lacy didn't die because she was ill. She was murdered on December twelfth. There was nothing you could've done for her."

His face never changed expression. "Let's take the elevator downstairs and get you set up. Would either of you like a cup of coffee?"

Luke looked hopeful. "No coffee, but I'd love a shot of tequila. Could you manage that?"

Wilkerson stared at him, still stone-faced.

"We don't need any coffee, thank you," Madison said hastily. "Let's go, Luke."

They followed the banker from the office toward the elevators. In a completely natural way and without even thinking, Madison took Luke's hand.

****

They sat at a round oak table in a softly lit private room within what Wilkerson had called *The Vault*. Deep in the heart of the bank, it was a cozy area, complete with piped-in classical music. A telephone was placed on the table in case they needed help, and between them, in the middle, was a legal-sized folder into which Luke placed all the items he'd taken from Lacy's safety deposit box.

Pandora's Box...

Now, as he stared at it, he didn't even bother to hide his feeling of dread from Madison. The man who always hid his true feelings behind a heavy-duty veneer of machismo and charisma wasn't hiding them now. Truth be told, at least at this moment, he no longer cared.

"Do you want me to open it?" she whispered.

He looked at her gratefully, but shook his head. His fingers trembled as he pulled the folder toward him and opened it quickly, then opened it wider and gazed inside at the contents. Taken all together, they appeared harmless enough, but he knew better. If Lacy had gone to this much trouble, she had a damn good reason.

Get this over with, Luke. You owe her.

He removed each item carefully. The first was an envelope labeled *To Luke: Read First*. Next an envelope labeled *Piper's Firsts*. Then one labeled *Do You Remember?* Then a thick envelope labeled *Legal*, followed by one labeled *Letter of Intent*. Finally, there was a manila envelope labeled, in permanent marker, *Open Last. Extremely Private.* Everything was handwritten, in Lacy's large, childish scrawl.

Madison picked up the envelope labeled *Read First* and pushed it across the table to Luke. Before he'd even touched it, she pulled her phone out of her purse and turned her attention to the screen.

Grateful for the privacy she'd given him, he tore it open, removed the folded letter, took a deep breath, and began to read.

November 27, 2022

My Dear Luke,

I'm sure this is the last time I'll be able to come to the Centurion Bank. If you're reading this (and I pray you are), then I know that Tia Carly has given you the banking information I asked her to, and you know now what happened to all your money.

Please don't be mad at me because I saved it, Luke.

I knew Piper wouldn't have anything, ever, if I didn't do that because I knew I wouldn't be alive very long. The truth is I've lived longer than I ever thought I would—or ever even wanted to. I knew if the dope didn't kill me, some john would. Or Tony Davila would. No matter how it happened, I wouldn't be alive very long, and I had to put something by for Piper. If I didn't do it this way, they would've gotten it.

So I'm counting on you to invest it the way you think best, Luke. You always were the smartest guy I ever knew. I've written a letter of intent, which hopefully will take the place of a will, because I don't want to go near any lawyers. You know how I am about that. I hate them with every part of me. But no matter what, I don't own anything except this money you sent me. I set it up so you can get it right now, and I know I can trust you to handle it right.

When Piper was born and I called you in December to ask you to take her, I wasn't trying to trap you. My only thought was to save her. But I was also trying to find a way to be sure you could know your daughter. And she is your daughter. You can run every test known to man, Luke, but you'll find it's true. Still, understand this—I've never blamed you for not taking her. You had no way of knowing she was your baby. You only knew what I was, and your reaction was understandable—and predictable.

I know exactly how you're feeling right now. You're feeling guilty, like this was all your fault, and you're trying to think of something you could've done to save me. You're blaming yourself for leaving me in the first place. Don't do that. You couldn't have changed a thing. You've built a great life for yourself, and I would've ruined that for you. I would've taken you down with me, and you knew that. You left because you had to leave. I've never blamed you, ever.

If you haven't found my closet hiding place, go to my house. It's in my bedroom. I've hidden some stuff in there for you. Don't let anyone see you take anything out. I need you to watch the DVD. You'll hate it, and I'm sorry, but it's the only way I can think of to save the children—because I don't know what's going on. I only know it's very bad and somebody important is behind it. Maybe you can figure it out. I can't.

Finally, I want you to know that I love you. I've always loved you, and I'll die loving you. When I finally get to that place where I'm taking my last breath, I won't see anything but your face. You gave me the happiest years of my life. You taught me what "safe" feels like. If it wasn't for you, I'd never have learned to read, write, play poker, dance, ride a skateboard, or drive a car. If it wasn't for you, I wouldn't know how to stick up for myself or how to protect my baby girl. I know it doesn't seem like I've protected her very well, but she's still alive—and that's thanks to you and everything you taught me. Now you've got to get her to a safe place.

Take care of our Piper, Luke. She deserves so much more than I've given her.

With More Love Than You'll Ever Know,
Lacy

As he blinked back tears and swallowed the lump in his throat, Luke folded the handwritten letter and slid it carefully back into its envelope. Madison looked up from her phone.

"Do you want to talk about it?" she asked softly.

"No. But I'd like you to read this." As he pushed the

letter across the table to her, he asked, "Can you find me her letter of intent, Madison?"

She located it in the stack of items and pushed it across the table.

He opened it slowly. What Lacy intended to pass as her last will and testament was simple and hand-printed.

November 27, 2022

I am Lacy Anne Potter Callaghan, and I am of sound mind and body on this day of November 27, 2022.

I was born on April 8, 1992, in San Antonio, Texas. I don't remember my parents, but I grew up in the Texas Foster Care System. I have one child, a daughter, named Piper Elyse Callaghan, who was born at home on October 13, 2016.

I bequeath all my worldly possessions and financial assets to my former husband, Luke Alan Callaghan, to use in providing for our daughter, Piper Elyse Callaghan, until she is twenty-one years old. This would include her physical care, her medical needs, her education, and a start to any career she chooses. If any funds are remaining, I want him to help her to invest them wisely.

I am leasing a house located at 827 Coronado Street in San Antonio, Texas. I want Luke Alan Callaghan, my former husband, to take possession of anything in that house he would like to have. He is free to sell anything or keep it for himself.

Please honor my wishes.

Lacy Anne Potter Callaghan

At the bottom of this letter was a copy of a Centurion Bank deposit slip, the scrawled unfamiliar names of two witnesses, and the stamped insignia of an unknown notary.

All at once, Luke was overwhelmed with shame—but not for the reason Lacy had thought. He was ashamed because he'd always believed he was smarter than she was, more together than she was, stronger than she was. But she'd proven him wrong, utterly and with total finality. She knew what courage was; he didn't. She knew what love was; he didn't. And she knew what sacrifice was—a sacrifice so great he couldn't have even dreamed it, much less lived it.

"Are you all right?" Madison asked softly.

When he saw the tears streaming down her cheeks, guilt slammed into him. Her reaction to Lacy's letter was normal. His wasn't. He felt frozen inside, as if an ice-slick glacier occupied the place his heart should've been.

But as usual, he didn't let on. "Pass me the rest of the stuff, will you?"

Madison pushed the other items across the table. He opened the envelope labeled *Do You Remember?* and pulled out a set of rabies tags he'd given Lacy when she was about ten years old and he was fourteen. He pulled out a tiny pair of pajamas she'd made for a frog, but then she'd given them to Luke instead to make him feel welcome when he'd arrived at the Spratt house.

And then…there was her wedding ring, a slender gold band he'd purchased in a pawnshop for twenty-five dollars.

He dropped the items back into the envelope before he could think anymore and grabbed the one labeled *Piper's Firsts*. Inside, he discovered a matchbox containing a lock of white-blonde hair with a tiny pink silk ribbon tied around it, a napkin with red crayon scribbles all over it and the words *Piper Callaghan, 18 months* scrawled at the bottom, and a cheap silver baby necklace with three tiny pearls placed evenly at the center.

In six years, this was all she could save of her baby.

Finally, he opened the envelope labeled *Legal* and discovered her final divorce papers, as well as the original court order requiring him to pay her temporary support for three months. A sticky note was attached to it with *You were right* printed across it.

He placed his briefcase on the table, opened it, and carefully stacked all the envelopes inside. All except for one, the one labeled *Open Last. Extremely Private.* He closed the lid and met Madison's gaze warily.

"I don't want to open this."

"Then don't," she suggested reasonably. "Wait until later."

He was silent a moment, then shook his head. "No. I need to do this now."

She pushed her chair around the table and sat down beside him, then folded her hands in her lap and waited.

Without wasting another second, he grabbed the envelope folded into a box-like shape and ripped it open. Four Polaroid photographs fell onto the table. He spread the pictures into a straight line and stared at them. Four children, two boys and two girls, all about six years old, all too thin, filthy, and stringy-haired, all with wide eyes as old as sin and just as burned out. They were neglected, clearly, but they had no bruises, no external signs of abuse.

Who were they? What was the common denominator? It had to be more than their obvious physical similarities. It had to go deeper…

What was it Lacy had written? Luke had to think a moment before it came back to him. *It was the only way*

I could think of to save the children.

She'd been talking about the DVD she'd hidden in her closet, but what children? These children?

He picked up the first photo—a little girl who promised to be beautiful in a few more years—and flipped it over. Written on the back, in unfamiliar handwriting, was *Savannah West, June 7, 2019.*

And then the second, a little boy with a freckled, impish face, but he didn't look mischievous or playful. He looked terrified, staring into the camera as if he'd seen the devil himself. *Toby Lee, August 20, 2019.*

The third, an emaciated little boy younger than the others, or maybe just small for his age, whose curly red hair was wild and hung nearly to his shoulders. *Bobby Grisham, November 22, 2021.*

And finally, a dark-eyed little girl with full, pouty lips and waist-length black hair, looking over her shoulder in a way that Luke found bizarre and mysteriously seductive. Embarrassed, he flipped her photo face down immediately. *Charly MacIntire, January 4, 2022.*

Less than a year ago…

He frowned. "Where would these kids have come from? What do the dates mean? And how would Lacy have gotten these photographs to begin with?"

Madison shook her head. "And why would she leave them here, for you? That's not her handwriting on the back, is it? I think a man wrote it."

"I don't know, but you're right. It's not hers." He paused. "Madison, the other night when you took me to Lacy's house and showed me the cop staking out Antonio Davila, you told me that years ago Davila used to pass Polaroids of children around in a pedophile network."

"Yes, but this isn't pornography. These are just very…sad."

"But they're Polaroids. Who uses Polaroids anymore? We all use our phones to take pictures now, right?" He stood up abruptly. "Listen, Madison, I need to get out of here. I need some air."

"Of course." She picked up the telephone, punched a button, and spoke into the mouthpiece. "Will you tell Mr. Wilkerson that we're finished?"

****

Mr. Wilkerson pushed the last sheet of paper across his desk and waited for Luke to sign his name for the final time. When Luke was finished, he stood up and pulled his wallet from his back jeans pocket.

"How much is the lost key fee?" he asked.

"Twenty-five dollars, sir."

Luke removed the bills from his wallet and handed them to the banker. He sat back down, waiting as Wilkerson filled out a receipt and pushed it across his desk.

"Mr. Callaghan, do you know who killed her?" Wilkerson asked.

"No, but we'll find out. You can count on it."

"Well, I hope so. She deserves a lot better than she got."

Madison spoke up. "Mr. Wilkerson, Lacy's funeral is tomorrow morning at ten o'clock. It'll just be a graveside service at the Sunrise Cemetery in San Antonio. You'd be very welcome if you'd like to come pay your respects. I'm sure I speak for Mr. Callaghan as well."

"Of course," Luke said quickly. "In fact, I'd

appreciate it if you'd come. You were a good friend to Lacy, and she didn't have many friends. You cared, and that means a lot."

Mr. Wilkerson looked at Madison, then Luke, and bit his trembling bottom lip. His eyes filled with tears. "I loved Lacy, Mr. Callaghan. I knew what she was, but I would've married her in a heartbeat. She didn't care about me. Not like that. She used to say you lived in her soul, and I knew there would never be any room for me. So I loved her from a distance." His voice cracked. "It wasn't enough, was it?"

"Mr. Wilkerson, you're a good man, and I'm sure Lacy knew it," Luke responded quietly. "Her life wasn't…well, it wasn't safe. She wouldn't have brought you into it, even if she loved you, too. And who knows? She might have."

Bryan Wilkerson stared down at his desk and flushed brick red. "Thank you, Mr. Callaghan. You don't know how much that means to me."

Chapter Seven

Madison pulled out of the bank parking lot, heading back to I-10 and San Antonio, and glanced over at Luke. His face was pensive, almost sad, but she could feel his tension.

"I'm going to call the house and ask Woodrow to pack some stuff for me," he said. "I'm hoping I can get up to my place at the lake after the funeral tomorrow and pick up my truck. I'd rather do that than rent a car. Do you think a week's worth of clothes would be enough?"

She nodded, keeping an eye on her rearview mirror as a super-lifted monster truck weaved in and out of traffic behind her. She grinned. "Believe it or not, we have a washer and dryer if it isn't."

"Maybe you could drive me out there tomorrow, and we could have lunch," he suggested. "I'll get your gas. I'd like to show you around."

"I'd love to. I hate funerals, so that would be nice."

"Oh, and by the way…I want to pick up a coffeemaker on our way home today."

"Not necessary."

"Oh yes, necessary. In fact, urgent."

She chuckled. "You don't like Whitney's coffee?"

"She says it's the hard water."

"Does she really? I guess that's as good an excuse as any. But…by all means, buy a new coffeemaker if it makes you feel better."

"Thank you, I will."

She noted with relief that the monster truck had pulled into a gas station right before the frontage road. She sped up and moved onto the freeway.

Once she was comfortably settled in the right lane, she glanced at Luke. "Do you want to talk about anything that happened today, or do you just want to be quiet? I can go either way, you know."

"It doesn't matter."

"Well, then, I have a question. I hope you don't mind."

"It's okay."

She gripped the steering wheel and took a deep breath. "Lacy said in her letter that you'd talked to her in December when she asked you to take Piper. So I'm a little confused. I thought you didn't know anything at all about Piper until after Lacy's death."

"I lied," he muttered.

"What do you mean?"

He stared out the side window. "She called me in early December and told me we had a baby girl. I told her there was no way she had any idea whose baby... Well, you can guess what I said. Anyway, I called her some choice names and hung up."

"When you said those things, did she argue? Did she defend herself?"

He shook his head.

"Did she say the baby was in danger or Davila had moved in or...anything?"

"Of course not. I made it pretty clear where I stood, and she knew me well enough to know she couldn't change my mind. Anyway, when I started making a little money on my second novel, I sent some to her. Not because I believed Piper was mine or I felt in the least bit responsible, but because I just wanted them both out of my life. That's the kind of jerk I am."

She sighed. "Don't be so tough on yourself, Luke. Under those circumstances, most men would've behaved the same way. At least you tried."

He was silent for a while, then suddenly turned slightly in his seat and looked at her. "I think I need to tell you about Lacy and me."

She caught her breath, unsure if she wanted to hear it. She wasn't even certain she'd understand. That kind of intensity, passion, connection—that was just *too much*. Some people longed for an all-consuming love like theirs, but not her. She enjoyed controlling her own life.

"It's all right, Luke. I don't need to know."

"Yes, you do. You deserve it."

He ruffled his hair until it was spiked up all over his head, a mannerism she was beginning to recognize as one of complete frustration, but she didn't understand what he was so frustrated about. She'd thought they were working together rather nicely...

"Luke, really. I read Lacy's letter today, and that's all I need to know."

"It would help me a lot."

She surrendered immediately. If it would help him explore what seemed to be an intensely unhealthy relationship of codependency between him and Lacy Potter, she had to listen. Talking it through might help him become a better father, and nothing else mattered to her.

"Of course, Luke. Tell me about you and Lacy."

****

Luke jumped in without hesitation. "Well, I first met Lacy in a foster home. She was six, and I was ten. Mr. and Mrs. Wilbur Spratt ran it, and they had several other kids, too. I think they took in the kids to get the extra money from the state—I'm sure you've heard that before."

"Oh yeah."

"Well, none of that money ever went to us. I'm sure you've heard that, too. Anyway, they lived in a run-down, three-bedroom house on the deep west side of the city. I remember we never had any hot water and we were always hungry. We never went to the doctor, never saw a dentist… We had one kid whose teeth were rotting right out of his mouth—he was in constant pain. The state finally took him away when his face swelled up so badly that he couldn't open his eyes and he was blind as a bat. So they took him out, but the rest of us stayed."

When he saw the look of disbelief on her face, he chuckled. "You're not shocked, are you? It happens all the time. I don't know why I was so surprised to hear Piper hadn't been removed from Lacy's house. Where else were they going to put her? In a place like Mrs. Spratt's? There's not much difference if you ask me.

"Anyway, this was where Lacy and I grew up together. I'd been taken from my mother when I was about two and lived in more foster homes than I could count by the time I was ten. The Spratt house was the last house I lived in. When I got dumped there, Lacy was the first kid I met. Even though I was older, we connected quickly because we had shared experiences—abuse, neglect, abandonment. But Lacy had experienced something I knew nothing about, something I couldn't understand if I lived to be a hundred years old…"

His voice trailed off. She'd been such a beautiful child, so trusting…

"It's okay," Madison said, resting her hand on his arm. "You don't need to tell me."

He scarcely heard her. After a moment, he continued, "She'd been raped repeatedly when she was real little. Nothing ever happened to the man, but she never got over it. When I met her, she was like a wild animal. An incredibly beautiful little girl, even then. She ran from everything, didn't trust anyone—except me. She trusted me. Completely."

"It was good you were there for her—"

"Don't start sounding like a head doctor, Madison. I was the worst thing that ever happened to her. I was bussed to LBJ High School, along with dozens of other 'underprivileged' kids, and I learned there that I just wanted to belong somewhere, to be like all these other kids who had families and homes…and cars. God, how I wanted a car! But that wasn't for people like me, and I knew it. So I found my niche…in athletics, in girls, in parties…in drugs. I learned drugs could get me anywhere I wanted to go. Drugs could get me money, power, and a feel-good high I just couldn't get anywhere else. But most importantly, they gave me a place to hide."

"Everyone has a reason for choosing drugs—"

"Well, that was mine. But as it turned out, who needed a hiding place even more than I did? Lacy. So who did her the big favor? Me." His voice was bitter with self-recrimination. "I turned her on to pot and pills when she was twelve, and I might as well have killed her right then and there. It would've been kinder. From the very first time, she loved it. But she wouldn't have had the nerve to do it without me, and it wasn't like I wasn't old enough to know better."

He was grateful for Madison's silence. She made no attempt to comfort him or tell him he was wrong. He needed to reveal this truth and purge his guilt by pinning all the blame on himself, where it belonged. She was a psychologist, and she probably understood his need to talk, but he hoped that right now she was listening as a friend.

The truth was for the first time in his life, he didn't want to be alone.

"I aged out of the system when I was eighteen," he continued finally, "so I got a job at a corner gas station and then rented a room right back at the Spratt's house just so I could keep an eye on Lacy. When she was fifteen, she told me Mr. Spratt had been sexually abusing her for years. After that, I tried harder to be around for her, but it wasn't easy. By the time she was sixteen and I was twenty, we were lovers. She was jail bait, and I knew how dangerous that was for me, but I couldn't help myself.

"Finally, when Lacy was nearly eighteen, we left the Spratt's house and moved in together. Spratt came to the gas station where I worked and threatened me because Lacy was still underage, but I told him I'd go to the cops about him and Lacy if he didn't get the hell out. So he left, and we never heard from him again. The day Lacy turned eighteen, we went down to the courthouse and got married.

"It was a crazy-stupid thing to do because both of us were crackheads. I took odd jobs, and she worked as an exotic dancer in some dive downtown. We lived in a two-room apartment about a block from a junkie hangout where most of our friends were, and we spent more time there, sticking needles in our arms and sucking on pipes, than we did at home.

"But then I got sick and spent quite a bit of time alone. I started writing a journal just to keep from going nuts, and I noticed I was feeling better. So I wrote down memories and feelings and things I hadn't thought about in years—and then I wrote a short story based on all that. I was no Hemingway, but that story was pretty good. When I wrote, I discovered my reality disappeared into a fantasy world, just like the places I'd made up when I was a little kid. Suddenly, I had a purpose, a reason to get up in the morning. I kicked the drugs and almost died, but I was determined.

"When I finally turned the corner and was strong enough, I wrote a mystery. A good old-fashioned whodunit, and I wrote it in six weeks. Then I went to the library and started taking an online writing course to clean up the story. When I was finished, I sold it, and I never used drugs again. But Lacy couldn't stop, not even for me. She didn't want to."

Madison touched his shoulder, reminding him she was still listening, and he was grateful for the contact. He continued with a catch in his voice.

"Lacy didn't want to live with a man who spent all his time cooped up with a computer—a man who lived in his own world and no longer shared any part of hers. She kept dancing and made good money doing it, but the drugs took their toll on her. I begged her to get help because she didn't eat and she never slept, but she didn't want any help. Finally, it was clear to me that if I didn't get away from her, I was going to die, too.

"But I didn't move out until she started bringing other men home, other users. That's why, when she called me the December after Piper was born to tell me I was the proud daddy of a bouncing baby girl, I laughed out loud. I didn't realize she had another, far more important reason for telling me. She figured I'd believe Piper was my baby *before* I'd believe some crazy story about a child-predator named Tony Davila moving in with them. So that's why she didn't even bother to tell me about him."

"You don't know that—"

"Don't misunderstand me," he interrupted quickly. "I'm not blaming her for not telling me about him. Every bit of this is totally my fault. She was a rare human being, completely free and child-like even after she was grown, no matter what had happened to her. I took that away from her when I gave her that first pill. I've spent the last several years trying to give it back the only way I knew how—with money. I couldn't give her myself—she needed too much—but I had plenty of money, and it didn't mean anything to me.

"See, Lacy was completely dependent on me. She was afraid of everything. Life, death, and everything in between. Every obstacle was a huge mountain she believed she couldn't climb alone. The drugs kept her from being so terrified, so dependent, so weak…she thought. I didn't have the patience to help her. And make no mistake—I could've helped her. That's the real point of this story."

"What is?"

"I don't know for sure who killed her, Madison, but it might as well have been me."

"That's not true."

"Why not?"

"Because Lacy was in charge of her own life and she

made her own choices. You did all you could to try to save her, but she wasn't having any. She even said so in her letter."

"Well, I appreciate that, I really do, but I'm a pretty heartless person when you get right down to it. You read Lacy's letter, and you cried. That's what a normal person would do. You looked at those pictures of beautiful little kids, and I watched your heart break in two. But I can't feel anything, Madison. Nothing reaches me. I may have a little girl who's been horribly hurt in inconceivable ways...but it's like I'm outside of it all. There's something wrong with me. I just don't know how to feel."

She reached over and patted his shoulder. "You will when the time is right, Luke. You'll feel more than you ever thought you could, and I guarantee you'll wish you couldn't. But when that happens, I'll be right here."

"You promise?"

She nodded, balled her hand into a fist, and tapped her left breast twice. "Absolutely. Cross my heart."

****

As Madison and Luke walked from the Walmart entrance toward the SUV parked nearby, she tucked her phone into a concealed pocket in her purse and hoped he didn't hear her stomach growling. "Whitney says everything is fine at home. Jared isn't coming for her until seven, so we can grab an early dinner if you'd like. Did you find what you wanted?"

"I did." He held up a large plastic bag containing a newfangled coffeemaker and a box of coffee pods. "Even Whitney can't ruin this coffee. All she has to do is stick a pod in there and turn it on. It was created for people who can't think before they've had their coffee in the morning."

"Well, that's all of us at my house. Thank you very much."

He chuckled. "Oh, I didn't buy it for you. I bought it for me. I have to have my coffee, and what I've been drinking…well, it ain't coffee."

She smacked his arm. "I'm going to tell Whitney you said that."

"She won't care. I just bought her the best coffeemaker in the world. She'll forgive me anything."

Madison laughed. As she waited for him to put the new coffeemaker into the back of the SUV, she tried to think of a quiet place they could go for a bite of dinner. She turned on the ignition once he was settled in the passenger seat.

"Are you hungry?" she asked.

"Starved. How about you?"

"Yes. Do you like Chinese?"

"Love it."

She pulled out of the Walmart parking lot and drove eight blocks to The China House Restaurant, one of her favorite places to grab an early meal. Once they sat in a booth near the rear of the dimly lit establishment and Madison requested a pot of hot oolong tea from a young waitress, Luke settled back and folded his arms across his chest.

"I thought I saw a big safe in your office this morning. Did I?"

"You did. Why?"

"I'm wondering if we can put the DVD and all this other stuff in it. I'd like to keep it all together. Does anyone have a key or the combination besides you?"

"No."

"Good. So would that be okay?"

"Of course. We'll do that as soon as we get home."

A tiny man about a hundred years old sidled up to the table with a grin on his wizened face. "How are you today, Dr. Wagner? We've missed you."

"Thank you, Mr. Hua. I've missed you, too. My friend and I are very hungry."

He bowed slightly from the waist. "I will take your order right away."

After Luke ordered sweet-and-sour chicken and Madison her favorite, spicy sesame chicken served with ice-cold, thinly sliced cucumbers, the waiter left them alone and the waitress brought their steaming tea. As Luke poured it carefully, Madison tried to think of the best way to say what she needed to say.

Honestly. Just say it honestly.

"Luke, I need to tell you something. Please don't interrupt, and please understand I'm very serious. I'm not flirting with you."

"Well…that's depressing."

"Shut up and listen. You had every right to leave Lacy, and you had every right to stay away from her afterward. Lacy's letter proves she understood that. You probably gave her more of yourself than you ever should have—I don't know. But what I do know is self-preservation is man's strongest instinct, and that instinct saved your life. You had every right to save yourself. I was wrong to say the things I said when I called you the other night. I had no right to judge you, and I'm so sorry."

She met his gaze steadily, holding her breath for what seemed an eternity, waiting for him to lob off a smart-aleck comeback that would rile her all over again.

But it didn't come. When he reached across the table and turned his hand palm-side up, like a cradle, Madison rested her own hand in it.

"Thank you," he said softly. "I appreciate that."

The arrival of their meal kept her from having to respond, and she was grateful. His dark eyes were too deep at that moment, like bottomless pools filled with secrets and unexpressed emotion. Her own senses were wild and chaotic; she had to pull back. She concentrated on sipping her now-tepid oolong tea.

He changed the subject to one safer and more comfortable. "Do you mind telling me how you and Whitney came to work together? You guys are like two peas in a pod..."

She smiled gratefully. "Well, I guess I can tell you a little bit. I met Whitney while I was working in a psychiatric hospital, and I was so impressed with her that after a while, I asked her to come to Hope's Home to help me run things. That was three years ago, and I've never regretted that spur-of-the-moment decision even one time. As you've probably figured out, her background in foster care really helps her deal with my kids."

"I can see that." He changed the subject abruptly. "Do you know anything about the attorney who wanted to take Piper home with him? Jared seemed to have no use for him at all, and Whitney got pretty fierce."

"Well, Ryan Neely is a real fighter for fathers' rights here in San Antonio. He commands top dollar, and he's highly respected—a pillar of the community, so to speak. He loves to go up against women who've pressed sexual abuse charges against their husbands in custody battles. For example, I did some work with an attorney named Bill Rogers a year or so ago. He represented a woman who believed her ex-husband had severely sexually abused her son, and he asked me to testify about the little boy's state of mind. Neely, who represented the father, cross-examined me. He's a brutal piece of work. I've only met him that one time." She paused, then added softly, "Thank God."

"Yet he's a pillar of the community?"

"His opinion, not mine. He just has a lot of money. People listen to him."

"But Jared said last night Neely wouldn't have taken any kid into his home or wasted his time representing someone like Lacy. That doesn't sound like a pillar of the community to me. Is he really that terrific an attorney?"

She bit her lip thoughtfully and didn't answer right away. During her one courtroom meeting with Ryan Neely, she'd learned he was focused, intense, calculating, arrogant, and as sharp as a switchblade. He was also incredibly attractive in an older, movie-star kind of way, and he clearly had no time for losers. As he cross-examined her, he'd prowled his arena like a caged animal, unwavering in his determination to trip her up, yet he'd been smooth and respectful. It had taken every ounce of strength, intelligence, and experience she possessed to beat him.

"Well, we won," she answered with a grin, "so he's not as great as he thinks he is. But do I think he really wanted to help Lacy or Piper? Not a chance."

Luke pushed his plate to one side and finished the last of his tea. "And yet he did. Why?"

"I don't know. But I'm sure it was for a reason that benefited him and no one else." She pushed her chair away from the table and picked up her handbag. "Let's go home and see what Lacy wants us to learn."

****

"Hi, guys!" Whitney greeted them at the kitchen entrance, drying her hands on a dish towel. "Did you have a nice day?"

Madison remembered Luke's request not to divulge any information to anyone, so she simply smiled, nodded, made her way to her office, and closed the door firmly behind her. As she worked the combination and opened the safe to place Lacy's items inside, holding on to only the four children's photos, she heard Whitney's squeal of delight in the hallway and Jared's answering laughter. She grinned.

Luke must've given her the coffeemaker. *Well, thank God for that.* She closed the safe door tightly and gave the combination lock a few extra whirls for good measure. *Maybe we can actually enjoy a good cup of coffee in the morning.*

"Luke got us a new coffeemaker," Whitney announced as Madison joined the others in the kitchen. "That was just so nice of him."

"It was self-preservation, pet, that's all."

Jared laughed aloud. "Are you ready to go, Whitney? Our reservations are at seven thirty."

"I sure am. I'm starving." Whitney turned to Madison, pulling her long silver-blonde hair over one shoulder as she shrugged into a black, suede, fringed, western jacket. "Listen, the security cameras are on. The alarm is set. The kids have been fed, bathed, and put to bed. The older ones are reading, but they'll be ready for sleep in about an hour."

"How did Piper do today?" Luke asked.

"About the same. I put Sasha outside a little while

ago, but she never left Piper's side all day. She'll come in through the doggie door when she's ready—she loves the cold—so you won't have to worry about her. What are you guys doing this evening?"

Madison met Luke's eyes over Whitney's head. "We thought we might watch a movie. Do we have any popcorn?"

"No, but we have a few brownies left over. They're in the pantry."

"That'll be great," Luke said, a little too enthusiastically. "Can we finish them off? We had Chinese for dinner, and I'm already hungry again."

"Be my guest. You ready, Jared?"

"Yes, ma'am. Y'all enjoy your movie. We'll see you later."

Chapter Eight

Luke stood at Madison's bedroom door but waited a moment before knocking. Staring down at the DVD in his hand, he tried to mentally prepare himself for whatever might be on it. Like any other normal, red-blooded, American male, Luke wouldn't be bothered much by pornography, even if Lacy starred in it, because he'd seen more than his share of it over the years. But the contents of this film had to be much more than that.

The question was, how much more?

The door opened, and Madison stood there silently, watching him. "Are you coming in?" she asked finally.

He cleared his throat in embarrassment. The last thing he wanted was for her to know how afraid he was.

"Come in, Luke. I've put all the kids down and turned their lights off, but we'll give it a few minutes before we start. I want them to be asleep before then."

He nodded, followed her inside, and closed the door behind him. She'd changed into a pair of comfortable sweats and didn't look a day over thirteen. He stifled a grin.

The room had clearly been an enormous master suite back in its day, and Madison had turned it into her own tiny house. One section, opening into a miniscule bathroom, contained a little electric refrigerator, a coffeemaker, and a small microwave oven placed on a round oak table. Beside the microwave, blending right in with the décor, was what might have been a small pistol safe. An antique cherrywood four-poster bed, complete with stairs because it was so high off the ground, was placed beside a set of french doors that opened onto an upstairs balcony overlooking the backyard. Finally, in a cozy little area practically hidden from his view at the door, were two comfortable chairs, a set of bookshelves filled with hardcover books stacked in a haphazard manner, and a small entertainment center containing a television, stereo, and DVD player.

"Would you help me pull this screen out?"

He gripped the end of a western-style room divider and held it steady as she set it behind the two armchairs so it blocked the view from the door.

"I spend a lot of time up here analyzing film and so on," she explained. "I don't want a child walking in and seeing something they shouldn't, so I keep the television screen hidden."

"Analyzing film?"

"Sure. Interviews with alleged child abuse or sexual assault victims primarily, but everything I do is documented on film—for everyone's protection. My office downstairs is primarily for client meetings or work I do with Jared and Whitney. It's very private up here. Oh, by the way…everything we have pertaining to Lacy and Piper is now locked in my office safe, so don't let me forget to put the DVD and photos back down there when we're finished."

Without a word, he handed her the film. She placed it on a small table between the two armchairs, alongside the envelope Luke recognized as the one containing the children's photographs, and ran her hand through her hair. He saw her fingers tremble and felt an answering twinge of tension.

"I'm going to pour a glass of wine," she said abruptly. "Can I get you something? A beer or maybe a soda?"

"A glass of water would be good, thanks."

"Okay. Get comfortable in one of those chairs, and I'll get this show on the road."

He couldn't even summon a grin for her feeble attempt at a joke. As he eased himself into the overstuffed armchair, he was only vaguely aware of the soft *whoosh* of the refrigerator door, the clink of glasses, the dimming of lights. He leaned his head back and closed his eyes, trying to ignore the thudding of his heart in his throat and the hot beads of perspiration dribbling into his hairline. His mouth was cotton dry, as if he had just crossed the Mojave Desert on foot in the heat of summer, and his hands shook. He clasped them tightly in his lap.

He'd never been so nervous in his life, and he didn't know why.

She set the glasses on the table between them, opened the DVD container, and put the disk in the player, then turned the lights completely off. After returning to her chair, she punched a few buttons on the remote and settled in.

In a few moments, an empty bedroom suite appeared on the blank screen. This obviously hadn't been filmed at Lacy's house, and the grainy texture of the picture showed that it was a copy. Filmy curtains covered a wall-to-wall sliding glass door, the massive bed was round with transparent material draped over a topless canopy, and the ceilings and walls were mirrored. Outside, beyond the balcony, a heart-shaped swimming pool was visible.

When Lacy entered the scene, Luke leaned forward and studied the screen intently. Nude, her deeply tanned body glistening with droplets of water, she was even more beautiful than he remembered. Magnificent silver-blonde hair cascaded down her back and concealed more than half of her buttocks. Her profile was perfect, her breasts high and firm, her abdomen taut, her legs long and slender. Even though he hadn't seen her in years, even though he'd spent yesterday with her lifeless body, her exquisite beauty still stopped his heart.

Madison whispered beside him, "My God, she's breathtaking…"

Lacy lay on the bed, ostensibly to sleep, and the camera lovingly caressed every lithe, supple inch of that sublime body. After a moment, she was joined by a naked man whose tall, muscular form gleamed with oil and perspiration. But before their lovemaking could become intense, another nude man and woman entered the room, fondling and stroking one another as they moved toward the bed.

Luke felt Madison squirming uncomfortably in the chair next to his, but he relaxed, realizing this film was going to move like a dozen other porno films he'd seen over the years. There was little dialogue, which was a good thing because the sound was lousy. Most of the audibles involved the usual slurping and sucking, moaning and whimpering, whispering and giggling… He couldn't help but grin as he closed his eyes.

Nothing to see here…

The movie ended, there was a moment of flashing static on the screen, and another film clip began. This scene took place in far more wretched circumstances—

now in a squalid room with greasy, nicotine-streaked walls and a stained mattress in the middle of the floor. The Lacy Callaghan who lay on the bed was no longer beautiful. Her dull blonde hair was matted and tangled, her pelvic bones jutted above the vulgar black leather G-string that nestled in her crotch, and those once-proud breasts were now shrunken and sagging. Visible, even from a distance, were angry track marks running up and down her arms. Luke knew they'd also be behind her knees, between her toes...

His heart pounded furiously, painfully, in his chest. His hands were icy.

A long-haired man entered the scene wearing a skin-tight, black leather outfit with chains draped around his narrow hips, up one arm, and clasped tightly in his hand. He moved toward Lacy slowly, deliberately, an evil leer slashing his face. She scrambled to her knees, cringing, and held out her arms in a gesture of pleading terror. His huge erection was obvious through the leather. When the camera swung in for a close-up of Lacy's face, Luke could see that the fear in her eyes was real.

"Oh dear God," Madison whispered, "I think that's Antonio Davila..."

He closed his eyes. The room spun; he was nauseated and drenched in sweat. As the chains thudded against her body, Lacy's pain-wracked screams ripped through the stillness.

Suddenly, Madison grabbed his arm. His eyes flew open.

Now a little girl, no more than five or six years old, hung from a contraption attached to the top of an enormous cage, her tiny wrists crossed and roped together. Her dark hair tumbled to her waist, partially concealing her nakedness, but her terror was unmistakable. As her thin little legs dangled helplessly in the air, her face contorted in a soundless scream as Davila approached her, carrying a long, metal instrument in his hand.

Luke swallowed vomit. His eyes burned with tears of rage and nausea. He reached for Madison's hand and gripped it, hard. He turned his face away from the screen.

The child's blood-curdling screams filled the room, pounded in his head, slammed into his chest with such force his entire body shook. As the shrieks of pain and terror dissipated into moans, baby-like whimpers, and finally silence, tears streamed unheeded down his face.

Suddenly, the screen went blank, and the only sound in the room was Madison's muffled sobs. But then, just as he reached for the remote to turn off the film, Lacy reappeared on the screen, now seated on the very mattress he'd seen in her bedroom yesterday.

She wore the gaudy silk nightgown he'd noticed draped over her mirror. She looked exhausted and ill, with only the fragile bone structure in her face reminiscent of her once-luminous beauty. She leaned forward, hands clasped in her lap, her purple-shadowed eyes filled with pleading and tears.

"I have to talk fast...I don't have much time. Luke, if you're watching this...please take Piper away from here. No one will listen to me..." Her smoke-husky voice cracked. "They're going to hurt her, and then they'll kill her..." She leaned even closer to the camera. *"You have to remember this—tip the piano man."*

And then the screen went black.

Instinctively, Luke stood up and pulled Madison to her feet; he pushed her face into his chest and held her close as she wept. Her sobs were ugly, gut-wrenching, from the depths of her soul. Luke stroked her hair, whispered what comfort he could, but nothing seemed to ease her outburst of pain.

"I'm sorry," she whispered. "I'm so sorry…"

"Don't be silly. If I could cry like that, you can be damned sure I would."

She hiccoughed before she moved away from him and headed for the bathroom. Hearing her splash water on her face, he envied her ability to release her hurt and rage. He didn't even know where to begin.

He walked to the DVD player, popped it open, and removed the disk. As he held it in his hand, he stared at it, and an image began to form in his mind—an image he was sure he'd never forget. Once again, he saw the little girl dangling in the air, her dark hair flowing down her back…and then it came to him.

The photo…that beautiful child with the seductive expression on her face…

The photo he'd placed face down on the table in the bank…

He crossed the floor in just a few long strides, grabbed the envelope off the table, and removed the photos. He found the picture he was looking for and held it closer to the lamplight. He was right—this was the child. He flipped the picture over.

Charly MacIntire. January 4, 2022.

"Madison?" Luke called, his voice throbbing with excitement. "Hurry up! I need to show you something!"

****

"Isn't this the same little girl we just saw on the film?" Luke asked.

Seated at the little round table in the kitchenette

section of Madison's room, each of them nursed a cup of steaming hot tea. She placed her phone beside her cup and stared blindly at the photograph. She couldn't take her eyes off it.

Finally, she nodded. "It is. It's her."

"You're the pro here. What can we do? We need to do something."

"We need to think. But let's don't say anything about what we've learned today to Jared or Whitney, okay? At least, not yet."

"Why not? I thought you said you'd trust them with your life."

She picked up the photo of little Charly MacIntire and gazed at it intently. She wasn't sure how to answer his question. She couldn't just come out and say, "Because I could be wrong…"

His voice was reasonable now. "Listen, at some point, you're going to have to bring in the cops. We don't have the expertise, equipment, or jurisdiction to handle this on our own."

"I know, but not yet. They're already involved in Lacy's murder and trying to find Davila, so let's just leave it there. For now, anyway."

"No worries on this end. Cops and I don't get along too well."

She gave a faint smile and changed the subject. "What do you think this date means, Luke?"

"I don't know. It must be either the date they took the photo or when they got the kid. What do you think?"

"I don't have a clue. It could be the date they started using her in films. Remember, Lacy said she wanted to save the children, but we don't know if she saved anyone or not. On the other hand, if this little girl is dead, this could be the date she died. God knows, they could've killed her in the film clip we just saw."

Luke shook his head. "If they killed her in that film clip, Lacy would've showed it. It would've been asinine to cut it. She wouldn't have done that."

"Yeah, you're right. Listen, I know a good private investigator if we need one. He sits on my board of directors. His name is Jerome Scranton."

"Does he work with the cops?"

"Of course, if he needs to. He used to be a homicide detective in SAPD."

Luke looked relieved. "Good. I guess the most important thing to do first is to find out if all these kids are alive. I know Lacy didn't write the info on the back of the photos, someone else did, so she must've risked a lot to get them and pass them on to me. She had to have a good reason to do that." He ruffled his hair until it stood straight up. "I have a question for you, Madison, and I hope you don't think I'm crazy."

"Try me."

He looked away from her and lowered his voice. "Since Lacy was obviously scared to death for the children—and probably Piper more than anyone else— do you think she might've made all those abuse reports herself?"

"Why would she do that? She never welcomed any follow-up—"

"Yeah, but do you think it's possible?"

She stared at him. "Well, of course it's possible. Anything's possible. I guess she could've made them in hopes of bringing Piper's situation to the attention of people who could help, but it sure seems like a hard way to do it."

He stroked his beard thoughtfully, then shook his head. "No, you're right. That'd be crazy. Why would she go to all that trouble, only to deny it when someone came out to investigate?"

But the more seriously Madison thought about it, the more sense it made.

"Well, she could've been afraid," she suggested finally. "She might've been able to make those reports in private, but then, when the caseworker showed up, she might not have been alone. She might've been counting on someone in authority just *seeing* the situation and *doing* something about it, which would've kept her and Piper out of danger, but it just never worked out that way."

He nodded. "I get that. She had to be terrified all the time. Davila lived in that house, and there was no way she could get away from him. That's clear from the comments she made on the film and from everything I read today. She knew she'd *never* get away from him, but Piper was a different story. I think she was willing to try anything, even if it meant she had to use the system itself. And you have no idea how much she hated the system. But I think she might've kept trying." He bit his lip. "It's possible she didn't stop trying until she was dead."

"That's true. The message she put on the end of that film—that's pure desperation. She had nowhere to go, no one to turn to…" Frustrated, Madison ran her fingers through her hair. "You know what? We might be coming at this all wrong."

"What do you mean?"

"She might've done this for your benefit."

Luke looked at her like she was nuts. "Well, that's

obvious..."

"No, I don't mean the film. I mean the entire situation. Think about it. That first film clip we saw shows Lacy was involved, at some time, in some pretty good hardcore pornography. When I say *good*, I mean the set was nice, she was beautiful... In other words, she would've been cool with it, right? She was a hooker, she did drugs, she needed money. Nothing unusual about doing porn to pay for that stuff. But later, when they got into kiddie porn... Even hookers draw the line at kiddie porn. Even junkies stay away. So, maybe, once they got into kids, Lacy tried to bring in the state, hoping to protect Piper from what they were doing. She was even willing to lose her child if it meant Piper was safe. And if the state got involved, the whole operation could collapse without her having to squeal on anyone."

Luke frowned. "I'm not following..."

"I know. Give me a minute."

Some little detail, something she couldn't put her finger on, was trying to break into her consciousness and wouldn't. Concentrating, she resorted to the technique she always used; she *became* Lacy Callaghan. Tall, slender, exquisite, she sold her body to men to support a drug habit, and as long as her child was safe, it didn't matter. She made pornographic films and shot the proceeds into her veins or handed it all over to Davila. In her world, there was nothing unusual—or even wrong—about that. But in a weird kind of moral juxtaposition, she saved all of Luke's money for Piper, probably so she could face herself in the morning...

Until they began using children in their movies.

That would've been the point where Lacy lost control. Her income wasn't large enough to cover the profits Davila and his crew could make by hurting children. So Lacy had to think of something else. She made abuse reports but couldn't risk backing them up. Who would protect her little girl if a sadist like Davila learned she'd talked to authorities?

No one.

Lacy *had* to stay alive. She was all that stood between Piper and Antonio Davila.

Until she was arrested just a few weeks ago—and bailed out by a powerful attorney named Ryan Neely a few hours later. The next morning another call about Piper came in to the Department of Family and Protective Services, and for some reason, someone in authority finally decided to act. But when that same attorney offered to take the little girl home with him—

And there it was, that nagging detail. Madison looked directly at Luke.

"Did Lacy know something about Ryan Neely and children that no one else knew? Why would she run from him, taking Piper with her? But she does, and she disappears—then turns up later with her throat cut. Sometime, and we don't know when, she puts this message about Piper and *tip the piano man* at the end of a DVD she's hidden for you. That's really crazy. It's almost as if she *knows* she's going to die, like she's given in...or, even, set it up."

"What do you mean, set it up? She'd never willingly participate in something like this—"

"You're missing my point, Luke. Lacy had to know she was going to die. Why else would she risk putting a message like that at the end of those film clips? What would've happened to her if Davila had found that DVD instead of you?"

"He would've killed her and gotten rid of the film."

"Exactly, and you know she knew it. Piper was the only reason she would've risked doing that. Take a walk in Lacy's shoes, Luke. She believes with her whole heart you're Piper's father. She's done everything she can think of to get your attention, but nothing's worked. Now she's very sick, and she knows she's going to die. She's got all her paperwork in order, and she's poured her heart out to you in a personal letter. She's ready to go, she's made her peace—but she has to see to it that her child is protected. She knows that won't happen if she just dies of natural causes. But if she's murdered, that will force the state to take Piper out of the house and bring you back home. I think that's what happened, Luke. I think she set it up that way. Not in the beginning, maybe, but at the end, when she was so sick. I think she realized her own murder would be her last chance to save her little girl's life." Madison paused, then finished softly, "It was a sacrifice she was willing to make, and she made it."

****

At that moment, Sasha began barking in the backyard and Luke jumped, startled. When Madison's security alarm blared on her phone at the same time, she instantly shut it off and placed her finger against her lips, then pointed to the french doors that opened onto the balcony. He nodded and slowly got to his feet as she rested her thumb on a small screen atop the gun safe next to her coffee cup.

There was a muffled *click*, and Madison opened the safe, removed her 9mm pistol, cocked it, and headed toward the balcony. When she reached the door, she flipped a switch, immediately flooding the backyard with light. In the distance, Luke could hear the wail of police sirens. He pushed the door open, then hunched over in an attempt to conceal his height, and made his way out onto the balcony. Madison moved close behind him.

Sasha stood on her hind legs with her front paws planted against the trunk of the enormous old elm tree, still howling and barking and snarling at a figure crouched above her in a wide crook in the tree, just out of her reach.

Grinning, Madison handed Luke her pistol. "I don't think he's going anywhere. Will you go down there and be sure she doesn't kill him? I'll wait in the front. The cops should be here soon."

"Be careful. He may not be alone. What're you going to tell them?"

"I don't know. Let's find out who he is first. This isn't our first break-in—he might not be a part of our problem at all."

Luke made his way down the stairs, pistol in hand, and out the back door into the yard, talking to the excited canine as he approached her and her hostage. "Good girl, Sasha! Look what you've done!" He kept the pistol aimed at the terrified man crouched in the tree. "Stay where you are, you idiot. She kills on command."

The sirens were silent now, and only Sasha's deep-throated growls were audible. Luke halted behind her and looked more closely at the intruder.

The man was actually little more than a boy—maybe eighteen years old, Hispanic, tall and husky with matted, shoulder-length black hair. His red hoody was dirty, and his jeans were ripped at the knees, but his sneakers were expensive and new. He pointed in terror at Sasha, shaking visibly from his head to his feet.

The back door slammed as two police officers accompanied Madison into the backyard. Once they reached Luke, he put the safety on the pistol and handed it back to Madison.

"He's just a kid," she said, clearly surprised. "Sasha, settle!"

Sasha immediately backed away from the tree and sat down, watching Madison expectantly.

"I'm sorry," the young man blurted. "Please don't kill me—"

She lifted one eyebrow. "What're you babbling about? No one's going to kill you. Sasha, come!"

Sasha pranced to her side, white plumed tail waving languidly over her back, and stood patiently as Madison got a good grip on her collar. "Good girl, Sasha, you're such a good girl…"

After one of the police officers had helped the trembling young man down out of the tree, the other cop frisked him thoroughly and found a switchblade in the back pocket of his jeans. "You got anything else?"

"No, sir."

Madison stood up. "May I talk to him before you take him?"

The older of the two officers shrugged, pocketed the switchblade, and nodded. "Sure, Dr. Wagner. Do you know him?"

"No, I don't. But I'd like to know where he came from. Let's go in the house, and I'll get us something to drink."

Chapter Nine

Luke took in the scene playing out before him with disbelief and more than a little amusement. Madison bustled around the kitchen like a little *hausfrau* taking care of her company—two burly police officers and one terrified kid who probably hadn't eaten in a week—while Sasha lay stretched out by the back door, sound asleep. The scene was so domestic and unremarkable that Luke could hardly believe he'd just spent the last two hours watching child pornography with this weeping woman, then holding an intruder at bay in a tree.

The young man bolted down a bologna sandwich.

"Don't eat so fast," Madison scolded. "You'll get sick. What's your name?"

"Rafe Gamez. Thanks for the sandwich. It's good." His words were tinged with a faint Latino accent mixed with a Texas twang.

"You're very welcome, Rafe Gamez. But you know…there's a price for that sandwich."

He set his sandwich on the plate in front of him and looked at Madison suspiciously. "Yeah…there usually is."

"Go on, eat. What's your story?"

"My story?"

"Why did you try to break in my house?"

He looked at her for a while, chewing rhythmically like a cow doubling down on its cud, clearly trying to understand her motives.

Finally, sandwich gone, he seemed to reach a decision, shook his head, and sighed. "I was going to turn myself in to Julian Alvarado tomorrow night and get clean. I just wanted a couple more fixes before I did that, but I didn't have any money. This is an old house, so I thought it might be easy to break into."

"You thought wrong," one of the officers observed wryly.

Rafe glanced at the snoozing Sasha. "Yes, sir."

"You scared of dogs?" Luke asked abruptly.

"Yes, sir!"

"Well, you'd better be scared of this one. I wasn't lying. She kills on command—"

"Julian Alvarado?" Madison interrupted. "I've heard that name, but I can't place it."

"He's a street preacher," the younger officer explained. "He has a ministry on the deep west side called Victory Church. He's been around for years. Junkies go to him when they're trying to get clean and can't afford rehab. He has a small center, but he'll actually take them into his home and get them straight right there on his living room floor if he has to."

"That takes some guts," Luke observed skeptically.

"And no brains," the officer responded. "But I've got to admit that he does good work. The drug world's small, you know? Everyone knows everyone, and everyone knows Julian."

Luke turned back to Rafe Gamez. "There are lots of old houses on this street. Why'd you choose this one?"

The kid shrugged. "Why not?"

Luke knew what it was to steal for a fix. He knew the desperation, fear, and physical pain that attacked in the early stages of withdrawal. That could be part of this young man's reason for breaking in, but it wasn't all of it.

He narrowed his eyes in suspicion. "Show me your arms."

The kid didn't argue. He pushed up a sleeve, revealing angry track marks on the inside of his arm and a mottled scar on his wrist. He glared at Luke. "Satisfied?"

Luke nodded. "For now."

But he wasn't. Something wasn't right with this kid, something he couldn't put his finger on. He was too affable, too chameleon. He didn't carry a gun, and he surrendered too easily. Why?

The younger police officer spoke up. "Enough of this, you guys. We need to go, Al."

Al yawned. "C'mon, kid. We'll see if we can get Alvarado to help you out when we get downtown."

Rafe nodded, but he didn't look hopeful. "Thank you, sir. I'd appreciate that."

He stood up and held out his hands, obviously accustomed to the procedure, and the younger officer cuffed him without comment.

Al winked at Madison. "Thank you for the water and the sandwich, Dr. Wagner. I look forward to catching your next intruder."

"You're welcome. I'm a terrible cook, but I can make a mean sandwich." She took a step closer to Rafe. "You call me if you get out of this stupid trouble you've gotten yourself into. I might be able to help you."

"Thank you, ma'am."

When the officers and their young collar had trooped out of the house, Madison looked at Luke and frowned. "Did you notice the scar around his wrist? Like a bad ligature mark."

"Yeah."

"Did you notice if it was on both wrists?"

"No, I wasn't paying attention. I was just looking at the track marks."

"Me, too. And another thing," she added softly. "Julian Alvarado."

"What about him?"

"Junkies go to him if they want to clean up. They stay at his house until they're straight. Everyone knows about him, but he stays out of the system. The cops pretty much leave him alone."

"So? What about him?"

"So…we need to find him. We need to see if he knew Lacy."

****

The next morning, Luke's face was serious as he looked at Madison from the passenger's seat in the SUV. "You know, you don't need to go with me to the funeral. I'm sure you have better things to do."

She glanced over her shoulder before she backed out of the driveway, then met his eyes with a smile. "Actually, I do need to come with you. Remember, I told you I had a super private detective on my board? I just talked to him, and he said I should definitely go. And as you well know, I always do as I'm told."

"Huh. I must've missed that part."

"No, you just weren't paying attention."

Once Madison had turned onto Broadway and was comfortably ensconced in the flow of morning traffic heading toward downtown, she glanced at Luke and sighed. The dark shadows beneath his red-rimmed eyes and his grayish pallor highlighted his lack of sleep, which she completely understood. She hadn't slept well, either. Hoping to hide her fatigue, she'd dressed carefully in an emerald-green business suit that flattered her copper-colored hair and fair complexion, but she wasn't really sure she'd done much good.

Luke hadn't even commented, but she understood that, too. His mind had to be on the upcoming funeral. She wouldn't be shattered by it—she hadn't known Lacy Callaghan—but the anguish on his face was heartbreaking.

"Like I was saying," she continued as normally as she could, "Jerome told me to watch the people who come to Lacy's funeral, just in case someone of interest showed up. I'm sure you know all about that, since you write mysteries and all."

He looked bewildered. "What're you talking about? Who's Jerome?"

"I told you last night…Jerome Scranton. He was a detective in SAPD for years, but he retired and does private investigating now. He picks his cases carefully, and he also sits on my board of directors. Since Whitney and Jared are going to visit Jared's folks tonight, I've invited him over to my house for dinner. I think you'll find him very interesting."

Luke frowned. "How much are we going to tell him?"

"Actually, I don't know. I do trust him totally. I just want to pick his brain. He's lived here all his life, and he worked undercover vice for several years on the force. He recently returned from a law enforcement conference he went to just so that he could keep in touch with all his old buddies and learn what's trending. He knows his way around."

Luke seemed to relax. "Sounds good. Are we still picking up my truck after the funeral?"

"Of course. We'll be home in plenty of time for dinner." She paused. "But I need to warn you about something."

"What's that?"

"When we spoke this morning, Jerome asked me if I trusted him, and of course, I said I did. But any time he asks me that, it means he's going to do something and I'm not going to know what it is until he's done it. Are you okay with that?"

"Do I have a choice?"

"No, not really. Neither do I. It's how he rolls. But, believe me, whatever he does will be for the best, and we just need to go with it."

Luke seemed to come to a sudden decision. "Madison, this is your ball game, not mine. I'm not going to second-guess any judgment call you make. I'm just concerned Piper may not be safe at the shelter. I'm really worried about that, especially since last night—"

"I know. So am I."

"Well, that surprises me—since you gave our bad guy a sandwich. I don't think I've ever seen that before."

She gave him a sheepish grin. "I know. That was probably stupid. But he was just a kid, and I thought I might get some information with a sandwich. After all, *I'll* tell you anything you want to know in exchange for food—especially if I don't have to cook it."

"I'll keep that in mind."

"And the name *Julian Alvarado* might actually be important for us."

"That's true." He changed the subject abruptly.

"Listen, I've been thinking. We could hide Piper up at my place at the lake without any problem. I have a housekeeper, a full security system, and I can bring a guard on if you want me to. You can take a look at it when we go this afternoon and tell me what you think."

"That may not be a bad idea."

She turned in slowly to the Sunrise Funeral Home parking lot and pulled into a slot near the entrance. She glanced in her rearview mirror to fluff her hair and check her makeup, then looked over at Luke. "Are you all right?"

"Of course. You look very nice, by the way."

She felt the heat of a blush and grabbed her handbag. "Thank you. We're a little early, but I want to speak to Martin if I can."

He nodded, got out of the SUV, and stood beside the door, his expression uncertain. Madison couldn't even imagine the demons he was battling this morning, but she knew there had to be plenty of them.

"Am I dressed all right?" he asked as he joined her at the front of the SUV. "I decided not to wear a suit."

"You look just fine," she assured him, tucking her hand in the crook of his arm. "Let's go see if we can find Martin."

She was too shy to tell him that he actually looked incredibly handsome in a white dress shirt with a turquoise-and-silver bolo clasped on black leather, black jeans, and much-loved gray cowboy boots shined to a rich luster. It was a western-style outfit that accentuated his silver-white hair and perfectly trimmed beard like a dream.

"Isn't that Mr. Gregory at the entrance?" he asked.

She breathed a sigh of relief. "It is. Let's hurry and

catch him while we still can."

****

Thoughtfully, Luke watched from a slight distance as Martin Gregory hugged Madison for several moments. Martin didn't speak until he'd finally released her and gestured for Luke to join them. The two men shook hands.

"I didn't think you'd want a limo, so I didn't order you one. We're only driving to the rear of the cemetery, and Lacy's casket is already set up there. There're only a few people here, and they've already gone to her location, so you can follow me. Is that all right?"

"Of course," Luke answered. "We appreciate your help."

"Madison, I thought Whitney would come with you."

She gave her tousled hair a discreet pat down after Martin's enthusiastic hug. "I've left her in charge of the children, but she sent her love."

"Please tell her I missed her. How are you, Mr. Callaghan?"

"I'm doing well, thank you."

Martin nodded. "I'm glad to hear it. Listen, I wanted to tell you I didn't know which minister to call, and there really wasn't anyone on our list I thought would be appropriate. I was going to open the graveside service to people who might want to share their memories, but I realized that choice could be dangerous... Anyway, out of the clear blue, I got a phone call yesterday from a street preacher here in San Antonio who knew Lacy pretty well, asking if he could do this service. I hope you don't mind, but I thought it was a perfect fit."

Madison caught her breath, and her fingers

tightened on Luke's arm, but she said nothing.

His response was calm. "No, that's fine, Martin. I just appreciate you handling everything. What's the preacher's name?"

"Julian...something. I'm sorry. I really hate this getting-old stuff."

"Alvarado?" Madison prompted softly. "Julian Alvarado?"

"That's it! Thank you. Do you know him?"

"No. I've just heard the name. And he said he knew Lacy?"

"Yes, he did. Are you sure you're okay with this?"

"It's perfect. Thank you so much."

"You're welcome. Are you ready to go?"

Luke nodded and covered Madison's hand on his arm with his own. "I'm as ready as I'll ever be."

****

Madison pulled out of her parking slot and drove slowly behind Martin's late-model white car. When a black SUV moved into place behind her, she instantly recognized it as one belonging to a detective. She touched Luke's hand and tilted her head slightly backward. "That's SAPD."

"You don't need to whisper," he responded with a chuckle. "He's just a cop." He pointed toward a large canopy with two rows of seating under it. "I guess that's us."

She nodded and pulled in next to the curb behind Martin. The black SUV followed suit, but the driver remained in the car. Madison didn't move, either, until she noticed Martin standing beside her window. Luke seemed frozen in his seat.

"Come on, Luke. They're waiting on us."

When Martin opened her door, she took his offered arm and walked with him up the sidewalk toward the canopy, Luke following closely behind them. She didn't notice any parked vehicles that looked out of place...nothing expensive, nothing souped up, nothing that would capture anyone's attention. When she saw an obese Hispanic woman sitting in the front row, a younger woman sitting beside her, she squeezed Martin's arm. "Isn't that Carlotta Martinez?"

"It is. I told her to sit in the family row with you and Mr. Callaghan. I believe that's her daughter with her. I hope that's all right."

"Of course. I guess they were as much family as Lacy had."

As they approached the canopy, Madison recognized Lacy's banker, Bryan Wilkerson, seated directly behind Carlotta in the second row, and a young woman wearing an expensive black suit with a blue fox fur collar sat next to him. Madison didn't recognize her but knew immediately she was no professional businesswoman—at least, not the kind she was trying to portray. Standing beside Lacy's rose-covered casket, next to a podium, was a shaggy-haired, casually dressed Latino man with a Bible in his hand.

When they'd reached the front row, Martin helped Madison into her chair next to Carlotta, then turned to murmur a few words to Luke and shake his hand before he walked to the back of the canopy. Luke sat down next to Madison and bowed his head.

Madison smiled at Carlotta, trying to hide her concern at the elderly lady's tear-swollen eyes and pallid complexion. She nodded at the young woman holding Carlotta's hand.

"Thank you for coming," she whispered.

When Carlotta's face crumpled, her daughter gathered her in her arms and held her close, murmuring to her in Spanish. The minister watched for a moment, a tender smile on his handsome face, then stepped behind the podium and began to speak.

****

As Julian Alvarado talked about eternal life and angels taking sinners to Heaven and all humans being children of God, Luke allowed his mind to wander. It wasn't that he didn't believe what he was hearing. It just didn't seem to make much difference.

He fixed his gaze on the closed coffin before him, then focused on the mechanical contraption beneath it. In just a few minutes, after everyone was gone, Lacy would be lowered into that ground and covered with the same cold, uncaring earth that had never given her a moment's peace while she was still living. Lacy had been so afraid of the dark, afraid of thunder, afraid of lightning—afraid of every element with which she would now spend eternity.

He felt a soothing touch on his wrist and looked down to find that his hands were balled into fists so brutal his knuckles were white. He forced himself to relax, opened his fingers, and allowed Madison's hand to slip into his. Like salt and pepper, he thought, bemused. Like Ma and Pa, bread and butter…like her hand belonged there.

He pulled himself out of his reverie when he heard Lacy's name. Now he might learn something. He looked up and realized with a shock that the minister was talking directly to him.

"I first met Lacy Callaghan at a Christmas Eve

service we held at Victory Church, three years ago. It was very cold, and she came inside, I think, just to warm up. Our little children's choir was singing carols, and Lacy sat in the front pew, just listening. I remember thinking how much like an angel she looked as she sat there, watching those children. We talked that night and many times after that, and I came to love her very much. So I wanted to share with you today the Lacy Callaghan I knew.

"Lacy's life was hard, and she made some bad choices, but she never blamed anyone but herself. She was one of the most loving people I've ever known—she loved her child, and she loved those people she considered her family. She believed in God. She was certain Heaven held a place for her, regardless of her choices, and I'm sure she's right."

Now Alvarado's expression grew intense, and his dark eyes bored into Luke's face.

"Finally, and maybe more important than anything else, Lacy Callaghan was a fighter. Most people didn't know that about her, but I did. She never saw a wrong she didn't try to fix or a person she didn't try to help. She wanted to make a difference in this world, no matter how small or insignificant others may have found it. She loved children more than anything else—more specifically, her own child—and she would've laid down her life for any one of them without a second thought. I think it's important you know that."

When Madison squeezed his hand, Luke understood. This street preacher knew a side of Lacy that even Luke didn't know, and apparently he'd come here hoping he could make Luke aware of it.

Julian Alvarado closed his Bible and held it next to

his chest. "Before we close, does anyone here have a memory of Lacy they would like to share with us?"

After a few moments, to Luke's astonishment, Lacy's banker stood up and made his way to the podium. Alvarado shook his hand and stepped back.

"I'm Bryan Wilkerson," he began quietly, "and I've known Lacy for several years. I certainly didn't plan to say anything today, but the minister's remarks about Lacy's love for children reminded me of something I'd completely forgotten until now. I'd like to share it with you.

"Last Christmas our bank ended a fundraiser we'd been running all year long to benefit children in the Texas Foster Care System who needed a little extra help. Our goal was a hundred grand, but we came up five grand short. Now, clearly, we'd raised a healthy chunk of change, and we were all very happy with that final total. But on that last day, Lacy called me and asked if we'd met our goal. I had to tell her we hadn't. She immediately donated the rest of the money, swore me to secrecy, and then told me something I never will forget.

"She said, 'Bryan, life is hard for everyone, but children are helpless. They're sitting ducks for whatever evil someone wants to do to them. Promise me if you ever see a child in need or in trouble, you'll do whatever you can to make a difference. Don't ever assume someone else is going to do it.'

"And so I promised her, and I'm making that promise again today. My condolences to you, Mr. Callaghan. I'm sure the world will forever be a darker place...for us both."

Luke mouthed *thank you* as the banker walked back to his seat, then bowed his head as Alvarado gave his closing prayer. When the service had finally concluded, Luke stood up and stepped to the side of the casket.

Oblivious to everyone else, he finally allowed the tears to come, but he wasn't grieving for Lacy. He felt with all his being that she was no longer inside that coffin. Her pain was gone; her needs were gone; her fears were gone. She was now an invisible and powerful part of the universe. She could play in the wind and the clouds like a free and high-spirited child, she could be the Lacy she'd always wanted to be, and she was no longer afraid of the dark.

Luke pressed his fingers to his lips for a long moment, then touched the casket in one last kiss. It was his final good-bye.

Chapter Ten

"May I speak to you a moment, Mr. Callaghan?"

Luke turned away from Carlotta and Madison, who were visiting quietly near the canopy edge, to meet the penetrating gaze of the street preacher, Julian Alvarado. His were the darkest, fiercest eyes Luke had ever seen. At that moment, he realized the man hadn't been intentionally focusing his intensity on Luke during the service. His presence was just so strong and commanding it had felt that way.

"Of course, Mr. Alvarado. I wanted to thank you for providing such a nice service for Lacy."

Alvarado bowed his head and nodded. "It was my pleasure, sir."

"How can I help you?"

"Mr. Callaghan, I need to speak with you, but we can't talk here. We can't risk being seen. Do you mind if I ask who the lady with you is?"

Luke frowned. "Her name is Dr. Wagner. Why do you ask?"

"I thought so. Mr. Gregson told me about her. Did she know your wife?"

"My ex-wife," Luke corrected with a tired sigh. "No, but she's working with me on something that concerns Lacy."

"Well, I was wondering if you'd follow me to my church where we can talk in my office. It'll be completely safe and private there. Please bring Dr. Wagner if you think it's appropriate."

Luke remembered the break-in at the shelter the night before. He wasn't as positive as Madison that it hadn't been part of a more complex scenario. "Are you sure your office is private and safe?"

"Well, let's just say I hope so."

At that moment, as the detective pulled away from the curb, followed by Bryan Wilkerson's car, Luke noticed that Madison was looking at him, a questioning expression on her face.

"Let me get Dr. Wagner, and we'll follow you out," Luke said. "We won't be but a few minutes."

Alvarado smiled. "I can wait, Mr. Callaghan. That old red truck over there is mine."

"Thank you. Be right with you."

Luke walked to Madison's side and made all the polite moves he needed to make without even thinking about them. He hugged Carlotta and her daughter, then shook hands with Martin Gregory.

Finally, after watching them make their way toward their vehicles, Luke grabbed Madison's arm. "Julian Alvarado wants us to follow him to his church. He needs to talk to us."

Her eyes widened. "Did he say about what?"

"No, but he doesn't want to talk to us here. Says we can't be seen together."

She nodded, and it seemed to Luke that once again she was all business and eager efficiency. "Okay, then. Let's go."

****

Julian Alvarado's office reminded Luke of his own: books stacked haphazardly from the floor almost to the ceiling, files piled high on a scruffy desk that had certainly seen better days, and Styrofoam coffee cups that should've been tossed out a week ago. But his walls were adorned by beautiful wrought-iron crucifixes decorated with colorful stones, probably created in Mexico, while Luke's walls were covered with maps, posters, and Texas memorabilia. Kitty-cornered beside a closet door was a podium with an old Bible resting atop it. It was a rather bizarre haven from the raucous rap music and pounding synthetic drumbeats emanating from the cars cruising up and down the streets outside.

Framed by a large window, white blinds pulled tightly closed, Julian sat in a swivel chair behind his desk. He leaned back, his fingers linked behind his head, while Madison and Luke faced him from the other side. Luke was not a religious man, but something about Alvarado made him sit up and pay attention. Perhaps it was his flashing coal-black eyes or thick, wavy dark hair touching his shoulders, but Luke thought he looked like portraits he'd seen of John the Baptist.

"No one followed you from the cemetery, right?" Alvarado asked suddenly.

"No, sir," Madison answered. "I don't think so."

Alvarado grinned. "Please, I'm not that much older than you. Call me Julian."

His teeth are too perfect. Luke was immediately ashamed. The truth was, he'd never met a preacher, lawyer, or cop he trusted. On the other hand, he reminded himself, this man seemed to have loved Lacy, and she must've believed in him, so he had to keep an open mind.

"Thank you," Luke said aloud, "but only if you call us Madison and Luke."

Julian nodded, but his mind was clearly somewhere

else. He leaned forward in his swivel chair and rested his elbows on his cluttered desk. "I know this has been a hard day for you both, and I don't want to make it any harder, so let me get straight to the point. What do you know about Lacy's death?"

Luke was a little shocked by the preacher's candor, but he welcomed it. "Not much," he admitted. "She was murdered, we know that for sure, and some guy named Antonio Davila is a person of interest. That's about it. But before you go any further, I have a question for you."

Madison shot him a nervous glance, but Julian just shrugged. "Of course."

"How did you hear about Lacy's death? Mr. Gregory said you called him and asked if you could speak at the funeral. We didn't put out an obit, so I think it's a little strange…maybe even a little too convenient…that you knew about it."

Julian cocked his head to one side and looked at Luke thoughtfully. Finally, he nodded. "Of course, you're right. The world of junkies, prostitutes, pimps…well, it's a small world, Luke. I'm sure you know that. Most of them don't read newspapers or listen to the radio or watch the news. But that doesn't mean they don't have friends or people in their lives they care about. They pass the word around, just like you would. One of the working girls I know knew Lacy. I don't know how she heard about it or from whom, but she's the one who told me."

Madison leaned forward. "Did she tell you Lacy was murdered?"

"No, just that she had died. But I knew she was murdered."

Luke's mouth went dry. "How'd you know that?"

"Because I saw her on December second, the day after she got out of jail, and she told me."

"She told you what?"

"She told me Antonio Davila was going to kill her. And then she said he'd film it."

****

As Madison stared at Julian Alvarado in disbelief, Luke released a sigh so explosive she guessed he'd been holding his breath. She didn't know what to say, but Luke didn't seem to have any such problem.

"Have you talked to the police?"

Julian shook his head. "Not yet. But I saw the detective at the service this morning, so they'll be coming around soon enough."

Luke nodded and ran his fingers through his hair in that now-familiar gesture of unspoken frustration. "Please start at the beginning."

"Like I said this morning," Julian began patiently, "I met Lacy three years ago on Christmas Eve. She worked several areas in the city, and this area—the deep west side—is one of them. I saw her often after that, and I watched her go downhill. I actually tried to help her kick heroin at least twice that I can remember, but Davila always managed to sabotage anything she tried to accomplish. And once she was on the crystal meth, there was nothing I could do. That stuff is pure poison, and Davila always saw to it that she had some. I couldn't compete with that, and neither could God. So by that time, she belonged to Davila. Totally. There was nothing he could do to her that she wouldn't take, as long as he kept her supplied."

"Did Lacy ever tell you that Davila is into kids?" Luke asked abruptly.

Julian's eyes widened, and he shook his head. "I suspected as much, but no, she never said that. All I know for sure is he's her pimp and her dealer."

"Did you know she had a child?" Madison asked quietly.

"Not until early this year." For the first time, Julian appeared uncomfortable. He tugged at his shirt collar as if he needed more air. "I hadn't seen her in several months, so when she showed up at my house, which is right next door to this church, I was relieved to see she was still living. That's probably the worst part of ministering to this group of people—you never know if you'll see them again, dead or alive. Anyway, when she showed up at my house—this was a few days after New Year's, this year—she was high as a kite, so I didn't pay much attention to what she was babbling about. I was more concerned about trying to help her down easy. But she was insistent, so I tried to follow what she was saying. She told me she had overheard Davila on his cell phone that morning, talking to someone, but she didn't know who, about taking a child from the Mercy Children's Home here in San Antonio."

Luke frowned. "From where?"

Madison stepped in. "The Mercy Children's Home. It's a foster care place that people can adopt children from. Children can live there for years. It's not a stopover place like mine. They have a very good reputation. Go ahead, Julian."

He folded his hands together and rested his chin on them. "I knew Davila couldn't have a good reason for taking a child from anywhere, but I didn't know what I could do about it. So I asked her what she wanted me to do, and that's when she told me she had a little girl. She said her daughter used to be able to stay with an old woman who lived next door, but Davila had put a stop to that, so she didn't have anywhere she could hide her child if she had to. She seemed convinced Davila was going to hurt this child that he was getting from the Mercy Children's Home, and somehow she connected that child's danger with a threat to her own little girl. So that's all she wanted from me that day, a place to hide her daughter."

Madison remembered the concealed area in Lacy's closet and wondered again if Davila had discovered it. Lacy must've been looking for a backup hiding place, just in case he had. She must've been out of her mind with fear.

"I assured her she could bring her little girl to me and my wife, Victoria, and she would be completely safe with us. Lacy calmed down a little, and then she left, but I wasn't even sure she'd remember our conversation the next day. She was obviously in very bad physical shape, and when that happens, mental issues can occur as well. She could hallucinate, hear voices, just forget everything... I knew if I saw her again, I probably wouldn't be able to reason with her."

"When *did* you see her again?" Madison asked.

"It was on the afternoon of December second. Nearly a year later. The only reason I know that date for sure is because I checked my diary this morning before I left for the funeral. On December second, Lacy showed up at my house with her little girl. I'm so sorry—her name escapes me."

"Piper," Luke muttered grimly. "Her name is Piper."

"That's right. Piper. Anyway, when Lacy arrived, she had a small bag and a little girl clinging to her hand,

147

and I could see they were in big trouble. I took them into this office immediately and locked the door. At first, when I asked her what was wrong, she told me she and Piper had run away from her old man and she wanted to get clean. I told her I didn't have any beds right then, but our Affirmative Outreach Rehab Center right behind my house would have a bed vacant in a day or two. At that point, she broke down and said Davila was going to kill her. She said she needed my help and she needed it fast, before Davila got back home and realized she was gone. She said he wouldn't care if *she* was gone, but he would lose his mind if Piper wasn't there. I'll never forget the way she said that. 'He'll lose his mind if he can't get to her...'

"I thought it was a weird thing to say, so I asked her why, but Lacy wouldn't tell me. All she said was Piper was in a lot of danger and they had to stay together. I was very upset because I wanted desperately to help, but I had no beds, not one extra inch of space. I even had junkies sleeping on my living room floor! I begged her to give me just a day or so to make some other arrangements, and then everything would be okay. But she just looked at me, so sad, and said, 'I thought I could count on you. I thought you'd take care of us.' I don't think anything else has ever hurt me that much because I just couldn't help her right then, and I didn't know anyone else who could, either."

"Why the hell didn't you just hide them in the bathroom or something?" Luke asked angrily. "Surely, you could've found some place—"

Even though she understood his frustration, Madison intervened gently. "Luke, it's irrelevant now. He has a family of his own and junkies living around his own kids. I don't think we have any right to point fingers at him."

Julian looked at her gratefully, but the sadness in his dark eyes was unmistakable. "Anyway, I promised her I'd take care of them both, but she had to give me a little time. She just looked me right square in the eyes and said, 'You don't understand. He's going to kill me, and he's going to film it.' Then she grabbed Piper and rushed back out on the street and made a phone call right on the curb. I ran out and did everything I could do to stop her, everything, but her ride showed up, and they got in…and I never saw them again."

He's going to film it.

Madison thought of the DVD and four children's photographs hidden in her office safe and fought nausea.

"You said the cops will come talk to you now," Luke stated flatly. "Will you tell them all this?"

"I don't know. If they ask, I guess. I won't have any choice."

"And if they don't ask?"

Julian bit his lip. "I don't think so."

"Good. I wouldn't, either. Not yet, anyway."

"You don't like cops?"

Luke flushed. "It's not that. I just don't trust them. And I don't trust anybody else right now, either. We want to do a little more digging on our own, and we're meeting a private detective tonight who sits on Madison's board of directors. Personally, I want to hear what he has to say."

Julian nodded again. "I get that. All right. I won't tell the police about this yet—unless I have to."

"Good. And if you do have to tell them, can you let us know?"

"Absolutely."

"Thank you. Oh, listen, just out of curiosity, are you familiar with an attorney by the name of Ryan Neely?"

Julian frowned and didn't answer for a moment, then nodded. "Yeah. He's a real creep."

"Really? I heard he was a pillar of the community."

"A legend in his own mind. Why do you ask?"

Madison decided to answer before Luke could. "On the night of December first, Lacy was arrested for solicitation and possession of methamphetamine. Ryan Neely bailed her out. The next day she came to you and asked if you could hide Piper if she needed you to. Did she happen to mention Neely when she saw you?"

"No, not a word. But I have a hard time believing he did that. Neely hates junkies."

She shrugged. "Well, maybe not so much. That same day, December second, protective services received an anonymous abuse report on Piper Callaghan—not its first—and decided maybe they'd better send a social worker out to check on Piper after all. But then, somehow, Neely found out about it. He called protective services and told them not to worry about it, that he'd take Piper into his home. He actually went to the house to get her, but no one was there."

Julian looked confused. "How'd he learn about the report?"

"No clue."

"Wait a minute. You said anonymous abuse reports?"

She nodded. "We're thinking Lacy might have called them in herself, trying to get help for Piper."

"Well, that's definitely something Lacy would do. But I don't believe for one minute that Neely offered to give Piper a home without some ulterior motive. Not Ryan Neely. The man is Lucifer's first cousin."

"Well, we know for a fact he offered," Luke said reasonably. "We also know that when he showed up to get Piper, Lacy and Piper were gone. But that's all we know."

"That must've been when they came to me," Julian whispered.

"Must've been."

Madison changed the subject abruptly. "Julian, do you know a kid by the name of Rafe Gamez?"

Julian lit up, instantly diverted. "Yes, I do. I've been trying to get him clean for months, and he just hasn't been interested. But he came to the Lord last Sunday, and tonight he's coming into our rehab program. He got into a little trouble the other evening, and I had to talk to a judge so he could be released into my center, but I've got my fingers crossed. Why do you ask?"

Luke spoke before Madison could. His lie was smooth and easy. "We met him a couple of days ago, and he told us about how you were going to help him, that's all. I was skeptical—"

Julian chuckled. "Of course you were. I get it. Rafe is typical of the people I work with. He's been on the street most of his young life. When he came to the Lord, I asked him if he wanted me to meet his parents. I like to do that. But he told me he had no idea where they were, so I didn't say any more about it."

Madison clasped her hands tightly in her lap. "Julian, does the phrase, *tip the piano man* mean anything to you?"

"No...I've never heard it before. What is it?"

Luke stood up and helped Madison to her feet. He

pulled a couple of business cards out of his wallet and handed them to the preacher. "We don't know, but we think it's important."

"Is Piano Man a person?"

"We don't know that, either."

Julian nodded, picked up his own business card off his desk, and handed it to Luke. "I'll ask around and call you if I hear anything."

"You be careful, Julian," Madison interjected with a smile. "Don't take any unnecessary risks. You're too important to this community."

"Getting out of bed in the morning is a risk, and I'm no more important than anyone else." But his dark eyes were perplexed as he met her gaze. "*Tip the piano man. Now, that's a strange one... I don't think I'll forget that anytime soon.*"

****

"You look tired, Madison," Luke said as they walked across the street to the corner lot where she had parked the SUV. "You want me to drive us up to the lake? I called my housekeeper this morning, so she's expecting us."

She gave him a grateful smile and handed him her keys. "Oh Lord, that would be wonderful. Thank you so much."

As he maneuvered the vehicle from the parking lot, she paid closer attention to the area as they drove toward Highway 90, the busy thoroughfare leading out of the city and toward the peace of Medina Lake. Victory Church was scrubbed gray adobe with only a simple banner hanging above the entrance, and next door on either side were small nondescript homes. One of them housed recovering drug addicts when the center was full, but no signs alerted passersby as to which house it was. Apparently, Julian Alvarado played everything very close to his chest, but that was one of the things Madison liked about him.

She leaned her head back against the headrest and yawned.

When Luke melded into the heavy freeway traffic heading out of the city, he asked, "You okay?"

"I'm fine, thanks. I'm just overwhelmed, I think. I'm looking forward to seeing Jerome tonight. He always grounds me. I'm hoping he may have news."

"Listen, if you think so highly of him and you trust him that much, let's just lay all our cards on the table, okay? I've been putting together a timeline each evening to help me keep my thoughts straight. We can give him a copy of that, along with everything else we have. It should give him plenty to start with, don't you think?"

"Absolutely. It's more than enough. But let's do it this way. You meet him, and then you let me know if you *don't* want him to come in. It's important to me that we be on the same page."

"I appreciate that, Madison."

"Of course. Piper's the one we have to protect here, so we should make the decision together."

About thirty minutes later, Luke exited the highway in the small, historical town of Castroville and headed east toward the lake. As they drove past well-irrigated farmlands and the occasional small business, the discordant sounds of traffic and road construction began to dissipate into the tranquil countryside. The two-lane road was smooth, and the dividing stripe was freshly painted. It was one of Madison's favorite drives, and she couldn't have asked for more perfect weather: sunny, crisp, and cool—typical south Texas in December.

"What did you think of our street preacher?" Luke asked as he let his window down.

"Julian? I think he's an extraordinary man. What did you think?"

"An extraordinary man…" He looked over at her thoughtfully. "Those are mighty big words, young lady."

She nodded her agreement. "I think he deserves them—unless I've read him all wrong. And apparently, Lacy felt the same way. She trusted him."

"Yeah," he muttered, "and a lot of good that did her."

"You know, Luke, you can be a thoroughly unlikable character."

He heaved a sigh and gave Madison a look so filled with feigned shame and remorse she laughed aloud.

"You're right. I'm a brat. I don't like cops, attorneys, or preachers."

"Well, I think we should give Julian a chance," she said after a moment.

"Agreed. That's very nice of you. Do you usually give men an extra chance?"

The question caught her off guard, and she looked at him quickly. When he lifted his brows in a picture of wide-eyed innocence, she relaxed and smiled.

"Oh, c'mon, Madison, 'fess up. You ever been married? Engaged? In love?"

She heard the laughter in his voice, but she felt the questions were serious. He'd told her a great deal about himself, and he'd been painfully honest, but she'd shared next to nothing with him. That made for a rather lopsided partnership.

"I thought I was in love once," she volunteered

finally, "but I was wrong."

"Indigestion, right?"

She nodded, grinning. "Something like that. The truth is I was always obsessed with school, then with my work, then with my shelter... I've just never had time, and I never met anyone who could put up with me. I'm kind of bossy, you know, and I know I'm driven—"

"No...really?"

She smacked his shoulder. "Smart aleck. Anyway, it would take a remarkable man to give me the kind of space I need to do what I do. I figure if someone like that comes along, I'll pay attention. But I don't expect it to happen."

"Well, then, it probably will."

Madison glanced at him. "That's what Jerome always says. Of course, he thinks he's my daddy. He's trying to get me married off as soon as possible because he wants to be a grandpa. I think that's a little pushy, don't you?"

"Oh, I don't know..."

She looked at him suspiciously, but the smile tugging at his lips made her heart thump a little faster. She ducked her head in embarrassment.

"That's enough about me," she announced. "I'm going to take a nap."

Chapter Eleven

Madison pulled herself from sleep as Luke turned onto a well-traveled highway heading up into the rolling hills and thickly wooded area near popular Medina Lake, then turned onto a dirt road and drove for at least another two miles. Finally, he halted in front of a swinging gate centered in a seemingly endless, white privacy fence.

"This be us," he announced.

She gave him a curious look as he drove slowly onto the property, but remained silent as she gazed around in disbelief. If she lived to be a hundred, she doubted she'd ever see another place as close to Heaven as this.

Acres of grass were brown and straw-like now, but she could imagine it in the spring—like a thick, rolling carpet of green velvet. Clumps of live oak trees, mesquite bushes, and cedar dotted the landscape as he drove up the dirt road. In the distance she could see a sprawling, two-story farmhouse.

"How many acres do you have here?"

"Just twenty. Do you like it?"

"It's gorgeous."

"Thank you."

"How far are you from Medina Lake itself?"

"Six miles exactly. I didn't want to be any closer than that. It gets too busy in the summer. But the Medina River runs right through my property."

She was amazed at the change that had come over

him. For the first time since they'd met, he seemed relaxed, comfortable, at peace in his little corner of paradise. He was a completely different man.

"If you look at that incline just ahead…on the other side of it is the Medina River. I love to go down there and write."

"Which you get to do so often from your condo in New York," she teased.

"Oh, I won't be in the city much longer. One of my childhood dreams was to live alone in a beautiful place out in the country, where no one could bother me. I wanted somewhere I could write my books and hide away if I needed to. Actually, my staff and I call this place *The Callaghan Retreat*. Corny as it sounds, this place is a dream come true for me."

"Who's on your staff?"

"Well, I have a yardman named Felix who brings his son in to help him keep up with all this landscaping. Then I have a wonderful housekeeper-cook named Doris Woodrow who thinks she's my mother—I just call her Woodrow, like in *Lonesome Dove*—and a secretary-researcher who comes in when I'm working. In the summer there's a pool guy who takes care of the pool, but I don't use it very much. I'm very well taken care of when I'm here. But lately, I've felt the need to be around noise and music and people—plus, my editor needs me. So I'm living in New York at the moment, but I'll be back before long."

"I don't think I could handle this much solitude."

Luke cut off the ignition and handed her the keys. "You get used to it. Besides, solitude is a necessity for a writer. That's why I have all the amenities and comforts of home around my house, but when I need to be alone with nature, I just walk over the hill and go down to the river. It's perfect."

Madison smiled, dropped the keys in her purse, and opened the door. When she stepped outside, she gazed in admiration at the white frame farmhouse.

As she looked more closely, she realized the descriptive term *farmhouse* was far from accurate. While the home itself was freshly painted an eggshell white and the front was accented with rustic cedar, the exterior seemed to be more glass than wood. Madison was sure each room had an enormous picture window affording the occupant a glorious view of every corner of this magnificent property.

Luke touched her elbow. "Let's go in the house. Watch your step. We've had rain out here, too. I'm sure Woodrow smelled me coming an hour ago and has an eight-course lunch on the table. Don't be intimidated by her. She's a thorny old bird, but I couldn't do without her."

"Does she live here all the time?"

"She does now. Mr. Woodrow passed away a couple of years ago, and she wasn't happy living alone, so I invited her to stay. She needed someone to take care of— they never had children—so I fit the bill, I guess. When I'm home, she bosses me around something terrible."

"You don't mind?"

He gave an affectionate grin. "Not really. She does it with love—like a mom would, I think—so I sort of enjoy it."

As they climbed the steps of a pillar-lined front porch that ran the length of the front of the house, she glimpsed a swimming pool, encircled by a high cedar deck, off to one side. Just beyond that was a white summer pavilion, complete with plush lawn furniture and two built-in picnic tables. Surrounding it all were ancient oak, cypress, and cedar trees, now barren of deep green leaves, that undoubtedly provided a canopy of blessed shade during the hot Texas summers. These were definitely the *amenities of home* he'd referred to.

All this luxury for entertaining and no visitors. Resentment inexplicably tarnished her admiration. *All this for one man...*

The front door flew open. "Well, glory be, Mr. C! What evil wind blew you in? We figured we'd never see you again—fact is the whole town's been wagerin' on it! Who's this?"

Madison stared, taken aback, at the woman Luke called Woodrow. She couldn't have pictured a more unmotherly looking individual if she tried. This woman was tall, probably close to six feet, with steel-gray hair flowing down her back and piercing blue eyes. Dressed in jeans, cowboy boots, and a man's red-and-black flannel shirt with a red bandanna tied around her neck, she was all bone and callouses and sinewy muscle.

"This is Dr. Wagner, Woodrow, remember? The lady I told you about? Madison, meet Woodrow, my right-hand person."

Doris Woodrow thrust out her hand and gripped Madison's fingers so tightly Madison thought she heard her bones crack. Before she could even respond with a greeting of her own, she was jerked through the front door and found herself standing in a cool, Mexican-tiled foyer.

"Howdy do, sweetheart!" Woodrow's smoke-husky voice seemed to reverberate off the walls. "Sure am glad to meet you! We don't get city folk out here much, that's for sure. Y'all hungry?"

"A little," he responded, watching Madison with an amused expression on his face. "Funerals don't do a lot for the appetite."

"Oh, good golly, I plum forgot about that! Y'all come on in the kitchen and have a little bite of somethin'. I didn't have time to make much. Pete had a foal come early this mornin', and I went over to help."

Madison managed a weak *thank you* and thrust her hands behind her back, massaging her throbbing fingers. At the very least, several ligaments were tangled.

As she followed Woodrow and Luke to the kitchen, barely listening to the housekeeper's raspy voice grinding on and on about phone messages and letters from New York, she tried to take in the splendid décor of this wonderful home.

She glimpsed a sunken living room, three Saltillo-tiled steps down from the foyer, with an enormous rock fireplace accented by cedar paneling and a set of dark wooden french doors that opened onto the front porch. She sneaked a peek into a rustic study-library just across from the living area, noting the packed floor-to-ceiling book shelves and sliding glass doors that led onto the cedar deck encircling the swimming pool. Every available wall was adorned by western art and Indian artifacts. The house was totally masculine; even its fragrance was that of real leather, natural wood, and the out of doors.

Woodrow's voice brought her up short as they entered a sparkling kitchen that must've contained every appliance known and coveted by a modern gourmet chef. She dragged her astonished gaze from the most complicated microwave oven she'd ever seen back to

Woodrow's face.

"This kitchen is great enough to make me want to learn to cook, Mrs. Woodrow!"

"You don't cook?"

"No, ma'am, I never really had time to learn."

"Good golly! I been cookin' for a houseful my whole life." She took an enormous chef salad from a computerized stainless-steel refrigerator. "Y'all sit down here and eat."

"Thank you, Woodrow. Just stop your fidgeting and relax. After we eat, Madison and I are going to take a little digestive walk down to the river, and then we're going straight back to San Antonio." Suddenly, Luke changed the subject. "Tell me something, Woodrow. If I brought a little girl back here for a while, would you be able to look after her? You said you've been cooking for a houseful your whole life, so I'm thinking maybe you'd be able to handle it."

Woodrow's eyes widened, and she didn't answer right away. But then, suddenly, a smile of pure joy exploded across her sun-lined face. "A little girl, Mr. C? I'd love that! You just give us a minute or two warnin', and we'll be all set!"

He grinned back at her, clearly relieved. "Wonderful! I'll let you know in a day or so. Did you get that bag packed for me?"

"I sure did. Casual and dressier. I also filled up the truck and had her checked out. She's all set to go."

"You're a saint, Woodrow. Thanks."

She cocked a sparse eyebrow and ran her fingers through that wild mop of gray hair. "Just doing my job is all. I'll leave y'all to it now." She thrust her hand straight out to Madison, who accepted it warily. "It's been a real pleasure meeting you, Doc. You come back and see us, y'hear?"

"Yes, ma'am, I will. Thank you very much."

Madison couldn't miss the speculative expression on the older woman's face as she looked from Madison to Luke, then back at Madison. Mrs. Woodrow gave a sudden grin, her blue eyes more piercing than ever, and Madison knew exactly what she was thinking.

She ducked her head to hide her smile.

****

When they'd reached the Medina River, Luke leaned against an ancient live oak tree and watched the crystal-clear water burble over time-smoothed rocks. Nothing relaxed him more than to stand in this very spot and allow the soothing sounds of nature seep into his core.

He glanced at Madison nervously. She seemed tired and a little out of sorts, but he had an important question to ask, and there wouldn't be a better time than this. He took a deep breath. "Do you think this place would make a good home for Piper?"

"Well, good grief, of course! Why would you even ask that?"

He shrugged. "I don't know. I've never been a dad before. I don't know what you guys look for—"

"Well, it doesn't have to be *this* nice," she interrupted, now clearly miffed. "We're not ogres, Luke. We're not all out to get you."

He held up his hand, grinning. "Easy does it, Dr. Wagner. What's wrong?"

She sighed and leaned against a nearby mesquite tree, gazing pensively into the water. "Nothing. I'm sorry. I'm tired."

"Madison, I get it. You're wondering how I can enjoy all this when there are so many children who have nothing. Especially when I was one of them. You're wondering, how could I have forgotten where I came from? How could I have not opened this wonderful place to every needy child I came across?"

She ran her fingers through her hair and looked up at him. "I'm sorry," she repeated in a whisper. "I'm really so tired…"

For a moment, as the sunlight danced over her hair and turned it into a shining cap of burnished gold, he thought she was the most beautiful woman he'd ever seen. The thought shocked him—he hadn't felt that way about any woman since Lacy. But it didn't matter right now. All that mattered to him was that she realized he wasn't as self-absorbed and narcissistic as she'd first believed.

The silence stretched for a few moments before he finally spoke. "Listen, you've been involved with kids for years. They're all you care about. I understand that. But until two days ago, I didn't know I could be anyone's father. I didn't know I could have a child who might be living out of garbage cans, getting the hell beat out of her, and being forced to participate in some kind of filthy movie business. It took all my energy to escape my own childhood, and I didn't intend to worry about someone else's. I certainly wasn't going to drag a hundred other kids into my life who'd do nothing but remind me of where I came from."

"They're not all I care about—"

"Let me finish. You, on the other hand, put yourself right in that sewer with them. You have no ulterior motives, nothing but pure love, and I've never seen that before in my life. So if it isn't too much trouble, give me a few minutes to get used to it, will you?"

She didn't say anything for a long time. Finally, she touched his arm. "I'm sorry, Luke. You're right. I can be a judgmental witch."

He took her hand in his and pressed it to his lips, pleased that his touch brought a flush of color to her cheeks. "Thank you," he said softly, "because I only want to hear you say one thing about me, and I won't be happy until I hear it."

"What's that?"

"I want to hear you say about me what you said about Julian Alvarado. I want to hear you say that I'm an extraordinary man."

****

As Madison merged into rush hour traffic on I-10, she kept Luke's truck in her rearview mirror. It wasn't hard because the vehicle was enormous and its deep burgundy color could be seen for miles.

She straightened her hands-free cell phone in its container and moved into her right lane.

"Whitney," she said loudly, then waited for Whitney's phone to ring.

Whitney answered quickly. "Hey, what's up?"

"Well, Luke's following me in his truck, and the traffic is horrible, so I thought I'd give you a call."

"Well, not much going on here. It's almost Christmas, so everything's shutting down. You know how it is."

"Yeah, I do. How's Piper today? Any change?"

"A little, I think. She seems a bit more interested in the other kids and what they're doing, although she doesn't join in, and she doesn't say anything. Sasha is stuck to her, so that's the same. They're like Siamese twins now. But I do think she may be catching a cold. She seems to have an earache, but of course she doesn't answer me when I ask about it."

"How do you know her ear hurts?"

"She cups her hand over it every once in a while and sort of rocks back and forth, you know? I put her on a heating pad and gave her some aspirin, which she took, but it doesn't seem to be helping. Anyway, I've asked Stacy to stay with the kids and keep an eye on Piper until Jared and I get back so you guys can do your work tonight without being bothered. We'll be leaving at seven thirty, so do you think you'll make it home by then? I don't want to leave Stacy here alone."

"I'm trying. Traffic is horrible, and this I-10 construction is making it worse. Could you call Dr. Weinstein for me when we get finished here and see if he can squeeze her in tomorrow? This is a good time to get her into the medical system."

"Okay, but tomorrow's Wednesday. He'll have to see her in the morning. He closes on Wednesday afternoons, remember?"

"That's fine. The earlier the better. Earaches are horrible."

"Okay, I'll call as soon as we hang up. Oh, Jerome phoned a little while ago and said he was running late. He's been down at the police station most of the day doing some research, so he thought he'd bring in a couple of pizzas for you guys when he comes over. He didn't want anyone to worry about actually fixing dinner. I told him you'd appreciate that."

Madison chuckled. "No, he just doesn't want me to cook. Pizza sounds great. Did he give you any idea what time?"

"He said he'd try for about seven thirty. Can't you get home any sooner?"

"I'm pedaling as fast as I can, girlfriend. Don't get your panties in a wad."

Whitney laughed out loud. "My panties are always in a wad when I have to go anywhere near Jared's folks."

"I know. I'm sorry."

"No biggie. Listen, you have to tell me. I'm dying to know—what do you think about Luke?"

Madison shook her head. "I don't think about Luke."

"That's a lie. Even *I* think about Luke. Is he as horrible as you thought he was going to be?"

"No, he's actually a pretty nice guy. Call Dr. Weinstein, Whitney. I have to go now."

Whitney made the sound of a crowing chicken and laughed.

Madison hung up.

It was about an hour before she turned onto her street and drove slowly toward the shelter. She pulled to the curb, braked, and got out of the SUV, then motioned for Luke to park in front of the detached two-car garage behind the privacy fence so his truck couldn't be seen from the street. Since it was a gorgeous new pickup, she was afraid it would entice potential auto thieves, as well as alert anyone who might be keeping an eye on the shelter to see if anybody new was staying there. Once they'd closed the six-foot gate and she was certain the truck was nicely concealed, she pulled her vehicle into its usual parking spot on the driveway and locked it up. She waited for Luke at a nearly hidden back entrance close to the gate.

"I want to give you the code to get you in the house," she told him when he'd reached her. She pointed to a black key pad above the doorknob. "It's easy. Just use 161616, and it'll unlock." She keyed in the code, and the lock gave an audible click. "Here we go."

"161616. Got it." Luke shifted his luggage to his other hand. "I never noticed this door before." He followed her into a good-sized laundry room containing an enormous washer and dryer and cleaning items stacked on a shelf beside an enclosure that stored a vacuum cleaner, a construction broom, and a heavy-duty mop. He looked around and nodded. "Very efficient."

"I'm glad you approve. If you go through that door by the closet, the stairs take you straight up to the second floor."

He chuckled. "I'll do that, then. I need to get my luggage up to my room. I don't know what Woodrow packed in here, but it weighs a ton."

"Feel free to unpack if you want. Whitney said Jerome was bringing pizza tonight because he was running late, so I'm sure you have time. He spent the day down at the police station doing some research."

"On what?"

She shrugged, a little curious herself. Jerome didn't really know much about Lacy's murder other than the fact she was dead and her daughter was in Madison's custody, but that might actually be enough information to send Jerome Scranton into a tornado of frenzied activity.

Luke answered his own question. "Well, I guess we'll find out soon enough. I'll see you shortly."

"I'm going to talk to Whitney and Jared for a minute. Will you stick your head in the playroom and check on Piper for me? Whitney says she might have an earache."

"Be glad to. See you in a few."

****

Madison opened the bureau-sized safe in her office and ruffled through a legal-sized box labeled *Callaghan*. Satisfied everything was in order, she pulled the box out and locked the safe door behind her. She had everything she needed to show Jerome—bank information, letters from Lacy, DFPS documentation, the DVD, and photographs. Madison made certain the lid was on tightly and carried the box upstairs toward her bedroom.

As she passed the children's playroom, she made a mental note to speak to Stacy about being certain no little ones made their way to her room, which they sometimes did when it was bedtime. Tonight, it was imperative that Stacy maintain order and keep them all corralled.

She let herself into her room, set the box on the round table in the small kitchen area, flipped on a lamp beside the bed, and quickly changed from her business suit into jeans, a white pullover sweater, and a pair of sneakers. It seemed eons since Lacy's funeral and their conversation with Julian Alvarado, but everything had happened today. *The longest day ever...*

No wonder she was so tired.

She heard the chimes of the front doorbell and hurried down the hallway. When she reached the playroom, she stopped and peered inside, looking for Stacy. But what caught her eye was Luke Callaghan sitting cross-legged on the floor, leaning comfortably against the wall, singing, "How much is that doggie in the window," with six children seated in a half-circle around him. Everyone was laughing as they apparently tried to remember the words. They seemed to be enthralled with this new visitor who appeared equally enthralled with them.

Her gaze slid to Piper, who was lying on a sofa with a heating pad beneath her right ear. She looked even more pale than usual, but still she watched Luke with interest as he sang with the other children. Sasha lay stretched out beside the sofa, sound asleep. Madison spotted Stacy and gestured for her to come to the doorway.

"Yes, ma'am?"

"Stacy, would you tell Mr. Callaghan that Mr. Scranton is here? And also, please keep the kids all together tonight. Don't let any of them out of your sight or let any of them come to my room unless the house is on fire. Can you do that?"

"Of course, Dr. Wagner."

"Thank you so much, sweetheart. And I appreciate you staying here so late. Do you have studying you can do?"

"Yes, ma'am. I have a psych exam tomorrow, but that's it. School's out for Christmas vacation on Friday, you know."

Madison's eyes widened. "Where has this year gone? We'll try to wind up at a decent hour, I promise."

"No worries, Dr. Wagner. Oh, by the way…did Whitney tell you Piper has a doctor's appointment at eleven in the morning?"

"Yes, she told me. I'm glad Dr. Weinstein was able to fit her in. Just send Mr. Callaghan to my room when he's finished with the kids. We're all going to be in there for the evening."

"Yes, ma'am, I will. Good night."

Madison nodded absently, watching as Piper's tiny hand dropped down to stroke the top of Sasha's massive head. Sasha instantly awoke and rolled over in anticipation of what she obviously hoped would be a belly rub.

Madison turned away, tears blurring her vision as she sent up a silent prayer.

Oh God, please let this child stay in that sweet, safe bubble for just a little while longer...

Chapter Twelve

Once everyone was gathered in her room, Madison was amused at the slightly intimidated expression on Luke's face as he stood eyeball to eyeball with a lean, tautly muscled man. Jerome Scranton wore a scruffy cowboy hat atop wavy salt-and-pepper hair that fell nearly to his shoulders. When he removed his hat, a shock of silver-white hair swooped across his forehead. As usual, he reminded Madison of Wild Bill Hickok.

"Luke, meet one of my dearest friends, Jerome Scranton. He was formerly SAPD, worked vice and narcotics undercover...eight years in homicide. He's now one of my most valued board members, a private investigator, and like a second father to me."

Luke offered his hand. "It's a privilege, sir."

As the two men shook hands, Scranton's voice seemed to come from the soles of his boots. "Thanks, son."

Jerome moved to one side to introduce a much younger, shorter man. "I hope you don't mind, Madison, but I brought my old partner, Darth. We call him that because he lives on the dark side, and now he's a permanent pessimist. He heads up SAPD's Special Victims Unit. Darth has a lot of experience in kiddie porn, pedophilia, and computers—all that nasty stuff. From the little bit you told me this morning, we're going to need his help."

Catching sight of Luke's uncertain expression, Madison decided to take charge and offered her hand to the younger detective. "Welcome," she said warmly. "I'm Dr. Madison Wagner. I'm so glad you joined us."

"Morgan Harris." He shifted his laptop under his arm and pumped her hand in a firm, no-nonsense handshake. "You can call me Darth. I appreciate the opportunity."

"Opportunity?" Luke asked.

"Yes, sir. I'm hoping we can help each other."

"I hope so, too," she responded uncertainly, wondering how they could possibly help him. "Before we eat, let's set up our workspace, shall we?"

As she issued orders from her position in front of the small refrigerator and brought drinks to the table, the men obeyed and placed everything where she wanted it within five minutes. The box containing Piper's documentation was set on the floor next to Luke's chair, Lacy's DVD was inserted into the DVD player in the living area, and their laptops were placed in front of their chairs at the conference table. An enormous pizza box served as a centerpiece.

Darth removed his gray zip-up hoodie and sat down beside Jerome. His longish auburn hair was shaggy and uneven, probably the product of a lousy haircut he'd given himself, and his emerald-green eyes were magnified by oversized spectacles with thick lenses.

"I think we're good to go now," Madison said finally. "Is everyone hungry?"

She opened the box containing a steaming-hot black olive and mushroom pizza. "I really appreciate this, Jerome. It looks wonderful." She placed a stack of napkins on the table. "Dig in, fellas. Do I need anything else? There's a couple of beers, a bottle of wine, and a few sodas in the frig over there when you're ready for something else to drink."

Luke popped the top on his can and took a long swig, then looked at the two men seated across from him. "Please don't take this the wrong way, Mr. Scranton. Madison said we need you, and I totally trust her judgment, but cops are already investigating the murder of my ex-wife and looking for this kid-freak, Antonio Davila. Do you mind telling me how you can help us?"

"If you call me Jerome, I'll be glad to tell you what *I* can do and the cops can't." He took a bite of pizza and chewed thoughtfully before he spoke again in a thick, West-Texas drawl. "Madison didn't fill me in on much when I talked to her this morning. She only said your ex-wife had been murdered, possibly by a known pedophile, and her little girl was here at the shelter. She also said the child refused to talk, and there were possibly missing children involved. Oh, and she said you were waiting on paternity results."

Luke nodded.

"What do you know about pedophilia, Luke?" Jerome asked abruptly.

"Not very much."

"Well, in my opinion, the most important thing you need to know is that you can't trust anyone. You have no idea who is…and who isn't…a pedophile."

"That's encouraging."

"Not so much, right? But between me, Darth, and Madison, I can promise you'll get a real education—the kind money can't buy and you don't want. But at the very least, you can probably use it in a book sometime."

"How do I know I can trust any of you?"

Jerome's piercing blue eyes twinkled. "Good. You're learning already. Maybe you can; maybe you can't. Only time will tell."

Madison refused to let that lie. "You can trust Jerome. He's a professional hater of pedophiles. He was ready to leave the force ten years before he actually retired because of pedophiles. If I get involved with a child who's been hurt by a pedophile, Jerome gets involved, too. It's just the way we roll."

"Well, I get that, but I would think cops—"

She moved her pizza out of the way and leaned forward intently. "Luke, listen carefully. In all my years of dealing with this kind of situation, I've learned a lot. One of the most important things I've learned is this— when it comes to children, you can't count on cops. I'm sorry to say that, Darth, but—"

Darth held up his hand and shook his head, then removed another slice of pizza from the box. "It's okay. I know where you're going, and you're right."

She nodded. "Luke, don't get me wrong—it's not that they don't care. They do. A lot. Sometimes too much. It's just the legal system has them bound and gagged. For the most part they're not educated enough about pedophilia, and pedophilia is a very secret crime. Once in a while there's medical evidence, but usually it's just a child's word against the perpetrator.

"The thing is cops like evidence they can see: vaginal lacerations, semen samples, photographs, alibis. Pedophiles usually don't leave that kind of evidence. They leave night terrors, demolished psyches, permanent emotional damage—but they seldom leave *anything* a cop can take into court. If they do leave physical evidence, the law too often prevents a cop from ever getting his hands on it.

"That's where Jerome comes in. Because he's a PI with more than a little creativity and nerve, he can get anything he wants, any way he wants to get it. And that's who we need working with us right now. Someone who's not going to let the law stop him from finding out what's going on, and someone who agrees with me that nothing's more important than the children." She gave Darth a long look. "I hope you understand what I'm saying. You're a detective, and you have to follow the law. Good luck with that. We've stumbled on a situation here, and all we care about are the kids. I'm not going to ask your permission to do anything."

Darth gave a boyish grin. "Somehow I didn't think you would."

"So whatever is said here, you'll keep to yourself, right?"

"Copy that."

****

Luke stared at her. On the outside Madison Wagner was feminine and seemingly fragile, but beneath that lovely exterior pounded the fierce heartbeat of a true crusader. If she trusted this Jerome Scranton so completely, then he, Luke Callaghan, trusted him, too. All they could do was hope this detective was everything Jerome Scranton said he was.

Darth seemed to read his mind and looked around the table. "Here's my background, just to make you guys feel better. After I graduated from UT with a degree in computer programming and graphic design, I spent four years in the service. I've been a cop since I was twenty-seven. I've always been a computer nerd, but I worked in the Computer Systems Operations Unit in the military and became totally obsessed—if I hadn't been before. I'm a detective in the Special Victims Unit now, but I've worked in homicide, vice, narcotics, and cybercrimes as well. I had a paper route when I was six and sold cars in high school. I'm not married, and I don't have any kids. No time for it. My work ethic is pretty ridiculous."

Luke was a little embarrassed, but he held his ground and refused to apologize. Darth hadn't told them anything personal, of course, because he was a cop, but the litany of job skills had at least eased Luke's apprehension. "Thank you for that. I appreciate it."

"Sure."

Luke sighed. "Go ahead, Jerome. I'm sorry."

"It's okay." He opened a folder and took another bite of pizza. "Here, Luke. This is what Darth and I did after I talked to Madison this morning. Darth is undercover right now, so he's got to decide if he's going to tell you what he's working on, but he ran Antonio Davila's rap sheet for me. And to answer what's sure to be your next question, no one's seen him. At least, not so far. But he'll show up. Freaks like him always do. He'll go where the kids are."

Jerome pushed several stapled sheets of paper across the table, and Luke skimmed them quickly: possession of methamphetamine with intent to deal, several assault charges, possession of child pornography, sexual assault of a minor, several stays in county jail, and one three-year term served in the Texas Department of Corrections in Huntsville for battery and rape. Luke pushed the papers back to Jerome, who placed them in his folder and removed another packet.

"Now, this is the police report for your ex-wife's murder and her autopsy report. There's a toxicology report, too, but it'll be at least another two weeks before we get it back. However, there doesn't seem to be much doubt about what'll be in it." Jerome handed the paperwork to Luke. "You'll see in the police report that two officers responded to an anonymous call—Officer Jamie Reed and his partner, Officer Sarah Linstrom—at 3:14 in the morning on December twelfth. They're both good cops, but they're young. Not real experienced. The autopsy report shows her time of death was approximately two in the morning—just an hour earlier. The deceased woman was found on the bedroom floor, lying on her side in a pool of blood, stabbed in the throat by a three-to-five-inch blade. A little girl was standing beside her. This tells us two important things right off the bat. One is that the killer knew what he was doing, and the other is that the attack was probably personal. If the stabbing was done right, she would've died in less than a minute." Jerome paused. "Madison tells me the little girl doesn't talk—probably too traumatized. I'm guessing she's your daughter?"

"I think so—"

Madison interrupted suddenly. "Jerome, is there any mention of the house being ransacked?"

"No. Why?"

She looked at Luke. "Then it was ransacked after her body was removed."

Jerome frowned. "Huh?"

Luke felt her steady gaze on his face and made an instantaneous decision that came straight from his gut. It was time to bring Jerome Scranton and Morgan Harris into the fold completely and let the chips fall where they may.

"Well, gentlemen," Luke began, "the day after I

arrived, Madison took me to the funeral home where we met Lacy's next-door neighbor, an elderly Mexican woman named Carlotta Martinez. Without going into a bunch of details, I'll just say that Carlotta gave me a package of what turned out to be bank information Lacy had told Carlotta to give me if something happened to her. Carlotta also swore she saw Davila leave Lacy's house very early that morning. After we left the funeral home, we broke into Lacy's house to see if she had a hiding place in her bedroom closet like one we'd built together when we were kids, and she did. We found a DVD hidden there. But the house had been totally torn up. Ransacked. Destroyed. We don't know if someone was looking for the DVD or Piper or both. I wanted to do a more thorough search of the closet while we were there, but there was a bad storm, and Madison refused to stay any longer."

Scranton stared at him; amusement battled annoyance as it played along the edges of his lips. Finally, he threw in the towel and gave a broad grin. "You guys broke into Lacy's house, for real?"

"I told him not to, Jerome," Madison offered weakly.

"I'm sure you did everything you could, my love. No doubt it was all his fault." He paused and gazed at Luke and Madison soberly before he finally spoke. "If you really want us to help you, someone has to bring us up to speed. Who's going to do it?"

"I will," Luke said quietly.

He opened his folder and handed over the timeline he'd been keeping since his first morning in the shelter, while Madison began removing items from a legal-sized box she'd placed beside Luke's chair. As they alternated in telling the story, Jerome paced back and forth like a nervous wolf, tugging on his right earlobe periodically when he seemed stumped, but he never interrupted. Darth removed his thick glasses and took notes.

Finally, Jerome spoke. "So are you saying you have in your possession now a DVD you found in a closet you didn't even know for sure was going to be there?"

More than a little self-conscious, Luke cleared his throat and nodded. "I know it sounds crazy, but—"

"More than crazy, son. But hey, I've been wrong before. The point is you found it, you got it here, and that's good."

When Luke glanced at Darth nervously, wondering if he doubted Luke's sanity, too, he realized that while the detective wasn't as young or geeky as he'd first thought, he was the kind of nondescript individual who could melt into any crowd and disappear. Five people would give six different descriptions. Luke could probably carry on an hour-long conversation with this Morgan Harris and not remember a single detail about it—or him.

"Are you working Lacy's murder case, Darth?" he asked.

"Not really. Antonio Davila is my focus—but not because of Lacy. We're looking for him because he's a predatory child molester and a serial sadist. A buddy of mine in homicide has Lacy."

A light bulb went off in Luke's head, and he looked at Jerome. "Now I understand why you brought Darth here. You think we could all be working on the same thing...just different aspects. This situation is beginning to remind me of a damned tumor...with a lot of fingers."

"Well, I guess that's one way to look at it," Darth

observed with a wry grin. "Scranton, go on. Let's see where the fingers lead."

"No, wait just a minute, Darth," Luke interrupted. "I want you guys to see a few photos."

"And Lacy's letters, too," Madison added. "They need to read those."

Darth looked puzzled. "Photos? Letters?"

Luke nodded as he pulled the relevant items out of the box labeled *Piper Callaghan.*

"Lacy wrote a personal letter to me and left it, along with a letter of intent to take the place of her will, in a safety deposit box at the Centurion Bank in Boerne. The package Carlotta gave me contained all the personal financial information I needed to gain access to this stuff. As you probably know, Lacy and I were married for a little while, but I've known her for most of my life. In her safety deposit box, she also left me this envelope with these four photos." He pushed the items across the table.

Luke leaned back in his chair, watching Darth's face as he scanned the documents and looked closely at each individual photograph. He couldn't read the detective's expression; it never changed. This man played his cards very close to his vest, just like Jerome. Luke was learning to trust that.

"Is this Lacy's handwriting?" Darth asked suddenly, pointing to the photos.

"No, sir."

Darth looked at Luke for a long moment, his expression probing and solemn. "These kids... Do you guys know anything about them?"

"No," Madison answered.

Luke added, "I know this is a lot of information to

bombard you guys with, but we can't work together if you don't know everything we have. So here it is. Take it slow. We'll wait."

Jerome picked up Luke's timeline and studied it. "Let's start with Piper's protective services file. May I see their reports?"

Madison handed the packet to him quickly, her gaze meeting Luke's across the table. Jerome remained silent as he went through the paperwork.

Finally, after what seemed like hours, he looked up. "So what this says is there were several abuse reports made over time, handed over to different caseworkers, tossed around in various staffings, and then pretty much ignored…until December second. Now, here, Luke, on your timeline, you say an attorney named Ryan Neely offered to take Piper home with him on December second so she could stay out of foster care. Are you sure about that name? Ryan Neely?"

"Yes, sir, positive. Do you know him?"

Jerome's face twisted with dislike, and he glanced at Darth. "There's not a cop in San Antonio who doesn't know Ryan Neely. Moving on. Can we see the letters and stuff from Lacy that you picked up at the bank?"

Luke passed the paperwork across the table and watched Jerome's face closely as he read Lacy's letter. Her words would be the kicker, he was sure.

After a few minutes, Jerome passed a couple of pieces of paper to Darth. "Well, Mr. Luke, I was wrong. No doubt that film was left for you. I never would've believed it. Have you seen it yet?"

"Yes, sir."

"Both of you?"

"Yes, sir."

Darth handed the pages back to Jerome, cleared his throat, and placed his glasses on the top of his head. "You said you wanted to stay and search the closet more thoroughly, Luke. Do you think there's something else there?"

Luke shrugged. "I don't know. I'd just like to go back and check. Lacy's letter said *I've hidden some stuff in there* and *don't let anyone see you take anything out.* It just sounds like more than one DVD to me."

Darth nodded. "Well, when you first said you broke into Lacy's house and discovered a DVD hidden in a closet, all I could think of was we couldn't use it because we got it without a search warrant. But this letter of intent from Lacy states unequivocally that everything in that house belongs to you, as well as all her money, so I think we just skirted that issue by the skin of our teeth. No one needs to know you found the DVD before you knew about this letter, and I can't imagine that the film itself isn't full of probable cause. But, please, don't go back by yourselves."

"We'll be fine—" Luke began.

"It's not about that. It's about the law, gathering evidence, and not being able to use it in court—the very thing Madison was afraid of. But I think we're all right so far. We can use Lacy's letters leaving all the contents in the house to you as our permission for taking the original film, as well as giving us permission to take anything from there in the future. But still, do you mind if I go on and get a solid search warrant for us so all our asses are covered? Then we can go through that closet again with a fine-tooth comb. As us old-timers always say, 'When in doubt, whip it out.' " He winked at Luke. "That's referring to search warrants, of course."

"Excuse me," Madison interrupted, "are we covered or not?"

"I think you are," Darth answered carefully, "but I'm not God. The judge is God. I need to be sure."

"Can I go with you when you go back?" Luke asked.

"I like that idea, but I'd have to ask you not to touch anything."

Jerome chuckled. "Like that's going to matter now…"

Darth sighed and looked around the table silently. His gaze landed on Luke and remained there. "Listen, you guys, I know how you feel about getting the law involved in this. For the most part, I feel the same way. But I really believe you've stumbled onto something here that may be a direct link to a case my team and I have been working for a very long time—and I need to be sure it's handled right. If it isn't, these pervs will walk…and I don't think any of us want to see that happen. So is it okay if I at least offer you a little guidance before you jump off a cliff on your own?"

Luke was humbled and ashamed. He'd been on the opposite side of this fence for so long that he had no idea how to partner up with a lawman now. Once again, just as when he'd first met Madison and stared fatherhood in the face, he realized he had no choice but to grow up.

"I'm sorry, Darth," he said sincerely. "We have no right to come in here and jeopardize your case just because we don't want to work within your legal parameters. You tell us anything you need us to know, and we'll do everything we can to do it the way you want. Is that fair?"

Darth grinned. "More than fair—and I'll do the same. Remember, there are things you can do that I can't, and there are things I can get that you can't. Scranton and I have worked this way for a long time. We know how to do it. In fact, Scranton trained me."

Luke nodded. "Well, getting in that closet won't take five minutes, so we can go whenever you say."

"I think we can get that search warrant easily from Judge Leonard," Madison interjected. "He's familiar with Piper and Lacy—he put Piper in my custody."

"That's good. I like easy." Darth paused, then gave a deep sigh. "We should probably watch this film now. Do you mind?"

She pushed the DVD case toward Darth. "Please do, but keep the sound down—at least until the end, when Lacy actually speaks. You'll need to hear that. And would you put the DVD back in this case when you're finished?" She sighed. "You don't mind if we skip this part, do you?"

"No, that's fine. We'll come get you when we're done."

"Just a minute," Luke said quietly, reaching across the table for the envelope containing the four photographs. He riffled through them, then pulled out the picture of the little girl with the wild dark hair looking seductively into the camera. He handed it to Jerome. "This is Charly MacIntire. Watch for her."

Jerome looked at the photo closely in the lamplight and nodded, then handed it to Darth. Darth paled but said nothing.

Madison stood up and rubbed her eyes. "I'm going to go check on Piper. Call us when you're ready."

Chapter Thirteen

When Darth opened the door and gestured for them to return to the room, Luke automatically cupped his hand around Madison's elbow and guided her inside. After they'd sat down at the table, Jerome leaned forward earnestly. When he finally spoke, his West-Texas drawl was even more pronounced than earlier.

"I want you to know that Davila's nightclub, La Ninfa, was closed about two years ago, and last I heard, the city wanted to tear it down. But it's still there. When I saw Davila on this film clip... Darth, we need to check that place out again."

"You're right."

"Excuse me," Luke said hesitantly. "We saw a detective at Lacy's house the night I arrived, and Madison said he was waiting for Davila. Do you still have someone over there?"

Darth thought a moment, then shook his head. "I don't think so because no one ever showed up—"

Jerome chuckled. "Yet Madison and Luke just walked in."

"Ouch. And we didn't find that closet—or no one looked close enough. I'll put someone back there right away."

Jerome turned his attention toward Madison, who was staring down at her hands as if she were a million miles away, and pulled a few more sheets of paper from his folder. He passed them across the table toward her and continued talking, apparently unconcerned when she didn't respond. Luke was puzzled by her disinterest. But when her shaky voice broke the stillness, he realized she'd been focusing on something else, something that had frightened her.

"Jerome, do you think Piper is safe here?"

The lawman didn't answer instantly but tugged on his right earlobe for a few seconds. Luke figured Jerome was looking for the right words.

She persisted. "Jerome, please. Do you think she's safe here?"

"You don't?"

"I don't know! Some kid tried to break in last night, and I really believe he's exactly what he said he was, but I can't be sure."

Jerome went pale. "What're you talking about?"

"Sasha treed a kid last night who was trying to break in," Luke explained quickly. "The kid said he was going to Julian Alvarado's rehab tonight and he just wanted a couple of fixes before he threw in the towel."

Jerome frowned and looked at a sheet of paper. "You didn't write that on your timeline."

"I'm sorry, you're right. I should've added it."

"Did he say why he came here?" Darth asked curiously.

Now Madison looked a little nervous. "He said this was an old house and he thought it would be easy. You think he was lying?"

"You don't?" Jerome countered.

Luke chuckled mischievously. "She gave him a sandwich. I thought she was going to marry him."

Jerome stared at her as if she'd grown another head.

"What the hell did you do that for?"

She glared back at him. "I thought I'd find out more about him and where he came from if I treated him like a human being. He's just a kid, for God's sake! You're thinking like a cop, Jerome."

Jerome's West-Texas accent accelerated. "And you're thinkin' like a bleedin'-heart head doctor, Madison! I've warned you and warned you about that. There ain't no doubt about it. You're gonna wake up dead someday." He paused and settled down. "What's the kid's name?"

"Rafe Gamez," she answered, a sulky expression on her face. "He's big and husky, like a football player, with long dirty hair. I don't think he's a day over sixteen or seventeen."

"Rafe. Short for Rafael?"

She shrugged. "I don't know. I didn't ask."

"You didn't ask. Was he arrested?"

Luke took pity on her. "Yes. He ate his sandwich, and the cops cuffed him and took him downtown. They did mention they'd call a preacher, Julian Alvarado, for him, which I thought was decent. We met Alvarado after Lacy's funeral this morning, and he confirmed that Gamez was coming into his program tonight."

"You met Julian Alvarado? That's not on your timeline, either."

Madison cleared her throat. "In Luke's defense, Jerome, he hasn't had a chance. We just met Julian this morning. Do you know him?"

"I sure do. Good man. One of the best."

Luke cocked an eyebrow. That was high praise, coming from someone as cynical as Jerome Scranton. Julian Alvarado, street preacher and John the Baptist look-alike, shot up several notches in Luke's opinion.

"Well, Julian's going to admit Rafe Gamez to rehab tonight—unless they keep him in jail," Madison said triumphantly, "so I guess maybe I'm not so stupid, after all."

"I never said you were stupid," Jerome responded wearily, "but you and Julian are cut from the same cloth. You both want to believe the best about people. On the other hand, Darth, Luke, and I see the world for what it is, which is probably a good thing. You and Julian can talk; the rest of us can fight. Two talkers on one side, three fighters on the other. Balance. That's what the world needs. More balance."

"Excuse me," Darth interjected, clearly fighting for patience, "but did you learn anything interesting during this meeting with Julian?"

Madison took a deep breath and dove in. "Julian said Lacy came to see him on December second, the day after she'd been arrested, and begged him to hide her and Piper from Antonio Davila. Julian told her he couldn't do anything that day, but to give him a little time and he'd find a place for them. Lacy said they didn't have any time, that Davila was going to kill her. She also said he'd film it."

Darth's eyes widened. "He'd film it?"

"That's what she said."

"You just found this out today?"

"Yes."

"Anything else?"

She nodded. "He also told us Lacy had come to see him last January, a couple of days after New Year's, and she was in bad physical shape, even back then. But she was really upset and told him she'd overheard Davila talking on the phone to someone at the Mercy Children's Home about taking some child out of there. Julian also said Lacy seemed to be afraid Davila was going to hurt this Mercy child and she somehow connected that with her own little girl, whom Julian didn't even know about until then. He also said that he didn't know Davila was a pedophile until I told him this morning. But even without knowing that, he did realize Davila couldn't have any good reason for taking a child out of Mercy."

Jerome looked puzzled. "I don't get it. Why would she go to Julian with that information?"

Madison shrugged. "Clearly, she trusted him. I guess she just wanted to be sure she could bring Piper to him if she ever had to, and he said she could."

"But then, when she did finally show up with Piper, he couldn't help her?"

"He had no room at all," Luke explained, suddenly feeling the need to defend the preacher. "He even had junkies sleeping in his living room."

Jerome gave a mocking grin. "And there was no room at the inn..." He shook his head. "Okay. Lacy actually said Davila was going to kill her and film it?"

"According to Julian, yes."

"Well, we know she was murdered, but we don't know if they filmed anything."

"Wait a minute," Darth said quietly. "Do you guys remember when Carlotta said she last saw Lacy alive? When Lacy gave her the bank information?"

"I think she said it was about two weeks ago," Madison answered. "That would've been the end of November, right?"

Darth nodded slowly. "Well, then, I think it's safe to assume that Lacy put this DVD together for Luke sometime between December first and December twelfth, the day she died. Otherwise, she would've put it in the bank package she gave to Carlotta. It would've been much safer for her to do that than for her to hide it in the closet. She would've been dead meat if Davila found it."

Luke looked at the detective respectfully. "I hadn't thought of that."

Jerome chuckled. "That's why he makes the small bucks. Now, about this Mercy Children's Home. We don't know anything about…no, wait. That's not true. I've got a friend on their board of directors."

"Of course, you do," Madison murmured.

"And I know their chief administrator—Wilhelmina Griffith. I think she has a crush on me. She runs the show, and everyone calls her Willie. You said Davila had this phone call from them around New Year's, of this year?"

"That's what Julian said," Luke answered.

Once again, Jerome tugged on his earlobe and pursed his lips reflectively. He twiddled his thumbs and narrowed his piercing blue eyes until they were little more than slits in his face. Luke would have given everything he owned to go inside this man's head and actually witness the way his brain worked.

Jerome snapped his fingers and reached for the photographs, selecting the one Luke had given him. He turned it over and stared at the label silently. The blood left his face.

He pushed the photograph toward Madison. "Little Miss Charly MacIntire. Luke spotted her in that film clip on Lacy's DVD, which Darth thinks was made between December first and December twelfth. We don't *actually* know when Charly's clip was made, but we do know that

Davila got a kid from Mercy Children's Home nearly a year ago, just a couple of days after New Year's—or at least that's what Lacy believed. The date on this photo here is *January 4, 2022*. We don't know if the child he took from Mercy is Charly, but if it is, that means her clip was made between January fourth and December twelfth, 2022. Almost a year. That could mean they used her in a lot of movies."

None of this made any sense to Luke. "How could Davila take a child from a children's home? He's a known pedophile—"

"I doubt seriously he went anywhere near that shelter to pick up Charly MacIntire or any other kid," Darth interrupted. "He would've picked her up somewhere else."

"I'm not following…"

"He would've arranged a more private meeting place."

Luke's eyes narrowed. "That would mean someone of authority at Mercy is involved in this, too."

"That's true," Madison observed. "We also don't know if anyone ever took her out of Mercy *before* January fourth and filmed her, either."

"I don't think so," Jerome said quickly. "She would've been too bruised and traumatized for them to send her back there. No, if Charly MacIntire is the child Davila took out of Mercy, she started filming after January fourth, 2022 and she never returned."

Luke's heart began to thud.

The crystal-clear image of that beautiful little girl hanging from a contraption in a cage, terrified and screaming as Davila approached her with a metal tool in his hand, flashed through his head like a bolt of lightning.

He choked against rage.

She could've been making those sick movies for almost a year. She could still be making them now…

But Darth was strangely silent.

When Jerome spoke, his voice shook. "It's the most recent date we've got, by the way. Two of the other photos are dated 2019, and one is dated 2021. So little Charly is going to be our best lead." Jerome looked at Luke expectantly. "Lacy was clearly counting on you to handle this. So…what do you think we should do next?"

Luke didn't hesitate. "I think you should call your girlfriend Willie—was that her name? See if we can find out if little Charly MacIntire was ever at Mercy Children's Home. If she was, when? Is she still there or not? And was she ever removed from the premises anywhere near January fourth, 2022? If she was, who took her? We need to do that, like, yesterday."

Jerome nodded in approval. "I'm all over it. What else?"

"We should see if any of these four children have been reported missing from anywhere, or if they've been reported dead, or if they're back home safe and sound. I guess you can do that in your sleep. It would take me a year."

"No problem. Anything else?"

Very deliberately, Darth removed his glasses from the top of his head, ran his fingers through his dark hair, and finally spoke. "You guys don't need to do all that digging on Charly MacIntire. She's no stranger to my unit. We've been looking for her since she was reported missing from Brackenridge Park back in January."

Luke was speechless, and the room went silent until Jerome finally released his breath in a strange sort of inverted gulp. "No kidding."

"I'm sorry. I know I should've told you right away, but I had to be sure your friends were who you said they were."

"Are you keeping anything else from us?" Madison asked.

He grinned and slipped his oversized spectacles into his hoodie pocket. "Well, I don't really wear glasses…"

Jerome's expression was stern. "This is serious, buddy."

"Okay. The truth is I know Charly's file inside and out. A social worker named Carole Black reported her missing. She'd turned her back for just a minute to find her phone while Charly played on the playground. When she turned around, Charly had disappeared. That happened on January fourth, about three in the afternoon. We've been looking for her ever since, but it's like she just vanished into thin air."

"Thin air?" Madison asked skeptically. "I thought it was your job—"

"It is, and I can't explain right now, but poor little Charly's been lost in all the crazy. I take full responsibility."

She sighed. "It's all right, Darth. Actually, this may be where we can help you. Did Ms. Black say why Charly was with her?"

"Well, apparently, Charly had a counseling session with a protective services social worker/psychotherapist named Goldie Newsom, and Ms. Black was taking her there. But then Ms. Newsom had to go to court or something, so Ms. Black thought it might be nice to just take Charly to the park for a while. She got permission from the director of protective services to keep her for the afternoon."

"Quinn Davis?"

"The one and only."

She grinned. "You don't like him?"

"I don't trust him."

Luke ruffled his hair nervously. "Do you know where Charly lived at that time?"

"At the Mercy Children's Home."

Jerome pulled his earlobe. "Darth, you guys have checked that place out, right?"

"Not well enough, apparently. I know it sounds terrible, but our plates are way too full. I have ten active cases involving kids going on right now. I'd like someone else to take a crack at this one. You guys up for it?"

Jerome nodded. "Love to. I'll call Willie at Mercy early tomorrow morning and try to set up a meeting." He glanced at Madison. "If they want us to come right away, can you do it?"

"No, I have to take Piper to the doctor at eleven. She has an earache. Then I'm sure I'll have to pick up some medicine. I probably won't be free before about five or so. Shall I just text you when we get in?"

"Fine. That'll give me time to do a little more research. Darth, if you can get loose, I think I'd like to go downtown tomorrow and see if there's any activity at La Ninfa."

"Good idea. Call me at the station in the morning. I'll try to break out and go with you."

"Excuse me, Jerome," Luke interrupted, "but what does La Ninfa actually mean?"

"Ummm…loosely translated—The Nymph."

Luke felt a little nauseated. "Madison, may I tag

along when you take Piper to the doctor?"

"Of course. I'd appreciate the help."

Jerome looked at Madison, an unspoken order on his craggy face. "We need to get into Mercy as soon as we can—it's the best place to start. Can we meet tomorrow night and make our plans?"

"Sure. But why do I need to go? Is there something special you need me to do?"

"You never know."

By now Luke was paying little attention to their conversation. He was too busy chasing a vague idea back and forth in his mind like a ping-pong ball he couldn't quite pin down. He drummed his fingertips against the tabletop.

"What's up?" Jerome finally asked.

Luke squinted at the lawman. "How many avenues are available for bad guys to find scared, isolated kids? Think about it for a minute. One would be homeless kids, runaways, teenagers on the street or at places like La Ninfa, where you say they prostituted kids out the back door. But I'm talking about really *young* kids, toddlers, even babies. I can only think of a few. One would be foster care establishments, like Madison's Hope's Home or Mercy Children's Home, or individual foster families, like my own Family Spratt, or even orphanages. Another avenue might be the children of addicts, whores, and women terrified of the law, their pimps, or their dealers. Children like Piper, moms like Lacy. But the easiest, believe it or not, would be through the foster care system itself…at least in my opinion.

"The state acts like there's a ton of oversight, but there isn't. It's all paper protocol, and it's underfunded. There aren't enough good homes. So as long as the paperwork is all right, no one pays much attention. I know this from experience. Consequently, attorneys who work with kids could get them. Judges. Pediatricians. Preachers. Teachers. Even protective services itself could pull kids who have no support system, no advocates, and farm them out. Since all those people are respected parts of the establishment, it could take a long time to nail the whole thing down. If ever."

Jerome stared at Luke, eyes wide. "And here I thought I'd be giving *you* the education. You just summed up my whole lesson plan. So let me ask you a question."

Luke felt like a kid who'd just pleased his hardest teacher. "Sure."

"Do you have any idea about what *tip the piano man* might mean?"

He sighed, deflated. "Not a clue."

"Madison?"

She shook her head. "Sorry."

"Darth?"

"Nope. I've never heard it before. I have an idea, but I'm not ready to talk about it yet. I will soon, though." He grinned and added, "I promise."

****

Madison's mind sped backward, and she thought of Quinn Davis, the director of the Department of Family and Protective Services. She thought of Piper's file with all the social workers' names redacted, including the supervisor who'd given permission for Ryan Neely to pick up the little girl. No one could do that except the director. She remembered how she'd tried to reach Quinn the day after Jared had brought her the file, but Quinn had been conveniently out of town. Whitney's harsh reaction to Jared's offer to call Neely had been strange as well, and she still didn't understand how Neely had known anything about Lacy and Piper Callaghan in the first place...

What was it Luke had said? *Attorneys could get kids. Judges. Pediatricians. Preachers. Teachers. Even protective services itself could get them and farm them out.*

How simple. How insidious and diabolical and sinister...but how simple.

She stood up. "I'm going to get another glass of wine. Anyone else?"

"I'd love a water," Jerome said absently.

"That sounds good," Luke muttered, shuffling through papers. "Thanks."

She carried the bottled waters to the table, returned to fill her wineglass to the rim with another chardonnay, and sat back down. She ran her fingers through her shaggy, cropped hair in frustration, then decided to ask a question as forthrightly as she could.

"Darth, you know about these pedophile rings. Do you think there's any such thing as a snuff film?"

"You mean, like, did Davila actually film Lacy's murder? Who knows? If he did, it's probably already circulating somewhere on the dark web and some creep is probably using bitcoin to pay for the privilege of watching it—that keeps the transactions virtually untraceable. Remember, these guys are like roaches. Everything they do, they do in the dark. Officially, the FBI says there's no such thing as a snuff film, but that's a crock. With the dark web being so layer encrypted and all, like a damn onion... Well, I don't see how there aren't any. It's just too easy, people are too sick, and

Rosetta Diane Hoessli

there's too much money to be made. In my field, we just follow the money. That usually takes you straight to the answer. Money…head of the snake. Almost always."

"You mentioned Ryan Neely," she responded carefully. "A big, important attorney like him, who already makes a fortune, could probably hide anything he wanted, don't you think? What do you know about him?"

"Not much."

Jerome twisted the cap off his bottled water, took a long drink, and wiped his lips with the back of his hand. "I know he's a full partner at the law firm of Joseph Cannon and Associates, Inc., and no one else there is as well-known as he is. Cannon himself is a widower, and he's getting old. I hear he's putting himself out to pasture pretty quick—I don't think he's been inside a courtroom in a couple of years. There are two other main attorneys, but I can't remember their names. The Cannon offices are in a three-story historical home in the King William District, and Neely himself lives in a castle in Terrell Hills. That's about all I know. Where are you going with this, darlin'?"

"Around in circles, unfortunately, but everything seems to lead back to Neely. Like Lacy said in her letter, someone important is behind this. He fits that."

Luke lifted an eyebrow. "There are lots of important people in San Antonio, and you can't get a search warrant on a guy just because he's rich."

"True, but nobody else important wanted to take Piper home or bailed Lacy out of jail or made his reputation by defending accused child molesters and helping them get their kids back—several cases pro bono that I know of. But Ryan Neely's done that for years."

As the three men stared at her, she knew she'd finally hit it out of the park. She leaned forward intently. "Can you think of a more perfect blackmail setup than that?" She answered her own question. "No, there isn't one. It's almost foolproof."

Darth's eyes narrowed. "Let me get this straight. Are you suggesting Neely takes on fathers who're fighting sexual abuse allegations in custody battles, doesn't charge them anything for his services, and then uses their children in a kiddie porn operation once he's won?"

"Exactly. In my business, there are child psychiatrists and psychologists known to be for sale. You can literally buy their testimony. We all know who they are. While no one would ever suspect Ryan Neely of doing anything like that, everyone has said he'd never offer his home to a kid like Piper without a reason or bail someone like Lacy out of jail with no strings attached." She looked around the table triumphantly. "So there's his reason. Lacy had something he wanted. He wanted Piper then, and I'll bet he wants her now."

Darth nodded slowly. "Maybe even more than Davila, and Lacy might've known it. Maybe that's why she risked taking Piper to Julian's. She must've found out protective services was going to let Neely take her."

"And that leads us back to my original question. Do you think Piper's safe here?"

"I think she's as safe here as anywhere. No one knows she's here, at least not yet. I wouldn't move her." Suddenly, abruptly, he pushed his chair away from the table and stood up. "Please forgive me. I need to leave now. Madison...Luke...Scranton... Thanks so much for talking to me. You guys have all been a huge help."

Luke and Jerome both stood, and the three men shook hands all around.

But Madison walked straight to the detective and gave him a long, genuine hug. "It was our pleasure," she told him sincerely. "I think we're going to do incredible work together."

Chapter Fourteen

The next morning, Madison opened the blinds in Piper's room and allowed the sunlight to stream inside, admiring, as she always did, little specks of gold dust dancing in the air. Sasha stood up, gave a long, contented stretch, and padded happily to Piper's bed. She nudged Piper's arm with her cold, damp nose and waited for the little girl to awaken. When Piper finally stirred and opened her eyes, Madison smiled.

"Good morning, baby girl," she said softly. "Do you feel better this morning?"

Piper rubbed her eyes and turned away, nuzzling her face against Sasha's thickly furred snout. Sasha gave her pale cheek a quick lick.

Madison opened the top drawer of the dresser and removed panties, socks, purple sweatpants, and a lavender sweatshirt. As she piled the clothing on a small table, she kept up a running stream of conversation.

"Well, it's a beautiful day, so I hope you're feeling a little better. We're going to see Dr. Weinstein, and he's going to make you feel just like new again. He takes care of all the children who live here." Seeing Piper's dark eyes widen in alarm, she added quickly, "I'm going to stay in the room with you, my angel. Have you ever seen a doctor before?"

She didn't respond but never took her intense gaze off Madison's face.

"You probably haven't, but that's all right. You'll like Dr. Weinstein. He's kind of old, but we won't hold that against him, right? And the ladies who help him are wonderful, too. You'll see. You'll be better in no time. Sasha, get out of the way. I'm going to trip over you and hurt myself. Piper, you want to look real pretty when we go, right? Let's get you into these sweats and your shoes and socks, and then I'll fix your hair."

She noted that Piper obeyed robotically, but her eyes were alert and sometimes even danced—with what, Madison wasn't sure. Amusement? Mischief? Maybe just happiness...or relief? Whatever it was, those enormous, thickly lashed, dark eyes were finally beginning to show signs of life, and she was content with that. At least, for now.

She took the little girl's hand, led her to a dressing table near the window, and helped her settle on a white-cushioned stool in front of a small mirror. She began to brush Piper's thin blonde hair, careful not to touch the sore ear, and reached for two flower-decorated rubber bands.

"Is your ear still aching, sweetheart?"

Piper shrugged.

"Well, we'll take care of it, okay? Let's do some dog ears, since you love puppies so much." She grinned at Piper's quizzical expression and created a straight part down the back of Piper's scalp. "You know what? I think you've actually gained a little weight! At least two ounces, and they look great on you." She touched Piper's cheek as she pulled one side of her hair into a ponytail, then the other, and straightened the rubber bands so the flowers showed. "There! What do you think?"

Piper didn't say anything, but she gazed at her

reflection with a soft smile playing on her lips. Madison took the opportunity to step back and look more closely at the little girl.

For the first time, she could clearly see the combination of Luke and Lacy in this lovely child. She had her mother's beautiful, fragile bone structure and full, pouty lips, with Luke's dark eyes, thick lashes, and straight-bridged nose. Piper seemed a little tall for her age, but both her parents were tall. She was still far too thin and pale, but now Madison could see the promise of Lacy's heart-stopping beauty blossoming in her child.

She leaned in so her face was next to Piper's and met her eyes in the mirror. "I want to tell you something because I don't want to keep any secrets from you." She paused, then smiled. "I know you can talk—in fact, you talk very well. Your Tia Carly told me that. So I'm guessing you just don't *want* to talk, and that's fine with me. You do whatever you want. But whenever you're ready, I'll listen to anything you say. *Anything.* Do you understand?"

Piper's dark eyes filled with tears, and her lower lip trembled, but she nodded.

"Good! Now, come on downstairs for breakfast, okay? Then you can brush your teeth, and we'll leave. Mr. Callaghan is going with us in case we need some help. Is that all right?"

Piper's tears disappeared as quickly as they'd appeared. She looked at Madison in the mirror and frowned, then cocked her head to one side. After a moment, Madison understood the question in the little girl's eyes.

"That's right! His name is the same as yours. Isn't that interesting? Anyway, come on down and have some breakfast. Maybe when we're finished at the doctor's office, we can go to San Pedro Park. Would you like that?"

With *Mr. Callaghan* apparently no longer an issue, Piper jumped off the stool and took Madison's hand, a wide grin on her face. At that moment, Madison glimpsed the animated, sparkling little girl Piper Callaghan could become if she was just loved, nurtured, and given an opportunity to grow.

What was it Whitney always said? *Children are resilient...*

A silent, repetitive prayer formed in Madison's heart. *Please, God, keep her safe... Please, God, keep her safe...*

Sasha woo-wooed with excitement, squeezing between them as they walked hand in hand down the hallway, her elegant tail wagging like a long, feathered plume over her back.

****

From his place beside the new coffeemaker, Luke grinned as he watched the children shovel their breakfasts down quickly so they could play outside. As he observed the loving way Whitney took care of them, giving each child a special bit of attention with their glass of orange juice or bowl of cereal, he was more convinced than ever that Whitney was completely loyal to Madison, the children, and Hope's Home. Once again, an image of the Spratt's squalid little house and his frightened wild-child, Lacy, banged at his memory, but he ignored it.

When Piper and Madison entered the kitchen, followed by the ever-present Sasha, Luke caught Madison's eye and winked. She ducked her head and blushed, a slight smile on her lips. But before he even had a chance to enjoy that unexpected reaction, his eyes widened in disbelief.

Little Piper, all ponytailed up and dressed like somebody loved her, walked straight to the table, pulled out a chair, and sat down as if she belonged there. She didn't acknowledge any of the other children, and she certainly didn't speak, but she sat with them, and that was enough for Luke. He couldn't hold back his grin.

Whitney, still in her bathrobe and fuzzy slippers, brought him a glass of orange juice and nodded toward Piper. "Take this to her," she whispered.

He took the orange juice and headed for the table. Setting the glass beside Piper's bowl of cereal, he said softly, "Here you go, Miss Piper."

She gave no indication she'd heard him, but he knew she had. He walked back to the counter where Madison was preparing her coffee, and touched her hand. She looked up at him and smiled.

Dressed in snug black jeans tucked into black knee-high boots and a turquoise turtle-necked sweater, she looked as young and casual as a college student heading off for a relaxing break in a coffee shop. Her tousled auburn hair streaked with burnished gold was stunning against her creamy complexion. Once again, Luke found himself transfixed by those beautiful blue-green eyes.

Nothing about her appearance hinted at the pressure she was living with now, but he could sense it. She was more vulnerable and less controlled this morning, as if she was teetering somewhere between composure and panic, and he felt even more protective than usual.

He spoke in a voice so low only Madison could hear him. "I think it's really cool how you tied all that about Ryan Neely together last night. I was a little embarrassed

I didn't think of it myself."

"That's silly. You're not in my business, so why would you?" She stirred a drop of french vanilla creamer in her coffee and took a sip. "Oh, my goodness, this is so good! Thank you, Luke!"

He laughed aloud. For some reason he felt like a kid on the first day of school, spotting the girl of his dreams in the lunch line and knowing he didn't stand a chance of winning her. He turned away to buy a little time and prayed she wouldn't notice.

Apparently, she didn't. "Luke, I was wondering if we could take your truck this morning. It's so big I can make Piper a really nice bed in it. I don't know what Dr. Weinstein will do, but she might not feel too well by the time he's finished."

"Of course. That's a great idea. As a matter of fact, let me get out there and set it up for her, okay? You just come on out when you're ready."

She touched his arm and spoke softly. "I told her we could go to San Pedro Springs Park when we're out. Is that okay? It's only about ten minutes from here. I'll tell Whitney if you don't mind taking us."

"I don't mind at all. Oh, and I'll just wait for you in the waiting room. Piper doesn't need me passing out if the doc gives her a shot."

She cocked an eyebrow and grinned.

****

"How are you today, Madison? I haven't seen you in a while."

"I'm very well, Dr. Weinstein, thank you. But my little friend here isn't. She has an earache and I think, maybe, the start of a bad cold. I wanted to catch it before it got any closer to Christmas and I couldn't get her in to see you."

Dr. Daniel Weinstein, the best pediatrician in San Antonio—at least in Madison's book—nodded and walked toward Piper, who was sitting on the examining table clutching Madison's hand with an iron grip. Her dark eyes widened, and her chin quivered as he drew closer. He halted and pretended to study some papers carefully.

Finally, he looked up and smiled. "I see your name is Piper. That's an interesting name. I like it."

Madison cleared her throat. "Dr. Weinstein, Piper doesn't talk, and we don't make her. I hope that's all right."

Dr. Weinstein's heavy brows arched quizzically. "Really? Well, of course that's all right. In fact, Piper, I don't blame you one bit. If I could stop talking just like that, you can bet your bottom dollar I would. I get mighty tired of hearing the sound of my own voice." He took another step toward her, then stopped once again when Piper's eyes widened. "But here's the problem, sweetheart. Dr. Wagner says you have an earache, and I can't help you feel better if you don't let me look at it."

Piper's eyes never left his face, and her hands tightened on Madison's fingers. Madison prayed she could get through this appointment without every tendon, bone, and ligament in her hand being shredded to bits.

She leaned closer to Piper. "Sweetie, Dr. Weinstein is a very old friend of mine, and he takes good care of all the children in my house. Won't you let him peek into your ear for just a minute? I'm going to be right here with you. I'm not going to leave you for even a second." She looked at Dr. Weinstein. "She sleeps in the room next to mine, so I can check on her all night if you think she needs antibiotics."

"We'll see… Can I look at your ear now, cutie-pie?"

Piper didn't move for a moment, then whimpered a little and turned her head so that Dr. Weinstein could examine her. Madison held her breath. *Don't let it hurt…*

The doctor took a few more steps toward Piper and gently cupped her face in his hands, positioning it so he could use his instruments without frightening or hurting her any more than he had to. "You let me know if I hurt you, okay?"

Piper's fingers tightened on Madison's.

"Your friends at Dr. Wagner's house all call me Dr. Dan, and I hope you will, too. I mean, as soon as you decide to talk to me. Yessirree, this ear is pretty inflamed." He glanced up at Madison. "I'm surprised she's not screaming in pain. She's got a pretty good tolerance."

"I imagine she does."

He glanced at her again, then turned his attention back to Piper. "Will you open your mouth real wide, stick out your tongue, and say, 'Ahhh?' That's always fun. I like to do that."

Piper looked at Madison, who nodded with a smile, and obeyed. Dr. Weinstein used the hated but necessary tongue depressor and was finished before Piper even had a chance to gag. He looked into her other ear. "Well, would you lookie here!"

Piper turned her head quickly and gawked at a shiny quarter Dr. Weinstein rolled between his thumb and forefinger.

Madison grinned at the familiar trick Dr. Weinstein used on all her children. "Dr. Dan pulled that right out of your eardrum! I bet there's lots more where that came from."

A tiny smile played at the corners of Piper's mouth, then widened into a full-blown grin when he held the quarter out for her to take. After a few moments, Piper released Madison's hand and grabbed the coin.

"Do you know if she's had any of her vaccinations?" Dr. Weinstein asked quietly as Piper tried to shove the quarter back into her ear. Then, a little louder, he added, "I'm going to give her a shot of antibiotics right now and some oral antibiotics as well. Give her one teaspoon in the morning and two teaspoons every night right before bed for the next five nights. They'll help her sleep, too, which will help you." He chuckled and patted Piper's shoulder. "We want this earache gone before Santa Claus gets here. I don't want him to be worried about catching a cold when he goes to your house."

Piper stared at the doctor. Madison knew from the little girl's wide, incredulous eyes that Santa had never come to her house before, bad cold or not.

"I think you're right, Dr. Dan." Madison lowered her voice so that Piper couldn't hear her. "I don't know about her other shots. Can you check with Metropolitan Health for me? It was hard to fill out your forms, to be honest. She has no social security number, no phone number other than mine, no school, no nothing. I don't think she's ever seen any kind of a doctor before."

"Not a problem. Let's schedule her for a well-child right after the new year, but you call me if this shot doesn't take care of her ear. I'm going to give you a prescription for some numbing ear drops, too. I'd advise you to keep them on hand, just in case. And baby aspirin if she spikes a fever, of course."

"When are you closing for the holidays, Dan?"

"From December twenty-third until January second." He touched Piper's arm and smiled. "But for this little girl here, my service will always find me."

"Thank you. Have a wonderful Christmas."

"And y'all as well."

He turned back to Piper and solemnly held out his hand. She looked at Madison, then at Dr. Dan, and finally seemed to reach a decision. She tilted her chin, stiffened her shoulders, took a deep breath, and allowed him to take her hand. Madison ducked her head as she blinked back tears.

His face broke into a wide grin. "I'll see you in a few weeks, Piper. You be a good girl, and when you come back, you can tell me what Santa Claus brought you. Is that a deal?"

And then, to Madison's disbelief, Piper smiled back and nodded.

****

Luke stifled a grin. When a pretty young woman behind the check-out window tried to return his credit card and his fingers touched hers, she looked so flustered he almost felt sorry for her. Finally, she stapled his receipt to some paperwork, jammed it all into a folder, and shoved it across the counter.

Madison cleared her throat. "Don't mind me, Luke. You just take your time. Piper and I are heading back to the truck. I don't think she slept very much last night, plus Dr. Dan gave her a shot, and I think it's making her a little sleepy."

"No worries. We're done here."

Madison slid the folder containing Piper's medical file and prescriptions into her oversized handbag and slung it over her shoulder, then took Piper's hand as they walked slowly from the office, Luke following close behind.

She glanced over her shoulder at Luke. "I doubt if Piper will care, but I promised her the park, even if it's only long enough to pick up her prescriptions. A drugstore is right across the street from the park. Do you mind?"

"Nope." Luke moved up to walk beside her. "Here, let me carry that bag. It's bigger than you are."

Piper yawned, and Luke put his hand on Madison's arm to stop her. He knelt in front of the little girl. Although she took a quick step backward and looked at him through worried eyes, she didn't seem frightened.

His heart hammered in his throat, but this was too good an opportunity to pass up. "Let me carry you to the truck, sweetheart. We have quite a ways to go."

Madison, in a soft but firm voice, intervened immediately. "It's okay, Luke. I've got her."

He shook his head slightly, kept his gaze on Piper, and waited. He could see the wheels turning in that bright little brain…

Who is this man? What does Dr. Wagner want me to do? I'm too tired to walk…I want to sleep…I don't feel good…

And still he waited. He wouldn't touch her until she agreed.

After what seemed an eternity, Piper released Madison's hand and took one tentative step toward him, then halted uncertainly. When he gazed into those dark, inscrutable eyes so like his own, he was filled with a sense of tenderness he'd never felt before. He took her in his arms and stood up, patting her back gently as she

211

wrapped one arm around his neck and rested her head on his shoulder. Luke glanced at Madison and grinned at the look of astonishment on her face.

"Do you think genetics speak to each other?"

"Could be. Here's where we cross."

He followed Madison down a glassed-in walkway connecting the third floor of the physicians' office building to the enclosed parking garage, Piper's limp legs dangling as he carried her. She was so light he hardly knew she was in his arms.

A six-year-old shouldn't be this light…

Luke had made Piper a very comfortable bed in the back seat of the truck, and he placed her in it with care. She barely stirred as he pulled a blanket up to cover her shoulders. He opened the door for Madison and bowed gallantly.

"You're not one of those women who gets insulted if a man opens the door for you, are you?" He gave her a crooked grin before he closed the door. "Are you in?"

"I'm fine, thanks." She pushed her bag under the seat and fastened her seat belt. "And no, I'm not. I think it's the least I deserve."

"Couldn't agree more."

Following Madison's instructions, Luke left the garage and drove toward San Pedro Springs Park, which wasn't too far from Hope's Home. It was a dismal side of town, old and run down, but the park itself was beautiful and well-manicured. Madison pointed toward a parking spot in front of a 1950s-style drugstore across the street.

Luke pulled in, turned off the ignition, and glanced over his shoulder. "She's still sleeping. Do you want me to go in?"

"No, I'll be right back. The pharmacist is a good friend of mine."

"Okay."

As he waited for Madison's return, Luke decided to step outside of the truck to get a better view of this unfamiliar part of the city. The temperatures were dropping, but the weather was still incredibly spring-like for December. It was what Luke loved most about central Texas. While the rest of the country was freezing, shorts and T-shirts were often sufficient here.

Suddenly, far down the street, the screaming sirens of police cars and fire trucks broke into his thoughts, and Luke looked off to the right of the park, toward the heart of old downtown. People moved casually to the sidewalk and peered in the direction of the mayhem, shading their eyes. He couldn't see what the ruckus was about, but it was clearly something important.

After a few minutes, Madison joined Luke on the sidewalk. "What's going on?"

He shrugged. "I have no idea." Peeking into the truck, he added with a chuckle, "Whatever it is, it didn't wake Princess Piper."

"That's good. Her prescription will be ready in about twenty minutes."

Before Luke could respond, Madison's cell phone rang with the bluesy ringtone of "Bad to the Bone." She glanced up at Luke. "Jerome Scranton," she explained with a grin.

He leaned against the truck, folding his arms across his chest, and nodded. "I'll watch the show while you guys solve the world's problems. Nothing like life in the fast lane."

****

"Where are you, Madison?" Jerome's deep voice reverberated in her ear, and she automatically turned down the volume. He could easily be heard in the next county. "Are you still with the doctor?"

She frowned. "No. We're at the drugstore across from San Pedro Springs waiting on Piper's prescription. Is everything all right?"

"Is Piper with you?"

"Of course."

When she heard him heave a huge sigh and whisper, "Thank God," her heart gave an extra thud.

"What's wrong?"

"Nothing for you to worry about—"

"Don't give me that, Jerome. There are a lot of cop cars and fire trucks heading toward somewhere not far from the park. What's going on?"

Luke glanced at her with a frown.

Jerome spoke quickly. "You know where that drainage area is about ten blocks or so down from San Pedro Springs? There's a historical marker near there."

"I think so. What's happened?"

"Madison, someone just found a child's body in the brush down in that ditch."

"Wait…what?"

"Listen to me. Y'all get Piper home as soon as you get those meds filled and lock up. I'm on my way to the scene with Darth now. I'll be at your place as soon as I can."

"Do you know who it is?"

"Not a clue. I'll see you tonight. Oh, and if you can make room for me somewhere, I'm moving in with you guys for a while. Do you mind?"

She was so relieved she was almost embarrassed.

"Of course not, Jerome. Please stay."

****

It had been a long time since Madison was involved in a situation where she had to wait for Jerome, but it wasn't hard to remember why she hated it so much. She wanted everything done *yesterday*, while he took his sweet time making sure every *i* was dotted and every *t* was crossed. He blamed it on his cop training. The other reason she hated it was because he was almost always right, and she almost never was.

Madison leaned back in her recliner in the living area of her bedroom, closed her eyes, and reached for the cup of hot tea next to her. While Piper was asleep in her room and Luke was playing in the backyard with Sasha and the other children, she finally had a moment to think. She was grateful for the respite. Things would start popping the second Jerome Scranton walked through the front door.

She'd showered, changed into fleece-lined sweats and fuzzy slippers, and locked herself into her room almost the moment she got home. The discovery of the child's body had thrown her for a loop, and she had to get herself together before Jerome arrived. He had no patience with what he called *all that estrogen...*

She shook her head. She was a woman, but she didn't see herself as hormonal. She didn't cry easily, and she very seldom panicked. But she *was* compassionate and empathetic, which was why she was good at her job. Yet now she was holding her breath, hoping against hope they wouldn't be able to identify this child...which was cruel and insane.

A tear crept down her cheek as a single name kept whispering through her consciousness, unbidden and unwelcome. And, hopefully, inaccurate.

Charly MacIntire...Charly MacIntire...

That horrifying clip in Lacy's film was the only reason Madison even thought it might be little Charly, but she could definitely be wrong. San Antonio was a huge city, and child abuse was a big problem. It certainly wasn't unusual to hear about missing or dead children.

But if this dead child was Charly MacIntire, it was almost certain she had no family to grieve her loss. Probably, no one would miss her. She must've spent every day of her short life wondering why she'd been put on this earth in the first place.

She heard a tentative knock on the door and recognized it immediately as Whitney's. Wiping away her tears, she opened the door and planted a smile on her face. "Hey, girlfriend. What's up?"

Whitney looked at her closely. "May I come in?"

"Of course."

Whitney followed her to the little round table in the kitchen area and sat down. She folded her hands in her lap.

Madison walked to the small refrigerator and opened the door. "Can I get you something? A water or anything?"

"No, thanks. I'm good."

"We actually ought to have a glass of wine. Jerome's moving in."

"That's what Luke said. Why is he moving in?"

"Luke didn't tell you?"

"No, and I don't think he intends to. That's what I wanted to talk to you about."

Madison sat across from her. "I don't understand."

Whitney's vivid blue eyes filled with tears.

"Something's going on here, and I want to help. It's my job to help you. But as long as everyone keeps me in the dark, I can't do anything. Why won't you tell me?"

Madison felt sorry for her friend, but there was nothing she could say. She leaned forward and rested her hand on the tabletop, palm upward. Whitney laced her fingers with Madison's.

Madison squeezed her hand. "It's Luke's call right now, not mine, but it's not personal. Piper is in danger, so he wants to keep the circle around her small. The fewer people know, the safer she'll be. We'll all be safer. Jerome's staying here because it's easier for him to work here, in this part of San Antonio, than from his ranch in La Vernia. It's a long drive for him."

"That's just a little too pat, Madison—"

"I know, but it's the way Luke wants it. For right now. Besides, all I need from you is for you to keep doing exactly what you're doing. Watch out for Piper and keep working with her. You're doing a fabulous job. She actually shook hands with Dr. Weinstein, and Luke got to carry her to the truck. No one else can do what you do here."

"Luke got to carry her?" Whitney pulled her hand from Madison's and leaned back in her chair. "That's amazing. But you can't tell me what kind of danger she's in?"

"No, not yet."

"Okay, I get it. But tell me as soon as you can. I need to know."

"Of course, but it's not up to me. Not really. Just remember he's almost surely Piper's father, and the emotions he's dealing with right now are new to him. He doesn't trust anyone. And the truth is there's no reason why he should."

"You're right." Whitney pushed her chair away from the table with a mischievous grin. "By the way, go take a look in the backyard. Your Luke has turned into the Pied Piper. I've decided that if you don't fall in love with him, I think I will."

Chapter Fifteen

Madison stood at the kitchen window and watched the scene Whitney had described—accurately, as it turned out. In the backyard, Luke and Sasha stood in the center of a circle made up of small children holding hands. Every once in a while, he would bark out an order that sent all the kids scurrying to obey. She smiled as she realized he was teaching them to play Simon Says.

She couldn't hold back a giggle. He was tall, well-built, and handsome enough to choke a grown woman, but no child in that circle was intimidated or impressed by him. When it was someone else's turn, he followed the directions of each child-Simon, falling to the ground, jumping up and down, screeching like an idiot right along with the rest of the children. Sasha ran around the circle, wearing her goofy malamute grin, licking sticky faces, and tugging at T-shirts. Clearly, they were both having a wonderful time.

An astonished baritone voice drawled behind her, "Well, would you look at that! Who woulda thunk it?"

She whirled around, nearly breaking her neck on her huge fuzzy slippers, and slapped Jerome's arm in frustration. "You scared me to death!"

He grinned down at her and removed his ever-present cowboy hat. He ran his fingers through his wavy mane of gorgeous salt-and-pepper hair and rubbed his eyes. "Where do I go, honey? I need to get cleaned up and—"

"Howdy," Whitney said in her usual sunny way as she entered the kitchen with no sign of her earlier distress. "Madison, Tessa's moving in with me. That way, Jerome can have her room. That would put him next door to Mr. Callaghan."

"Are you sure that's okay with Tessa?" Jerome asked. "I don't want to upset any kids."

"Tessa and I are best buds. We'll have a ball." She paused and grinned. "Then, when you're done settling in, come on down, and I'll throw a cold supper on the table. I'm presuming you're hungry."

He rubbed his hands together in anticipation. "I haven't eaten since dawn, so I'm starving. From the looks of the party outside, Luke's going to be in the same boat."

Whitney seemed pleased she was once again included in a small social gathering—at least, somewhat. She went to the back door and threw it open. "Come inside, you guys! Bath time!" She turned to Madison. "The kids have all eaten, so I'll get Stacy to help me."

Madison touched her shoulder gratefully. "Thank you so much, sweetie. Will you have supper with us?"

"Of course! I'd love that. We'll eat in about an hour."

****

Grinning, Jerome leaned back in his chair and gave a discreet belch. "That was great, Whitney. Thank you. I didn't know how hungry I was."

"You're more than welcome."

She smiled at him and stood up to clear the table. Luke immediately did the same and gathered plates and glasses, then followed her to the dishwasher. As he worked beside her, admiring the way the soft overhead lighting sent shimmers of silver through her mane of blonde hair, the tiniest seed of an idea began to ripen in his mind.

"Whitney, is your hair naturally that color?"

"Huh?"

He chuckled and dried his hands on a dish towel. "I don't mean to be rude, but I really need to know. Is your hair naturally that color?"

"It's actually lighter, sort of like yours. But that makes me look like an aging albino instead of pretty and distinguished, like you. So I have it streaked with some light brown every few months or so, which tones it down and keeps me from sticking out like a sore thumb."

"Do you think that would work for me?"

Jerome chuckled. "You saying you don't want to be pretty and distinguished anymore?"

"I'm saying I don't want to stick out like a sore thumb."

Jerome's laughter ceased immediately, and his eyes narrowed. "I get it. You could shave your beard and darken your hair a little... Yeah, that would work."

"You think?"

"Why would you want to do that?" Whitney demanded. "You're famous for that hair..."

Madison stood up quickly. "Anyone want something more to drink? Iced tea, soda...a water?" Her voice ended on a note of desperation.

Luke glanced at her in concern. "Are you all right, Madison?"

Tears sparkled in her blue-green eyes as she shook her head.

He felt like a selfish idiot. She was aching to learn

the identity of the little body found in a ditch—and terrified at the same time. He didn't need to decide right now whether or not to disguise himself. That could come later.

He opened the refrigerator and peered inside. "I'm getting a soda. Can I get you anything, Madison?"

"Iced tea, thanks."

"Anyone else?"

As everyone made their requests, she sat back down and clenched her fingers together in her lap. When Luke set the glass of iced tea in front of her, he patted her shoulder before he returned to his chair.

She slapped her hand against the tabletop, obviously out of patience. "What happened today, Jerome?"

When Jerome's questioning gaze landed on Whitney, Luke said quietly, "Go ahead. It'll be on the news tonight anyway."

"The discovery of the child's body will be, but not her identity. They have to track down either family members or dental records to make a positive ID. But I recognized her."

Luke swallowed, hard. "Her?"

"It was little Charly MacIntire. I'm sure of it."

Madison paled and didn't move.

"What's going on?" Whitney asked impatiently. "Who's Charly MacIntire?"

Luke couldn't answer.

Charly MacIntire. He hadn't realized how much he'd been hoping there was no connection between that terrified little girl in the film clip and the dead child. Still, he had to keep his emotions to himself—at least, until he was certain Whitney could be trusted.

But Jerome didn't miss a beat and answered her

question smoothly. "She's been missing for the last few days, and I've been doing some work for her parents. I was with Darth when the call came in about a child's body being found downtown, so I rode with him. I was able to identify her immediately."

Whitney didn't overreact. She just seemed relieved. "Well, it's good you were there."

Luke hated leaving her out of the loop; she was too important. She knew children and how their minds worked, which was more than he could say for himself, and he desperately needed her expertise. But he had no choice right now. He dug around in his mind for a quick change of subject and seized on it.

"By the way, Jerome, I googled Joseph Cannon and Associates, Inc., the law firm you said Ryan Neely worked with. I wanted to see who the other attorneys in the firm were. I discovered two other full partners, Mr. Sebastian deWynter and Mr. Curtis Allen. Apparently, Mr. deWynter is young and single, and Mr. Allen is middle-aged and married. That's about all I could find out."

Whitney cleared her throat tentatively. "I can help with that. Curtis Allen is a religious fanatic. He and his family go to church three or four times a week, his kids go to a private Christian school, and his wife doesn't go anywhere. None of them do."

"How do you know all this?" Jerome asked. "Even I didn't know that."

"I'm just naturally nosy."

"What about Sebastian deWynter?" Luke inquired. "What kind of name is that anyway? Sounds like a male stripper."

Her eyes danced. "Well, he *is* sort of in the

entertainment industry when he's not being a lawyer. He's very good-looking, and he plays the piano at a nice bar right down the street from the courthouse. He's got quite a following, actually. Even tourists know about him. They call him Piano Man, like that song by Billy Joel."

As the silence stretched, the blood slowly left her face. "I'm sorry," she said finally. "Was it something I said?"

****

Madison and Luke sat at the conference table in her upstairs suite and waited for Jerome to speak.

"Is Whitney all right?" he finally asked, his weathered face concerned.

Madison nodded. She still felt guilty, almost like a traitor, but she really had no choice. "I talked to her earlier, and she understands we're not free to bring her into the loop right now. Her feelings are a little stung, but she gets it. Now, tell us what's going on."

Jerome looked relieved, and Madison understood. He hated dealing with upset women.

"Okay, you guys, here's the plan," he began. "We have an appointment with Max Rybeck, my friend at Mercy Children's Home, tomorrow afternoon about four thirty. We'll use their conference room and see what we can find out."

Madison frowned. That didn't make much sense to her. "Darth already said they knew Charly came from Mercy, they knew exactly when she disappeared, and they knew the last person to see her. They actually know a lot. Why do we need to go back?"

"Because he also said he wants someone else to take a crack at it," Jerome answered. "Fresh eyes, in other words. So that's what we're going to do. We're going to get cracking."

"What are we looking for, specifically?" Luke asked.

"I want Charly's backstory. I want every bit of information about her we can find. When did she arrive there? Who showed interest in her? Who did she hang out with? But we need to keep her name to ourselves, and we can't let on that we know she's dead. We also need to find out if there's any connection between Mercy Children's Home and the other kids in those photos."

"How are we going to get that information?" Madison asked reasonably. "Your friend isn't going to just hand it over. There's a privacy issue. Plus, most boards don't work like ours, Jerome. All our members have some expertise in child abuse, foster care, or law enforcement. It's not unusual for me to call on any one of you to help me with something if I'm not qualified to do it. But most boards are made up of members with money, political pull, name recognition, media experience...stuff like that. So your friend probably won't have a clue how to find out what we need—just saying he's inclined to help, which he probably won't be."

"Ordinarily I'd agree with you, but this time you're wrong. This time the success or failure of this mission rides on you." He paused, then grinned mischievously. "No pressure."

"Me? What're you talking about?"

"Seems my friend is a fan of yours. When I was trying to make this appointment, he wanted to put it off until after the new year. But when I told him you were coming with me—*the Doctor* Madison Wagner—he changed his tune and set our meeting for tomorrow."

"Why?"

"It seems he attended a series of lectures on child abuse and childhood trauma you gave a couple of months back, and he was super impressed. Besides, he likes women—especially little ones."

"Well, she is that," Luke murmured.

Madison shot him a look. "What's my reason for coming with you tomorrow?"

"Max knows I sit on your board of directors. He knows Hope's Home is your shelter, you only have twelve beds, and your children can only stay for up to six months. Finally, he knows the foster care system in Texas, like everywhere else, is overburdened and many of the foster families are dangerously underqualified. So I told him we're looking for another reputable children's home we could recommend or use ourselves in the event we didn't have room. What Max Rybeck is going to do tomorrow is try to sell you on Mercy Children's Home." He paused and lifted an eyebrow. "So any specific information we need, *you're* going to have to charm him into giving you."

She chuckled. "I can do that. What can you tell me about him?"

"Max is a real estate developer. Have you ever heard of Rybeck Land Development, Inc.?"

"Of course."

"That's him. He's married and has a son named Devlin who attends the University of Texas as a business major. Max's wife, Catherine, can't stand either of them. He's probably received every civic honor known in this city, so he runs in the right circles. But he really *is* a generous guy—especially when it comes to kids, animals, and old folks. If anyone can introduce us to important people, it would be Max. And he knows Mercy like the back of his hand."

"Seems you've thought of everything."

"Nope, not really. I don't know how you're going to get more info on little Charly MacIntire or those other kids."

"Leave that to me. But, Jerome, even if your friend wants to help, he can't give us private information. You'll have to steal it."

"Then keep him occupied while I do that. Now, listen. Darth wants to come over here tomorrow evening about eight thirty. He's got some stuff he says we need to see. Is that okay?"

"Of course."

"Good. I'll call him when I get to my room. Oh, Luke, I nearly forgot. You can't go in as a celebrity writer, and your name is far too recognizable. Let's change it to…how about Luke Gallagher?"

"That's fine. I'll just add it to my list of aliases."

Jerome gave a tired grin as he pushed his chair away from the table and stood up. "I need a shower, folks, and I'm beat to a pulp. I hope you don't mind if I say good night now."

"Wait." Madison's voice was tentative. "About Charly. Did you see… Could you tell…"

Jerome walked around the table to stand behind her and rested his hands on her shoulders. His voice was shaky when he finally spoke. "I'm not going to lie to you, Madison. It was brutal. I've never seen anything like it."

The tears spilled over, and she ducked her head. "I think Lacy knew what was going to happen to Charly, and she was terrified it would happen to Piper." She reached for Jerome's hand and pressed it to her cheek. "What can I do to protect our girl?"

Jerome pulled the chair out next to her and sat down. "Honey, look at me. These people are animals, and we have to stop them. Focus on that. Nothing else. Just that."

****

When Madison came down to the kitchen the next morning, Luke was nowhere to be seen. Whitney poured her a cup of black coffee and handed her a boiled egg before she ushered her to the table.

A deep voice boomed from the doorway. "Can I have some of that coffee? Where are the kids?"

"Good morning, Mr. Scranton! Of course, you can. They're all in the playroom with Stacy. Tomorrow is her last day until after the new year, so she came in early to see them."

"Thank you, ma'am." Jerome sat next to Madison and sipped his coffee. "Damn, this is good! You've finally learned to make coffee, Whitney!"

"Not really. Luke bought us a new coffeemaker."

"Well, remind me to give him a kiss, will you? I don't think I've ever had a decent cup of coffee here!"

"Speaking of Luke, do you know where he is, Whitney?" Madison asked.

"Not a clue. I got down here about eight thirty, and his truck was gone."

"When do you think you'll get his paternity test results back?" Jerome drained his cup. "Jeez, could I get some more of that java, Whitney?"

Madison answered his first question. "I just sent it in two days ago, but I got a confirmation they'd received it this morning. So probably early next week. I'm hoping before Christmas. Since this is Thursday, the nineteenth,

I don't know if I'll get that lucky, but maybe... I'm a good customer, after all. I don't use anyone else."

Whitney set a second cup of coffee in front of Jerome and sat down. "I think Luke's going to be disappointed if Piper isn't his daughter. And that makes me really happy."

Madison nodded. "Me, too. She's such a special little girl. How's her ear this morning?"

"Much better. She slept all night."

A throat cleared in the doorway, and Madison looked up, startled. For a moment she had no clue who she was looking at—until he gave that familiar lopsided grin. Her mouth dropped.

Luke Callaghan was clean-shaven, exposing a chiseled jawline and full lips she hadn't noticed before. His tousled hair was a natural shade of sandy blond, as if it had been carelessly kissed by the sun. His contemporary wire-rimmed glasses completed the new guise. He looked nothing like himself.

"What do you think?" His inquisitive gaze roved around the table but lingered on Madison. "Will I do?"

She prayed he couldn't see the pulse throbbing in her throat as heat crept up the back of her neck. She glanced at him from the corner of her eye, admiring once again the way his hair fell in soft waves just above his collar. Something about him made her catch her breath and her heart race a little faster. He didn't have to say or do anything. All he had to do was sit close to her, stand beside her, look at her in a way no one had ever looked at her before.

"Very nice," she murmured.

Whitney, true to form, wasn't so shy. "Be still, my pounding heart! You look fantastic!"

He winked. "Calm down, young lady. You're going to hurt yourself."

Jerome got to his feet and stood in front of him, giving him the once-over. Finally, he nodded in satisfaction. "You'll fly under the radar with no trouble at all. And the ladies seem to like you."

"Story of my life."

Madison stood up. "Well, if you guys don't mind, I need to start getting ready if I have to charm the khakis off this poor guy." Then, hoping he'd think she'd just noticed him, she added, "You look really handsome, Luke."

After checking in on Piper, who was still sleeping, Madison headed to her own room where she stared blankly into her closet. She felt slightly claustrophobic, as if all the information and memories she'd accumulated over the years were slowly closing in on her. Her life and academic experience had prepared her to help traumatized children or adults grappling with childhood abuse, but she'd never planned to get involved with perpetrators and perverts. She was no mystery writer like Luke Callaghan, who seemed to relish this unexpected opportunity to change his appearance and become someone else. She was no peace officer/private investigator like Jerome Scranton, to whom danger and violence had long been a way of life. She was just a child psychologist stepping far out of her comfort zone, and the worst part of it was if she made a mistake, she could create untold amounts of tragedy.

When the names *Peter Scully* and *Shannon McCoole* slid like strips of oily scum into her mind, she was forced to look at that memory head-on. She'd had to study the behavior of those two twisted individuals in depth when internet technology had become so sophisticated that predatory men like them could perpetrate their crimes for years without detection. Not all that long ago, she hadn't had to deal with the layers of onion-like encryption and security that protected child pornography websites on the dark web to find out where the threats to children were, but now she did.

Everyone did.

The evil of both men was palpable, and the way they'd used the secrecy of the dark web to hurt children, even little babies, was beyond diabolical.

Peter Scully was a middle-aged Australian who'd gone to the Philippines where families were starving and children lived on the streets. Their abject poverty had enabled him to actually purchase youngsters from desperate parents and set up a multi-million-dollar pedophile network on the dark web. Here he and two of his girlfriends had live-streamed the torture of young children, including an eighteen-month-old baby, selling viewings of each horrific event for about $10,000 a pop.

Shannon McCoole, another Australian, was a child protection worker, a respectable position that gave him unfettered access to children in the state of Queensland. He was also the head administrator of a highly sophisticated global child pornography website located deep in the heart of the dark web. The helpless children he victimized while live-streaming into thousands of private computers were all in state care and ranged in age from eighteen months to no more than three years old. When the Queensland anti-pedophile task force finally found and closed down McCoole's network, they did so by locating and targeting a highly encrypted internet bulletin board that boasted more than forty-five thousand members.

While both men had been captured and put away, their perverted endeavors still invaded her nightmares—and she knew many more sick souls resided in that black hellish abyss Scully and McCoole had come from.

To her, those men just illustrated how *normal* those people always seemed to be, and how no one was above suspicion. McCoole had been just thirty-four years old when he was arrested, a pedophile who presented so perfectly that no one ever suspected he was a threat to children, and Scully had been hiding out in the Philippines from Australian authorities—who only liked him for fraud charges. No warning signs, nothing. The individuals paying thousands of dollars to watch this sick online brutality against children were clearly very wealthy, and many members of both men's global pedophile networks were powerful political and legal people.

These people are animals, and we have to stop them, Jerome said. Focus on that.

He was right. Her father had always told her to never allow doubt to creep in to anything she wanted or needed to do, to remember there was nothing she couldn't do if she wanted to do it, and her self-doubt, like that of all human beings, was her worst enemy.

She took a deep breath and began combing through her closet for the perfect outfit. She was entering an arena she'd never thought to enter, but she was uniquely qualified to do it. She'd come up against men like this Max Rybeck many times in the past—in private homes, family therapy sessions, seminars, workshops, and especially courtrooms. She knew how to project fearlessness and confidence directly at people who tried to intimidate her. And she would project it now.

She had no intention of ignoring Lacy Callaghan's desperate plea for help. And she had no intention of losing. Charly MacIntire had been tortured to death, and Lacy had sacrificed her own life in what seemed to be a wasted effort to protect her. Darth had been involved in this fight for a long time, Jerome knew what he was walking into, Luke was determined to defend his child, and she would use her knowledge any way she could. They'd be an army of only four, but together they'd be powerful—because they cared.

Finally, these people would be put on notice.

****

Madison dressed more daring than professional for her upcoming meeting, but she knew from the admiring-yet-concerned expression on Luke's face when she entered the front foyer that she'd made the right choice.

She wore a long-sleeved, V-necked soft gray cashmere sheath dress that just skimmed her slender figure, stopping a few inches above the knee. Her silver-tinted stockings set off her expensive charcoal gray pumps. A single pearl dangling from a fragile silver chain around her neck drew the eye to a healthy exposure of cleavage. Her shaggy cap of copper-tinted auburn hair, usually brushed smooth and close to her head, was curly and tousled, emphasizing high cheekbones and large, blue-green eyes outlined by thick dark lashes and smoky eye makeup. Her full lips glistened with a natural gloss that accentuated her smile.

She hoped she'd managed to pull off *classy yet sexy as hell* because she *needed* to attract Max Rybeck's attention and keep it.

Meeting Luke's appreciative gaze with a smile, she

turned slowly, arms straight out, and teasingly parroted his greeting from earlier that day. "Will I do?"

He cleared his throat as if he couldn't quite find his voice. "Oh yeah. You look lovely."

In an exaggerated show of seduction, she gave him a slow smile and batted her eyelashes. "I don't want to look *lovely*," she said in a low, husky voice. "I need to look *hot*."

He flushed. "Okay. You're smokin'. Smokin' hot."

"Thank you. That's more like it."

Whitney and Jerome entered the foyer together, Jerome shrugging into a black leather jacket, and Whitney squealed with disbelief. "Good grief, girlfriend! You're so hot!"

Luke and Madison looked at each other and broke into laughter.

Jerome cocked his head to one side and studied her as if he'd never seen her before. "Rybeck's gonna tell you everything without knowing he's telling you anything."

"Well, that's the goal, right?"

"I'm happy to say, darlin', our man don't stand a chance."

She sobered. "I'm afraid to leave Piper, Jerome. What if something happens? What if someone breaks in?"

"She'll be fine," Luke said gently. "Let's go now. The sooner we leave, the sooner we'll be home."

Chapter Sixteen

Luke pulled into the parking lot on the side of Mercy Children's Home, turned off the ignition, and stared at the red-brick and white-shuttered administration building. The driveway in front of the structure was circular, and the winter-brown lawn all around it was well-kept, but the attempt at creating a homelike façade failed utterly. Like every foster care facility he'd ever seen, except for Madison's shelter, this place looked like a juvenile detention center—hostile, cold, unwelcoming.

"You've never been here, Madison?" he asked.

"No. I've been invited to a few functions, but I could never go. This looks nice, don't you think?"

He looked at her in surprise. Nice? Really? Apparently, she judged the children's home by the exterior, while he judged it by the loneliness and isolation he knew resided within. No foster care facility would ever look inviting to him, no matter how it appeared on the outside. He'd always recognize it for its true function. A place to keep children confined and victimized—out of sight, out of mind.

"I forgot to look before we left, you guys," he said quickly, "but do y'all know the names and dates of those children in the photos? Just in case we run into something?"

"I do," Madison answered instantly. "There's Savannah West, June 7, 2019. Then Toby Lee, August

20, 2019. Then Bobby Grisham, November 22, 2021. And Charly MacIntire, now deceased, January 4, 2022."

He looked at her in admiration. "How do you know all that? I can't even remember when I was born."

"It's my job to remember stuff."

Jerome spoke up. "Don't forget Darth wants us back at the shelter by eight thirty."

She grimaced. "I won't forget. I want out of this outfit as soon as possible."

He opened his door with a chuckle. "Let's go, Miss Hottie. We have a job to do."

Luke offered his arm to Madison as they all walked together toward the administration building. The Mercy Children's Home had to be about a city block long, he decided, and it appeared to be a community within a community. He saw a little chapel, an infirmary, and several small houses strategically scattered around the main building. As they drew closer, he realized the houses were actually duplexes, probably living quarters for children and their caretakers.

Nice touch, he thought grudgingly. Let the kids think they actually have a place to go to, and it looks good to folks on the outside. Little *Welcome, Friends* placards on the doors, Christmas lights outlining the rooftops...all so saccharine sweet it nearly made him sick.

When Madison spoke in a low voice, he had to lean down to hear her. But when he did, he knew she was thinking along the same line he was.

"How easy would it be to take a child from one of these little houses and return him when you're finished? If you know the schedule or, better yet, have access to the right computer so you could check him out of the home without anyone knowing, no one would even realize you left..."

Luke nodded in agreement but didn't answer.

When they reached the building, Jerome held the door open for them. "Let's see if we can get our bearings a little until Max catches up with us."

When they entered a glossy-tiled lobby, Luke admired a beautifully decorated, ceiling-high Christmas tree in the middle. Two doors were side by side on one wall—one labeled *Library* and the other *Supplies*. To the left of the tree, a hallway led to what appeared to be conference rooms, and a hallway on the right led to offices. Jerome gestured toward the right.

Luke and Madison followed him to an office door labeled *Wilhelmina Griffith, Chief Administrator*. Between this office and the boys' restroom was a wall covered by glassed-in shelves displaying trophies, awards, and large photographs. At the end of this hall appeared to be an auditorium.

A short, rather heavyset man threw open the chief administrator's office door. "Jerome Scranton! How the devil are you? Y'all come on in!"

A smile planted on his craggy face, Jerome turned around.

Max stepped out of the office and closed the door behind him. "Naw, come to think of it, let's go on down to a conference room. No one'll bother us there."

Before he led them toward the opposite hallway, Max Rybeck sidled toward Madison, halted, and allowed his gaze to travel lazily up and down her slender body. Luke's fist clenched involuntarily.

Jerome jumped in. "Max Rybeck, this here's Dr. Madison Wagner and her good friend, Luke Gallagher.

He's visiting for Christmas. We sure do appreciate you seeing us on such short notice."

"Howdy do, Dr. Wagner. Good to meet you, Luke."

Madison offered her hand to him, apparently unaware of his blatant attempt at sensuality. Luke felt a twinge of distaste when fat fingers curved around hers, and he instantly noted a wide tan line on the naked ring finger of his left hand.

A player, used to getting what he wants... Well, I don't think he's going to get it this time.

"Please call me Madison," she said softly, her voice even huskier than usual. "It's a pleasure to meet you."

"Likewise...Madison." Rybeck's tone caressed her name as he tucked her hand in the crook of his arm and guided her in the direction of the conference rooms. "I sure do hope we can work together."

Scowling, Luke followed them, barely noticing how Jerome stayed several feet behind him. Instead, he was focused on the fact Rybeck couldn't have been more than four inches taller than Madison, if that much, and outweighed her by at least a hundred pounds. His black, curly hair was obviously dyed, and his rear end was as flat as a piece of toast. A thoroughly unattractive man, Luke thought, disgusted, but Madison seemed to disagree. Apparently, she was enthralled with some story Rybeck was telling in a low voice that no one else could hear.

"Here we are, guys!" Rybeck pushed a door open and flipped on an overhead light. "Y'all take a load off. Madison, come sit by me."

Seating himself at the head of the conference table, Rybeck leaned back in his chair and folded his arms across his chest. "Before we start chewin' the fat, I want to invite you to stay and hear our little Christmas program. The kids have been practicing since this summer. All our benefactors and major donors will be here, plus foster families, so it'll be a perfect opportunity for you to meet everyone who's anyone at Mercy."

"And who might that be?" Jerome asked curiously, pulling a chair out beside Madison. He sat down.

Rybeck pursed his pouty lips thoughtfully. "Well, let's see… One man I'm sure you know, Madison, is Quinn Davis, Director of Protective Services. He always comes. And of course, all our board members—Ryan Neely is an attorney, Marjorie Honeycutt with the *San Antonio Tribune*, Kevin Lindsey with channel four news—just folks like that."

Madison gave an uncertain smile. "We'd love to stay, but are you sure we'd be welcome?"

"Of course! I invited you, didn't I? Besides, it was Willie's idea, not mine."

Luke seated himself across the table from Madison. "I'm sorry, I've forgotten. Who's Willie?"

"Wilhelmina Griffith. She's the chief admin around here. Nothing happens at Mercy she doesn't know about, so if you have any questions, feel free to ask her."

"We really appreciate that, Max," Jerome said sincerely.

"Sure. There'll be a little buffet-type thing, too, so you can have a light supper if you want. Now, Madison, tell me exactly what you're looking for and how we can help you."

She leaned forward intently, resting her elbows on the table and her chin on her hands, exposing an even healthier amount of cleavage. Although Rybeck seemed to be paying attention, a faint sheen of perspiration glistened on his forehead.

She spoke in that low, throaty voice. "My shelter, Hope's Home, only holds twelve children, but I'm licensed to house them for up to six months instead of just ninety days. I don't have to shy away from problem kids. I'm a child psychologist, as you probably know, and my board members are all active in children's fields, so my shelter is a little more specialized and proactive than most. But a few times in the last year or so, I've run into a situation that makes me very uncomfortable, and this is where I hope you can help me."

She paused as if she was waiting for a response, so Max sat up a little straighter in his chair. "Of course! Just name it."

She looked down at the table, her expression one of shy uncertainty. "Thank you so much. A few times I've been asked by a family court judge or a visiting judge from an outside county to take a child into my shelter, but I haven't had the room. I've had to turn down the request, and you can imagine how that made me feel. I've heard wonderful things about Mercy Children's Home, so I wanted to see if we could work something out where you might be able to give one of my children temporary housing—just until a bed opens up. Do you understand what I mean?"

As she looked at him pleadingly, Rybeck managed a nod. "Of course! I'm sure we can help."

"I can't tell you how much that would mean to me, Max," she said with a catch in her voice. "Late last year I had to turn away a beautiful little girl with a horrific family story, and it really broke my heart to do it. If I had it to do over again, I'd move a healthier child from my shelter into a place like this so I'd have a vacant bed. I never learned what happened to her, but I made up my mind it would never happen again. I've been looking for other places during the last several months, but I haven't found anywhere I'm comfortable with—if you know what I mean."

Luke leaned back in his chair and watched this game of cat and mouse, bemused. The truth was Max Rybeck was the kind of man she could chew up and spit out with no problem at all, but he clearly had no idea. She played him like a pro, and he didn't even put up a fight.

Jerome's chair scraped the floor as he stood up. "Max, you got a john around here? My coffee's going right through me."

"Next to Willie's office, by the trophy wall. You remember where that was?"

"Sure. Thanks."

Luke glanced at Jerome, then settled back in his chair as if he had all the time in the world. He turned his attention back to Madison.

"Max, what type of safeguards do you have in place here to protect the children?" she was asking casually. "And I'm sure your background checks are very thorough, right?"

"Of course. Everyone from the director to the janitor goes through them. No one's exempt, not even our board members."

"What's your dismissal policy? I mean, if someone does anything…wrong…with a child…"

"Instantaneous. No questions. No recourse."

"Does law enforcement look into that? Are charges filed?"

"Absolutely."

"Do you have any orphans here or children whose

foster families couldn't handle them?"

Luke admired how she'd slipped that question into the conversation so subtly—it was the most important question on the list.

Rybeck frowned. "Willie could answer that, at least about the orphans. I do know some foster children have had to be moved around until they're settled in with the right family. Of course, you understand that."

"I do." She turned her attention to Luke. "I'm sure this is very boring for you. Why don't you take a look around the grounds for me? You wouldn't mind talking to me alone, would you, Max?"

He grinned and leaned forward, resting his fleshy arms on the table. "Feel free to wander, Mr. Gallagher. We're an open book around here. Madison and I will catch up with you in a little while."

****

Just as Luke rounded the corner, Jerome walked out of the boys' restroom. He held a finger to his lips and gestured toward the office door labeled *Wilhelmina Griffith, Chief Administrator*. Luke nodded and reached Jerome as he was turning the knob. The door opened easily, and from beyond a half wall that shielded a secluded workspace, Luke could see the faint green glow of a computer screen.

"Either someone's coming right back," Jerome whispered, "or they forgot to turn the computer off. No matter what, we got to do this quick."

With Luke on his heels, Jerome headed straight for the computer located on a wide sectional desk beside a closet. Jerome opened the closet door quickly, found it empty, and closed it. The *click* of the doorknob seemed to reverberate through the office.

"Go stand outside by the trophy wall and stop anyone who looks like they're going to come in here, will you? This shouldn't take long."

"Happy to."

In the darkening office, Luke maneuvered his way carefully between shelves, equipment, and file cabinets until he finally reached the door. He opened it, peered into the hallway to be sure no one was coming, and breathed a sigh of relief. As soon as he stepped outside, recessed ceiling lights working on some kind of a timer flickered, then illuminated the murky hallway. He stood at the trophy wall, pretending to be engrossed in the awards and photos.

"Excuse me, are you lost?"

A strident, raspy voice nearly sent him through the roof. He bit back a fluent stream of completely inappropriate curse words and met the dark, direct gaze of the most Amazonian-looking woman he'd ever seen in his life.

"Are you lost?" she repeated impatiently, her voice elevating a notch.

He shook his head, giving her a slow, lopsided grin that didn't appear to faze her in the least. "No, ma'am. I'm Luke Gallagher. I'm here with Dr. Madison Wagner, but she's with Max Rybeck right now, so I thought I'd check out your trophies. I hope that's all right."

"Oh, of course!" She thrust out her hand and clasped his with an iron grip. "I'm Willie Griffith, chief admin of this little shop of horrors. Max told me y'all would be coming today. Did he remember to invite you to our little shindig tonight?"

When she finally released his hand, he gently flexed his fingers to be sure they still worked. "He did, thank you. We're looking forward to it."

"That's wonderful. Can I show you anything?"

He almost turned her down, then remembered Jerome. Luke didn't know what was taking so long, but he did know he had orders to keep this woman away from her office. Jerome had to leave without anyone seeing him, but Luke needed to remain near, just in case...

He moved closer to her. "You know," he said confidentially, "I was a foster child myself back in the day, but I didn't get to stay anywhere as nice as this."

She took his arm and gently guided him away from her office toward the tall Christmas tree in the lobby. "I understand. I stayed with so many foster families I don't even remember all their names. Walk with me, Mr. Gallagher. I'd like to show you something."

"I need to stay close by if it's possible, Miss Griffith, in case Max and Dr. Wagner come looking for me."

"Call me Willie. It's just a little something I'd like you to see in the library. I'll get you right back."

Luke remembered the library was in the foyer—a little farther from Jerome than he liked—but he had to allow the determined woman to take him there. She obviously wasn't accustomed to refusal, and he wasn't man enough to offer any.

Willie opened the library door and flipped on the lights. "Come with me."

Like an obedient child, he followed her across the library and finally stopped before one long wall covered by sheets of manila paper containing assorted family trees. At the top of each family tree was a name printed in large block letters.

Beside each printed name was a child's photograph.

"As you probably know, many foster kids have problems with self-identity," Willie explained, "so we wanted our children to understand they each have a history, both physical and emotional. We talked to them about DNA, ethnicity, and how they all have a place in this world. It seemed to comfort them, make them feel as if they belonged somewhere. It's been a valuable lesson for all our kids."

Luke nodded, stood still, and took in each picture. His eyes were drawn to the photo of a smiling, chubby-faced little boy with dancing blue eyes and curly red hair. As he stared at it, he concentrated on keeping his face expressionless. Lacy's photo had shown a skinny, terrified child with wild red ringlets hanging to his shoulders, but that didn't matter. Luke would've known this little boy anywhere.

Bobby Grisham.

He pointed at the photo. "Willie, is this little guy still here?"

She looked at him curiously. "No...why?"

"I just wondered. He looks really familiar."

"He was here last year. He was one of my favorites, but a family out near Medina Lake actually adopted him. They lived outside the little town of Mico, I think it was. We can check my records if you want."

He thought of Jerome slinking around her office doing God knew what and shook his head. "No, that's all right. I was just curious."

"Are you sure?"

"Absolutely, but I appreciate the offer." He wanted to get off this subject as soon as he could and asked quickly, "Isn't it tough to get a foster child adopted?"

"Are you asking about Bobby specifically?"

"Well…not really. Like I said, I was in the foster system myself and never knew who my parents were, but no one ever asked to adopt *me*. Of course, I was a pretty bad kid…"

She chuckled and patted his forearm. "Not your fault, Mr. Gallagher. Older kids usually aren't adopted, but Bobby was lucky. We have a grant writer/consultant named Sage Winslow who also lives near Mico. She actually became very close to Bobby and talked his mother into terminating her parental rights, which wasn't difficult if I remember correctly. Then, early last year, he was adopted. I don't remember the details, but it all went pretty fast. He was only here about six months. Sage will be here tonight if you want to talk to her."

Luke thought quickly. *Lucky, huh? He was just a throwaway kid, like Piper, probably like Charly…no support system, no family…*

"He was lucky she took such an interest in him," he said aloud.

"He was. At least his mother recognized that she couldn't take care of him and gave him to a family that could."

Before Luke could respond, someone knocked on the library door and pushed it open. Jerome poked his head inside. "Willie, is that your voice I heard?"

"Jerome! What a surprise! I didn't know you were here."

"Well, I am. I was in the bathroom with a…stomach issue." He joined them at the wall and looked closely at the drawings. "Hey, Luke, I wondered where you went. Aren't these interesting?"

Luke nodded slowly, but he couldn't pull his gaze away from the photo of the chubby little boy and the colored-in branches of the child's family tree. He did his best to speak in what he hoped was a steady, unconcerned tone.

"Yes, sir," he said finally. "They sure are."

****

Madison sat in the last row of cafeteria chairs in the small auditorium, Luke on one side of her and Jerome on the other, waiting for the children's Christmas recital to begin. As people straggled in, she tried to observe each person who entered without being too conspicuous.

Quinn Davis would be here, Max had said, and Ryan Neely...

She hadn't even thought about Quinn Davis during the last few days—there hadn't been time—but she certainly hadn't lost interest in him. In fact, he was the person she wanted most to speak to. He'd know who'd contacted Ryan Neely initially, when the decision was made to place Piper into foster care right before her mother was murdered, and he'd know why she hadn't been protected from the very beginning.

Just then, Jerome patted her arm. "There's Quinn," he whispered. "If you can, will you see if he'll be in his office Monday?"

"Hey, look at this!" Luke interrupted, pointing to a name printed at the top of the program.

She took the program from him and peered at it closely. At first the name didn't register. *Sebastian deWynter, Piano Accompanist.* But then Whitney's words rang through her memory.

They call him Piano Man, like the song by Billy Joel.

She glanced at Luke and cocked an eyebrow. "Maybe we can meet him after this."

He nodded but didn't answer as the lights began to

dim. When the spectators had settled down, a tall well-built man dressed casually in a pair of black jeans and a white western-cut shirt strode to the front of the auditorium.

Madison recognized him immediately and tapped Luke's hand with her program. "Feast your eyes," she whispered with a grin. "We've been blessed with the presence of Ryan Neely."

Chapter Seventeen

The attorney looked around the room for a few moments, as if preparing to give a closing argument, then bestowed upon his audience a slow half smile clearly designed to warm them up. He spoke in a practiced baritone voice Luke was sure reached every corner.

Yet there was something *off* about this man, something he didn't like. It wasn't because Neely was an attorney, although that didn't help. He was arrogant and pompous, as Madison had claimed, but it was far more than that…

"Good evening, everyone. I'm Ryan Neely, and I sit on the Board of Directors of Mercy Children's Home. Y'all didn't come to hear me talk, so I just want to welcome you to our sixth annual Children's Christmas Recital and let you know our kids have been rehearsing for this since the Fourth of July. Our pianist is one of my law partners, Mr. Sebastian deWynter, and our grant writer, Sage Winslow, graciously consented to lead our choir this year. Everyone's been working very hard, so please let the kids know how impressed you are. When the program is over, please join us in the cafeteria for some refreshments." He held out his hand toward a long line of children trooping down a side aisle toward the front of the auditorium. "Now, without further ado, let's give it up for the Mercy Children's Choir."

Luke heard applause, murmuring, and quiet laughter

as a tall, slim man seated himself at the piano and a young woman walked to the stage from the back of the room.

Sage Winslow.

This was the woman who'd orchestrated Bobby Grisham's adoption, Willie had said. Luke leaned forward for a better view, but her back was already to the audience as she helped the kids find their places. All he could determine was that she was short and slender in a shapeless black dress and wore her long dark hair in a haphazard bun clasped to the top of her head.

She looked ordinary enough to him, but she had to be pretty persuasive to talk a mother into terminating her parental rights. She wasn't an attorney, so what did she have to offer?

She held her hands in the air and prepared to begin.

As he closed his eyes and listened to the children singing familiar Christmas carols, a tiny grin played across his lips. He'd never participated in anything like this and had never even wanted to, but now he couldn't help but wonder what it was like. The kids' voices were reed thin and off pitch, but they were obviously thrilled to be the entertainment for this evening.

As the children launched into a rollicking version of "Frosty the Snowman," Luke let his mind meander back to the photo of little Bobby Grisham in the library—the little boy's story was beginning to nag at him. Willie Griffith said he was adopted in early 2021 and the adoption had moved forward quickly. Lacy's photo of that hungry, terrified child was dated *November 22, 2021.*

So unless Willie had been mistaken about the actual time of year Bobby left Mercy, he'd been healthy and happy until he was adopted. So who adopted him? And what happened after that?

Charly MacIntire had been tortured to death and her body dumped in a drainage ditch. Would Bobby's body turn up next? Would it ever turn up at all? Both children had lived in Mercy Children's Home, very possibly at the same time, and both children were now gone. That wasn't by coincidence.

That was by diabolical design.

He pulled his attention back to the children on the stage. The lights dimmed further, and Sebastian deWynter began playing the sweet, haunting melody of Luke's favorite Christmas carol, "O Holy Night." When a splendid feminine voice suddenly soared high above the voices of the children, he was astonished to realize Wilhelmina Griffith had joined them on stage and was now singing solo as each child held up a battery-operated candle. It was the only religious moment in the entire concert, but Willie's voice was so beautiful he had to swallow a lump in his throat.

When the last poignant notes had faded away, the auditorium was silent—then erupted in a roar of applause as the audience arose to its feet, Luke with them. For the first time in his life, and in spite of the heartbreaking situation in which he now found himself, he felt the warmth of love and redemption that Christmas had always seemed to promise—to everyone but him.

****

Once they'd reached the cafeteria, Madison watched as Jerome engulfed Willie in an almost overwhelming bear hug. "Good golly, Miss Willie, I had no idea you could sing like that! You gave me goose bumples all up and down my spine!"

251

He took her hand as they moved toward the food tables, and his voice floated back toward Madison. "Can I get you some punch? Or maybe a sandwich?"

"Thank you so much, Jerome. I appreciate that."

Madison looked up at Luke and shook her head in disbelief. "My God, Luke…he's flirting with her!"

Luke gave her a wink. "You think?"

"But why? Why would he do that? I think she really likes him!"

"Well, good! He'll get a lot more information from her if she likes him than if she doesn't. Come on. If I get you some punch and a sandwich, will you like me, too?"

He held out his hand, and she took it, following him toward a long table outlined by Christmas lights and covered with finger sandwiches, relish trays, fruit dishes, and holiday cookies. But before they could reach it, a deep voice stopped them, and Max Rybeck put his hand on her shoulder.

"There you are, Madison! I wondered what happened to you. What'd you think of our little show?"

Madison squeezed Luke's hand, pulling him up short. "I loved it, Max! Thanks so much for inviting us!"

He beamed. "You're more than welcome. I have someone here I'd like you to meet." He turned to the young woman Madison recognized as the choir director and said, "Sage Winslow, this is Dr. Madison Wagner. She owns Hope's Home, a children's shelter in San Antonio. Madison, Sage is a grant writer for Mercy, but she does it on a freelance basis. Since you said you run your shelter primarily on donations and your outside work, I thought you and Sage might be able to do some business. She's very, very good."

Madison smiled and studied the woman more

closely. They were about the same height, but the resemblance stopped there. Where Madison's cropped and highlighted hair was fashionable, Sage's was perched carelessly on top of her head by a large barrette, dark tendrils straggling around her face. Her large black-framed glasses couldn't have been more unflattering, her dress was too long, and she wore matronly black pumps more appropriate for a grandmother with bunions than a woman so close to Madison's age.

But something told her that Sage Winslow's look was done on purpose. She was far more attractive than she wanted anyone to know.

Madison offered her hand and was impressed by the firmness of Sage's handshake. "I'm very happy to meet you. So you go after grants?"

"That's my primary source of income, but I also do freelance work online. Every little bit helps, you know what I mean? Most of us writers starve to death."

Madison grinned. "That's what I hear, but I can't write my way out of a paper bag, so I wouldn't know. I've never actually hired a grant writer, but that sounds like it might be a good idea. Maybe we could get together soon and discuss this further?"

"I'd love to! I'd love to see your place and maybe meet your children…"

Without warning, Luke exploded into a sneezing fit so violent it sounded like the top of his head might explode. Madison looked at him in alarm as his face grew redder and redder, and tears streamed down his cheeks. He grabbed Madison's shoulder and shook his head vehemently.

"Jeez, I'm so sorry!" He sneezed again. "Jeez!"

Instantly, Madison dropped the subject of a meeting

with Sage and turned her attention back to Max Rybeck. "Max, have you seen Quinn Davis this evening? I really need to speak to him about one of my kids."

"Not yet, but I'm sure he'll be here. He always comes. Let's get our supper and find a table, all right?"

Madison met Luke's bloodshot eyes and lifted an eyebrow. "Are you okay?"

He sniffled and nodded. "I'm fine. So sorry. I think some kind of expensive perfume must've drifted by. I'm deathly allergic to that stuff."

Max chuckled. "I'm just allergic to the price tag." He steered Madison toward the food table. "I see Willie sitting over by the Christmas tree with Jerome. Shall we join them?"

****

Luke leaned back in his chair, wiped his mouth with a small napkin, and grinned. The chairs were clearly for children, not people over six feet tall, and the round table scraped against his knees. Even Willie Griffith had to squirm to make room for her long legs, and Max Rybeck's belly made it nearly impossible for him to get food to his mouth. Only Sage Winslow and Madison appeared comfortable.

"I heard you sneezing across the room, Mr. Gallagher," Willie commented suddenly. "I do hope you're not catching a winter cold. There's something going around, you know."

Luke rubbed his nose and hoped his eyes were still bloodshot. "No, I'm fine. Something just fired up my allergies."

"One of our little girls came down with a bad sore throat last night, and I wanted to get her in to see the doctor this afternoon, but he was booked. We'll have to wait until Monday. Keep an eye on yourself, Mr. Gallagher."

"You can get her in to see Dr. Daniel Weinstein tomorrow morning, I'm sure," Madison offered. "His office is open on Saturdays. In fact, I'd be happy to give him a call for you—"

Willie looked surprised. "You know Dr. Dan, too? We've used him here for years. I won't use anyone else. No, he's booked until Monday, but thanks for the offer. We'll be fine."

"Oh, okay. No problem." Madison glanced at the delicate silver watch on her wrist. "We can't stay much longer, Jerome—"

A surprisingly deep baritone voice broke into the conversation. "How are you this evening, Max? Where's your lovely bride tonight?"

"Howdy do, Sebastian! Cat's already gone home to spend Christmas with her family. I can't go. Folks, this here is San Antonio's own Piano Man, Sebastian deWynter." After completing the introductions all around, Rybeck grinned and added, "Care to try to squeeze into a chair and join us?"

"I'd love to, thanks." Sebastian pulled out a chair and lowered himself onto it carefully. He looked at Madison and Luke. "So what brings y'all out here to see us?"

"I just wanted to talk to Max about a couple of things, and he was kind enough to invite us," Madison answered. "We really enjoyed your show. The kids were terrific."

Luke hoped Sebastion couldn't hear the nerves in his voice as he jumped in. "So you're San Antonio's own Piano Man. Do you play anywhere we might be able to go and hear you?"

"I play at Durdy Molly's tomorrow night, down on the river. I start at nine. It's just a small piano bar, very quiet and intimate, but you might enjoy it."

"That sounds like fun. We'll see what we can manage—"

A familiar baritone interrupted, and Luke looked up to see Ryan Neely standing behind Sage Winslow's chair, gazing down on them. "Merry Christmas, everyone! Good evening, Willie. How do you think our kids did tonight?"

Willie gave a broad smile. "Fantastic! I'm very proud of them. Y'all, this is Ryan Neely, another one of our board members. Ryan, meet Dr. Madison Wagner, her friend Luke Gallagher, and my good buddy Jerome Scranton. Jerome sits on Dr. Wagner's board—she owns Hope's Home. Have you gotten anything to eat?"

"Not yet. I've been trying to circulate a little."

"Well, grab a chair and join us for a minute."

"Thank you, I will."

Luke narrowed his eyes, studying Neely more closely as the Christmas lights on the tree and around the cafeteria winked like stars blazing rich color. He was grateful for the opportunity because *something* about the man literally made his skin crawl, but Luke had no idea what it was. Still, the warning antennae he'd cultivated on the streets over many years was screaming now, and he knew better than to ignore it.

When Neely's hand closed cozily around Sage's shoulder for just a moment before he moved away from her chair, Luke had no doubt what that intimate gesture meant. Ryan Neely and Sage Winslow were an item.

Luke wondered if anyone else knew it.

"You look awfully familiar to me, Dr. Wagner," Neely was saying as he sat down. He squirmed awkwardly in the small chair. "Have we met?"

"Oh, I doubt if you remember me, Mr. Neely. We had a run-in in a courtroom a couple of years ago."

"Really? Who was my client?"

As Madison cocked her head to one side, apparently trying to remember, Luke waited for the lie.

"I honestly don't remember. It was a custody case, though. You represented the father, and I testified for the little boy." She grinned mischievously. "But I do remember...the mother won."

"You must've been formidable, because that hardly ever happens."

Sebastian shifted in his chair. "She might've won because she had a good case, you know. Just saying..."

Neely held up his hand. "I'm sure you're right."

Madison leaned forward, exposing so much cleavage Max Rybeck nearly fell down the front of her dress. "I heard a radio commercial about you the other day, Mr. Neely. When did you begin specializing in fathers' rights?"

"Well, I've always done that when I could, but I didn't start publicizing my special interest until recently. When it comes to custody battles, fathers are still pretty much overlooked in favor of moms. When a case comes to my attention that seems to highlight that injustice, I take it to give the dad a fighting chance if I can."

Luke's lip curled. *Your special interest...I just bet it is.*

Madison gave a slow nod. "I admire that, Mr. Neely, and I'll keep it in mind. I've run into that a few times myself."

"Well, don't hesitate to give me a call if I can ever help with anything."

"Excuse me, folks," Jerome interjected, "but I see Quinn Davis over there, and I need to talk to him about something real quick."

Madison stood up. "I have a meeting tonight at eight thirty, so we all need to get a move on. We'll meet you at the truck, Jerome."

"Sounds good."

With that, Jerome disappeared into the milling crowd, and Luke eased himself to his feet. "It was a real pleasure meeting all of you. Willie, thank you so much for showing me around earlier."

"Not at all, Mr. Gallagher. I enjoyed it."

Sage Winslow touched Madison's arm. "Give me a call when you want to get together, Dr. Wagner." She handed Madison a business card. "I'd love to work with you."

Madison tucked the card in the front of her handbag and smiled. "Thank you so much, Sage. I look forward to it." She turned to Max Rybeck and offered her hand. "I can't tell you how much I appreciate all your help today, Max. I'll be in touch very soon."

****

When Madison opened her suite door, Jerome, Luke, and Darth trooped inside and headed straight for the small conference table. While Luke seemed quiet and subdued, Jerome was close to leaping out of his skin. Since Madison could count on one hand the number of times she'd seen the lawman actually excited, she was dying of curiosity herself.

Even Darth gave him a quizzical look as he placed his laptop on the table. "What's up, cowboy?" he asked as he pulled out his chair and sat down. He opened his laptop and dragged it closer. "Did you run over a bad guy on your way home?"

"Better'n that."

Darth leaned back in his chair. "I'll bite. What happened at Mercy?"

"Wait a minute." Jerome glanced at Madison. "Is everything okay with Whitney and Piper?"

"They're fine," she answered. "Piper's sleeping—Whitney said she ate like a horse—and now Whitney's watching a movie with Tessa. No one'll bother us. Go ahead."

The truth was Madison was thrilled with Whitney's report about Piper. The little girl had eaten every bite of her dinner, swallowed her medicine, and gone to sleep with Sasha right next to her bed, all without a fuss.

No big deal if a child doesn't have night terrors, but this is wonderful. Maybe just a reprieve, but still...

She pulled herself back to the issue at hand when Jerome took a good-sized flash drive out of his jacket pocket and held it up. "We stayed for a recital tonight and got to meet some very important people—or at least they seemed to think they were. But earlier, while Madison was busy enticing Max Rybeck, I got into Willie Griffith's office. She's the chief administrator. Anyway, I managed to download tons of files, and I hope Charly's was one of them. What I tried to get was admissions info, the histories and profiles of all board members, and everything I could find on each employee—from the janitor to the bigwigs."

Darth whistled. "And all without a search warrant... God, I love your job. Let's see what you found—even if we can't use it."

Jerome inserted his flash drive into a USB port on his computer and opened a file labeled *2018-2021 Admissions.* Darth scooted his chair closer, and Jerome positioned his laptop so they could both see the screen.

"There!" Darth said suddenly. "MacIntire, Charlena. I bet that's our gal!"

Jerome nodded. He clicked on the file and waited for it to load. Finally, he spoke. "It says she was born April 2, 2016 in San Antonio, Texas."

Nodding, Darth moved in closer. "Well, here's what my team and I already know. Charly's mother's name is Fiona MacIntire. She's serving a life sentence in Huntsville for murdering her brother. She was a prostitute and spent a lot of time down in New Orleans. Charly was placed in Mercy Children's Home by protective services after Christmas in 2019. The family she was with couldn't handle her."

He paused, read silently for a moment, then looked up from the screen, his brow furrowed. "But I didn't know this. Quinn Davis apparently took a personal interest in her, beginning when she entered foster care. He had a thing worked out with a social worker/psychotherapist—that Goldie Newsom I mentioned earlier—to hold counseling sessions with her. There's a marginal note here that Charly should always be released to Quinn's care upon his request. All he had to do was sign her out and sign her back in. I'd imagine that includes anyone else he approved of as well, like the social worker Carole Black who was with her on the day she disappeared."

Once again, the name *Shannon McCoole* of Australia slithered like a python through Madison's memory. McCoole had been a trusted worker in the

Queensland child protective services, and no one had ever even looked into his easy access to very young children, or what he did when he had them. Quinn Davis would be his equivalent, no question.

"What does it say about her disappearance?" she asked aloud.

Darth shrugged. "Just what happened is all, and a reference to the cops who took the report."

"No other mention of Quinn Davis?"

"No."

Luke pulled the photo of little Bobby Grisham from the box beside his chair labeled *Piper Callaghan* and passed it to Jerome. "Is there anything about him in there? Willie said he was at Mercy in 2021 and adopted outright toward the end of the year."

Jerome clicked through files. He glanced at Darth. "Here it is."

Madison cocked her head to one side, frowning. "Wait a minute. What would Willie know about Bobby Grisham?"

Luke pulled out his phone and swiped the screen. He finally stopped and passed it to Madison.

"I snapped this picture in the library at Mercy tonight. I only got the chance because Willie was so hot for Jerome she completely forgot about me. Bobby Grisham once lived at Mercy. This picture was taken before he was adopted and left the home. You can see how wonderful he looks. Chubby, bright eyes, shiny red curly hair. But the picture Lacy left for me…well, he had to be on starvation rations to get that thin in so little time. And I don't think he ever bathed, either."

Jerome held up his hand. "Get this, y'all. Bobby Grisham was born on May 29, 2016 to Marilyn Grisham, age fifteen, no baby daddy listed. Bobby was pulled from her home a couple of months later, and lived in two foster homes until he finally entered Mercy on January 14, 2021. His adoption was finalized on August 15, 2021 by the Joshua and Katherine Walker family out in Mico, and he left Mercy for good on September first." Jerome looked on the back of Bobby's photo. "The date on this picture is November 22, 2021. So…he went to hell in a handbasket somewhere between September first when he left Mercy, and November twenty-second. That's just two-and-a-half months."

Madison's mouth went dry, and her heart began to hammer. "Did Willie say anything about how Bobby happened to be adopted so quickly?"

Luke rubbed the cleft in his chin. "Willie said that Sage Winslow—the woman who directed the children's choir tonight—got close to Bobby right away and talked his mother into terminating her rights and putting him up for adoption. Willie said he was adopted very quickly and she hasn't seen him since. She also said he was one of her favorites."

Darth drummed his fingertips on the table. "Sage Winslow? What kind of hippie name is that? Is she their choir director?"

"No," Madison answered uncomfortably. "She's a grant writer, primarily for nonprofit children's groups. She wanted to talk to me about helping us, but Luke nearly blew his head off sneezing. He clearly didn't want me to bring her here, so I just said I'd call her."

"Good catch, Luke," Darth said. "Madison, you don't want to bring any strangers in here to scope out your kids right now. Don't let the fact that she's a woman fool you. Some of the most vicious perpetrators I've ever dealt with are women." He turned his attention back to Jerome. "Do they show an address for the adopting family out in Mico? The Walkers?"

"Let me check." Jerome scrolled down the screen, then nodded. "Here it is. 107 County Road 218. Joshua and Katherine Walker."

Darth snorted. "Mico? Who the heck lives in Mico?"

Luke chuckled. "I have a place not too far from there. But you're right. In Mico itself, there's a population of about eighty-four, and half of that is armadillos. But don't let the addresses fool you—most of them aren't actually in Mico."

"Well, then, that has to be our Walker family." Darth scribbled the address on his notepad. "Is there any information about Bobby's mother, Marilyn Grisham? I'd like to know why she gave up her rights so quickly."

Jerome rubbed his eyes. "Let me see. Their comments are hidden unless you click on them. Okay, wait. Here we go. It says Marilyn left her parents' home not long after Bobby was taken from them and went to work for an escort service that provided very young girls to wealthy men. She was only fifteen when he was born, remember? By the time Bobby landed at Mercy, Marilyn was a drug addict and had contracted AIDS. My guess is she hadn't seen him since he was taken from her." Jerome looked up and tugged on his earlobe. "That's why she terminated so quickly, Darth. She was dying. She was probably relieved to know he'd be taken care of."

"But what about the grandparents?" Darth glanced at Madison. "If they were still living, wouldn't they have had an opportunity to adopt him first?"

"Well, you'd think so," she answered, "but you said

he was taken from their house when he was a baby. There must've been a reason for that. My guess is they didn't want him back or they might not have been well."

"I wonder how this Sage Winslow knew Marilyn Grisham and how to find her. A grant writer and a hooker with AIDS. Weird besties."

"Jerome, is there a file on Sage Winslow?" Madison asked.

"Just a second. Here's a folder labeled *Board Members 2017-2022*. Here we go. Unmarried, no children, University of Texas dropout…" He shook his head. "Other than that, nothing we don't already know."

Luke cleared his throat. "Well, I think she's got a thing with Ryan Neely. Just a feeling, nothing specific— except the way he touched her shoulder tonight. Intimately, you know?"

Darth narrowed his eyes and nodded. "That would be interesting. What's her address?"

"Ummm…also Mico, 91 CR 218." Jerome looked up, granite-faced. "We can google it, but those addresses seem close together. Luke, do you know where that is?"

"Not exactly. I think it's about ten miles from my place. I'm at the intersection of County Road 218 and Big Tree, much closer to the lake."

Darth spoke in a strangely still voice. "Let's find out if Marilyn Grisham has passed on, okay?"

Jerome nodded. "Give me a sec."

"But what's the common denominator between Charly and Bobby?" Darth persisted.

Madison stared at the cop in disbelief. "Are you serious? The common denominator is as clear as the nose on your face. Both kids lived at Mercy, both disappeared from there, and both were alone in this world. That's not enough?"

"It's a start," Darth agreed grimly, "but I need a whole lot more than that."

Chapter Eighteen

Madison subsided when Jerome held up his hand and spoke. "Okay, you two, shut up and listen. Marilyn Grisham died on August 1, 2021, and Bobby's adoption with the Walkers was finalized on the fifteenth. So the pathway to Bobby must've been set up by someone who knew the system and could work through it fast."

"The entire lake area is a tight community," Luke observed. "It's likely these two women knew each other. Everyone knows each other out there."

Madison gave a little cough and leaned in closer to Jerome. "Jerome, is Quinn Davis mentioned in Bobby's file?"

"I don't see his name anywhere. Oh, I forgot to tell you...Davis put me off about a meeting on Monday. Said something about having to go to Dallas for some kind of child abuse award some organization is giving him."

Such a glory hog... But aloud she said only, "Well, we can't miss that, now can we?"

"You don't like him, either?" Darth asked.

"I don't like the way his name keeps popping up."

"Okay, one more thing, Jerome," Darth said. "These other two photos—little Savannah West and Toby Lee, both labeled *2019*—anything on either of them?"

Jerome searched for several moments, then shook his head. "Nope."

"Okay. They didn't come from Mercy, then."

Luke reached into the box at his feet, pulled out Piper's protective services file, and pushed it across the table toward Darth. "This is my daughter's file, and you'll see most everyone's names are blacked out. Do you see anything there that might connect Piper with Charly or Bobby?"

Darth looked at each page carefully, then shook his head. "Not really, but it looks like Quinn Davis signed off on everything. I'd like to know if Carole Black or Goldie Newsom handled any part of your daughter's case back when someone was making those anonymous reports you mentioned." He pushed the file back to Luke. "Madison, you said your attorney brought Piper to you. What's his name?"

"Jared Ross. Yes, he did. The cops called him when they couldn't find a place for her to stay, and he called me. We contacted Luke the next day because of some paperwork the cops found in Lacy's house, and we hoped he might be her father. We'll know for sure in a few days."

Darth nodded. "Was it normal for Jared to bring a kid like Piper to you?"

"Under these circumstances, yes. He's done it a few times before."

Jerome looked up from his screen. "Are we through with these files for right now?" he asked abruptly.

"If you want us to be," Darth answered. "What's up?"

"Well, I'm just thinking… I know you're familiar with the nasty stuff. I'm wondering if we might be able to find the whole film with Charly MacIntire on it. I mean, we don't know when Lacy made that clip. Could Charly have been killed at the end of it and then dumped in that drainage ditch? Could it have been posted online somewhere? Could it be that recent, or am I way off?"

Darth rubbed his chin thoughtfully. "Jerome, you're talking about a snuff film. And whether it's posted somewhere or not, we'll probably never find it. It's hidden too deep. It'll cost too much."

Madison's surroundings suddenly felt surreal. *Is this really happening? Surely, this is a nightmare. Surely, I can just get up and walk out, and it will all disappear...*

Jerome's voice dispelled that illusion. "If they murdered that little girl and we can find it on film—"

"Well, we'll keep our eyes open, of course. You never know. But Lacy was clearly scared to death about somebody getting to these kids—as well as Piper—so that has to be our focus right now." Darth looked around the table. "Now, listen...I'm going to ask you again. Does *tip the piano man* mean anything to anybody?"

"Well, we met an attorney tonight who's a partner of Ryan Neely's," Madison answered. "Whitney told us yesterday he's quite the pianist and his following around town calls him Piano Man. Like Billy Joel, you know? His name is Sebastian deWynter."

Darth didn't hesitate. "A little too convenient, if you ask me."

"Why?"

He sighed. "Nothing I say here can leave this room, you understand?"

"Of course."

He tapped his computer. "This is my personal laptop," he began, "and all the agencies working this case with us know it's mine. They can get on the same sites I can, communicate with the same people I do, and see everything I see. I brought it tonight in case we need to get online. I don't want any of this smut to get anywhere near your computers, and I don't want these people to know who or where you are."

Luke frowned. "You mean the agencies?"

"No. These pervs. They're located all over the world, and they recognize me when I show up online. They think I'm one of them, and that's how it needs to stay."

"Smut," Madison repeated nervously. "What kind of smut?"

"Hardcore kiddie porn. We've been working on this for nearly a year."

"A year! How do you stay sane?"

"What makes you think I'm sane? We're all crazy as loons."

She grinned in sympathy. "Well, I'm a psychologist—here to help if you need it."

He nodded, then turned back to the others, once more all business. "Now, I'm not going to explain how the computer stuff works—it's complicated—but I will explain what's happening as we go along. Before I do that, though, I need to let you know a couple of very important details.

"Understand that I'm not going into this blind. I told you guys earlier that I've got an idea about what might be going on here. What I was referring to, specifically, was the name *Piano Man* and the phrase *tip the piano man*. If I'm right, what you've stumbled on here may be the first serious crack in our local portion of a global kiddie porn operation we've been investigating for months. Madison, you and Luke come stand behind me so you guys can see what I'm doing."

They obeyed. Once they were situated, Darth began

punching keys on his laptop. Madison could feel his tension swell as screen after screen popped up.

Finally, he gave a long sigh. "Now we wait."

Jerome moved his chair and leaned in closer to Darth. "What're you doing?"

"I'm deep in the dark web now, and I'm going to a website called PattyzPlaypen. It's not pretty. It's a website I actually had to pay to get on. There are thousands of them. Owners and administrators can make millions of dollars just giving these pervs a secret place to do their nasty stuff. Madison, feel free to step out if you need to."

She swallowed nausea but lifted her chin defiantly. "I'm fine, thank you. I need to know everything you can find out."

"All right." He turned back to his screen and punched a few more keys. "So my username on this site is *Kidbanger40*. Most of the people here trust me, and I'm going to try to use that to our advantage, but I doubt I can go much farther than I already have. Something like this requires a lot of secrecy, and I haven't done much to encourage that kind of trust…at least not yet."

"I don't understand," she said.

"Well, for example, one of the organizations back in the 1990s, called Wonderland Club, was so exclusive it had special entrance requirements. Potential members had to be sponsored by other members, they had to be computer literate, and they had to upload their own personal hardcore images of children being abused—*at least ten thousand images per member*—before they would be admitted to this group. And they had to continually upload new images during a select period of time on a regular basis, or they'd be thrown out of the club. I haven't had to do that yet, and I hope I'm not going to have to. These days we can sometimes use computer sleuthing methods to name and locate pervs rather than actually getting down and dirty like we used to. It's much faster these days, and we can save more children."

Luke spoke from his place beside Madison and leaned in a little closer to Darth's computer. "You had to produce your own stuff to get into these groups? How could you even do that?"

"I told you we sell our souls to do this job. There was even an official task force in Australia that produced and administered its own kiddie porn website so they could catch these guys in the act. But here's the bottom line. I'll do whatever I have to do to save children from pedophile rings like the Wonderland Club. Most of us will. Fortunately, we don't have to do it that way nearly as often anymore."

"Oh my God..." Madison whispered. "I thought I knew about this stuff..."

"It's changing all the time. The minute we think we have a handle on it, they change it. The dark web, which was initially invented by the government to protect foreign dissidents and whistleblowers, is now primarily used for criminal operations of all kinds, not just child pornography. You can't keep up with it.

"On the other hand, never forget that those old-school ways of passing nasty images around—videos, Polaroids, floppies, even brag books containing trophies—are still used today just because they're so personal and pervs still like to keep their victims close." He cleared his throat. "Now, you're welcome for the free lesson, but I can't waste any more time. It's already nine thirty. I have law enforcement connections watching us right this minute, so I'm just going to throw both *Piano Man* and *tip the piano man* out there and see what happens."

"Fingers crossed," Jerome said. "By the way, what's the *40* for in *Kidbanger40*?"

Darth gave a wicked chuckle. "So glad you asked. It's part of my badge number."

Jerome rolled his eyes. "Guaranteed to keep you from being charged with entrapment, right? Okay, tell us what you're looking for."

"Well, even though Lacy didn't say anything about someone in particular being Piano Man, my gut tells me Piano Man may actually be a username. *Tip the piano man* may be a secret code that pervs who want to watch child torture have to use to get into the sub-room of a specific kiddie porn site. I'm zeroing in on child torture because of what I know about Tony Davila, the film clips Lacy left Luke, and the terrible condition of little Charly's body.

"Some pervs call 'child torture porn' *hurtcore*, short for a now-closed website called Hurt2theCore. It won't be easy to find, but it's out there. If you see that word, get my attention immediately, because that's what it refers to. Most pedophiles won't have anything to do with it. I'm sure Lacy didn't know any particular website name or she would've told Luke. She must've overheard someone mention *tip the piano man* and didn't know what it meant but realized it couldn't be good."

Madison felt like a huge wad of cotton had been jammed into her throat. She'd always believed she knew all there was to know about the abuse of children, but she knew now she was dead wrong. She hadn't even scratched the surface.

Darth continued softly. "Still, even though I've been all over the dark web, I've never heard anything about a Piano Man. That could mean it's all fairly new, or it's deeper into the dark web than I've gone so far, or Lacy was wrong and there's nothing to it. I'm praying someone'll answer fast, but I'm not counting on it. These guys are like mushrooms. They grow in the dark and flourish in shit. On the other hand, if God smiles down on us and someone bites, one of our cyber guys will move right away to try to find out who and where they are—or, at the very least, who the administrators are."

Madison glanced at Luke. His face was pale. "This is insane," he managed. "A sub-room? *Hurtcore?*"

Darth nodded. "There's no way I can make this pretty, and I apologize for that. You can't clean this up. It's real, and it's happening now, and we have a chance to stop it...for a minute, if we get lucky. So here's what I'm trying to tell you. Some kiddie porn sites have sub-rooms—highly encrypted areas that have several layers of security. You have to get through all that before you can even talk to someone. In these rooms, the torture of children can actually be live-streamed to computers all over the world. You can even request what you want to see—for a phenomenal fee, of course—and the children are forced to do it."

Madison closed her eyes. She'd seen many abused children during her career, but not like this. *Is this what little kids, little sexual slaves, live with day in and day out?*

"My gut feeling," Darth continued, "is that the phrase *tip the piano man* will get you into a room like that—only because Lacy said it specifically, and she lived with a serial sadist-pedophile. Other sub-rooms have members who exchange files containing gruesome photos or films of children being abused, but nothing is done live. I'm ashamed to say it, but the United States is the largest consumer of child pornography and the entire child sex trade itself in the world. As long as that's the case, this is the battle we're going to fight. No matter what, once you get into that stuff, it's going to cost you a fortune—and I don't mean just in money. I mean, it's going to cost you your soul. This work has practically cost me mine." Darth paused a moment, then snapped his fingers. "Bingo, here we go. I'm in."

Madison leaned closer to see the screen more clearly. For a moment she couldn't make sense of the home page. It was actually delightful, like a magical playground with splashes of vivid color, a flamboyant carousel in the center, and the words *PattyzPlaypen* emblazoned on a banner across the top. Beneath that heading, Madison read *Preteen Porn/Click Here*, on the next line was *Child Porn/Click Here*, then, finally, were the words *Child Porn Hardcore/Click Here*.

Darth pointed at the screen. "See? Don't let anyone tell you they accidentally stumbled into a hardcore kiddie porn site. You can't get there by accident. You have to pay a subscription fee to even go this far. You know what you're getting into right away."

Darth highlighted *Child Porn* with his cursor and clicked on it. The home page was replaced by an old-fashioned list of chat rooms by title, a forum briefly cataloguing the subject matter of various conversations, and a register of usernames rolling up and down the side.

The usernames caught Madison's attention. Enraged her. Broke her heart.

Babybugger. Cherrypickr. Lilboylovr. And those names were the tame ones…

Who are *these people?*

She felt as if rose-colored glasses she hadn't even known she was wearing had suddenly been ripped away from her eyes, exposing her to a bloody and blistering truth about human beings she'd never even considered before. But how could that be?

After all, she specialized in traumatized children, and she'd always been fascinated by how people had become the way they were—especially perpetrators. Had a pedophile been molested as a child himself? Did a sadomasochist hurt himself or others because of a lack of control in his life? Was a serial rapist trying to regain the power he'd lost in his childhood?

Well, whatever. She no longer gave a damn how those people had become the way they were. They were evil, twisted, sick, and they had to be stopped. The damage they did to children was unfathomable.

As the list of usernames continued to roll down the screen and Madison continued to read them, she waited for that familiar, self-preserving desensitization to set in. But it didn't happen. Every descriptive username ripped her heart out.

How will we ever stop them? There are so many of them and so few of us…

Luke's hands rested lightly on her shoulders as he moved more closely behind her. "Are you all right?" he whispered.

Her eyes filled. "We can't find them, Luke. Look how many there are! And Darth says there are thousands of websites like this one…"

Darth held up his hand. "Stop talking! I understand

how overwhelming this is, Madison, but stay focused. The organization we've been looking into has roots in every country, but every national investigative agency involved has their own area of expertise. The work can be tedious, but it's always effective. When they brought down Shannon McCoole in Australia back in the day, they identified him in films and photos by a single freckle on his effing finger! Can you imagine how long that took?"

Madison's eyes widened. What kind of people were these investigators? What kind of determination and fortitude did they have to be so meticulous? She didn't have it…not even close.

"The organization we're investigating uses runaways, throwaways, or kids who're just plain desperate…or at least that's all we've found so far," Darth continued. "These kids are older, and they think they're invincible, so they come into cities with nowhere to go and nothing to eat, which makes them sitting ducks for pervs like these. They're easily kidnapped and trafficked all over the world."

Darth paused a moment, then added, "By the way, I don't like the word *trafficked*. Human trafficking, child sex trafficking—those are clean terms that allow people to be untouched by and impervious to the reality of what truly happens. Pure and simple, these are sex slaves, kids and adults, and like I said before, the United States is the largest consumer in the world.

"Sorry. I didn't mean to get off on that. Anyway, I've learned that pervs make stupid mistakes. They get overconfident and think cops can't catch them—but then we do. There may be no connection between the organization I've been watching and the one you've stumbled on, but that doesn't matter. We'll never know if we don't get in there. Someone's going to make a mistake, Madison. Wait for it."

Luke spoke up. "Darth, I'm just curious here. Have you ever worked a case where someone used actual blackmail as a means of gaining access to a child?"

"You mean, like Madison suggested for Ryan Neely? I've never worked one quite like that, but I've worked cases where parents sold their kids outright to pornographers or pimps or used them in their own personal organizations. Why?"

"Well, I'm wondering if someone, maybe like this Sage Winslow, convinced Marilyn Grisham that she had to give up her son. And as soon as the papers were signed, Bobby could've been adopted by a family that was also involved in this kiddie porn organization. Then he would've been in their films, and there would've been no way out for him. They might've even tried the same thing with Lacy."

Darth didn't answer. Instead, he held up his hand and gave a long whistle, then touched a name on the screen. A profile instantly appeared.

"Holy Mother of God," he whispered. "Do you guys believe in miracles?"

Madison leaned in closer to get a better look. There it was, plain as day.

PianoMan74.

Madison's legs went weak. "What does his profile say?" she asked, her voice shaking.

Darth chuckled. "Don't get excited. I'm sure it's fake. But let's take a look, just for fun. We'll see how creative he is." He clicked on the username's profile. "Creativity isn't his strong suit. Name is Bobby Oliver, lives in Chicago, computer programmer—"

"There's no DOB listed," Jerome interrupted quietly, "but his birth year could be 1974, if you go by his username. That would make him around forty-eight. Do you guys think Sebastian deWynter could be that old?"

"Yeah, maybe," Luke answered. "This guy also says he's divorced, no children. Do we know any of that about Sebastian deWynter?"

Darth picked up his cell phone, punched in a number, and put a finger to his lips. After a moment he spoke quietly. "Start checking the IP address for *PianoMan74.* I'm moving forward. Three names to watch for: Sage Winslow, Sebastian deWynter, and Ryan Neely. Yeah, you heard me right." He ended his call abruptly and placed his phone face down on the table. "Okay, let's see if I can engage this guy. He's in a chat room called L'il Orphan Annie."

As Darth began typing in a comment, Madison realized the detective was completely literate in "chat-speak," so he could talk to people who lived on computers. The communication ensued rapidly, and she had to translate to herself so she could follow it:

Kidbanger40: ?4u
PianoMan74:Wat?
Kidbanger40: My lil gurl needz piano lessns.
PianoMan74: How old?
Kidbanger40: Is 2 y/o too yng 2 strt?
PianoMan74: No.
Kidbanger40: Polite 2 tip the pianoman? LOL. So,
thnx.
PianoMan74: Sure.
When Darth's cell phone rang, he answered right

away and listened closely, nodding periodically. When the caller finished talking, Darth's response was terse and clipped. "Just keep at it. We didn't expect this to be easy."

Ending his call and setting the phone face down on the table once again, he shook his head in disgust. "They're running into barriers right and left. This guy's encryption is phenomenal, and his IP address is scrambled to hell and back. It's okay, though. We'll figure it out—we have one of the best hackers in the business. In the meantime, they're going to try the admins and see what feathers they can ruffle."

Suddenly, a private message box popped onto Darth's computer screen, and Madison caught her breath when she saw the message *9:45 p.m. PianoMan74 wants to private chat with you. Accept or decline?*

Darth gave a soft whistle. He moved forward and clicked *Accept.* When he leaned back in his chair, he folded his arms across his chest. "Okay, boys and girls, are we ready? Let's see what this miserable dirtbag wants with me."

****

Luke discovered he was holding his breath as he waited for the man to return to the chat, and concentrated on slowly releasing it. He dropped his hands from Madison's shoulders and took a step back. She needed to pay attention, study, analyze. The last thing he wanted to do now was crowd her space.

Darth spoke up. "Madison, would you go on Facebook and check out the pages of everyone you can think of, including Mercy Children's Home? Especially Sage Winslow. Luke's right. She may have played an active role in Bobby Grisham's quick adoption. Also, check out Ryan Neely and Quinn Davis. See if there's any connection on social media between the two of them."

"Sure." She moved away from her position behind him, returned to her chair, and sat back down. She fired her laptop back up. "Just give me a minute."

"Thanks. I'll let you know if I need you—and I probably will."

Luke's heart gave a nervous thud when Madison answered, "It's fine if you do. I promise I'm not a little lady who needs to be protected from the seedier side of life. I can handle it."

Darth chuckled. "I don't doubt that, but this isn't busy work. You know the names of these people better than I do. Sometimes people post stuff on Facebook that seems innocuous to everyone except that one person who knows what to look for. The same is true for Twitter, Instagram…" He paused and drummed his fingertips on the tabletop. "This guy is taking his sweet time getting back to me. He's doing his homework right now."

"What homework?" Luke asked.

"He's looking up everything he can find about me online. I have a heavy footprint for him to follow—he'll love it."

"Yeah?"

"Yeah, I'm a children's photographer. I have a high-dollar studio on Broadway, and my photos have been displayed all over the country. There's nothing sleazy about me. Even parents have written rave reviews online about my work and my treatment of their children. I'm much-loved. In my off hours, I teach English to Mexican toddlers, and I'm a Big Brother to two foster kids, one boy and one girl. I'm not picky."

Suddenly Luke felt sick. *What if…*

Chuckling, Darth nodded. "Good. You don't trust me. You shouldn't. We brought down two ICE agents a few years ago in Cambodia who were supposed to be working with a Cambodian child protection organization to stop American tourists from molesting Cambodian kids. Let's just say, those ICE guys weren't doing their jobs. Watch me closely. I don't mind."

Luke gave a weak grin and tried to relax.

Madison spoke up. "Mercy Children's Home seems to be all about donations, and that's it. Sage Winslow has a page that advertises her grant business, and Neely is just part of the Joseph Cannon and Associates, Inc. page, along with all the other attorneys. But Quinn Davis' personal page does have a link to Ryan Neely, specifically in reference to his work with fathers fighting custodial issues. That's kind of weird. Sebastian deWynter has a page that advertises his gig dates and locations, and it seems to be a place for him to touch base with his female groupies. The only Facebook page that's even remotely interesting is Katherine Walker's."

Jerome glanced at her. "Who?"

"The woman who adopted Bobby Grisham."

"Oh. What about her?"

"Maybe nothing, but if you go back through her photos, you'll see that she and her husband lived in a really old, dilapidated farmhouse on their property in early 2021. But in September of that same year, they must've come into some money, because now they have a beautiful new home on the same property."

"Any pictures of Bobby?" Darth asked.

"Not one. She has several dogs and lots of photos of them, but not a single picture of her newly adopted son."

Darth drummed his fingertips on the table. "Good catch, Madison. New money, but no kid. Nothing anywhere else?"

"Not really. I googled the address and found a map showing that the property is twelve acres with no businesses around it. I also learned the property has been in Mrs. Walker's family for three generations. Otherwise, nothing."

"Okay. Thanks, Madison."

When the chat box suddenly flashed on the screen, Darth held up his hand once again and gave that low whistle between his teeth.

"Here we go, boys and girls, here we go…"

Chapter Nineteen

Madison closed her laptop and returned to her spot behind Darth, leaning in to better see the small lettering. She clasped her hands together, held her breath, and began to read.

PianoMan74: Ur pix r good.

Kidbanger40: Yea? Thnx. Cheese pizza iz my spchlty.

"Cheese pizza?" Madison whispered.

Darth nodded and translated, "Cheese pizza. CP. Child pornography. *Child pornography is my specialty.* Don't let these journalists or so-called fact-checkers tell you that these creeps don't talk in code. They do. They have to." He chuckled. "How else could they communicate?"

The conversation continued.

PianoMan74: U don't post much?

Kidbanger40: Enuf.

PianoMan74: Not 4 me.

Kidbanger40: LOL

PianoMan74: Is 1 urs?

Kidbanger40: Kid?

PianoMan74: Yea.

Kidbanger40: Yea. 1 is mine. Foster.

Darth looked at Jerome and shook his head. "This guy is young and inexperienced, so I doubt he's the Piano Man we're looking for."

"Why do you say that?"

"Because he's asking me about a kid right out of the chute. That's stupid. I could be anybody."

"You *are* anybody, squid bait. Could he be using the Piano Man name to try to sound important?"

Darth looked doubtful. "Well, I guess… Oh wow. He's not wasting any time. Look at this."

PianoMan74: A/S/L

"What's that mean?" Madison asked.

"Age. Sex. Location. Let me see if I can get him to commit."

"Commit to what?"

"Something specific."

Kidbanger40: 2 y/o, gurl, can trvl

PianoMan74: Need 2 hear her play

Kidbanger40: Sure. U n Chicago?

PianoMan74: No. How mch $ 4 2 hrs?

Darth nodded, satisfied. "Now he's committing with money, but he doesn't want to tell me where he is. Let's see how he wants to do this."

Madison's stomach churned. It wasn't that she didn't realize this happened—she'd just never been so directly involved.

Apparently, Darth was surprised as well—and wary. "This guy either really believes he's anonymous and untouchable, or he's playing me to see how much I know about the phrase *tip the piano man.* He hasn't responded to that comment of mine at all. I'm going to tell him I want to watch."

Madison's lip curled with disgust.

Darth punched in a few letters with two fingers and waited. The man's response was swift.

PianoMan74: Sure. I like tht 2.

Darth nodded again. “Let’s see if he bites on live-streaming.”

Madison swallowed against the bile burning the back of her throat.

Kidbanger40: $ dpnds / more $ 4 live

PianoMan74: I cn do tht. Snd mor pics

Darth rubbed his eyes wearily. “Okay, guys, I’m going to take a risk here. I’m going to send a few kiddie porn pics from a law enforcement stash of photos and pray he’s never seen them before. I think he’s stupid enough for me to get away with this.”

“What if he isn’t?” Luke asked anxiously.

“Then I’ve blown it. But if I’m right and he’s inexperienced, I’ve drawn him out without using any new pics. I like that. I want to get him to ask for a date and a location.” Darth brought up a file list, highlighted three photos, and clicked *send*. “Cross your fingers.”

Kidbanger40: 3 pics cmng 2 u

PianoMan74: Thnx

Darth whistled softly and crossed his fingers. It wasn’t long before the man reappeared.

PianoMan74: Yr lil gurl?

Madison caught her breath. Here it was. What if Darth was wrong and this creep had seen these photos before?

Kidbanger40: No. My lil gurlz nu

PianoMan74: Me 1st?

Kidbanger40: Yea. Yu like?

PianoMan74: Yea. Whoz n these pics?

Kidbanger40: Jst a kid. U hav pics?

PianoMan74: Yea

Kidbanger40: Snd?

Darth spoke to no one in particular. “He’s going to

send photos, and I'd rather you guys didn't look at them. I'll see if they match any of your missing kids as soon as we can download."

Madison nodded. "You're the boss."

She walked to the refrigerator and leaned her forehead against the cool metal, closing her eyes.

Someone touched her shoulders gently. Luke turned her toward him. "I'm sorry you have to go through this."

She gave a feeble smile. "It's all part of the job, but I don't have to like it. And I never want to get used to it. When that happens, if it ever does, I'll close my doors."

"I understand."

Darth muttered something under his breath and punched a few keys on the keyboard.

"What's up?" Jerome asked.

"I don't know. He says he's gotta go for now, but he'll be back soon. I don't want to lose him. It's already ten thirty."

Madison was startled when Luke's cell phone rang. He took it from his shirt pocket, looked at the name on the screen, and frowned. "Julian Alvarado…" He put the phone to his ear and spoke softly. "Julian! Is everything okay?"

Madison heard Julian's voice but couldn't decipher his words, so she busied herself pouring more drinks and straightening papers on the table, keeping an eye on Luke's face. She became more concerned as his expression grew darker. Something was definitely up.

Her heart pounded.

She felt Jerome's questioning gaze on her, but she could only shrug. When Darth swore again, Jerome leaned in toward the computer and muttered something unintelligible.

Darth touched the screen. "There's a little boy in this picture. I need to make the image sharper if I can. Then we'll try to figure out where he's located. Do you have Lacy's photos handy, Jerome?"

"Sure do."

"See if you can spot anything in this room that matches with your pics."

"On it."

Darth cleared his throat. "Madison, can you help me here?"

She walked to the table and stared at the screen, trying to disassociate herself from the pain and terror so visible on this little boy's face. A young man stood beside the bed. Chiseled and blond, he was a perfect Aryan specimen. His body, shiny with oil, was slim but well-muscled, like that of a highly trained swimmer.

A heavy-duty chain was wrapped around his right hand.

There was no question about what he intended to do to his young victim, but the photo itself wasn't pornographic. She focused her attention on the background of the room.

A double bed with a metal headboard. A stained mattress, no sheets. No visible windows, a scarred hardwood floor. The little boy was handcuffed to the headboard.

"Are those blood stains on the mattress?"

"I don't know," Darth answered gruffly. "Maybe."

Her heart sank. *This could be anywhere.*

But Darth didn't give up. "Madison, you ever seen this little boy before?"

He enlarged the face of the terrified child, and she looked more closely. Silky brown hair, green eyes with long, luxuriant lashes, cherubic cheeks…a healthy little boy. *Fresh meat…*

She shook her head. "No, I'm sorry. I've never seen him before."

"That's all right. If you remember anything…tell me. I'm going back online now. Maybe our friend is there." He glanced at Luke. "Everything okay?"

Luke cleared his throat. "Houston," he answered in a perfect imitation of Jerome Scranton's West-Texas accent, "I think we have a problem."

Luke sat back down at the table and waited a moment before he spoke. "Remember Rafe Gamez? The kid who tried to break in here the other night?"

Madison frowned. "Of course."

"Well, Julian Alvarado said he just checked on him and his room is empty. He wondered if we've seen him."

"Why would we see him?" Jerome asked. "It's not like he would've come here for a visit."

"Julian said the clients in his center aren't allowed to leave the premises at all, so he was going to go through Rafe's stuff in a minute and try to get an idea of where he might've gone. He's just checking around, that's all. I told him to call me back if he needed any help."

"This guy's sure taking his time," Darth muttered. "I asked him if he had any more pictures, but he hasn't answered. Where'd he go?"

While they were waiting, Madison's mind returned to the terrified little boy in that squalid room. Even though the man with him wasn't Antonio Davila, it could've just as easily been. God only knew how many times he'd hurt a child in just this way…and filmed it.

Madison remembered exactly how Carlotta Martinez had described Antonio Davila.

I took one look into his eyes, and I knew he was the most dangerous man I'd ever meet in my life.

That was no exaggeration, she was sure. How many children had he hurt—or worse? And how much pleasure had he taken in it? More than she could comprehend, because control and power defined Antonio Davila. Without it, he was nothing.

This was the man with whom Piper had lived for nearly six years.

That little girl had to be aware of so much...so much they now desperately needed to know.

She had to get Piper to talk. And fast.

Luke's phone rang again. He answered right away, listened, then spoke firmly. "You stay where you are, Julian. We're leaving now." He listened again, then answered, "You don't need to do that. I'm bringing two detectives with me. Just wait."

He stood up and slid his phone into his shirt pocket. "We have to go."

Darth didn't hesitate. He pushed his chair away from the table. "What's up?"

"I'm not sure. Julian says he's gotten into Rafe's computer and we need to come now."

Madison's heart seemed to stop as the full impact of Luke's words settled in. "Should I go with you?"

"I don't think so," Darth answered. "In fact, I'd rather you stay here and keep an eye on Piper. Don't, under any circumstances, answer the door. And no matter what happens, don't go outside." He put his hoodie back on, closed his laptop, and slipped the four children's photographs into a concealed pocket inside the jacket. "I'm going to leave one of my guys in a squad car out front, just in case."

She managed a tired smile. "Thank you. Luke, may I speak with you a minute?"

"Sure. I'll meet you guys downstairs. We can take my truck."

When Darth and Jerome had left the room, Luke walked to Madison and looked down at her questioningly. "Is everything all right?"

"I wanted to tell you I've been wrong. I have to get Piper to talk right away. There's no telling how much she knows. So I'm going to start concentrating on that first thing in the morning. I'm sure she's sleeping."

"You should do the same."

"I will, but wake me when you get back, okay?"

Luke looked down at her with such wistful tenderness she could hardly breathe. As his dark gaze wandered over her lips, she couldn't ignore the question she read in his eyes. She began to tremble.

"Madison..." He caressed her name in his whisper. "Madison..."

She knew what he wanted, and she didn't hesitate. She didn't ponder, analyze, worry about how it looked or what he'd think. She closed her eyes, went on tiptoe, and tilted her head back. When his lips met hers, his kiss was featherlight and tentative, but she needed him to *want* her—the way a healthy man wanted a woman. She yearned for his touch, ached to feel him against her body—the immensity of her need terrified her. She took his face in her hands, drew him down to her, parted her lips, and pressed them softly, then more insistently, against his. As she tangled her fingers in his hair, he moaned and wrapped his arms around her. His heart pounded against her chest. She couldn't breathe.

Suddenly, Luke stepped backward and held her

away from him, his face flushed with passion and desire. "I'm sorry… Forgive me…"

"Please. Luke…"

"Madison, wait." His voice shook. "You're upset, and I won't take advantage of that. I want you. I want you more than you know. But not now. Not like this."

She took a ragged breath and stared at the floor, appalled at her own desire. She'd gone after him like something wild, something maniacal—and he'd rejected her. She turned away from him, humiliated and ashamed. "Of course, you're right. I think I lost my mind a little bit." She tossed a rueful grin over her shoulder. "It'll pass. I'll be okay in the morning."

He looked puzzled. "I didn't mean—"

She held up her hand so he wouldn't say anything else and spoke in a firm, distant voice. "Good night, Luke. Please forget this ever happened. It'll never happen again."

****

"Julian's rehab center is located on Southwest Military Drive," Darth said from the back seat of Luke's truck. "Just get on the freeway up here and head west. I was out there a few weeks ago, so I know where it is. By the way, don't panic if it looks like we're being followed. We are. I've got two SVU detectives right behind us."

Luke nodded, but his mind was elsewhere. He could still taste Madison's kiss on his lips, desperate and demanding; his heart still pounded in his throat. He'd been shocked to discover he wanted her with every fiber of his being—he hadn't realized it until he held her in his arms and felt her lips part eagerly beneath his own. Then, his body had responded to her need for him with breathtaking and overwhelming power, but he knew all she really yearned for in that instant was a normal, healthy connection with a man who wanted her just as much as she wanted him. The pulsating and fierce desire he felt for her had been so potent it was all he could do to remain standing. But he understood she was far too vulnerable in her heartbreak and pain to be capable of making such an important decision.

Luke gave a mental shake of his head. Here he was, the playboy-celebrity who didn't care about anyone, now wanting to be more important in one woman's life than anybody else in the world. The way she trembled at his touch had stolen his heart, yet he'd known immediately he couldn't have her until she wanted him for the right reason.

For the first time ever, Luke Callaghan wanted a woman because of *who* she was and what she stood for, not because of her creamy flesh and mysterious blue-green eyes. Madison Wagner was lovely, but he wanted her because of her huge heart, her deep ability to love, her astute intelligence, her innate understanding of partnership. Unlike Lacy, she'd never need him to complete her. She could be happy and fulfilled without him—but he wasn't at all certain he could say the same for himself.

All he could do now was pretend nothing had changed, like she hadn't just turned his world completely upside down. He had to be cool, as if the earth hadn't shifted beneath his feet. It would be the most difficult thing he'd ever done.

Darth's irritated voice interrupted Luke's thoughts. "Did you hear me, Luke? Take the next right!"

"Sorry," he muttered. "I was just thinking—" He made the right turn and slowed down as they entered the neighborhood.

"Julian's house is on the left here, next to the little church," Darth directed. "Follow his driveway all the way to the rear. That's the Affirmative Outreach Rehabilitation Center." After Luke had parked near the door, he added, "Follow my lead, you guys. I don't know what we're getting into, but my team is on this, so we'll be fine."

They clambered out of the truck just as Julian appeared at the entrance, holding the door open.

"Come in, Mr. Callaghan," Julian said quietly, not offering his hand to the group until after he'd locked the door behind them. "Are you two gentlemen police officers?"

"We are." Darth pulled his badge from inside his hoodie jacket pocket. "I'm Morgan Harris with SVU, and this here is my good friend, Jerome Scranton. He's retired homicide. I have two more SAPD officers outside and a couple of Texas Rangers on call. We're pretty well covered."

When Jerome reached for his badge, Julian shook his head. "Not necessary. Madison mentioned you sat on her board of directors when I met her the other day. If Luke and Madison vouch for you guys, that's good enough for me."

This unexpected compliment pleased Luke, but he couldn't help wondering if there were strings attached to it. After all, Julian was just a street preacher whose background was more than a little sketchy, and the company he kept was definitely problematic. For all Luke knew, Julian Alvarado could even be a part of this organization.

Then, out of the blue, he heard Madison's words

once again.

I think he's an extraordinary man.

If she thought Julian Alvarado was extraordinary, who was he to question the preacher's motives for anything? All he wanted was for her to think the same of him.

Julian handed Darth a sheet of paper Luke hadn't noticed he was holding until now. "This is a standard release form I have every patient sign when they enter this facility. It says I'm free to go through their belongings, listen to their phone conversations, read all their email, and examine their computers if they have them. I'm also free to kick them out if they break any rules, but I didn't kick Rafe out. He's just gone. I did a bed check about six thirty this evening, and he seemed fine. I did another check about ten thirty, and he was gone. So I went through his stuff, hoping to get a clue about where he went. I'm giving you this paperwork now so you'll understand how I came to find what I found."

Darth nodded politely, folded the paper without even looking at it, and slipped it into his hoodie pocket. He glanced at his watch. "It's just now eleven fifteen. How did he get out without you seeing him leave?"

Julian shrugged. "I'm here by myself tonight, but everything is locked up tight. I don't have a clue."

"What do we know about this Rafe Gamez?" Darth asked.

"He just turned seventeen, and he has no family. He's lived on the streets most of his life. That's it. Now, please. Follow me."

When Luke met Jerome's somber gaze, a sense of dread slowly settled over him like a canopy of ice. The affable lawman was no longer a slow-talking West-

Texas cowboy. He was an alert rattlesnake, primed to strike.

As they followed Julian through a waiting area and down the short hallway, Luke tried to take in his surroundings, looking for exits, doors, windows. The facility was very small, probably no more than ten beds, and beyond austere. No pictures adorned the walls of the waiting area, which contained only straight-backed chairs and a cheap coffee table. The floors were covered with stained linoleum, and there were no vending machines or snack boxes. The facility appeared neat and quiet. Luke knew from unfortunate experience that a junkie trying to get clean didn't really need more.

"Here we are." Julian inserted a master key into the door and opened it. He flipped on the overhead light and gave them a long, sober look. "Before I show you what I found, I need you to understand something. Addicts know about the dark web, and they know there's a special server they have to use to get there. Whenever something like this happens, the first thing I do is look to see if my patient has gone deep to make a drug connection, buy a weapon, or try to get money. All those things are easily found there. So when I discovered Rafe was gone, that's what I did. I made sure the webcam on his computer was closed before I got on it, and then I clicked his cursor key to see if I could get on the dark web. Ordinarily I would've been asked for a password, but this time I wasn't. A website came right up. Apparently, Rafe left so fast he didn't even log out."

Julian made his way to a small table and chair near an unmade twin bed. An open laptop was on the table. "Be careful you don't accidentally X out here—we don't know the password. He probably has it written down somewhere, but I don't know where that would be. At least, not yet."

Darth nodded and punched a single key on the computer. Julian took a step backward and motioned for Luke and Jerome to join him. As they all grouped around the computer, a merry-go-round containing pastel-colored animals began gliding across the screen. Luke stared in disbelief at the words dancing at the top of the monitor.

PianoMan74, welcome back. You last visited at 10:25 pm.

Darth gestured for them to follow him out of the room and into the hallway. He spoke in a whisper, even though they were completely alone, and Luke leaned in slightly to hear his words.

"Julian, I believe I was talking to this young man earlier this evening on *my* computer—I was talking to someone who called himself *PianoMan74*. He sent me a few kiddie porn photos and went offline at about ten thirty or so. He never came back, you called Luke, and here we are." He glanced at Jerome. "We need to get a search warrant before we can get in this computer."

"No, you don't," Julian objected. "I'm giving you permission. We don't have time—"

"Darth, we've got plenty of probable cause," Jerome interrupted. "Go ahead."

Darth shook his head and pulled out his cell phone. He was now all business. "I'm going to call someone to get a search warrant for Rafe's room and computer right now. You okay with that, Julian?"

"Of course."

"Thank you. And you have no idea how Rafe might've gotten out of this place or where he went?"

"No."

Darth spoke softly into his cell phone, flipped it closed, and put it back into his pocket. "The warrant will be here in a few. Let's get to work."

Darth pushed the bedroom door open and walked back inside. He pulled the chair away from the table, sat down at the computer, and tapped a single key.

Instantly the screen went blank, turned blue, and rolled line after line of mainframe language down the page. Luke's palms began to sweat as he recognized the nightmare of every computer user. *The blue screen of death...*

"What's happening?" he whispered.

Darth held up his hand, then pointed to the screen. After a few moments, the title of an unfamiliar website flashed across a magenta-hued heading box. *Little Lolita Land.* Down the center of the screen were topical headings. *Downloads. Safety. Privacy. Forums. Messages. Chat. Applications. VIP applications.* Usernames for people already online were listed in the chat box.

There was nothing amateur about this website.

Darth clicked on *Downloads* and waited, but not for long. Within seconds video and image files began to appear, and the titles of those files left nothing to the imagination. Julian turned away, sweaty and paste-white, but Darth leaned forward intently.

"Whoa!" he whispered, highlighting a file. "Would you look at this?"

Luke forced himself to look.

The file was labeled *Tx_Angel_Chld.jpg*.

Darth clicked it.

An image began to load slowly and appear on the

screen, bizarre and distorted. After a moment it focused into painfully sharp detail.

Her face was bony, her eyes dark and huge, and her mouth was open in a silent scream of terror. She was tiny, no more than five years old, and her naked body was covered with bruises. A tall, well-built man wearing only a leather thong and a black leather mask held the helpless child in the air by her hair.

Luke knew who the man was, and he knew the little girl.

Antonio Davila...and Piper Callaghan.

Chapter Twenty

Luke began to shake. For the first time in his life, he truly understood the meaning of the word *rage*. He understood the term *killer instinct*. He understood the descriptive phrase *blood in his eyes.*

Suddenly, just as Madison had predicted, he felt it all. He couldn't stop feeling it. It washed over him and sucked the breath from his lungs. It buckled his knees.

But before Luke could make a sound, the cursor began moving on its own. Darth swore beneath his breath. The computer screen went dark. Then, after a few moments, a comment box appeared, followed by a single sentence. *Are you ready to play?*

Darth answered immediately. *Yea.*

Words?

Darth sat very still, chewing on his bottom lip, and then, finally, shrugged. "It's now or never," he whispered.

He began to type. *Tip the piano man.*

After a few seconds, the comment box disappeared, and a small, dark room slowly came into focus. A narrow bed with a wrought-iron headboard, a stained mattress, and no sheets were in the center of the room. On the bottom left-hand corner of the screen was a time stamp, *11:32 p.m./12/19/2022.* On the bottom right-hand corner was the word *LIVE.* On the upper left-hand corner was the website title, *Little Lolita Land*, and on the bottom

299

right-hand corner were the words *Next Show at 3:30 a.m. Central Time.*

"Central time narrows it down for us a little, doesn't it?" Luke whispered shakily. "Location-wise, I mean?"

Before Darth could answer, a male voice began to speak from within the computer. "Good evening and welcome! You folks know the drill. Once you've paid in the usual way, preferably by bitcoin, you may begin to make your requests. You can private message Piano Man for prices, and he'll decide which requests to honor."

An unseen door off to the side of the screen opened, and a tall, muscular man, his body slick and shiny with oil, entered the room. Long, wavy black hair cascaded past his shoulders. A little girl, naked and fighting tears, clung to his hand.

"Oh holy God," Julian whispered.

Luke frowned. She seemed familiar to him, but he didn't know why. He was sure he'd never seen her before.

The man was a different story altogether.

Antonio Davila.

"Tonight, we are presenting you with a very special little someone," the voice continued. "Savannah is her name, and she's eight years old. Let's get started, folks. Begin your requests."

Savannah... Her full name rushed back to Luke on a tidal wave of nausea. *Savannah West.*

Jerome moved closer to Luke. "Is that our Savannah? The one in the photo Lacy left you?"

Luke didn't trust himself to speak. He managed a nod.

Davila picked up the little girl, placed her gently on the bed, and handcuffed her to the wrought-iron railing behind her. She turned her head to the side, as if to hide her face from the camera, but she didn't cry out. She just seemed resigned, accepting, sad.

"Where the hell is this?" Jerome whispered.

Darth spoke in a low voice. "This computer is remotely connected to another computer, but we don't know where it is…not yet. We can see them, but our webcam is closed, and they can't see us. What I want to know is, where's Rafe Gamez? How did he get out of here? Why did he leave so fast? He can't be the Piano Man these guys are talking about. He's way too young, too stupid. I think the *74* on his username must separate him from the Big Guy. These folks must think they're still talking to him. As crazy as it sounds, I don't think they realize he's gone."

Darth stood up and turned to Julian. "Listen, Rafe and Antonio Davila clearly know each other. I'm sure Davila put Rafe here—maybe because he knew Lacy came to you to protect Piper. I don't think Davila knew for sure where Piper's staying, so he covered all his bases, but by now he might know exactly where she is. We've got to get back to Dr. Wagner's place in case he does, but I'm leaving two detectives here to watch this building. Lock yourself in and don't leave under any circumstances. You're in danger until we've found Davila. Do you understand?"

"Yes, sir. You don't think *Davila* is Piano Man, do you?"

"No. Davila has a very bad, very long record. Too many people are watching him all the time. This Piano Man person has to be clean. You stay low 'til the dust settles, okay? I don't want to be worried about you, too."

"Don't waste your time on me—just find that little

girl. Lacy started this. You finish it."

Darth removed his cell phone from his pocket, hit one number, and spoke. "Do we have that search warrant for Rafe Gamez' room and computer yet?" He waited, then nodded. "Good. How about the one for Lacy Callaghan's house? Excellent. Come on and get started. Julian will let you in. We've only got about three hours to find this little girl. And whatever you do, don't let anyone in or out of this building."

****

Madison was exhausted, but she couldn't sleep. It was bad enough she didn't know what was going on at Julian's place, but now she'd thoughtlessly destroyed any chance she might've had to make Luke see her as anything other than a lunatic. When she saw him again, she had to apologize for behaving like a crazy woman.

If she saw him again.

Wearing sleep-inducing flannel pajamas and fuzzy slippers, she padded downstairs to the kitchen and put the kettle on for a cup of hot tea. Waiting was the one thing she'd never learned to do gracefully—even waiting for a light to change drove her crazy. She just couldn't waste time with a clear conscience—life was too short. The kettle began to whistle, and she removed it from the stove before it could wake up the whole house.

She was glad no one else had any problem sleeping. Whitney, the only true insomniac of the group, had actually been snoring when Madison checked on her and Tessa about an hour earlier. Piper's fever had finally broken, and she was still sound asleep while Sasha snoozed peacefully on her pillow beside Piper's bed. Madison hadn't heard a peep out of anyone, which made her feel uncharacteristically lonely and sorry for herself.

What's going on at Julian's?

Finally, sighing in resignation, she flipped off the light and carried her mug of steaming chamomile tea upstairs to her room.

She turned on her bedside lamp and climbed into bed, snuggling down into feather-soft pillows and a fluffy comforter. She closed her eyes and willed herself to sleep—until a faint squeak, like a lovesick cricket, shrieked through the silence.

She sat straight up, swung her legs over the side of the bed, and waited. When she didn't hear the noise again, she decided to check on Piper to be sure she hadn't awakened. After she opened her door, she looked up and down the faintly lit hallway. Everything was still. For a moment she considered taking her pistol with her but decided she didn't need to bring a 9mm handgun into a child's room—especially a child as unpredictable and easily frightened as Piper.

She used her phone as a flashlight as she made her way to Piper's room. She opened the door and shined the light up and down the walls, although it wasn't really necessary. Piper had three nightlights to ward off the bogeymen. Finally, Madison pulled a little chair to Piper's bed and sat down.

She's so peaceful when she sleeps...so beautiful...

In the few days since Piper had first come to Hope's Home, the angles in her face had begun to soften, her cheeks were flushed, and her hair actually seemed thicker. If she was changing so quickly on the outside, maybe a slight change on the inside would be possible as well.

Madison decided to take advantage of her own sleeplessness to try an experiment. She would attempt a little suggestion planting—her own variation of hypnotism. She'd found it effective in the past, so maybe it would work this time, too.

She leaned forward to speak softly near Piper's ear, but she didn't touch her.

"Sweetie, there are children who need your help, and you're the only one who can help them. You might think no one tried to help you, but that isn't true. Your mama tried very, very hard. If she ever told you anything at all, you can tell me. Or Mr. Callaghan, or Miss Patterson. Even if it doesn't make sense to you, angel, please tell us. We all want to help you, and you can trust us..."

Piper's eyes opened slowly; she seemed slightly confused. Madison moved backward and waited.

The little girl's face cleared.

"I'm sorry if I woke you, angel. I just heard something and wanted to check on you."

Piper closed her eyes again. Without thinking, Madison stroked the hair away from her forehead.

She caught her breath. *Oh dear, I shouldn't have touched her...*

But Piper sighed deeply, once again sound asleep.

When the security alarm blared on Madison's phone, she punched a button to silence it. Immediately, a low, threatening rumble came from Sasha's dog bed. For all her size, she'd moved from her sleeping position as silently as a stealthy feline and now crouched, deep in her pillow, eyes on Madison, alert and waiting.

The door opened slightly, and Whitney poked her head inside. "Oh, sorry...I didn't know you were in here. Did you hear that noise?"

Before Madison could respond, Sasha gave a wet

snarl and stiffened, every muscle taut with tension.

Whitney eased herself into the room, closed the door softly behind her, and held up her pistol. "Let's just stay with Piper, okay? The cops will be here in a minute."

Madison nodded and whispered a command to Sasha. "Settle, girl. Settle."

Sasha relaxed and submitted, but she never took her gaze off the door.

****

When Luke turned onto Madison's street, Darth's cell phone rang, and he answered instantly. "John? What's up?"

Darth listened for a moment, then whispered for Luke to drop his speed and turn off his headlights. Luke obeyed.

"Okay," Darth said into the phone, "we're coming up on the house now. Did anyone see you?"

Luke glanced in the rearview mirror in time to see Jerome reach for a pistol he had holstered beneath his jacket.

Darth listened a few more moments, then shook his head. "No, don't take him downtown. Just hold him until we get there. We're parking in the drive now."

But before Luke could turn off his engine and open his door, a police car turned into the driveway and parked behind him. There were no lights, no sirens, no warning. Two officers climbed out, guns drawn, and approached the driver's side of the truck.

Darth's voice was calm. "Don't say anything. I'll handle this. John has an intruder in the backyard. He says he thinks a car is waiting in the alley behind the house, maybe a couple of doors down, but I don't want to alert the driver if we can help it." He passed his badge to Luke.

"Hand this to the cops. Whatever happens, stay out of the way and keep quiet."

Nodding, Luke let his window down, thrust the badge toward an officer, and pointed at Darth, who immediately opened the truck door and stepped out. After a few moments of low-voiced conversation between the three men, Darth moved ahead. Luke and Jerome followed.

Darth opened the gate and eased himself behind the tall shrubbery next to the house, the others close behind him. After just a few steps, Darth peered around the corner, then removed his gun from its holster and cocked it. Two men were clearly illuminated in the moonlight, one holding a pistol on the other. Darth stepped away from the shrubbery and out into the open backyard, holding his own gun in both hands as he walked toward them, followed by Jerome and the other officers.

Following Darth's instructions, Luke held back. These cops didn't need him getting in the way. He didn't know if this intruder had been trying to enter the house— or if he'd already finished his business and was leaving. But no matter which it was, Luke intended to get upstairs to be certain Madison and the children were all right.

Luke keyed in the code Madison had given him a couple of days earlier and entered the house through the back door. He stomped up the stairs to make as much noise as he could.

"It's Luke," he called out as soon as he reached the second-floor landing. "Where are you guys? Everyone okay?"

Whitney poked her head out of Piper's room. "Get in here! I was going to turn Sasha loose. What's happening?"

Luke shrugged as he stepped into the bedroom. "Not sure. The cops have an intruder cornered in the backyard." He looked around the room until he spotted Madison sitting quietly in a child's chair beside Piper's bed. He moved toward them casually, careful not to further alarm Piper, who sucked her thumb furiously and watched him with wide eyes. Sasha gave a soft warning growl.

Luke ignored the dog and knelt beside the bed. "Are you girls all right?"

Madison nodded. "We're just fine. Aren't we, Piper?"

Piper's chin quivered.

Taking every ounce of self-control he had, Luke managed not to reach for the child. He didn't touch her. He just willed her to trust him. "Everything's fine now, Piper. Do you hear the door opening downstairs? Those are police, and they're with us. They're not going to hurt you, I promise."

Piper loosened her grip on Madison's hand.

Luke heard footsteps thudding on the stairs and quickly stood up. "I'm going to get them all into your room, Madison. I don't want them coming in here. We'll wait for you there."

She seemed unable to look him in the eye as she mumbled, "Okay. Go."

"I need to check on the other children," Whitney said quietly. "Will you be all right here, Madison? Do you need me to stay?"

"Of course not." She patted Piper's hand. "We'll be just fine."

****

Darth shoved a disheveled young man into

Madison's room, followed by Jerome and a police officer Luke didn't recognize. Darth closed the door.

"Everyone okay?" he asked.

"Everyone's fine," Luke answered. "Where are the other officers?"

"I told them we'd handle this. I think you know this guy?"

Luke gave the kid a dirty look and nodded.

Rafe Gamez smirked.

Luke was going to speak—he had plenty to say—but Darth's warning expression froze him into immediate silence.

"Slim, would you guard the door? Thanks." Darth turned his attention to the kid. "We can arrest you right now, but I'd rather talk to you. Why are you here?"

Rafe lifted an insolent eyebrow.

Darth pushed him toward the conference table and fished through a pocket inside his hoodie. He pulled out a small metal card. "Sit down. I'm sorry you're not interested in cooperating, but I'm going to read you your rights anyway—"

"I know 'em."

"You have the right to remain silent. Anything you say can and will be held against you in a court of law…"

As Darth finished Mirandizing the kid in that cold, bored voice, the magnitude of who Rafe Gamez actually was and what he'd done exploded into Luke's consciousness. Whatever evil game these people were playing with defenseless little children, this kid was a part of it. Maybe even an instigator puffed up by just a scrap of power…

Darth's voice broke into Luke's thoughts. "Do you understand the rights I've just read to you? With these rights in mind, do you wish to speak to me?"

"No."

That did it. Luke saw red. He jammed his fists into his jacket pockets and completely forgot Darth's warning to stay quiet. "Who are you? Who sent you here? What do you want with my little girl?"

The kid curled his lip—Luke guessed in a desperate attempt at bravado—but he failed. He clasped his hands together on the tabletop, but he couldn't hide their violent shaking. Shuddering, he scratched an armpit. Perspiration dribbled down his forehead and disappeared into an eyebrow. He looked miserable and smelled worse. "I don't know nothin'."

Darth leaned across the table. "Now, you listen to me. I've seen your computer. I know what you are. You diddle babies. You're a creep and a coward, but coming here was pretty brave, regardless. This place is armed with a silent alarm, and you knew that. There's a dog here that wants to kill you, and you knew that, too. You're so scared you stink. So you need to tell me who ordered you to come here from Julian's place, how you got here, and why you followed those orders. You don't have the stones to do something like this on your own."

Snot streamed from the kid's nose. "I don't diddle babies," he muttered.

Luke stepped closer to the table, watching curiously as more perspiration beaded up on the kid's forehead and ran down the sides of his face, vanishing into oily strands of dirty dark hair. He felt detached, like he was floating outside his own body, but he recognized the terrible suffering Rafe Gamez was going to experience very soon.

Darth seemed to know, too, but apparently it didn't

bother him a bit. "You're in trouble, pal. Your nose is gonna run, and that itching's gonna get worse. A lot worse. You're gonna double over with cramps real soon. If you don't start talking, we're gonna take you downtown, and no one there is gonna care how bad you need a fix. We'll charge you with attempted kidnapping, breaking and entering, child endangerment, possession of an illegal firearm—hell, possession of a roll of toilet paper—help me here, Scranton! Can you think of anything else?"

The kid wiped sweat from his brow with the palm of his hand and rubbed it against his filthy jeans. He crossed and uncrossed his legs, now clearly going into withdrawal. "Who's Scranton?"

"He's an old cop, and he's got nasty ideas about how things should go down with baby diddlers. Understand what I mean by that?"

Rafe shook his head.

"Well, he really, really hates people who hurt kids. I mean, he *hates* them. I figure you're one of those people."

"I don't hurt kids…" He hunched over the table. The room reeked of sweat and terror.

Luke spoke up. "I'm going to leave Mr. Big Shot here with you guys for a while, okay? I'm sure he's got a lot to tell you, and I don't want to get in the way."

As Darth and Jerome walked toward the table, nodding, Rafe eyed them warily. Luke didn't know how much of the kid's discomfort was withdrawal and how much was fear, but he almost felt sorry for him.

Almost.

The police officer guarding the door opened it and moved aside. Luke stepped into the hallway.

****

Madison returned to the small chair beside Piper's bed. "May I sit down, angel?"

Piper pulled the comforter away from her face. Her eyes remained squeezed shut, but Madison knew she was aware of everything going on around her. She tried to get comfortable in the child's chair and folded her hands in her lap.

God, please give me words…the right words…

"Angel, I want you to know a little bit about those police officers Mr. Luke was talking about. They're here to keep us all safe. Not just you, but all of us. They're on your side, baby girl. And they need our help."

Madison paused, waiting to see if Piper would respond at all, but the child didn't move an eyelash. She hardly breathed.

"I know you're listening to me, Piper, so I want to tell you just a couple of things. You don't need to answer me…I understand. But I want you to know you're a very good girl and you've never done a single bad thing in your whole life. Not one thing. You've had bad people around you sometimes, and they've done bad things to you, but *you're not bad*, and none of this is your fault. I hope you understand that. *None of this is your fault.* Now, remember when I told you that I know you can talk like a real big girl and I'll listen to anything you want to talk about?"

Madison paused again, waiting. Piper didn't move, but Madison sensed her intense concentration. She was tuned in to every word.

"I meant that, Piper, and we're going to do everything we can to help you. But we need *your* help, too. There are other little kids like you, but we don't

311

know where they are. If you can tell us anything at all about where they might be…you'd be a superhero. Would you like that?"

Piper's eyes bored into Madison's face.

She kept talking in a casual, easy tone. "If anyone made you keep a secret and told you not to tell anybody, not even Tia Carly, you don't have to be quiet anymore. Secrets like that are very bad, angel. They're very dangerous. You can tell me anything you want, because no one's going to hurt you now."

A single tear slid down Piper's cheek. She reached for Madison's hand with little fingers as cold as ice.

Madison had an idea that might just work. She could throw out a name, any name…

"Do you know a man named Ryan Neely?"

Piper shook her head.

"How about Rafe Gamez?"

Now she looked a little irritated and shook her head again.

"Do you know someone named Tony Davila?"

Piper's body went rigid. Her eyes bugged. She went limp.

And then she wet the bed.

Chapter Twenty-One

Oh my God, what have I done?

Oblivious to the consequences, Madison instinctively gathered Piper in her arms and held her close, whispered loving apologies in her ear, and rocked her back and forth as tears streamed down her own cheeks. How could she have been so stupid? She'd just made a mistake a first-year psych student might make, not a full-fledged psychologist in private practice for the last several years. She'd wanted an answer so badly, something they could run with...

Then she realized Piper's arms had tightened around her neck, and the terrified child was patting her, comforting her like a little mama. Madison pulled back and gazed deeply into Piper's eyes, relieved to see the fear was dissipating. She kissed the soft cheek.

"I shouldn't have done that, Piper. I was wrong."

Piper put her hand over Madison's lips and whispered just one word. *"Barn."*

Before Madison could respond, the door opened and Whitney peered inside. "Luke's out here, and he says the guys need you, sweetie. It's important."

Piper's arms tightened around her neck.

"I'll be right next door, my love," Madison whispered, "and I'll be back soon. Can Miss Patterson stay with you?"

Piper shook her head, whimpering.

Whitney stepped into the bedroom and closed the door behind her. She tiptoed to the bed and knelt beside Madison. "I've got a really cool idea, precious. How about if we draw some pictures together? It's time to start making Christmas stuff, so maybe we could do that until you get sleepy again." She patted Piper's back with a feather touch. "I can't believe it with all the racket we made, but the other kids are still asleep, so it would be just you and me. Would you like to do that?"

Madison felt incredibly stupid. Art therapy. A perfect way for children to communicate when they couldn't or didn't want to…

But Piper's arms tightened into a stranglehold around Madison's neck.

Madison turned her head slightly so she could see Whitney's face and mouthed *barn*. Whitney frowned, then nodded rapidly.

"What do you think, Piper?" Madison asked softly. "I need to leave for just a minute. I'll be right next door."

Whitney touched Madison's shoulder. "Piper's a real big girl, and she understands how important this is. You go. I'll stay here. We'll be fine."

Luke pushed his chair away from the cluttered table and stood up as soon as Madison entered. He crossed the room to take her hand. "Sorry to bother you, but Rafe won't talk to anyone but you," he whispered. "And Darth says we need you."

Madison stood still and stared at the young man in disbelief. He met her eyes miserably, then looked down at his hands folded on top of the table. She could feel his shame and embarrassment.

She needed a moment to gather her wits. "Do you guys mind if I get out of my pajamas? It won't take but a minute."

"Of course not," Jerome answered, "but hurry. We don't have much time."

"I'll be right out."

In her bathroom, she dressed in a pair of jeans and a warm sweatshirt, her thoughts running around in her brain like frightened mice in a maze.

Where is the barn Piper mentioned? Who's in it? Is it even real?

Why is Rafe Gamez here? Who sent him? How did he get out of the rehab center?

Someone is giving him orders... Who? Tony Davila? Julian Alvarado? Quinn Davis?

Madison shook her head as she stared at her reflection in the bathroom mirror. It was useless. She looked frazzled and exhausted. She returned to the group, sat at the table, and fixed her probing gaze on Rafe Gamez.

Seeing him up close like this, so still and frightened, gave Madison a fresh view of this man-child. He was so terrified she could smell him from across the table; he emitted a rancid odor like old urine. His shoulder-length black hair, parted in the center and wet with oil and sweat, stuck to his head. His gray sweats, soiled and stinking, reeked of stale tobacco.

Well, he was in the midst of trying to kick dope, and she'd seen enough of that to know it wasn't a pretty sight. The stench made sense—he was heroin sick—but why had he even thought he had the physical strength to kidnap a child? Why not wait until he was stronger and actually stood a chance of succeeding?

Someone had scared him within an inch of his life; she was sure of it. But *who*?

"Why do you want to talk to me?" she asked finally. "I can't do anything for you."

His gaze slid away from her.

She decided to be blunt. "Piper told me there was a barn. Do you know what she meant by that?"

"Piper can't talk!"

"Really? That's interesting. Why would you say that?"

Darth moved to a spot behind Rafe's chair and dropped his hands lightly onto the kid's broad shoulders. Rafe's face contorted with fear when the detective leaned down and whispered something in his ear. The silence stretched.

"Someone lied to you," Madison said finally. "Piper talks just fine."

Darth pushed an open laptop toward Rafe. "I'm done playing around with you, kid. We know this computer is yours. Julian Alvarado gave it to us this evening. You left so fast you didn't even log out. Truth is, you're really stupid."

Rafe went white. "You can't get into my computer! I know my rights!"

"You have no rights, kid. You signed them away when you entered Mr. Alvarado's premises. You gave everything to Mr. Alvarado, and Mr. Alvarado gave everything to me. You know exactly what we're going to look at on this computer, don't you? Madison, would you come over here, please?"

Madison joined him and held on to the back of Rafe's chair with an iron grip, terrified of what she was going to see.

Darth's breath tickled her ear when he leaned down and whispered, "Did Piper actually say *barn*?"

She nodded.

"Perfect." He barked at Rafe, "Click on that file!"

Rafe's fingers trembled so badly she couldn't see how he could click on anything. His face was so sweaty-pale she thought he might upchuck on the table. Suddenly, he dropped his hands in his lap.

"No. I won't."

Darth squeezed his shoulder. "Yes. You will."

Madison looked at the screen, trying to decipher the file name.

"*Tx_Angel_Chld*...Texas Angel Child? What *is* this, Rafe?"

He didn't answer.

Darth touched the file with his finger and waited until the photo of Antonio Davila and Piper had completely downloaded. Madison stared at it in disbelief, fighting a surge of nausea as she remembered Piper's outburst of terror at the mere mention of Davila's name.

She looked at Darth with tears in her eyes. "This explains so much."

"I thought it might. That's why I wanted you to see it. This is probably the tip of the iceberg. You know this isn't the only one we're going to find."

Holding up her hand, she nodded and walked to the other side of the table. She leaned in toward Rafe. "Do you know who that child is?"

His head shot straight up. "No, ma'am."

"Yet you came here to kidnap her? That's Piper Callaghan."

Rafe looked bewildered. "So?"

"Do you know who the man in that film is?"

"Tony Davila."

Madison pointed at Luke. "Do you remember this man? You know who he is?"

"No."

"Sure, you do. That's Piper's daddy. He could kill you and get away with it."

Rafe shrugged.

Luke's voice was dangerously soft. "Do you *want* someone to kill you?"

Again, a shrug.

"I'll be happy to do that for you."

And then, in a bizarre moment that made no sense, the kid looked up and grinned.

In one fluid, synchronized movement, Jerome kicked Rafe's chair and Darth jerked him straight up and out of it, then dropped him on the floor. Rafe scrambled to his feet, fists clenched, swaying as he attempted an awkward fighting stance. His pale face was oily with sweat. Darth and Jerome wore pitying smiles on their faces as Luke slowly arose to his feet.

"Don't, Luke! He's sick!" Madison's voice cracked. "Rafe, you're going to talk to us, aren't you?"

Darth stared at her for a moment, clearly a little disconcerted by her sympathy. He moved to Rafe's laptop, sat in his chair, and tapped a key on the bottom left-hand corner of the keyboard. He gestured for Madison to join him once more. She walked swiftly to his side and gazed down at the computer, unsure at first of what she was actually looking at.

When it finally registered, her fury was as intense and all-consuming as an uncontrolled prairie fire. She didn't know what to do with so much rage. She had to find a way to detach herself—she would be useless otherwise. She couldn't think of these children as real people. If she did, she'd lose her mind.

But she couldn't tear her gaze from the screen. A little girl, lying on a stained mattress, was handcuffed to a wrought-iron headboard in the middle of a small, dark room. Even though the child's face was turned away from the camera, Madison could feel her sadness, her resignation, like she knew it was useless to fight.

Just as Rafe obviously knows now...

What kind of kidnapper was he anyway? He tried to act like a belligerent rebel, but he obeyed orders like a well-trained canine. He didn't fight back when he was hauled into a house by cops and ridiculed by a woman he didn't even know. Not only that, but he seemed almost *relieved* they'd caught him and stopped him from doing whatever he'd been sent to do...

Suddenly, with crystal clarity, she understood his terror, the scars she'd seen on his wrists, his blind obedience, and his acceptance of punishment. Even his use of the name *PianoMan74* was probably an attempt to impersonate someone with immense power...possibly power over him.

As Madison continued to stare at the screen, the little girl slowly turned her face toward the camera. There was something vaguely familiar about her, something that tickled at the edges of Madison's memory. And then she knew.

She grabbed Darth's shoulder. "That's Savannah West, isn't it?"

"I don't know—"

"I wondered about that earlier," Jerome interrupted. "The man said her name is Savannah, which is kind of an unusual name, and she's eight years old. It has to be her."

But before Madison could even react, she spotted a time-stamp in the bottom left-hand corner of the screen, *1:02 a.m./12/20/2022.* The word *LIVE* barely registered in her brain, but the words *Next Show at 3:30 a.m. Central Time* jumped out at her and ran like a permanent recording over and over in her mind.

Next show... Next show... Next show.

Oh, sweet baby Jesus, we have to find her...

Suddenly, an invisible man's voice broke the tension. "The requests are coming in fast. I have to tell you—some of them are really mind-boggling. It's going to be a good night for some of us—"

Madison ripped herself away from the screen. Moving quickly to Rafe's side, she took his hands in hers and spoke in a gentle but urgent voice. "Rafe, listen to me. I think I understand now, and I can help you. Tell me the truth. Don't be afraid. How long have you known these people? Have they hurt you?"

He glared at her. "Nobody hurts me."

She looked closely at his wrist and gently traced the scar that wrapped around it. "You were kept in handcuffs for a long time, weren't you?"

"No."

"No handcuffs?"

"No."

Jerome jerked Rafe's arm toward him and looked closely at his wrist. "Technically, he's telling the truth. This is a serious ligature burn scar. It's not from handcuffs."

Rafe pulled away.

"Lift your shirt up," Jerome said suddenly.

"No."

Madison spoke quietly. "It's all right, Jerome. Rafe,

I don't think you want to hurt anyone. But you feel like you have to because…well, where will you go if you don't? These people have been your family for a long time, haven't they?"

"I don't know what you're talking about. There's money on the street for Piper Callaghan; that's all I know. So I came for her."

"I don't believe you. This is what I think. Until now, you've been forced to do whatever they wanted you to do. Until now, none of this has been your fault. But from here on out, anything you do is *your choice*. You're a strong young man. You can do the right thing. You can stop this. In fact, you're the only one who can. *You* can stop it. *You* can talk to us. *You* can save the little girl locked in that room because you know what's going to happen to her. *You* can keep our Piper from falling into their hands. But if you choose not to help us, we won't help you. No one will. You'll pay the penalty, and your so-called family won't care. It's entirely up to you. You have all the power, Rafe. Right now, they have none."

He met her gaze with narrowed eyes, but she stared back, unintimidated and unimpressed. Then, slowly, he took a deep breath, lifted his chin, straightened his shoulders, and sat back down at the table. He was ill, but he seemed determined to overcome it. Madison watched in astonishment as he appeared to come into his own right before her eyes.

She understood. She'd given him *choices*, and that had probably never happened before. She'd empowered him, and he responded like the man she'd hoped he could be.

She closed her eyes and said a little prayer that came from the depths of her soul.

Oh dear Lord, let me be right. Please don't let this be a mistake...

****

Cold and detached, Luke observed the scene playing out in front of him. Madison had somehow tapped into this boy's story, but he didn't care. He didn't feel anything except raw hatred.

When Jerome spoke up, Luke could tell he was unmoved as well. He stepped closer to Rafe. "Who's Piano Man?"

"I don't know."

"Why do you call yourself *PianoMan74?*"

Rafe dabbed at the beads of sweat on his forehead with the back of his hand. He sniffled. "I don't. Somebody else set that up. I just monitor the boards."

"Who's *somebody else?*"

He sniffed again. "I don't know."

"Why did you answer Darth with that request for a private chat?"

"He said he wanted piano lessons for his little girl. I thought it was weird. It's my job to answer stuff like that."

Jerome's lip curled. "Your job?" he asked sarcastically. "You have a job?"

"Yeah."

In a flash, Jerome changed the subject. "Who sent you here tonight? Who let you out of the center? We know this wasn't your idea."

"I just told you—I don't know! After Lacy's funeral, Tony told me to get ready to go into rehab at Julian's place. So I did. Yesterday I moved in, and Tony told me to wait for his call. So I did. Then he called me tonight and told me I could get out through the back door at the center, so I should leave and get in a car waiting for me in the alley behind the rehab. So I did. He told me to get the kid out of here. I guess I didn't do that so good."

Luke's fists clenched. "The kid?"

Rafe flinched. "I mean, Tony told me to come here and get Piper."

"How did Tony know she was here?" Madison asked suddenly. "No one knew except us."

"I think some doctor…"

Madison gasped. Luke understood immediately. Dr. Weinstein had seen Piper just yesterday. He'd know where she was and maybe even where she was sleeping. He'd definitely know she wasn't talking.

Luke challenged Rafe. "Dr. Weinstein called Tony? I hardly think they're in the same social register."

"I don't know anything about social registers, mister. All's I know is this doctor told someone the little girl was here and she couldn't talk. I guess that someone told Tony, and Tony sent me here. I didn't want to come because I already tried once and I'm scared of dogs, but Tony never listens to me. He don't listen to nobody."

"Did Tony send you here the first time?" Madison asked.

"Yeah, but he didn't know anything for sure back then. He was just scoping out this place because he thought she might be here."

Jerome scowled. "So now you're supposed to take Piper to Tony. Where's Tony? And how are you supposed to get her there? You can't just carry her down the street."

"There's a car waiting for me in the alley behind this house—and I know he's getting nervous because I've been gone so long. They weren't worried about Piper making any noise because she can't talk."

Jerome grabbed his arm. "Get this straight, squid bait. Piper talks."

Darth cleared his throat in warning. "Was it Tony's idea for you to go to rehab at Julian's place?"

"Yeah."

"Why?"

Rafe sniffled again. "I don't know. But he knew Julian was after me to get clean, so he might've used that to get me out of his hair. Anyway, he told me to go there and get religion and sit tight. So that's what I did."

"Did you know Julian wanted to help Lacy hide Piper there?" Jerome asked.

"No. I don't know anything about Lacy."

Luke spoke up. "Do you know if Tony killed Lacy?"

"No. Probably. Maybe."

Luke was silent a moment. "If he did, would he have filmed it?"

"Sure, if he could. But if he did, it's already online. You'll never find it."

Darth stepped in. "Why don't we go down to the station and you give us a written statement? Since you're being so helpful and all, I think I can help you, too."

"You can't help me. Besides, they'll kill me if I do that."

"Then tell me this, kid. Is Savannah West in that room?"

Rafe was silent.

Jerome took up the slack. "Look, kid. We've already got you for kiddie porn—you're going down for that no matter what. You give us a written statement telling everything you know, and we might can work a deal for you. So let's try this again. Is Savannah West in that room?"

Sweat rolled down the side of the kid's face. "I think so." His voice cracked. He cleared his throat and tried again. "Maybe."

"And where is that room?"

"I swear, I don't know." Rafe looked around the table pleadingly. "You guys, I'm really sick—please help me…"

Luke's head pounded with rage because he was sure the kid wasn't telling everything he knew. But then, suddenly, he felt a flutter of empathy, as if he'd reached down and touched his own core. All the horrific experiences in his life fell into place and made sense.

If I'd been a weaker kid, if I hadn't kicked the dope, if I hadn't found something I loved to do…I could've been Rafe Gamez. There, but for the Grace of God, go I…

"Don't be afraid," he said aloud. "We can protect you. Haven't you prayed that someone would help you? I did. Remember this, kid. Learning to be a man is a continuing education program. It'll take your whole life, but you can start now. Now, for the last time, is that little Savannah West?"

****

Madison fought fatigue and spoke softly. "Piper said something about a barn, Rafe. Is that little girl in a barn?"

He shrugged. "I don't know. The driver's the only person who knows for sure."

"So you were supposed to take Piper out to that car and just hand her over?"

"Sorta. I have to go, too."

Jerome's lazy drawl was unconcerned but decisive. "Well, now. I just don't see how that's going to work, do you? You're not taking Piper out of this house."

The room fell silent. Despair set in. Piper was too fragile to be used for bait.

The thought popped into her head almost like a message from God, and Madison spoke up. "I've got an idea."

Luke got to his feet gingerly and massaged the small of his back. He cocked a questioning eyebrow.

Darth looked at her hopefully.

Her heart sped up. "You're going to think I'm crazy, but hear me out. I'm five feet tall, and I weigh ninety-four pounds. That's clearly bigger than your average six-year-old, but if you wrap me in a blanket and throw me in the back seat, no one would know it. They think Piper doesn't talk, remember? So I don't have to say a word. And Rafe's big enough to carry me out without it looking too weird."

Luke stared at her. "Absolutely not!"

"I don't remember asking your permission."

"No way," Darth stated.

"Wait just a minute," Jerome objected. "This could work. I know Madison. I know how she thinks. Rafe, what was the plan? You're just supposed to take Piper to Tony, right?"

"Yeah. Tony said if he had two little girls, it would be a great show and a surprise for everyone watching. But if it didn't work out and it was only Savannah, that'd be okay, too. But I don't know where they are."

Darth took a step forward. "If you're lying—"

"I'm not! I. Don't. Know."

Madison held up her hand like a traffic cop. "Stop! Think about it, you guys. You could follow us. Grab the driver and Rafe once they get there, then bust into the room without me. It would work. You know it would."

"It's too dangerous," Darth objected. "We don't use civilians as bait—"

"You do, too," she interrupted. "You wire civilians, don't you? But it really doesn't matter. Darth, you're the only one in this room who actually works for somebody. Jerome and I do our own thing. So just turn your back on us. Don't listen. Don't be a part of this plan. Because, believe me—you're not going to stop me."

He looked down on her, a half smile on his face. "Okay, got it. I won't see you leave this house." He turned to Rafe. "I need to get a written statement from you, but I don't have time right now. I've recorded everything on my phone, and that'll have to do. We'll follow you guys to Tony."

"You can't! He'll kill me—"

Darth's face went stony. "I can. Or I'll kill you myself."

"You don't know where they're going," Luke protested. "That area's so isolated—they'll spot a tail five miles back. And we don't know this kid. He could change his mind and hurt Madison. Maybe even kill her."

But Madison wasn't having any. Her voice was calm as she methodically shot down each argument. "You could tail us from a pretty good distance. I'll be okay." She patted Rafe's shoulder absently. "Rafe's not going to kill me."

Luke looked at her and knew she wasn't going to budge. This was her playing field, her life, her purpose. Not only would it be impossible for him to change her mind—he had no right to even try.

He moved close to her and took her face in his

hands. "You be careful," he whispered. "Don't do anything stupid."

She covered his hands with her own. "Don't worry. I'll be fine."

"Madison, I—"

Just then, a faint knock sounded on the door, and Whitney poked her head inside. "Excuse me," she said softly. "Piper's drawn a couple of pictures that I think you might find interesting. Do you guys want to see them?"

Chapter Twenty-Two

Burning with embarrassment, Madison dropped Luke's hands and stepped away from him. "Whitney, where's Piper? She shouldn't be alone—"

Whitney lifted an eyebrow. "She's asleep with Sasha. I just want to give you these pictures."

"We don't have time to look at a little kid's art project," Darth began, then backed up in record speed when Madison shot him a look. "Of course, I'm happy to take the time…"

"This 'little kid's art project' could help," she said quietly. "Piper doesn't like to talk, but she might draw."

"I knew that. I'm sorry."

"It's all right. Show me, Whitney."

Whitney closed the door softly behind her, walked to Madison's side, and handed her the first page. "I asked her to draw whatever she loved most in the world so we could put it on a Christmas card, and she drew Sasha. I doubt there's symbolism here."

Madison saw nothing revealing, either, and passed it back. "What else?"

"I've never seen anything like this before, so I thought I'd better show you. She just seemed to draw it out of nowhere."

She handed another sheet of paper to Madison, who looked closely at the drawing and frowned. What she saw made no sense.

Three children. Little stick figures without faces. No arms, no hands...

A barn. An enormous door, an even bigger padlock, a roof-high pitchfork...

Another stick figure...a man. Solitary, huge, threatening. Reaching toward the children, fingers curled like talons. Gaping mouth, sharp teeth. Colossal erection crayoned in red...

Madison handed the drawing to Darth, who studied it for a moment. "Is this literal?" he whispered. "I don't know—"

"Ordinarily, I'd say we need to study this because children often use symbols. But I have a feeling some of this could be literal. She said the word *barn*, and she's drawn a barn. See the big pitchfork? She could be trying to tell us the pitchfork was used in something bad, or simply that there are farm utensils around the barn. See the smaller figures without faces? No mouths, no eyes...these are children. She's saying they're imprisoned, invisible, without voices."

"Why no arms or hands?"

"I'm not sure. If it's literal, they're probably tied or cuffed behind their backs. If it's symbolic, she's telling us the children are helpless. They can't defend themselves."

A question was clear in Darth's eyes, but it appeared he was too much a gentleman to ask.

After a moment, Madison took pity on him. "The erection in red signifies power, physical cruelty, strength—this man is dangerous. Maybe it's Tony Davila, controlling the children through terror and dominance."

"In a barn?"

"Yes, in a barn."

"Excuse me," Whitney interrupted softly. "I have one more picture."

She shoved the last drawing into Madison's hands and turned away. As Madison looked at it closely, everything in the room seemed to come to a screeching halt.

"What?" Luke asked.

Fingers trembling, she placed the paper on the table.

In childish scribbling, Piper had sketched an old house that took up half the page. Off to one side of the house were two headstones enclosed by a flimsy fence…maybe chicken wire. Like a private family graveyard. A smaller building was set farther back, on the other side of the house. A pitchfork leaned against the door.

The barn.

But what held Madison's attention was the stick figure of an enormous man with an extremely long penis standing by a table in front of the cemetery gate, a knife in his hand. On the table was the stick figure of a child, arms raised in pleading. A vacuous, sharp-toothed smile sliced the man's face. At his feet was a mound of stick body parts; an open-fingered tiny hand thrust through the pile and reached toward the sky.

"Holy Mother of God," Luke whispered. "You sure this isn't something out of a bad movie she's seen?"

Madison shook her head. "No…too much detail. I think she's telling us that somewhere a child—or more than one child—was dismembered and buried. She may *never* be able to verbally describe it, even if she wanted to, but she's trying."

Now desperation surged through her body. She

331

grabbed Luke's arm and held it with an iron grip. "Please get me in that car...now. Wrap me in a blanket and dump me in the back seat. If Rafe doesn't come out carrying *something*, little Savannah won't survive the night. They've killed children, you guys. That's what Piper's saying. You have to follow that car and stop whatever's happening—before it happens again."

"I don't want you—"

"Luke, she's right," Darth interrupted. "I'm not supposed to do this, but we have no choice. My partner, Cole Sutton, is outside waiting. My captain will provide backup. We'll also contact the Medina County Sheriff's Department, and they'll provide at least one deputy. We'll alert the Texas Rangers as well. Between all of us, she'll be okay. Jerome, will you call Ranger Tommy White for me?"

"Will do."

Madison turned to Whitney. "Put these drawings in the office safe, will you? And don't leave Piper alone until we're back. The squad car will stay out front, and you reset the alarm as soon as we leave."

Whitney's voice shook. "Where are you going?"

"That's not important, Whitney. Just do it."

"Please be careful. I won't leave Piper. I love you."

"I love you more."

Finally, Madison released Luke's arm and took his hands in hers. "This is what Lacy discovered. This is why she brought you back. She wanted you to save the children. We can't let her down."

****

"What the hell took you so long?"

"Sorry about that," Rafe answered. He shoved Madison unceremoniously into the back seat and slammed the car door closed, then slid into the front passenger seat and shut the door. "They have this crazy dog, and then I had to hide, and then—"

"Cut to the chase, kid. Everything okay?"

Rafe chuckled. "It is now."

"How about her?"

"She'll be fine. What's your name?"

"They call me Frankie."

"Hey, Frankie. I'm Rafe."

"I know who you are."

Frankie flipped the radio to a Tejano music station, apparently signifying the conversation had ended. As Rafe attempted to keep time by banging on the dashboard, Madison struggled to breathe through the comforter Luke had wrapped around her.

Hopefully, she could get her bearings, but it wasn't going to be easy. She couldn't see anything, didn't know which direction they were heading, and had no idea whether they were being followed successfully or not. To add insult to injury, she was developing a migraine.

What the hell possessed me to do this?

She closed her eyes and moved her head carefully to try to open a breathing space. On the radio, the announcer spoke Spanish a mile a minute, which did nothing to alleviate Madison's clanging nerves. She clenched her fists to keep from screaming out loud until finally she felt a whisper of cool air against her nose. She sighed in relief.

Then, suddenly, as if he'd read her mind, Rafe spoke up. "Would you turn the radio off? I don't speak Spanish, and I have a splitting headache. I need to think."

"Think? If I were you, that's the last thing I'd do."

"Yeah, I know. But this is the first time I've ever

done this, and I don't want to make any mistakes."

"Don't worry about it. All we're going to do is pull up to the house, honk, and wait for someone to come out for the kid. Is she asleep?"

"Nah. I hit her in the head. She'll be out for a while."

"You didn't mess up her face, did you?" Frankie sounded genuinely afraid. "Tony hates it when that happens."

"Yeah? Well, Tony don't scare me. I got skills."

"Skills?" Frankie imitated Rafe in singsong tone filled with mockery and scorn. *"Tony don't scare me...* You got a lot to learn, kid. If you're not scared of anything else in this world, you damn well better be scared of Tony."

"Yeah, I guess you're right." Rafe shifted in his seat, making it much easier for Madison to hear his words. "Where're we going anyway?"

"Don't you worry about it, kid. We'll get there soon enough—and then you'll be crying to leave."

"I don't cry."

"Oh, that's right. You got skills. You know Tony, kid?"

"Yeah, I know him real well. Do you?"

"No, and I don't want to. I just bring him kids and take my money. It's none of my business. Look for a County Road 218, will you? I been out here a dozen times, but I always miss it. It's off here somewhere. My GPS don't work right now, and my eyes ain't so good, neither."

Hastily, Madison began connecting the dots.

CR 218... The Walker family property is on CR 218, and Bobby Grisham lives with the Walker family. Sage Winslow lives near the Walker family, and they all live near Mico...

Oh God, it never even occurred to me we would head up here.

Oh God, are the guys behind us?

Oh God, what was I thinking?

Madison struggled to remember the road to Luke's property but drew a blank. She'd been exhausted that day and spent most of the drive with her eyes closed, so all she could recall was that the highway heading to the lake had two lanes and was well traveled. She couldn't even remember if there were any lights on CR 218 itself since it had been afternoon when they left for home. All she'd really paid attention to was Luke's gorgeous estate and how handsome he was, not how they got there.

But...Luke had said he didn't live far from either the Walkers or Sage Winslow. Even if Darth couldn't safely tail Madison on this dark road, he'd written the addresses down in his notebook earlier, so that could help in a pinch. Or Luke might be able to keep them from getting lost...maybe. And if Darth realized where they were heading, he could call for backup from San Antonio...maybe. If he had time. All maybes...

"I think that's CR 218 up there at that intersection," Rafe said suddenly.

Madison heard a tremor in his voice and stiffened. *Don't get scared now...*

Frankie heard it, too. "Thanks. You okay?"

"Fine."

"Is that a car following us?"

Pain shot through Madison's eyeball. She wished she could breathe.

"I don't know." Rafe's voice was hoarse. "You could pull over and let him pass."

Frankie was silent a moment. "We're almost there," he said finally, "and I'm running late. Don't want to piss Tony off. I'll just slow down and see if this guy goes around."

Madison felt the car ease up and held her breath. She didn't like the way Rafe sounded.

But after a few seconds, he chuckled. "There he goes—all the way up to the stop sign. Big hurry to get nowhere fast, right?"

"That's the way it usually is. Oh, he turned into that drive up there. Mama must be holding dinner."

"At two in the morning? More like breakfast."

Madison's heart sank. That car wasn't the tail after all. As the road became bumpier and curvier, Frankie slowed his vehicle.

"When they say 'dark' out here, they mean it," he grumbled. "Here we are. Good, they left the gate open for us."

Rafe cleared his throat. "How much do you make bringing kids out here?"

"A thousand bucks a kid."

"A thou—wow! You think I might be able to do that?"

"Maybe. They been talking about expanding their business, whatever that is."

"You don't know?"

"Naw, I don't want to know. I just bring the kids."

Madison heard the crunch of tires against gravel as the car slowed to a crawl. She strained to hear nighttime sounds…wildlife, insects, even the wind…but it was as silent as a crypt inside the car. Except for the men. Their voices reverberated, like the deep bass sounds of kettle drums.

She felt the first stirrings of real terror. Her heart slammed so hard and fast against her breastbone that she couldn't catch her breath. The comforter smelled burnt-sweet, sort of like charred marshmallows, and her throat was so dry she couldn't swallow. She desperately needed to pee. She began to shudder with icy, uncontrollable tremors that engulfed her from head to toe.

Stay alert...don't panic. It's just adrenaline...

The car stopped. Frankie turned off the ignition and honked. She heard the faint smack of a door slamming in the distance.

Be calm. Pay attention.

Frankie let down his window. Heavy footsteps in gravel coming toward the car sounded like cannon fire.

The night stillness was broken by a man's voice so deep and congested that it could've been a lubricated growl. "Hey, Frankie! We was worried. Everything okay?"

"No problems."

"Glad to hear it. Tony's a little antsy, and that ain't good. Here's your payday." There was a pause, then some chitchat as money changed hands. The man coughed, then sneezed. "Are you Rafe Gamez?"

"Yeah." His voice sounded weak.

"Okay. Tony says you know where the barn is and how to get in. He says take your package in there and stay 'til someone tells you different. Got that?"

"Yup."

The man sneezed again. "This cedar's killing me. Gotta get inside. Thanks, Frankie."

"Sure. Rafe, you want me to pull up closer to the barn?"

"No, I'm good."

Madison heard Rafe get out of the car and slam the door. The door nearest her feet opened, and Rafe pulled her toward him, then bundled her in his arms as if she weighed no more than a safety pin. As he carried her toward the barn, only one thought rolled around in her mind.

He knows where the barn is, and he knows how to get in...

Rafe Gamez had lied to her. He'd been here before.

****

Luke sat in the back seat of Darth's small black car next to Jerome and kept his eyes on the taillights in front of them. Suddenly, muttering an epithet, Darth stepped on the gas and passed the car like a shot. He glanced over at his partner, Cole Sutton.

"I think they made us, so I'm pulling into the next drive I see. Keep your eye on them so I can get back on the road ASAP."

Cole leaned forward. "Do we know how big this property is?"

"When Madison googled the address earlier, she said the map showed twelve acres with no businesses around it. The Walkers' Facebook page showed pictures of an old farmhouse and a big new house. Piper drew a barn and a family cemetery. So all I know is there's a lot of room out there."

"How're we going to know where they took Madison once we get there?" Luke asked nervously.

"We won't know until we find her," Jerome answered, "but we'll find her."

"He turned left at that intersection," Darth interrupted, "so that must be 218. Pulling out now. Reach in my jacket, Cole. My notebook has both addresses out here, just in case we need them."

"Where'd you get the addresses?"

"Mercy Children's Home," Darth answered, peering off to his left. "A couple of these kids came from there. I think the address Rafe is heading for is where at least one of the kids lived. Once."

Luke's leg bounced nervously.

"Have a little faith, bud," Jerome whispered. "We've been doing this a long time."

"I know. But she's little, and that man is brutal… If anything happens to her—"

"Nothing's going to happen to her. She's my heart. Between all of us, she's in good hands."

Darth pulled up to the stop sign and made a left turn on CR 218. There didn't seem to be an actual streetlight for the next twenty miles, but a pair of taillights were visible ahead. When that car made a slow right into a wooded area, Luke sent up a quick prayer they would be able to determine exactly where that turn had been. Portions of the land on these county roads were so densely forested that entrance gates often went completely unnoticed.

Darth turned off his headlights and inched the car forward. Luke's heart began a steady thud.

"We can't just follow this guy onto the property," Darth said quietly, "so I'm going to pull over down here, beside the fence, and wait for him to come back out. Then we'll move on up, park near the gate, and go in on foot."

"Is this the Walker property?" Jerome inquired.

Darth nodded.

"What if he doesn't come back out?" Luke asked.

"I think he will. We'll give him a few minutes and

see what happens. I need to touch base with my captain anyway—if I can get a decent signal." He put his cell phone to his ear.

"Don't hold your breath," Luke muttered. "They don't call this area 'BF Egypt' for nothing."

"Yes, sir, Cap'n," Darth said suddenly. "Just checking in. Cole is with me, and so is Jerome Scranton. I also have a male civilian here who knows the terrain in the Medina area very well. His daughter's the little girl they tried to kidnap from the shelter tonight." He listened a moment, then chuckled. "Well, sir, he's a big guy, and he seems pretty calm to me. Yes, sir, I'll tell him. Thank you, sir." He glanced over his shoulder at Luke. "Two of my guys have gone into Lacy's house to search the closet, and the captain is sending four more out here to us. We have to wait for them."

"That's crazy! We can't wait—"

"They're on their way," Darth interrupted. "It won't be long. In the meantime, we'll move in closer."

As if on cue, a car appeared at the end of the entrance and made a rapid turn away from them. Darth waited until the vehicle disappeared down the road, started his car once again, and inched his way down the fence line until they could see the drive. The gate was open.

"Good, the gate swings toward us. Seems he was in a hurry, huh? Don't make a sound when you get out of the car. Once we get to the entrance, we'll check out the lay of the land. Luke, stay with me. You're more familiar with this terrain than we are."

Luke had never been any good at taking orders, but he knew he had to begin now. Too many other lives depended on him. Madison was somewhere on this property, and she'd placed herself in harm's way without a second thought. With her was a young man who might or might not be on her side. Luke owed it to her, just as he owed it to Lacy, to save this little girl—and all the other children who might be imprisoned somewhere on these grounds.

He moved carefully to the opened gate and peered around the tall mesquite bushes bordering the fence line. The night air was crisp and clean, the sky was brilliantly illuminated with stars and a nearly full moon, and the drive leading into the property was clearly visible. This enabled them to see the farmhouse without difficulty, but they would also be easy targets when they tried to make their way across the grounds. As Darth joined him, Luke acknowledged him with a nod.

"My guys are about five minutes away," Darth whispered. "Are you ready?"

"Hell, no, but I'll do everything I can not to get you guys killed. Do you have a plan?"

Darth nodded. "You and Jerome go to the barn. Piper's drawing showed it to be to the right of the farmhouse as we're facing it, so I think that's the farmhouse at the end of the drive. When we get there, you and Jerome veer off toward the barn and try to get in. If I remember the picture correctly, she drew a huge padlock—although that could just be the way she saw it—and you guys might have a hard time getting in. Unless we get lucky and that's where Madison is. Cole and I, along with my guys, will take on the farmhouse. I think that's where the little girl's being held and the film's being made."

Luke squinted to see the farmhouse at the end of the drive more clearly, but all he could see was the glowing tip of a cigarette near what was probably the front door. He pointed. "Someone's standing outside."

"Armed for sure. Someone's probably at the back door, too. Here come my guys."

Luke turned to see a black SUV pull in behind Darth's little car. No lights. No sound. The doors swung open, and four well-armed men stepped out. Darth joined them, spoke quietly with more hand gestures than words, then pointed toward Luke and waggled his finger. Luke hastily made his way toward them.

Darth glanced at his watch. "It's nearly three—this show starts in thirty minutes. Boys, this is Luke Callaghan. His little girl was nearly kidnapped from a children's shelter tonight to be used in a nasty movie they're making here right now. He's been working with me and my team on a pedo ring in San Antonio, and he's been a huge help, so take care of him. Also, somewhere on these grounds—maybe in that barn—is a female civilian who's here for the children, so we need to take care of her, too. Luke, these men are snipers, and they're going to keep us from dying. I hope."

He paused for a moment. "Okay, the creep's tossed his cigarette. Let's go."

Chapter Twenty-Three

Rafe Gamez gently placed Madison on the ground and began removing the comforter from around her body. When she was free, he took her hand and helped her to her feet. She looked around the barn in shocked disbelief—and gagged.

Located on top of a rickety table near a side door was an ancient kerosene lantern sputtering a dim, ghostly light over several small children. Next to the table was a rusty slop bucket filled with urine and excrement. The children sat against the wall, sagging with exhaustion, hands behind their backs. Barefoot and wearing only underwear, they were painfully thin and covered in filth. Their little faces were frozen into blank, staring expressions. They didn't move. They didn't react at all to her presence. They were either in shock or drugged...or both.

Just like Piper's drawing...

Suddenly, she remembered and gripped Rafe's arm. "You lied to me. You said you didn't know anything about this place—"

"I said I didn't know where the driver was taking Piper. That's not the same."

She didn't have time to argue. "Do you know if Darth and the others are here yet?"

"No idea. But probably."

She couldn't seem to stop shaking. "Rafe, can I trust

you? You're not going to turn on me, are you?"

"No, ma'am. I promise."

"Then tell me what you know about this place."

He was silent for a moment. "There's a guard on the front porch and at the back door of the farmhouse," he said finally. "There's another one inside, at the door where the little girl's being held. Sometimes—I don't know about tonight—there's a live audience of four or five sitting in the hallway, looking through special glass like what the cops use...you know, mirror on the kid's side and glass on the other so people can watch. If that's set up, you can hear everything going on in that room."

Nausea burned her throat. "Did you see any cars when we came in? I mean, like, for an audience?"

"No, and I looked. If we're lucky, all we have to deal with are these three usual guards and Tony."

"Do any important people ever come here?"

"Nah. They're not crazy. All they care about is the money. They watch on their computers. Usually."

"Can you get out of here and look for our guys without being seen?"

"Tony told me to stay here."

Madison tightened her grip on his arm. "Rafe, we need to get all this information to Jerome and the others. We can't use a phone. Can't you sneak out of here and find our guys?" She looked up at him pleadingly. "I know you're scared. I am, too. Please try. If you don't, I will."

Shaking, teeth chattering, he turned away from her. "I'm not scared. I can do it."

Her heart thudded an extra beat. *He's too sick...*

"Are the children handcuffed?"

"No. Just rope ties. They're hooked to a clasp

attached to the wall." He held out his scarred wrists and gave her a long look. "I've tied them up before. I can untie them."

She frowned. She'd never seen a living being so pale in her life. "What if we tried to get them out of here? Could we do that?"

"No. You got cops outside, and as soon as Tony realizes it, all hell's gonna break loose. You don't want these kids stuck anywhere near all that crazy. Keep them in here and let Mr. Darth handle it. We'll just be sure they're free to run if they have to."

Madison had no doubt he was right. She moved closer to the group, looking for just one leader. The flickering kerosene lamplight bounced off knife-like farming utensils, casting grim and intimidating shadows around the barn. All she could see clearly were five children about six years old.

Finally, she selected a boy who looked stronger than the others and knelt before him. He flinched and turned his head. Up close, Madison couldn't miss the dark purple bruising around his neck.

She spoke loudly enough for all the children to hear, but tried to keep her voice low. "We're not going to hurt you. What's your name, sweetheart?"

"Toby Lee."

The name was familiar, but she didn't have time to question why. "Okay, Toby Lee. We're going to get you out of here just as soon as we can. This young man's going to cut you loose. But…and this is very important…keep your hands behind your back so it looks like you're still tied up, no matter what. In the meantime, don't move and don't make a sound. Our friend here will leave us for a little bit, and I'll stay with you. Do you understand all that?"

She was relieved to see a nod or two, but she knew they needed to move quickly. It was cold, and the children had been in this barn for a long time without heat, clothing, or food. They were too traumatized to help themselves. They were no longer frightened, hungry, or even aware of what was happening to them.

Somehow, she had to make them care about their safety again. She had to make them care enough to fight for their lives.

"Cut them loose, Rafe," she ordered softly. "They're either in shock or drugged. But either way, we don't have much time."

****

Crouching low, Luke and Jerome zigzagged through tall grass toward the barn, dodging limestone rock and tall ocotillo cactus as best they could, using thorny mesquite bushes as cover from moonlight that now seemed as glaring and bright as daybreak. When a side door on the barn opened and a figure stepped outside, Luke and Jerome squatted behind a thick mesquite bush and peered around it. Jerome cocked his pistol.

Luke grabbed Jerome's shoulder. "I think that's Rafe."

Jerome kept his pistol leveled and didn't answer.

"Hold up. He's waving. It *is* Rafe." Luke lifted his hand but stayed behind the bushes.

"You better hope it is," Jerome muttered, keeping his pistol aimed at the husky figure as it ran toward them. When Rafe was clearly outlined in the moonlight, running toward the shrub line, Jerome lowered his firearm and moved over slightly.

Rafe squatted beside him. "I'm gonna hurl," he

muttered.

Jerome grabbed his arm. "No, you're not. Where's Madison?"

"In the barn with five kids. We've untied them so they can get out if they have to, but she's staying with them 'til this is over if she can. She sent me to find you."

"Why?" Luke demanded. "She shouldn't be in there by herself."

"She's safe for right now. It's the farmhouse that's dangerous."

Jerome shifted his position and grunted. "I'm too old for this crap," he muttered. "What can you tell me about the farmhouse? Wait. Let me get Darth, and you can tell him what you know."

As Luke listened to the whispered conversation taking place on Jerome's cell phone, he kept his eyes glued to the farmhouse. To the left of it, according to Piper's drawing, was a family cemetery, which he couldn't see, and to the right was the barn. The only guards, according to Rafe as he described the layout to Darth on the phone, were in and around the farmhouse. But the man they'd seen on the front porch still hadn't come back outside, so they were all going to have to take their chances and run.

Now.

"Excuse me, sir," Rafe whispered into the phone, "I can't do that. I have to go back to the barn. Tony's orders were for me to stay with Piper...sorry, I mean Madison. Yes, sir, I'll tell them."

Luke heard the crackle of Darth's voice, but the orders were unintelligible.

Rafe handed the cell phone back to Jerome and leaned in toward Luke. "Sir, the detective says for you to go straight to the barn from here and stay with Miss Madison. He says for you to go now while the guard is still gone. Snipers are already in the front and back to get good shots at the doors."

Luke forgot all his good intentions about following orders. He frowned. "That's crazy. I can help, you know."

"Those were his orders."

Luke thought fast and decided to act as if those orders meant something, but in truth they didn't. He could do more than hold his own in a fight, and he wasn't going to bed down in a safe place for the night.

Aloud, he said only, "Do I go in through that big door in the front?"

"No, sir. There's a door on the right side of the barn. It's unlocked. Go in through there."

Suddenly, they heard a series of sneezes, then a muffled cry. The slam of a door. A yelled curse and stumbling. A thud, then silence.

Luke shot out from behind the mesquite brush and ran for the farmhouse. Someone hollered for him to stop, but he kept running. Finally, chest on fire, he reached the broken-down structure and flattened himself against the side as he caught his breath. Darth had said snipers were stationed near the front and back doors, so he had to be careful. He inched his way through the darkness toward the back of the farmhouse. As clouds whispered across the moon, the silence was eerie and thick. He could almost taste it. Reaching the end of the house, he stopped and peeked around the corner.

The back porch was dark. Empty. Silent.

Suddenly, a roar came from inside the house, followed by a crash, then silence. The back door slammed open, and a figure dashed out, down the back steps, and around the corner. Luke pressed himself against the building and watched the figure run across the yard, toward the road leading away from the property.

Who the hell is that?

Without warning, another figure charged from behind the tree line, attacked, and wrestled the man to the ground. Within seconds the man was still, lying in the dirt. His assailant stood up and headed for the farmhouse without a look backward. It was all accomplished without a sound.

As Luke moved cautiously around the corner, he heard a voice behind him.

"You're not supposed to be here, big guy," Jerome said quietly, passing him up with his gun drawn. "But it's too late now. We don't have much time, and I can use the help. One guard down and two to go."

Luke nodded, grateful for the armed backup, and followed Jerome toward the back porch. They went up the steps quickly and entered the farmhouse. From beneath a door down the hall, a sliver of light appeared, and Luke heard a deep voice from within that room. Jerome glanced at his watch.

"It's almost three thirty."

Suddenly, the dark hallway was flooded with light. Luke was momentarily disoriented until he realized the light was coming through a large window beside him. It was the two-way mirror that Rafe had described.

He gaped in disbelief. A naked little girl, her hands roped above her head to a wrought-iron headboard, turned her face to the wall. Beside the bed was a huge cage—he recognized it as the one he'd seen in the film clip. Antonio Davila stood beside it, a knit ski mask hiding his face and his muscular body encased in black leather, swinging a long metal pipe in his hand.

A deep, disembodied voice came from inside the room, clearly a recording. "This is last call for requests, suggestions, and payments. Piano Man is waiting for you. We'll begin in two minutes."

At the sound of the man's voice, the little girl visibly stiffened until every inch of her stick-thin little body was as rigid as petrified wood. Then there was silence. She began to cry, softly, hopelessly.

Luke looked at Jerome in desperation.

Without warning, he was startled by the loud firecracker *pop, pop, pop* of gunshots near the farmhouse. The front door crashed open, and Darth's voice exploded through the house.

"San Antonio Special Victims Unit! Tony Davila— come on out!"

"Back here!" Jerome yelled.

Darth and his partner Cole Sutton raced down the hallway and stopped in front of the room just long enough to get a good look at the scene unfolding behind the two-way mirror. Darth nodded at Cole and kicked the door in. Antonio Davila took a step backward and lifted his arms in the air, clearly unworried. Two more officers piled in behind Darth and Cole, but Davila remained where he was.

Darth spoke directly to him. "Turn that camera off and get that ridiculous mask off your face." He waited until Davila had followed his orders, then motioned to his team. "Y'all come cover this child up and get her out of here. There's a towel on that chair in the corner." His gun still pointed at Davila, Darth moved toward the live-stream camera gear set up near the foot of the bed.

Finally, he spoke quietly to his crew. "I'm going to go live here in just a minute, and I don't want anyone seen but me, understand? I'm sitting on the foot of this bed—hurry up and get that child out of here, you guys— and everyone else stay on the other side of the room. Davila, you're gonna start the camera when I say, or I'm gonna lay you out. Any questions?"

In just a few minutes, Darth's orders had been carried out. Luke stepped aside so that the little girl could be removed from the room, then moved in closer. Whatever Darth intended to do with Tony Davila...well, Luke didn't want to miss it.

Darth pulled a baseball cap down on his forehead and slipped on a pair of sunglasses, never moving his gun away from Davila. "I'm ready, Cole. Take this twisted creep to the camera so he can turn it back on. Use your phone to record what he's doing. We don't want anyone to say we touched that camera."

Smirking, Davila followed Darth's directions, then made final preparations with the webcam and external microphone set up on a tripod beneath the two-way mirror.

Cole Sutton finally spoke. "Okay... And...go."

Darth leaned forward, a big welcoming grin creasing his face. "I'm Detective Morgan Harris with the Special Victims Unit somewhere in this great US of A. I know you paid a lot of money to see this show, but your money's all gone now. There won't be any show. Cops around the world just ended it. *You're the show tonight.*" With that, Darth ran his index finger across his throat. "Just to be clear, we know who you are and where you live. Sleep well. We'll be seeing you soon. You won't know where. You won't know when. But...wait for it...it'll happen."

Luke felt a chill race up and down his spine—a chill of excitement and victory. Then, in his mind's eye, he watched with vindictive satisfaction as panicked customers shut down their computers...

...and screens all over the world faded to black.

****

"Did you hear those gunshots?" Rafe asked anxiously from his self-appointed guardian position beside the barn's side door. "Should I go see—"

Madison glared at him, bleary-eyed. She sat Indian style with the children close to one another in hopes of keeping them warm, but it wasn't doing much good. Her own teeth were chattering, and her feet felt like glaciers. "Calm down and stay where you are. You look like you're going to die. I've got to figure out how to get these kids warm. They're freezing to death."

"Do you want my jacket?"

"Give it to one of the child—"

"What was that?" Rafe interrupted. He grabbed a hammer off the step of a ladder nearby and held it in both hands, as if poised to do cranial damage to any intruder. "I heard a noise!"

Flashes of color danced before her eyes. Her migraine pain was intense. "Good grief. Stop. Someone will come for us anytime now."

"You just don't get it, do you?"

"What?"

"Tony Davila isn't going down easy. No way."

She covered her left eye with a cupped hand. That helped ease the pain a little. "Well, I guess we'll find out soon enough, won't we? He can't take on all these cops by himself."

Little Toby Lee squirmed nearer to Madison. She instinctively put an arm around him and held him close. "It's almost over, sweetheart," she whispered, "and then we'll get you out of here."

"I'm hungry, Miss Madison."

"I know, baby…"

"Madison? Rafe? Hello?"

Her heart skittered with relief. "In here, Luke!" She squeezed Toby in excitement. "See? I told you!"

****

Luke tromped into the barn, Jerome close behind him, and took in the situation with one glance. But when he saw Madison cuddled up with a little boy, joy swept over him in such a rush he nearly hit the floor. He was so focused on her it was like the previous hour had been nothing more than a bad dream. He had to take a few moments to regain his composure.

Finally, Luke crossed the barn and knelt beside her. Although he longed to take her in his arms and assure himself that she was unhurt, he knew he wasn't free to do that. "Are you okay?" he asked finally.

She nodded. "Can we go now? These kids are freezing."

"Sure. They can wait in police cars until the ambulances get here."

Swaying, Rafe set the hammer down. "Ambulances? Who's hurt?"

Luke gestured toward Jerome. "We've got two wounded guards—one with a head injury compliments of this old man—and the other guy was shot in the ass when he was trying to run. The third one broke his ankle tripping over his own feet in the dark out by the cemetery. We'll send the kids to a San Antonio children's hospital for observation."

"I'll ask Darth to have a car brought up here for them," Jerome said. "Just a minute."

Luke couldn't stand it anymore. He had to touch her; her blue-green eyes seemed clouded and unfocused. He took her hands in his. "Are you sure you're all right?"

She managed a smile and a nod. "I'm just cold, and I have a migraine. Is Savannah okay?"

"She's already in a police car with an SVU female detective. I think she's more scared than anything else."

"She has a right to be."

Jerome dropped his phone back into his jacket pocket. "Cole's bringing a car around for the kids. Come on, munchkins. Let's see if you can all stand up."

Luke helped Madison to her feet. Together they gathered the children into a group and made their way to the door, using Luke's cell phone as a flashlight.

Rafe followed them from the barn. "I'm telling you, Mr. Luke, this has gone down way too easy. Get the kids in that car as quick as you can and away from here, okay?"

"Of course."

When a black SUV pulled in front of the barn and the driver stepped out, Luke herded the children into the vehicle as fast as their frozen little legs could move. After the driver took some blankets and a few teddy bears from the back of the unit, he and Jerome began making the children as comfortable as they could. Within a matter of moments, the car had turned around and disappeared toward the road in a cloud of dust.

Luke walked back to Rafe and Madison, shrugging his jacket off. He placed it around her shoulders and gently pulled her closer to him. She leaned against his chest and gave a long, exhausted sigh.

Suddenly, Rafe grabbed her arm. "There's Tony! Dr. Wagner, do you think you could get Mr. Darth to let me talk to him? Please?"

"You can do that later, Rafe—" Luke began.

But Madison stopped him. "Confrontation is very important, Luke. It wouldn't take but a minute. Can't you ask Darth?"

"Really, Madison...I just think—"

"No, Luke, he's right. You know how the legal system overlooks victims. He might never get a chance like this again." She finished in a whisper, "Please, Luke. He deserves this. What he did, he did while he was sick. Really sick. Please."

Against all the warnings screaming through his head, Luke couldn't resist her. He looked down at her with a soft smile and shrugged. "Okay, just for a minute."

Darth and Cole Sutton walked on either side of a handcuffed Tony Davila as they made their way to a police car now parked in front of the farmhouse, lights flashing. In the distance, Luke could hear the sirens of approaching ambulances.

He headed for the trio, convinced he was making a huge mistake.

Let's get this over with...

****

Madison nudged Rafe's arm. "Get going. Make it quick."

She'd dreamed of coming face-to-face with Antonio Davila many times over the last few days, but when it finally happened, it was nothing like she'd anticipated.

He was actually model handsome with chiseled features and wavy black hair, but his eyes were dead.

Soulless.

Chilling.

And her response to him was equally cold.

She felt no hatred, no rage, no desire for revenge. She only wanted to be away from him.

Rafe stepped in front of her. His arms hung at his sides, and his fists were clenched. "This is a good night for the world, Tony. I'm glad I got to see it."

"Enjoy it while you can, *pendejo*. You know I'll be back."

"Where you're going...you'll be there a long, long time."

"Prison's the perfect place for me. Everything I know I learned in prison."

"I wasn't talking about prison, Tony. I was talking about Hell."

And then, with one effortless motion so fast it was a blur, Rafe's hand shot out, and his concealed stiletto sliced deeply into the left side of Davila's throat. Blood spurted from a severed carotid artery, then gushed as the big man toppled slowly, almost gracefully, to the ground. He groaned, wheezed, gurgled, then lay still and silent. As Darth tore his jacket off and tried to stem the bleeding, Rafe stared down at Antonio Davila with smiling disregard.

"He doesn't get to say when it's over. I do."

Then he dropped his knife on top of Davila's lifeless body, placed his scarred wrists together in preparation for the handcuffs that were coming...and waited to be confined.

Again.

Chapter Twenty-Four

Madison stood naked in her bathroom, studying a bruised hip in the steamy mirror—probably received when she'd been tossed into the back seat of a car like the proverbial sack of potatoes. Three days had passed since that terrible night, and she was only just now beginning to feel like herself.

She slipped into a pair of fleece-lined lavender sweats and a matching sweatshirt and gave her reflection a half-hearted smile. All her jeans were too snug to slide easily over her sore hip, so these loose sweatpants were the best she could manage. She would be participating in her annual Christmas decorating party for the children tomorrow evening, and she hoped she'd be up to it, but right now she still felt like something tossed out into the cold.

She leaned closer to the mirror and studied her face more carefully. The dark-purple shadows beneath her red-rimmed eyes emphasized her sleeplessness. *Nothing's going to cover up this hot mess.* She chose moisturizer and blush instead of foundation and ran her fingers through her hair, making a mental note to get to her hairdresser as soon as possible. She needed a haircut and highlights…

She sighed. Her attempt at mental normalcy was pretty pathetic. There was nothing normal about her life.

Someone knocked lightly on her door three times.

Madison recognized it as Whitney's signal for *this is important*.

She limped to the door and opened it. "Good morning, sweetie. What's up?"

Whitney gave her usual open grin and said, *sotto voce*, "I just checked the email, and I think Luke's paternity test is back."

Madison's heart skittered for a second. "Is he here?"

"Yeah. He's out in the yard with Sasha and the kids."

"Good. Don't let him go anywhere. Anything else?"

Whitney nodded and headed for the conference table. "Yeah. It's really busy for a Sunday. Judge Leonard called and asked if we could make room for these kids for at least another week, once the hospital releases them later today. Maybe even until February."

"What'd you tell him?"

Whitney sat down and stretched. "I told him we moved bunk beds into two bedrooms, so we could handle six more children for a little while longer—as long as he gave his official approval. He was really glad because he knows they're going to need a lot of therapy, and they won't get it in foster care. The hospital's done rape kits and full-body exams on all the kids, and the cops are finished with their preliminary interviews, so that's good. But he's going nuts trying to work through all this, especially during the holidays."

"I can imagine." Madison sat across from Whitney and shifted her weight cautiously to her right buttock. "Anything else?"

"Well…actually…yeah. Jerome met Darth at the police station this morning, and he called here a few minutes ago. They want to know if they can pop in about one. They've got something they need to go over with you and Luke."

Madison's heart skipped another beat. "Did he say what it was?"

"No, it seems to be pretty hush-hush. But I've got plenty to do this afternoon to get ready for this get-together tomorrow night, so don't worry about me. Oh, and that reminds me of something else."

Madison closed her eyes. Whitney's buoyant energy was exhausting. "What's that?"

"Well, Jared is coming by in a couple of hours to help us bake cookies and string popcorn. Our kids can't wait for that. He's been with Judge Leonard, helping to get all the paperwork together so the new kids can stay here longer, but he's nearly finished."

"Bless his heart," Madison said softly. "I really don't know what I would do without him. We need to get him something really special for Christmas. Anything else?"

Whitney nodded. "Well, you know that yesterday we invited Carlotta Martinez and Julian Alvarado to come tomorrow night. They called this morning and accepted, which really surprised me because it was such short notice. But Julian said he was going to visit Rafe at the jail tomorrow afternoon anyway and he would just pop over here when he was finished. Carlotta said her daughter would bring her."

Rafe. Madison still couldn't think about Rafe.

She pushed her mind away from that chilling memory and met Whitney's understanding gaze. She glanced at her watch. "Well, go ahead and get Luke, okay? It's almost one."

****

Luke sat at the conference table in Madison's room and stared at her laptop screen, hesitant to click on the envelope containing his paternity results. He'd been thinking about this moment almost nonstop since he'd returned from the farmhouse, and he'd come to view it as a do-over. It was an opportunity to make things right, no matter which way these cards fell.

Feeling Madison's gaze from the chair next to him, Luke looked at her soberly. "I've made a decision."

"What's that?"

"I've decided I'm going to raise Piper, no matter what these results say."

Madison gaped at him. "Are you serious?"

"Of course, I'm serious. You'd be in my corner, right?"

"Absolutely. Are you going to open that or not?"

Without giving himself another second to hesitate, Luke clicked on the envelope and waited for the email to load. Once it had, all he could do was stare at the final results in disbelief.

In all analyzed PCR systems, Luke Alan Callaghan does show the genetic markers which have to be present for the biological father of the child Piper Elyse Callaghan... The probability of Mr. Luke Callaghan being the biological father of Piper Callaghan is > 99.9999%. Conclusion: based on our analysis, it is practically proven that Mr. Luke Callaghan is the biological father of the child Piper Callaghan.

Luke dragged his gaze from the screen and looked at Madison through tears. "Lacy knew, and I never gave her a chance. She was right all the time."

Madison reached for his hand and cradled it in her own. "Don't beat yourself up about that, Luke. Lacy knew you'd come and handle things, and you did. I was wrong about you, and you were wrong about her. Let it go now."

"The thing is, Madison, this all went down so much more easily than I ever thought it would, and we have you to thank for it."

"Don't be crazy—"

"No, really. If you hadn't insisted on coming with us, we'd still be sitting in your room trying to figure out what was going on. You probably haven't even thought about it, but all of this was brought about by superhero women: you, Whitney, and Piper. At some point I'm going to write a book about you ladies—"

"Don't forget Lacy," she interrupted sternly. "She was the biggest hero of us all."

He nodded. "You're right. We can never forget Lacy. But there's something else, Madison—"

When Whitney's knock came lightly on the door, Luke tried not to groan out loud. If he didn't tell Madison how his heart was filled with her, he was going to lose his mind.

Whitney poked her head around the door. "Jerome and Darth are here, and they're biting at the bit to see you guys. Can I bring them up?"

Madison nodded and squeezed Luke's hand. When his eyes met hers, he was relieved to see that her expression had softened into one he'd never thought to see for him.

It was a look of affection. And right now, he'd take that.

****

Madison yawned as Darth carried a box to the table, Jerome close behind him, and prayed this wouldn't take too long.

"So what's got you guys so antsy?" she asked.

When Darth set the box down on the table with an air of determination, she eyed it warily.

"Is Santa Claus coming early?"

"What *is* this?" Luke asked. He pushed himself closer to the table.

Darth sat down. "This, my friend, is the box we found in Lacy's closet the other night...the one you missed the first time."

Luke released his breath in a *whoosh*. "So there was one, huh?"

"Yessir, there sure was," Jerome answered. "Although how in the world Lacy kept it from Davila, I'll never know. She's been collecting this stuff for a long time."

"What stuff?" Madison asked nervously.

"First of all," Darth said, pulling a folder out of the box, "this is information about their website, Little Lolita Land. It took our guys a while to figure it out, but what matters to you would be who their assistant administrator is." He held up his hand and grinned. "I won't even make you beg for it. Does the name Quinn Davis ring a bell? That's their assistant administrator. And by the way, he makes a fortune off this website. So his job at protective services gives him access to any kid he wants, and he just funnels them over to Little Lolita Land. And he's not the only one. His social workers and therapists—like the ones who handled little Charly MacIntire—got a cut as well. But their day is over. Even your Dr. Weinstein is going down...hard. It's only a matter of time now."

Madison blinked back tears. Dr. Weinstein was the hardest pill for her to swallow. Sweet Dr. Dan with the disappearing coins...how all the children adored him! She'd never even questioned his loyalty or love for his little patients, and that just proved she could be as naïve as the next person. How many children's names and locations had he passed on to pedophile rings, setting those little ones up for terror and pain unlike anything she could even imagine? How many trusting families and innocent childcare workers had he betrayed?

It had been so easy for him...

Swallowing the huge lump in her throat, she pulled herself back from the edge. If she allowed herself to dwell on her own bad judgment, she might never work again.

And these children needed her.

So, Rafe, you were wrong. It's not over yet. You don't get to say, either...

"You said Quinn was the assistant administrator," she said aloud. "Do you know who the head is?"

Jerome nodded soberly. His Texas twang became unusually thick. "Yep, we do, but it don't please us none. The chief administrator of both PattyzPlaypen and Little Lolita Land, as well as a couple more, is Sage Winslow over there at Mercy Children's Home."

Luke whistled between his teeth. "A woman? Are you sure?"

"I told you some of the most vicious perps I've ever run into are women," Darth answered. "By the way, the username *Piano Man* belongs to Sage Winslow, and she set up Rafe Gamez as the eyes and ears on the website. She called him *PianoMan74* just to make him feel important." He held the folder in the air. "You guys want to see this?"

"No," Luke muttered. "Thanks anyway."

Madison shook her head. "I don't get it. How did Lacy know Sage Winslow?"

"I don't think she did," Jerome answered. "I think Tony Davila wanted Piper when she was a baby—when he moved in and pimped out Lacy. Somehow, he got involved with this pedophile ring—I'm not sure when— and that's how he linked up with Neely and Sage, who worked with Quinn Davis and Dr. Weinstein. I think Lacy was battling everyone in the dark. She recognized names but didn't know them personally. Bad guys like them stay above reproach. Always."

"So what happens with them now? Quinn and Sage?" Madison asked.

"We're still building our case against them," Darth answered. "I want it air tight. They've got the best attorneys that money can buy, and they won't hesitate to use them. But Lacy kept all this initial paperwork from when they were first developing their websites, and my guys are using it to put our cases together. She also left several films that forensics are analyzing now. I'm sure they'll contain the full films of the clips she put together for Luke. And best of all, she kept several of Davila's trophies—hair clippings, a pair of panties, stuff like that. Hopefully, we'll be able to connect them to his victims."

Madison couldn't believe her ears. "Yet, even with all this evidence, they're still operating?"

"The live-streaming has already been shut down, so the torture will stop. The FBI will close down the main website once the other agencies we're working with around the world finish with it. In the meantime, we keep building our case. We'll pick Quinn and Sage up in the next day or two, I'm sure. They know we're on to them, so we have to be careful. Right now, the whole farm is a crime scene, and it has to be shut down for the dust angels to work their magic. We need lots more search warrants because I'm sure there are more bodies—"

Luke reached for Madison's hand. "What about Ryan Neely?" he asked quickly.

Darth leaned back in his chair and clasped his hands behind his head. "Well, your little boy—Toby Lee—had quite a story to tell about Mr. Neely. Apparently, it was just like you suspected, Madison. Toby Lee's daddy was being blackmailed into letting Neely use him in his films. But there's even more to it than that."

Darth paused and looked around the table. "Neely is the one who got Quinn Davis involved in the first place—after Davis was accused of sexual abuse and lost his son in a custody battle. Davis was a computer engineer and programmer before he became a social worker. Neely needed his expertise, so he took Davis' case, won it, and got Davis to start up the websites, hide the members, all of that.

"Anyway, when Davis saw how much money was generated, there was no way he was going to stay out of it. The only good thing I can say about Davis is he refused to let Neely have access to his son, so they just made all their money off other people's kids."

"And Lacy knew that, too," Madison murmured. She looked at Luke. "We were right. She realized, when Julian Alvarado couldn't hide her and Piper, it was all over for her. She knew Neely was going to get Piper and she couldn't stop him. All she had left was you."

"Darth, can you corroborate little Toby Lee's story?" Luke asked. "I'd hate to see him have to testify."

The detective nodded. "Yeah, we can. Lacy recorded a conversation with one of her johns early in her investigation—an Alan Lee—who told her about Ryan Neely and what he was doing. Toby was his little boy. He also suspected Neely was blackmailing several other fathers, but he didn't have any proof."

"Her investigation…" Luke repeated quietly. "She must've been living in this sewer for years. She was a long way from a dumb whore, wasn't she?"

Darth didn't answer. He placed the folder back in the box carefully, pulled out a notebook, and held it in the air like a preacher with a Bible. "This is a client list. A written-by-hand—complete with addresses and phone numbers—client list."

Luke frowned. "Of Lacy's johns, you mean?"

Jerome looked at him like he'd lost his mind. "No, you idiot. Who cares about that? Of members. Every single person Lacy knew about, I reckon. Little Lolita Land members. Customers and clients. People who like to watch. Fetishists. Participants. Even buyers, sellers, and transporters. Locations all over the world. It reads like the who's who of child sex trafficking. The DA has the original. Do you want to see this?"

Madison swallowed hard. "No. Put it away. So how big is this, Darth? Did we help your work? Was it worth it?"

"Absolutely. We can bring this organization down now. Somewhere it'll start up again, you know that, but your Lacy put a serious dent in their ability to do what they want without any fear. A lot of these people are going away for a long time. Even Ryan Neely. And these people don't do well in prison."

She blinked back tears. "I wish I could say otherwise, Darth, but she wasn't *my* Lacy. What about the four photographs she left for Luke? Did they actually mean anything?"

"Well, now, that's interesting," Jerome mused. "Someone mentioned that she wasn't much of a housekeeper, and she was so disorganized that she left her divorce papers in her kitchen cabinet, but each one of those kids represented an aspect of this organization. Like those fingers on the tumor Luke mentioned. Charly represented a permanent children's shelter—Mercy Children's Home—which implicates Quinn Davis and Dr. Weinstein. Bobby Grisham represented forced adoption, which implicates Sage Winslow and the Walker family. Savannah West represented an individual foster family, which also implicates Davis and child protective services. And finally, Toby Lee represented an attorney/client collaboration, which implicates Ryan Neely and Sage Winslow. So your Lacy was a long way from disorganized. She knew exactly what she was doing."

"Speaking of Mercy," Luke said slowly, "did Willie or any of the other board members know what was going on? Besides Sage Winslow, Quinn Davis, and Ryan Neely?"

"I'm not sure yet," Darth responded, "but I don't think so. Willie's already opened all their computers to us—she's been a huge help."

Madison closed her eyes, remembering Piper's graphic drawing of the Walker property. All this good news was terrific, but she had to ask the question no one else had asked. She took a deep breath. "Have you found any sign of little Bobby Grisham?"

"Not yet," Darth answered, "but we've got forensics out at the property now. They're working at the cemetery because there were two new graves there."

"Two?" she whispered.

"Yes, but we don't know anything yet. However, the Walkers were arrested this morning. My gut tells me they'll sing like birds when all the chips are in, and that'll be a direct connection to Sage Winslow."

Luke cleared his throat. "Has anyone claimed little Charly's body? Or Bobby's, if it comes down to it?"

Jerome shook his head. "Why?"

"If no one else claims them, please let me know and release them to Martin Gregory at Sunrise Funeral Home. I'd like to bury them near Lacy. I'll take care of the cost."

Madison blinked. She hadn't even thought about that. She squeezed Luke's hand gratefully. "And Rafe? What will happen to Rafe?"

"Rafe is talking to the DA now," Jerome answered, "and I'm sure they're going to offer him a deal. Maybe not a good one, but a deal. Of course, if it turns out he's got a lot of information and he could help the feds, he might be granted complete immunity and even placed in witness protection. Don't get excited now, Madison. I'm just speculating here…"

But she stared at him, appalled. "Witness protection! Do you know how much therapy that boy needs? If he goes into witness protection, he'll never get it, and that could make him a very dangerous man."

"Do you think prison would be any better?"

"Of course not. But he can't just be turned out onto the street like witness protection would do. Therapy needs to be mandated by the court—"

"Therapy?" Luke stared at her in disbelief. "Are you volunteering?"

Madison didn't answer for a very long time. She did

what she'd refused to do for the last three days; she relived Rafe's murder of Antonio Davila. Once more she saw him raise his arm, stiletto in his hand, the deep gaping wound in Davila's neck...and she finally understood why that memory so disturbed her.

Rafe's movement had occurred in a flash—too quick and experienced for him to never have performed it before.

It was just like Lacy's neck, an expert, deep laceration across her throat...

Could he have murdered Lacy? Was that even possible?

If he had, Tony Davila had been there. With his camera. Probably live-streaming.

"Are you volunteering?" Luke asked again.

She didn't voice her thoughts but said only, "I know I should, but I can't. I'm sorry."

"Good. If my opinion means anything, please concentrate on the kids you're going to have here. They need you."

She managed a smile. "I agree. That's exactly what I'm going to do."

"Well, I think that's it for us," Darth said, clearly uncomfortable with this new, a-little-too-friendly twist in Madison and Luke's relationship. "I guess we'll see you tomorrow night."

She nodded. "I'm looking forward to it."

"So what are you guys doing today?"

Luke helped Madison from her chair. "I'm hoping to take Piper out to visit her mother's grave. What do you think, Dr. Wagner?"

"That's a wonderful idea. Let me go get her."

****

As Luke and Madison walked toward Lacy's gravesite, little Piper between them clutching Madison's hand, Luke felt at peace with the world for the first time in years. The grounds were beautifully manicured, with many sites already decorated for Christmas by loving friends and families. He carried a white poinsettia in his arms.

"Oh, look, Luke." Madison pointed toward Lacy's resting place. "Mr. Gregory already has her headstone installed. It's an angel. I love it."

He stopped and turned to her. "Wait, Madison. I want to tell you something."

She looked up at him expectantly, still holding Piper's hand.

He spoke in a rush, before he lost his nerve. "I'm moving back to my place at Medina. I talked to my editors and agent yesterday, and they'll handle my business affairs. A friend of mine is closing down my condo. I just want you to know that."

"That's wonderful, Luke! I'm so glad!"

"I need you to help me establish a sort of summer camp on my property for foster kids. I hope we can get together right away to start working on it, okay? I want to do this, Madison." His voice trailed away uncertainly at the stunned expression on her face. "Have I said something wrong?"

Madison blushed furiously, clearly embarrassed to her core. "No, of course not," she said softly. "I'm just glad you're staying." She looked up at him and smiled. "I don't know how you've done it in such a short period of time, Luke, but I really want to see where this leads us. I don't think I've ever met anyone quite like you."

As joy rushed through him, Luke didn't care that his

daughter stood beside them, watching their interchange curiously. If Dr. Madison Wagner thought he might be good enough for her, he was going to do his utmost not to disappoint her.

Luke gave a sigh of relief. "I was afraid you were going to laugh me out of Dodge."

"Not a chance, big guy. Come on, Piper. Stop staring."

When they reached Lacy's gravesite, Luke knelt in front of the headstone with a small angel perched on top of it. Engraved in a flowery script were the words *Lacy Callaghan, A Beautiful Soul, 1992-2022.*

Luke held out the poinsettia for Piper. "Sweetheart, would you like to put this on your mommy's grave? I think she'd like that."

Piper looked at him solemnly for a moment, then took the plant and placed it on the fresh mound of dirt. Luke tried to swallow a lump in his throat. If he didn't accomplish anything else in his life, he wanted his child to know how brave her mother had been. He never wanted her to feel a moment's shame about where she had come from.

He turned and looked into Piper's eyes. "Piper, can I talk to you a minute?"

She didn't answer, but she didn't look away.

Luke fought the urge to touch her, to take her hands in his. "Piper, I found out something important today, and it made me real happy. I hope it makes you happy, too."

Piper's wide-eyed gaze remained fixed on his face.

Luke's heart pounded so hard he could barely breathe. "Piper, I found out today...well, here it is. I'm your daddy, pumpkin. You probably don't know what that means, but it means I'm going to take care of you. As long as there's breath in my body, I promise I'll protect you and no one will ever hurt you again. I'm so happy to be your daddy. I hope one day you'll be happy, too."

Piper stared at him, unblinking, expressionless.

He tried to keep the desperation from his voice. "I want you to know, baby girl, that you can stay with Miss Madison until you want to come live with me. You don't have to do anything you don't want to do. Do you understand?"

Piper's lower lip began to tremble. She looked away from him.

He was terrified. *Am I too late? Will she ever let me into her life?*

Panicked by her threatening tears, he reached into his jacket pocket and pulled out a small box. He opened it carefully, then removed the little inexpensive necklace Lacy had left in her envelope labeled *Piper's Firsts*. He straightened the chain so the three small pearls were evenly centered and held it up.

His voice was thick with tears he couldn't hide. He wasn't even sure he wanted to. "Your mommy left this for you, Piper. It was yours when you were a little baby. Would you like to have it now?"

She touched the pearls, ran her finger over the tarnished silver chain, then looked at him with those wide, unblinking eyes. And then, to his amazement, she nodded. Luke handed the necklace to Madison, who gently clasped it around the little girl's neck and straightened it so the pearls were even.

Suddenly, out of nowhere, Piper spoke. Her voice was just above a whisper, but she spoke. "Mama said you would come back."

Finally, Luke fought tears and lost. Tears of immense sorrow. Tears of joy. A tsunami of every emotion he'd ever felt surged over him all at once, and he experienced it in the moment, just as Madison said he would.

And she was with him, exactly as she'd promised.

She knelt beside him and took his hand in hers. "I want you to know something, Mr. Callaghan." She stroked his sandy-blond hair away from his eyes and kissed a tear off his cheek. "I want you to know…I think you're the most extraordinary man."

Afterword

In March 1984, we discovered that a little girl in our family (I'll call her *Kayla*) had been sexually assaulted by her next-door neighbor for more than three years, beginning when she was just six years old and ending after she told her parents.

This predator (I'll call him *Rob*) was middle-aged, respected in the neighborhood, and much loved by children up and down the street. He was retired from the military, a business owner, and married with three children—the youngest of whom was Kayla's best friend. Kayla's parents had trusted Rob and his family, even leaving Kayla in their care overnight when her grandfather was dying, never realizing they had handed their precious baby girl over to a predatory pedophile with their blessing.

It was 1984, after all, and people didn't talk about these things.

Yet as Kayla revealed a few more devastating details every day (as if testing her family's ability to endure hearing the additional information), I knew people *had* to begin talking about these things—with their children, their parents, their communities. And as we tried to help Kayla and her family maneuver the minefield of her jumbled nine-year-old emotions, I realized I didn't know anything about pedophilia. I'd never even heard the word. But it was an enemy far more prevalent and widespread than I'd ever imagined.

I thought, like most people even today, that you could pick out a child molester in a heartbeat, no problem. If a child just *happened* to be molested, we were all convinced she would come to us right away and spill every detail, Johnny-on-the-spot. We also believed the legal system would come racing to our aid like the proverbial knight on a white horse, protecting our children and locking up their perpetrators by the end of the next day. It took me about five minutes to learn that isn't true, and the suburban bubble I'd been living in exploded.

My life was forever changed.

In 1984, when Rob was arrested, the cops didn't think to search his house for photos, pornography, or videotapes—standard procedure today. Few police knew anything about *brag books* (a pedophile's scrapbooks containing trophies, pictures, and memorabilia of his various victims) or to actively search for those items in a closet, under a bed, even in the freezer. They didn't understand that pedophiles yearn to socialize and reminisce with other pedophiles, or that they could be found anywhere that children were: arcades, playgrounds, Sunday Schools, classrooms, scout groups, and summer camps—to list just a few.

In 1984, when Kayla first told us about Rob, there were no Special Victims Units in local police departments (or on television), the National Crime and Information Center (NCIC) computer hadn't been updated for general law enforcement use, and there was no sex offender registry. Computers weren't enjoyed by every household. (In fact, the first Apple MacIntosh didn't even go on sale until 1984.) We didn't use cell phones, and most people didn't have cable television. Words like *Google*, *Wi-Fi*, and *internet* were unheard of.

Consequently, those of us struggling through the perpetual battle of child sexual abuse and its repercussions on our daily lives struggled alone. We lived in a vacuum devoid of knowledge, history, and support. We watched little Kayla suffer the agony of betrayal by a man she'd loved and trusted, and didn't know how to help her. We held her when she cried, cursed, and acted out. We couldn't find anyone to guide us. We fought our own demons as well—guilt, self-recrimination, an un-Christian desire for vengeance— and discovered that no one wanted to talk about it.

But it's part of my writer's nature to research anything I don't understand, so I forced myself into the tragic arena of child sexual abuse to learn all I could. I sought out social workers, child psychologists, attorneys that specialized in child abuse cases, prosecutors, defense attorneys, victims, and perpetrators. I met community leaders in the forefront of the fight against child sexual abuse, family advocates that accompanied terrified little victims to court, and even politicians eager to make a difference (or at least eager to appear that way).

It's also my nature to try to turn lemons into lemonade. The more knowledge and experience I gathered, the more I wanted to share it. Our children don't deserve to be left alone in a wasteland of pain and self-blame. To this very day, they're crying out for help, understanding, compassion, support. I began to write, speak publicly, reach out to the families of other victims, and work with organizations actively involved in the war against child abuse.

I even participated in successful battles to make Texas laws fairer to children, the first of which benefitted Kayla. She was permitted to videotape her testimony and use anatomically correct dolls to demonstrate her abuse. It was this videotape that convinced Rob to enter a guilty plea, thus sparing Kayla from having to testify in public. The use of videotaped testimony from young sexual abuse victims is a common practice today.

But as the old saying goes, the more things change, the more they stay the same. Before I led a discussion one evening in the cafeteria of a Catholic school, a sweet-faced Sister asked me if I could "leave the sex part out" of my talk about child sexual abuse. Of course, I told her as gently as I could that the "sex part" was the most important part of our conversation. But when the Catholic Church priest scandal broke many years later, that Sister's question floated through my memory. How many children might have been spared that nightmare if parents hadn't "left the sex part out"?

This verbal exchange, as innocent as it was, heightened my determination to bring the scourge of child sexual abuse into the open. I just didn't know how I was going to do it.

In 1986, I went to court as an advocate in three different sexual abuse cases, all part of custody battles, and found it strange that the same attorney (well-known and powerful in San Antonio) represented all three fathers, each of whom had been accused by their ex-wives of sexually assaulting their children. As time passed, I discovered that this attorney seemed to use the testimonies of the same pediatrician, the same child psychiatrist, and the same social worker. It was like a good ol' boys' network; where you found one, you almost always found the others. And unfortunately, this attorney (and his unrecognized team) usually won.

Later, while I was in the office of a local child abuse organization, a woman arrived carrying a folder from a well-known one-hour photo business. She gave several pictures containing child pornography to the president of this organization. The woman was an employee of the photo company and had tried to give the photos to the police, but they hadn't seemed interested. The president called a contact of hers in the FBI and gave the pictures to him.

This was the first time I'd ever tied child sexual abuse to the use of Polaroid instant photos or considered how fast-film-developing companies could be of assistance to law enforcement. It was also the first time I ever thought about how missing children might be located by officers who were fighting kiddie porn.

Finally, a major "mover and shaker" in San Antonio was accused by his ex-wife of sexually abusing his little girl. To make a long story short (and it's a *looonng* story), he won custody of his child and destroyed his ex-wife—with the help of the aforementioned legal team.

And that's where the basic premise of *Tip the Piano Man* began.

What if young throwaway children were being victimized by an organized pedophile ring headed up by the very people who were supposed to help them?

I wrote my first rough draft in 1989 and researched the novel's foundation in depth for the next few years, then put it away. It was too painful to delve into, and little had changed. Computers still weren't an issue; there wasn't a dark web, deep web, undernet, or dark net to contend with. I'd never even heard of live-streaming or web cams. There were no *.onion* sites that I was aware of—highly encrypted websites, usually sporting extremely illegal content, that could only be reached by using a special browser. I'd never heard of *bitcoin*, a method people can use to keep financial transactions secret. In my naivete, pedophiles were still society's outcasts, lurking in dark alleyways or cruising the streets in windowless cargo vans.

Then one day in 1998, I learned how pedophiles were beginning to use the internet to share hardcore kiddie porn; *Operation Cathedral* hit the headlines. This was a well-organized police operation led by the British National Crime Squad that broke up a major international child pornography ring called The Wonderland Club operating over the internet. This case received widespread attention, partly because 1,500 officers from thirteen other police forces around the globe arrested 104 suspects located in those thirteen countries. Another reason for the attention was the high number of images that law enforcement discovered were possessed, produced, and distributed by club members—750,000 images and 1,800 videos, to be exact.

The landscape was changing.

Fast-forward to 2017.

Three Australian men named Shannon McCoole, Peter Scully, and Matthew David Graham invaded my sphere of consciousness; *Tip the Piano Man* exploded from my brain in an entirely different form.

Shannon McCoole is a thirty-three-year-old South Australian governmental childcare worker in Queensland currently serving thirty-five years for sexually abusing seven children as young as eighteen months old. Trusted and loved by parents and coworkers, he was also head administrator of a 1,000-member global child pornography website. More than 50,000 images of hardcore kiddie porn were found on his computer.

The case of Peter Scully illuminated for me, for the first time, how diabolical a man can be when he's in an evil, symbiotic partnership with a computer. Scully fled to the island of Mindanao in the Philippines from his native Australia after being found guilty of fraud. Before long he (and his girlfriend) began to build a lucrative international pedophile ring that offered pay-per-view live-streams of children being tortured and sexually abused on the dark web.

Without going into all the grisly details, I will say that Scully procured his victims (one only four years old) by promising their impoverished families work and education. He's now serving a life sentence in the Philippines and remains on trial for numerous other crimes against children, including the production and dissemination of child pornography, torture, and murder.

Matthew David Graham, the third Australian, was one of the largest purveyors of child pornography known on the dark web. Only twenty-two years old and working out of his bedroom in suburban Melbourne, Australia, Graham (known online only as *Lux*) operated a suite of *hurtcore* (short for *Hurt2theCore*) child torture and sexual abuse websites he called his *Pedoempire*, receiving about 400,000 hits per day. What interested me most about Matthew David Graham, however, was how Europol, Queensland's anti-pedophile warrior Task Force Argos, Victoria police's Astraea Task force, and the United States FBI all worked together to bring down this massive network of child torture/sexual abuse websites.

This, then, is the new face of pedophilia. Hiding in plain sight are charismatic and personable young men and women, intelligent, educated, and tech savvy—the direct opposite of the stereotypical old man hanging out on the schoolyard in a raincoat.

Now, as I finally close the last chapter of *Tip the Piano Man*, I hope I've successfully shown how vulnerable our children are to the greed and power lust of adults who see them, not as human beings, but as voiceless chattel to be manipulated, sexually assaulted, and even tortured for the enrichment of others. I hope I've shown how the landscape has changed, but also how it's more important than ever that we go back to basics and *talk* to our children, *listen* to them, *supervise* them, and *love* them so they have no need to go online and find it elsewhere.

Finally, I hope I've shown how urgent it is for all adults everywhere in the world to stand up for children, demand legal protection for them, and petition officials to not turn a blind eye to the suffering of a child when the next case breaks.

Because it will. It will never stop. And because of that, we are all that stands between our children and...them.

A word about the author...

Rosetta Diane Hoessli (called "Ronni" by her friends) has been a freelance writer since 1985, publishing articles in McCall's, Christian Herald, and many other smaller forums. A winner of national and state-wide writing contests, she has served as senior feature writer, columnist, and executive editor for three (3) regional publications—two in San Antonio and one in Houston, Texas.

Ronni also collaborated with New York socialite Jeanette Longoria in Longoria's self-published book entitled *Aphrodite and Me: Sensuality and Romance at Any Age*, co-authored biographical novel *Falling Through Ice* with Carolyn Huebner Rankin, and edited and compiled a book of short stories, *Working on the Wild Side*, by Florida Fish and Wildlife officer Jeff Gager.

Today, Ronni focuses most of her attention on writing historical fiction and traveling with her husband, Kevin, in their RV. They reside in San Antonio, Texas, with one fur-kid, near their daughter and two grandchildren.

Whispers Through Time was Rosetta Diane Hoessli's first solo novel. You can find out more about her and her work online at:

http://facebook.com/RosettaDianeAuthor